KU-098-295

CHRISTMAS AT THE FOYLES BOOKSHOP

London, 1917. After her parents died in a tragic accident, Victoria did everything she could to keep her siblings safe and off the streets. Working at the Foyles bookshop with her best friends is a dream come true – but now the war has put everything she holds dear in danger.

With her brother fighting on the front line, Victoria wants to do her part. Little does she know that volunteering to spend time with injured soldiers at Endell Street Military Hospital will reward her in ways she could never have imagined. There are family secrets to uncover, along with love, once lost but never forgotten.

This Christmas, all the Foyles girls want is their loved ones back safe and sound...

ELAINE ROBERTS

CHRISTMAS AT THE FOYLES BOOKSHOP

Complete and Unabridged

Stockport Library
and Information Service

003212472   CLL

MAGNA
Leicester

First published in Great Britain in 2019 by
Aria
an imprint of Head of Zeus Ltd
London

First Ulverscroft Edition
published 2021
by arrangement with
Head of Zeus Ltd
London

Copyright © 2019 by Elaine Roberts
All rights reserved

This is a work of fiction. All characters, organizations, and
events portrayed in this novel are either products of the author's
imagination or are used fictitiously.

A catalogue record for this book is available
from the British Library.

ISBN 978–0–7505–4892–2

Published by
Ulverscroft Limited
Anstey, Leicestershire

Printed and bound in Great Britain by
TJ Books Ltd., Padstow, Cornwall

This book is printed on acid-free paper

In loving memory of my wonderful husband, Dave, he started this journey with me but was unable to finish it.

You are loved and missed more than words can say.

1

Victoria Appleton's slender fingers clutched the brown envelope in her coat pocket, while the other hand gripped the wooden handle of her black umbrella. The wind tussled it from side to side, trying to whip it away from her. It was March 1917 and the war was still raging on. No one could see an end to it. The longer it went on, the more she worried she wouldn't see her younger brother, Stephen, again.

Then there was Ted, the first real love of her life, a love that had never faded over the years. She remembered writing her name and his on any spare bits of paper she could find, and they were always accompanied by lots of hearts. She'd always thought their names were meant to be together, Victoria and Edward Marsden. Practising her signature had brought it all to life until her teenage dream had tragically unravelled. When Ted wrote from the frontline, asking for her forgiveness, she had been thrilled to receive his letter. Her dream had been reignited, but now writing to him just reminded her of what was unobtainable. There had been no messages of love from him.

Perhaps everyone was right, it was time to move on. Victoria reluctantly let go of the envelope, to hold the umbrella steady. Her breath came out in grey wisps, blending into the low clouds. There was no rhythmic patter as the rain pounded against the fabric of the umbrella. She pulled it lower, the icy rain spiking at her face. The puddles and the rivers of water running down Tottenham Court Road were testament that it had been raining all night. Victoria immediately thought about her brother, sitting in the trenches on the frontline. He often wrote about standing up to his ankles in water, with rats for company, as he waited for the Germans to attack them, or for orders to go over the top. She shook her head, shaking away the images she had conjured up. She couldn't allow herself to think about the war. Since it had begun in 1914, she had only read about death and destruction on the frontline.

The Horseshoe Brewery came into view. Victoria was grateful that the weather had dulled the usual stench from the spent grain left fermenting in the storage bins outside. She quickened her pace as she crossed New Oxford Street. Traders and their barrows were already set up. The aroma of vegetable soup followed her down the road, along with the chorus of voices shouting into the wind, offering their wares. The door to the popular George Tavern, on the corner of George Yard, was ajar as a grey-haired woman wearing a mob cap shook out a piece of rag.

'Morning luvvie, init miserable today?'

Victoria nodded. 'It certainly is.'

'You take care now and mind you don't catch your death, being out in this.' The lady nodded and waved her piece of rag around, before disappearing inside the public house.

A smile formed on Victoria's lips. That was something her own mother would have said to her on a day like this, but she only had her memories to give her comfort now.

Victoria frowned. 'Get a grip, what's with all the maudlin thoughts today?' She shook her head. 'Right, only happy thoughts from now on.' Smiling, she

2

looked around and wondered if anybody could hear her talking to herself. Laughter rippled through her as she imagined what Molly would have to say about it. Today was her friend's first day back at Foyles Bookshop; the three of them were back together again. Despite the cold wet weather, she smiled again. Alice, Molly and herself were like the three musketeers. She giggled as her thoughts started to run away from her. What was the saying? Oh yes, 'all for one and one for all'.

'Victoria.'

She turned to scan the people walking along Charing Cross Road, their faces hidden from view as they bent their heads against the weather. Tilting her umbrella back a little, she saw Alice rushing towards her, holding her own umbrella high to avoid it clashing with others approaching her. The puddles splashed out with each step and covered the toes of her black ankle boots. Victoria waved at her friend. 'Isn't it awful? I'll be glad when the summer arrives.'

Alice smiled. 'Indeed, it will be nice to take Arthur to the park and let his little legs run around, to tire him out.'

Victoria turned and adjusted her umbrella. 'Bless him, I can't believe he'll be two in a few months.'

Alice jumped aside as a car drove through a puddle. The dirty water splashed up over the foot of her boots, falling just short of the tops.

The girls breathed a sigh of relief when the familiar sign of Foyles Bookstore came into view. Its large white lettering stood out in the greyness of the day. 'Novels 3d and 2d Given on All Returns'.

Alice beamed as she glanced across at Victoria. 'I'm quite excited to have Molly back working with us today.'

'Yes, me too.' Victoria tried to sidestep a puddle that was spreading across the pavement. 'I wonder how her wedding plans are going?'

Alice chuckled. 'I'm sure we'll hear today.'

The girls took turns to close and vigorously shake their umbrellas.

'Morning, Miss Appleton, Mrs Leybourne.' Mr Leadbetter, their grey-haired manager, frowned at them as he watched them from just inside the doorway.

'Morning, sir,' the girls chorused in return.

Mr Leadbetter smiled at the girls. 'I'm sure you are aware that your partner in crime is back today.'

The girls giggled.

Victoria began unbuttoning her coat. 'I don't know what you mean, sir.'

Mr Leadbetter chuckled. 'I'm sure you don't.'

Victoria glanced back outside at the pelting rain. 'It doesn't look like it's going to be the weather for putting the book racks outside today.'

Mr Leadbetter frowned. 'Not at the moment, but it might clear up later.'

They carried on walking through the towering shelves of books that were all around them, following the drip marks on the tiled flooring, out to the back of the shop, to hang up their coats and to clock on. The usual musty smokiness of the second-hand books was buried beneath the dampness of wet clothing.

'Morning!' Victoria yelled to the ladies milling around and received a chorus of replies. She slipped her coat off and hung it on a peg, before turning to walk away.

A dong rang out as ladies inserted their cards into

4

the clocking in machine. Molly came rushing in. 'Oh goodness, I'm not late, am I?' She took off her narrow-brimmed hat and ran her fingers through her long blonde hair.

The women all giggled at Molly's flushed cheeks. There was a chorus of welcome back from around the room.

Victoria grinned at her friend and stepped forward to give Molly a hug. Molly's usual floral scent was overpowered by the dampness of her coat seeping out onto the sleeves of Victoria's white crinoline blouse. 'Nothing changes.' She laughed and turned back to her coat, thrusting her hand inside one of the deep side pockets. She pulled out the brown envelope, studying it for a moment, before folding it in half and pushing it into the pocket of her black calf-length skirt.

Molly poked out her tongue.

'Yes, very grown up. As I said, nothing changes.' Victoria plucked her card from its slot, along with Alice and Molly's and passed theirs over to them. 'In all seriousness, it's great to see you back here where we can keep an eye on you.'

Molly's lips lifted at the corners. 'Thanks, I think I'll take that as a compliment, because you've missed me.' She unbuttoned her coat.

Alice laughed. 'Remind us, what time did you get to work at the munitions factory?' She also stepped forward to wrap her arms around her friend. 'Best get yourself ready, before Mr Leadbetter comes looking for you.' She stepped back. 'It's lovely to have you back.'

Molly took off her coat and gently shook it, before hanging it on a coat peg.

The three of them stood in line, the clock constantly

5

clicking, as each person in turn put their card into the slot and pulled it out again.

Molly stood behind Alice, patiently waiting her turn. 'Your hair looks nice, Alice, have you had it cut again?'

Alice turned and patted her dark hair. 'I had it cut to just under my ears, because every time I pick up Arthur, he grabs a handful.' She chuckled. 'I did think that at this rate, I'll have no hair by the time I'm twenty-five.'

Mr Leadbetter appeared in the doorway. 'Come on, ladies, there's no time for chatter. The doors need to be opened for customers, even in this miserable weather, so I need you all in your positions.' He nodded as they all drifted past him one at a time. 'Morning, Miss Cooper.'

Molly squared her shoulders, wondering how much trouble she would get into this time around. 'Morning, Mr Leadbetter.'

'I want you to follow me to your new workplace.' Mr Leadbetter peered down at Molly. 'I've placed you in the children's section, so I hope you enjoy the delights of working with them. Miss Appleton, I would like to see you, once I have organised Miss Cooper.' Mr Leadbetter turned on his heels and, without a backward glance, he left the room.

Molly glanced at Victoria. 'What have you been up to?'

Victoria's hand came up and rested at the base of her neck. She shrugged. 'I've not done anything.' She frowned. 'At least, I don't think I have.'

'Miss Cooper.' Mr Leadbetter's voice travelled through to the staff area.

Molly clenched her jaw. 'I'd better go. Don't worry,

6

Victoria, it's probably nothing.' She almost ran to the doorway. 'I don't want to keep old Leadbetter waiting and get off on the wrong foot from the first day.' She stepped through the open doorway, almost knocking Mr Leadbetter off his feet. 'Sorry, sir.' Gulping hard, she wondered if he'd heard her. Molly looked down, her mouth dropping open as she noticed she was still clenching her clocking in card. 'Oh, sorry, just realised I haven't punched my card.' Molly turned on her heels and ran back into the staff area.

Victoria and Alice watched her with wide eyes as she brushed past them and put her card in the slot. She waited for the dong, to show the card had done its job, before pulling it out and placing it back inside the wooden cardholder. Without a word, and straight-lipped, she ran back into the shop and her manager.

Mr Leadbetter eyed her for a moment. 'Hmm, I know you are excited to be back with your friends, but don't let me regret giving you back your job, Miss Cooper.'

Molly looked down at her ankle boots, momentarily getting distracted by the wet dirty toes.

Mr Leadbetter cleared his throat.

Molly jerked and stared hard at the books on the shelves in front of her. 'No, sir, I do appreciate you letting me return.' Colour filled her face. 'I do love being around books, but the excitement just got the better of me.'

Mr Leadbetter smiled, showing a row of creamy white teeth. 'Then you are in the right place, but the real question is, do you like children?'

Molly glanced at him through her eyelashes. 'As you know, before I left, I spoke to you about working with the children, so they would come to love books

7

the way I do.'

Mr Leadbetter nodded and stepped forward. Molly automatically followed him, weaving in and out of the bookshelves. He suddenly stopped and Molly just managed to not bump into him.

'Sorry to be a nuisance, but I wondered if you could help me?' A young girl stood in front of the two of them.

Mr Leadbetter gave her his best smile. 'Of course, what can we do for you?'

'I want to buy my mother a book and someone told me she would enjoy *Howards End* by E. M. Forster.' She looked up high on the bookshelves and indicated the area the book was in. 'I think that's it, but I can't reach it.'

Molly and Mr Leadbetter looked up to where she was pointing.

Molly nodded. 'I can see it.'

Mr Leadbetter easily reached up and pulled the book from the shelf. The books either side looked like they were going to topple down, but he managed to push them back with his other hand.

Molly smiled at the young girl. 'That's a lovely choice of book and I hope your mother enjoys it.'

The girl laughed. 'I don't know, but my friend said her mother had read and returned it for her tuppence refund.'

Mr Leadbetter examined the book. 'Well, the cover is full of some lovely greenery over a large house, so it looks like it could be a good read.'

Molly laughed. 'It's about a strong intelligent woman, so if it interests you maybe you should read it afterwards.'

The girl beamed at them. 'Thank you, I will.' She

took the book from Mr Leadbetter and they watched her make her way to a wooden counter for a bill payment slip.

'That was a good show of knowledge, Miss Cooper.'

Molly smiled. 'I told you I love books.'

Mr Leadbetter nodded. 'Actually, I don't know why I'm taking you to the children's section, when you know Foyles like the back of your hand. I'm sure I don't need to tell you what to do, or explain how we feel about our customers — you remember the customer always comes first, so please be helpful and remember you do not handle any money, under any circumstances. There's a counter to the left as you arrive in the section, and that's where you will be, but when things are quiet, please tidy and dust the shelves.'

Molly nodded. 'Yes, sir, don't worry, I will work hard.' She frowned. 'After the munitions factory, this will be a joy to do.'

Mr Leadbetter softened his tone. 'It must have been hard for you.'

Molly gave a faint smile. 'It was physically hard, but repetitive.' Her eyes welled up. 'There were some good people lost in that explosion.' She pulled a plain cotton handkerchief from her black calf-length skirt and dabbed her eyes. 'Some people lost everything they had, including their homes. This war has a lot to answer for.'

Mr Leadbetter lifted his arms a little, before letting them drop by his side. He cleared his throat. 'It sounds like it's a good job you are back with your friends.'

Molly nodded. 'Yes, and thank you again for letting me come back.' She took a deep breath. 'I best get on

9

and let you find Victoria, I mean Miss Appleton.'

'Yes, yes.' He turned to walk away, stopping to look over his shoulder at the blonde-haired girl he liked to think was the daughter he never had. 'It's good to have you back, Miss Cooper.'

Molly smiled and gave a slight nod. 'Thank you, sir.'

Mr Leadbetter turned to walk back to the payment booth, where he knew Victoria would be sitting. He watched her serving an elderly lady, giving a ready smile and chatting to her. The customer leant in and smiled after she had spoken. He nodded. Yes, he'd made the right choice. There had been a desire to choose Mrs Leybourne, but Miss Appleton deserved a chance, and to have something good happen in her life. He wanted to help give her something else to think about and this was the only way he could do so.

Mr Leadbetter indicated to another member of staff to follow him, as he walked towards the payment booth. The door to the wooden and glass kiosk was always locked, the occupant keeping the key at all times. Mr Leadbetter was an upright man in his sixties, who was very popular with the customers. Since the premature death of his wife, not long after the loss of their only child at the Somme, he hadn't been short of offers for meals and company, but he missed his family too much to think of any other companionship. He loved his position at Foyles, but it had been recognised that he needed help. The war hadn't slowed down the business of selling second-hand books.

'Miss Appleton.'

Victoria looked up, her eyes damp with unshed tears.

Mr Leadbetter looked at the customer waiting to

be served. A little girl was hanging onto the woman's skirt and a smaller child was in her arms. 'My apologies, madam, but we just need to relieve Miss Appleton for a moment.' He peered at the child in her arms. 'Would you like me to hold him, while you pay for your books?'

The lady's face lit up. 'That would be wonderful, thank you, but I'm afraid he's quite heavy.' She gently passed the baby over to him.

Mr Leadbetter opened his arms to take the child. The boy stared at him with big brown eyes.

'It's so difficult trying to carry a child and have one hanging on your skirt all the time. The trouble is, they miss their father.' She sighed. 'We were lucky he came home for a few days, but then he got shipped out again and that's how I ended up with this one.'

Mr Leadbetter smiled at the woman, before looking back at the child. He could feel his throat tightening. 'They are a precious gift. I know it's hard, but try to enjoy them, because one day they will be away from you and the family home forever.'

The woman stopped hunting for the change in her purse and momentarily looked up at him. 'That sounds like a voice of experience.'

Mr Leadbetter's lips thinned. 'It is, madam.'

The lady put her purse away and picked up the bill payment slip. She opened her arms, for the child to be placed into them. 'Thank you for your kindness, sir.'

Mr Leadbetter smiled at the young woman. 'You take care of yourself, and your children. Hopefully, your man will be home soon, safe and sound.'

The lady nodded, before turning away. She glanced over her shoulder at Mr Leadbetter, smiling as she nodded her thanks again.

Mr Leadbetter cleared his throat. 'Right, Miss Appleton, I wish to talk to you. Follow me.' He turned and walked towards the back of the shop, to the staff area.

Victoria looked around her with wide eyes. She caught Alice staring in her direction. Her friend shrugged her shoulders, before giving a reassuring nod. Victoria could feel her tears were not far away. Since Mr Leadbetter had said he wanted to see her, her mind had been moving like a film reel going over everything she might have done wrong. He had never wanted to see her away from her position before. She hoped she wasn't going to get the sack. She was thrilled Molly was back at Foyles, but she didn't want to lose her job just so Molly could have one. Memories of how poor her family were not so long ago bubbled to the surface. Nausea rose up her throat as she remembered the humiliation of pawning her parents' possessions, that had become so important to her, just so she could put food on the table. Was she about to be catapulted back to those dark days? Seven years ago, when a sixteen-year-old Victoria had been told the devastating news her parents had died in a train derailment it had crushed her. She hadn't had time to grieve for what was lost; she was immediately thrown into being a parent to her younger sister, Lily, and brother, Stephen.

Victoria felt herself wilt under the weight of responsibility, which sat heavy on her slim shoulders.

'Miss Appleton.' Mr Leadbetter frowned as he looked at her pale features. 'Come on, you're not going to your death.' He looked around him, before continuing. 'I don't know what's got into you three today, not that Mrs Leybourne has done anything,

12

but when one of you is affected by something, then all of you seem to be.' He shook his head. 'Let's hope I've made the right decision.'

Victoria gingerly stepped forward. 'What . . . what decision?'

Mr Leadbetter sighed. 'If you come with me, you'll find out. It's meant to be good news, but I'm beginning to wonder.' He turned and headed into the staff area again.

Good news. Victoria trotted behind him. 'I'm sorry, sir.'

The room was empty of people, apart from Mr Leadbetter's large frame sitting at a table. He stood up and pulled out a chair, indicating for Victoria to sit down. She did as she was bid and the old wooden chair scraped on the tiled floor as she adjusted her position. Victoria pulled back her shoulders and clasped her hands together on her lap. She could feel the beads of perspiration forming on her forehead.

'Now.' He looked down at her fingers pressing hard into her hands. He looked up again. 'I don't know why you're so worried, it's not as though you're in trouble.' He paused for a moment. 'Is there something I should know?'

Victoria shook her head. 'No, sir, it's just that you have never had concern to call me to one side, so I thought you were going to give me the sack.'

'The sack? No, dear girl, far from it.' A smile hovered on Mr Leadbetter's lips. 'Although the three of you do drive me to distraction at times, but I suppose I wouldn't have it any other way.' He chuckled. 'As for Miss Cooper, well . . . ' He shook his head. 'Anyway, that's not what we are here to discuss.'

Victoria suddenly realised she had been holding

her breath and gasped for air. 'No, sir.'

Mr Leadbetter cleared his throat and smiled at Victoria. 'Now I want to make you an offer, it's a serious one, so I want you to give it proper consideration.'

Colour rose in Victoria's cheeks. She coughed and wrapped her arms around her waist, wanting the ground to open up and swallow her. 'Sir, I don't think it's a good — '

'Wait, you haven't heard it yet.' Mr Leadbetter leant forward, resting his forearms on the table. 'I want you to become a floor manager. I can't promise it will be a permanent promotion, but it will give you valuable experience. You are very good with customers and you get on well with other staff members.' He laughed. 'Mind you, it might be wise to leave Miss Cooper to me for the time being.'

Victoria stared at him, shock holding her rigid.

'What do you think?' Mr Leadbetter studied her for a moment. 'I know it's a big step, because you've been in that payment booth for a long time, and it is difficult dealing with some of the staff, especially if you get on well with them.'

'To be honest, I can't believe you're offering it to me, but I am very grateful for the opportunity.' Victoria loosened her grip from her waist. 'I thought — '

'Yes well, now you know it was good news.' Mr Leadbetter blustered. 'You always act professionally, as indeed do I.' He scraped back his chair on the tiled flooring. 'Can I assume it's a yes?'

'Yes, sir.'

'Good, you can start today.' He smiled. 'If you have any problems or situations you are not sure about, then come and find me.'

'I will, Mr Leadbetter.'

'Remember, it's all about the customer. We want them to return to Foyles, war or no war.'

Victoria stood up, the scraping of her wooden chair across the floor filling the silence. She shook her head as she watched him leave the staff area. How could she have ever thought he was going to act inappropriately, and what did that say about her? Pulling the envelope from her skirt pocket, she ran her fingers over it, smoothing out the creases where she'd held onto it so tightly. She was desperate to read it, but now was not the time, so she thrust it back into her pocket.

2

Victoria's black shoes clipped the red and black floor tiles as she stepped towards the doorway of the shop. She stopped and looked over her shoulder at the table where she had just been sitting with Mr Leadbetter. There was no evidence that they had been there or of the conversation that had taken place. She hoped she wouldn't let him down. A tingle ran through her and a smile lit up her face; she was going to be a floor manager. She had the urge to jump up and down, clapping her hands. She couldn't wait to tell Daisy later, or write to let Stephen know. It would be good to have some real news in her nightly letters to her brother. Victoria wondered if her parents would have been proud of the three of them. She blinked quickly; of course they would. Her hand slid inside her black skirt pocket. Her slender fingers came into immediate contact with the crumpled envelope. Taking a deep breath, Victoria pulled back her shoulders, lifting her head slightly, ready to step through the doorway. Voices filtered through to the staff area. She froze. Would she know what to do? Her eyes widened. She folded her arms across her waist, gripping her sides tightly, crumpling the soft cotton in her fists. Victoria shook her head. Alice or Molly had better experience to do this job. She had only sat in the payment booth.

A man's gravel voice reached her. 'I see the newspapers are saying the Germans are on the retreat.' His words were quickly followed by several deep coughs.

'Let's hope so,' a deep voice responded. 'It's been

nearly three years now and the longer it goes on, the less chance there is of my sons coming home — '

'Are you all right?' a woman's frail voice interrupted. 'Shall I get someone?'

The coughing and wheezing continued.

Without a thought, Victoria rushed into the shop, not noticing the gathering of people watching the scene in front of her. She grabbed one of the many wooden slatted chairs that were scattered around the edges of the shop, for the man to sit on. 'Sit still and I'll get you some water.' Rushing back into the staff area, she quickly turned on the cold tap. The water gushed noisily into the sink, drenching everything in its path, including her white blouse. 'Damn.' Victoria jumped to the side and quickly turned down the tap, before filling a clean cup. She stared down at her wet blouse, hoped no one would notice it then she rushed back into the shop.

The man's hacking cough was causing some customers to stop and stare, while others shook their heads and continued about their business.

Victoria rested her hand on the back of the elderly man's thin wet coat. 'Here, sip this.' She fought the urge to wipe her hand down the side of her skirt.

The man closed his eyes for a second, before reaching out for the cup. His fingers gripped the handle tightly, his knuckles almost visible through the translucent skin. He took a couple of tentative sips, before rubbing his eyes with a piece of grey rag. 'Thank you.'

Victoria turned her head away slightly, as his smoke and coffee-filled breath wafted in her direction, mingling with the stench of his damp clothing. She nodded. 'Is there anything I can get you? You can sit for as long as you want to.'

The man cleared his throat. He gave a faint smile, baring his brown stained, jagged teeth. 'No, I'm fine. Thank you for your kindness.'

Victoria forced a smile. He sounded anything but fine.

'Is everything all right here?' A familiar voice came from behind the gathering of people.

Victoria watched as the customers broke apart, allowing Mr Leadbetter to come through. 'I think so, sir. This gentleman has a terrible cough, so I fetched him a drink.'

Mr Leadbetter nodded, turning his attention from Victoria to the man sitting on the chair. 'How are you feeling now, sir?'

'Much better, thank you, I don't know what came over me.'

The owner of the frail voice stepped forward. 'It's all this talk of the war.'

A small boy tugged at the lady's long coat. 'Will my daddy be home soon?'

You could have heard a pin drop. The old lady bent down as low as she could, to talk to the child. 'Hopefully, young man, all the daddies will be home soon, and when that happens, we'll have a party. Would you like that?'

The boy beamed, showing the gaps where his two front teeth once were. He shyly nodded. 'Will we have jelly?'

Everyone laughed.

'Of course, you can't have a party without jelly.' The lady groaned, as she pulled herself upright and ruffled the boy's hair. 'Now, I must get on before I forget what I came in here for.'

Victoria grinned at the boy's innocent smile. He

18

looked up at his mother. 'Can we really have jelly when Pa comes home?'

The young woman forced a smile that didn't reach her watery eyes. 'Of course you can.' She grabbed her son's hand and shook it. 'Come on, let's go and find you a book.' She paused for a moment and looked across at Victoria, who nodded her encouragement. 'Your father will be pleased when he hears how well you can read.'

The boy's face lit up. 'I love jelly.' His voice faded as they moved away.

Victoria chuckled as she watched them go. Molly would be at her best, helping them. A wave of sadness washed over her, as it dawned on her that the years the men had been gone would be lost forever.

The man with the gravel voice nudged her elbow. 'There you go, love.' He passed her the empty cup. 'It seems to have worked a treat. Thank you.'

Victoria took the cup and the man pushed himself up off the chair. 'Please go careful, sir.'

The man nodded and disappeared through the lines of bookshelves.

Mr Leadbetter watched Victoria for a moment. 'Are you all right, Miss Appleton?'

Victoria jerked round to face him. 'Yes, sir.' She looked down at her shoes. 'I'm sorry, I haven't moved very far, so I'm afraid I haven't done very much.'

Mr Leadbetter smiled. 'On the contrary, Miss Appleton, you have achieved a lot. Those customers will be telling everybody what you've done and of your kindness, so they, and others, will be back.'

Colour immediately began to fill Victoria's cheeks. 'Thank you, sir. I must admit, it feels strange not being in the payment booth.'

Mr Leadbetter chuckled. 'You'll soon get used to it.' He turned and walked away, stopping only to talk to a customer.

Molly's laughing tones broke into Victoria's thoughts. 'I knew it was you that boy was talking about, in between the jelly and the old lady.'

Victoria turned and gave her friend a huge hug, trying to force a frown, but the smile won. 'What are you doing over here?'

'I have just shown a customer where to pay, and said I'd wait and take her back to collect her book.' Molly giggled. 'Truth be known, I was desperate to find out what old Leadbetter wanted to see you about.' Molly raised her eyebrows and her eyes widened. 'Why aren't you in the payment booth? Oh God, he hasn't fired you has he, because if he has, I'll leave. I didn't want my job back so he could get rid of someone else — '

'No, he hasn't and you're rambling.' Victoria chuckled. 'I've missed you. I'm so glad you're back.'

Molly quickly looked over her shoulder. 'I've got to be quick, I can't get into trouble on my first day.'

Victoria shook her head. 'It won't be just with Mr Leadbetter, either.' She paused for a moment. 'I've been promoted, to help Mr Leadbetter.'

Molly's jaw dropped a little. 'What? Are you kidding me?'

Victoria watched her friend's eyes widen, as she stared intently at Molly. 'No, I'm not.'

A smile lit up Molly's face. 'Oh goodness, now I am in trouble! Still, we can't let your promotion break up a wonderful friendship.'

Victoria burst into laughter. She stopped abruptly and frowned. 'Do you think Alice will mind?'

'Why should she?'

Daisy stretched her neck, as she ran her fingers around the stiff, white shirt collar, tugging it away from her throat. The black tie felt like a noose around her neck. She studied herself in the gilt-edged mirror hanging above the fireplace, turning her head one way, then the other. The framed photograph of her parents caught her eye. She picked it up from the cold marble mantelpiece and stared at their poker-straight faces. Daisy shook her head. It wasn't how she remembered them; they had been full of fun and laughter, before they had been lost to them forever. She tilted the picture slightly and gasped. She hadn't noticed before, how much likeness there was between Victoria and their mother. The grandfather clock chimed in the hallway.

'Sorry Ma and Pa, but I'm going to be late if I don't hurry up.' Daisy carefully placed the frame back down. 'I don't feel like this today.' She sighed. 'Hopefully, I'll be working with Lily; you know, we have quite a laugh when we're together. She's not as serious as her older sister, Alice.' She paused as she placed the narrow-brimmed hat on top of her brown hair, which had been neatly rolled up. 'At least we won't be on the 'women of the night' watch.' She giggled. 'I suppose there could be a 'women of the day' watch.' Her laughter faded, as she studied the photograph again. 'You know, Victoria has done a wonderful job keeping us together as a family, especially as Ted disappeared just after you died.' Daisy's vision blurred. 'I don't know what we'll do if Victoria ever meets someone and gets married.' Laughter suddenly erupted from her. 'Hark at me, Ma, twenty-one years old, most women have a family at my

21

age.' She paused. 'Well, they did before this so-called Great War robbed us of our menfolk. I'm not sure how many eligible men there will be when it finishes, if it ever finishes.' A small sigh escaped. 'You know, I could spend my life as a spinster, never knowing the love you and Pa had together.' She shook her head and reached for her navy-blue jacket. Glancing towards the window, Daisy took a couple of steps towards it. The rain hadn't given up. It pounded against the glass panes, before driving down the glass to join the rivers that had already formed. People were rushing by, avoiding the puddles and not stopping when the tips of their umbrellas clashed. She looked up at the grey clouds swirling in the wind; the rain was here to stay. Daisy straightened the long, green curtains that Victoria had carefully sewn by hand. A cold draught rippled through them and Daisy shuddered, wishing she didn't have to go out patrolling the streets. She pulled them closer together.

The thud of the door-knocker dropping made Daisy jump and release the material, as though her fingers were burnt. She stepped across the brown, thread-bare carpet, into the hallway, wrinkling her nose as she passed the highly polished oak coat stand and console table. The only sound was her black leather shoes as they gave the occasional squeak on the tiled floor. She took a deep breath as she reached up, to turn the handle.

'Hello, Daisy, I thought I'd give you a knock. It's a miserable day out here.'

Daisy smiled at Lily, huddled underneath her black umbrella, the rain bouncing off it. 'Come in, before you catch your death.'

Lily stepped forward, closing her umbrella as she

did so. A puddle began to form on the floor. 'I'll leave this on the doormat, otherwise you'll have drips all through the hall.'

There was a click as Daisy shut out the awful weather. 'You're just in time. I was thinking about leaving, but I've been putting it off for as long as I dare.'

Lily laughed. 'It's certainly miserable, and it doesn't look like it's going to stop.' She pushed down the collar of her black winter coat, pulling it into place. 'Alice was beside herself with excitement this morning.'

Daisy gave a knowing chuckle. 'So was Victoria. I don't know if Molly realises how pleased they are to have her close by. Anybody would think she had moved to the other end of the country, instead of just changing jobs.'

'I wouldn't mind, but it must be quite boring working in a bookshop.' Lily smiled, as she thought about what their older sisters did for work. 'Judging from the number of books Alice has bought, she must be their main customer.'

Daisy giggled.

'I wouldn't mind. I helped her sort them out on the day she gave birth to Arthur, bless him.' Lily smiled as she thought about her nephew. 'We sent loads to the men on the front line, but now she has the same amount again, if not more.'

Daisy frowned as she led the way into the sparsely decorated front room. 'I wish Victoria would spend more money on herself.' She paused and turned to Lily. 'I know we don't have much, but we do manage now, thanks to you talking to me about joining the Police. That was quite a turning point.'

Lily smiled. 'It's not thanks to me. You made the

23

step that has improved things for both of you.'

Daisy shook her head. 'You encouraged me.'

'Well, let's face it, out of the war work that was open to us, it was one of the better choices available, and after what Molly went through, we now know how dangerous working at the munitions factory is.'

Daisy picked up her umbrella. 'I think that's why Victoria and Alice are pleased Molly is back at Foyles with them.'

Lily nodded. 'Are you ready to go out and face this awful weather?'

Daisy shrugged. 'As ready as I'll ever be.'

Lily reached out and rested her gloved hand on Daisy's arm. 'Is everything all right? You haven't had any news I should know about?'

Daisy gave a faint smile. 'If you mean Stephen, no. As far as we know, he is still at the front, but it will be good to have him home again.'

'So what's the matter?'

'I don't know, I'm just not looking forward to this today.' Daisy shook her head. 'It's probably the weather.'

Lily eyed Daisy with a glint of suspicion, before forcing a smile. 'Well, it won't be the first time we've been soaked through to our underwear.'

Daisy giggled. 'Ain't that the truth.'

* * *

John Appleton gripped his chest. His breathing was laboured, in between the coughing. The playing cards he was holding fluttered down onto the small table in front of him. His throat tightened as his breath was ripped away from him.

24

'John, John, here let me help you.' An elderly lady quickly crossed the room, moving away from the large bay window and the sea view, with unusual agility for her advanced years. In her haste, she collided with the dark oak sideboard, causing two of the family photographs to fall over and a figurine to wobble precariously. She grabbed the ornament, thankful that it hadn't broken.

John held up his hand, stopping her in her tracks. His wheezing was getting worse. He closed his eyes and tried to take some small breaths. His voice was weary when he eventually spoke. 'It's all right, Grandma.' He opened his eyes to see worry on her wrinkled face. 'Are you all right? Have you hurt yourself?'

'I'm fine, just clumsy as usual.'

They both jumped at the sound of his grandpa's booming voice. 'You need to get out and get some of that sea air in your lungs; it'll do you a power of good.'

John opened his mouth to speak, but his grandma turned from putting the silver framed photographs back in position and beat him to it.

'Herbert, you know John can't go outside with his condition, especially in this weather. He'll freeze to death, it's March for goodness' sake.' She shook her head in disgust. 'Have you looked outside and seen the people wrapped up against the cold? The sky looks full of snow and there's a thin covering on the ground. You must be able to hear the wind rattling against the windows.'

'Nonsense, Beatrice, you mollycoddle him. He only has to wrap up against the wind.' Herbert stubbed out his cigarette in the nearby glass ashtray.

John looked from one to the other. The urge to protect his grandmother consumed him. 'I am here, you know. I'm not a child anymore, I'm eighteen and whatever you may think, I'm not going out for a walk along the beach.'

Herbert leant forward in his wingback armchair, by the side of the unlit fireplace. The oak mantelpiece dominated the room, along with the shiny, green brick-tiled surround. He folded his newspaper in half, before slapping it into the palm of his hand. 'You, young man, will do as you are told. You don't know how lucky you've got it. There are men your age, and younger, fighting on the front line, risking life and limb for this country, and you sit there moaning about going outside and breathing in some good sea air that would soon sort out this nonsense about your chest.'

John felt his body fold inwards at his grandfather's words. He wrapped his arms around his emaciated body. Anger surged through his veins, knowing he should be able to ignore his grandfather's rhetoric. It was the same every day. 'Don't you think I know people are dying? It's not my fault that my health doesn't allow me to fight. As for lucky, you try living with it for eighteen years and then let me know how lucky I am.' He slapped his hand on his chest. 'Yes, I'm lucky to be living in Brighton. The clean air has probably kept me alive, but sorry, I don't consider living with this condition all my life as lucky.'

The drawing room door gave a small creak as Tom pushed it open. The air was filled with tension. His glance ran over the three of them. He slung his rucksack down on the floor as memories came tumbling into his mind; he was glad to be leaving this house. Pangs of guilt rushed at him. 'Everything all right?'

Herbert ignored his youngest son. He dropped

the newspaper onto the side table and jumped out of his chair in one fluid movement, but his face was contorted with rage. 'You, young man, need to learn some respect. I'll not have you answering me back in my own home.'

Beatrice gave a slight nod to Tom, before moving tentatively towards her husband. She reached out and rested her hand on his arm. The fine wool of his jacket was soft against her fingers as she squeezed his arm. 'Herbert, please.'

Herbert shook off her hand. 'I am not putting up with it, Beatrice. I will not be mocked in my own home.' He ran his hand through his thinning grey hair.

Tom took a step further into the room and forced a smile to his voice. 'I'm off, Pa.'

Herbert glared at Tom. 'Thomas, this is not the time, or are you too stupid to realise I am taking your nephew to task.'

Tom glared at his father. Count to ten a voice screamed in his head. 'I'm not stupid Pa, but I do have a train to catch.' He paused for a second. What the heck, he had nothing to lose; his father didn't like him anyway. 'It's about time you stopped picking on your children, and your grandson, otherwise you'll die a lonely old man.'

Beatrice turned away. 'Please stop, Tom, I don't want you leaving us on an argument. I want you to feel you can come home to us.' Her eyes pleaded with her son and grandson to be the bigger men, even though she knew her husband was in the wrong.

Herbert glared at the two boys. 'I'm sick of the lot of you.' He stared at John. 'You need to show more appreciation, before you end up on the streets for good.'

John hesitated for a moment, letting his gaze rest on his grandmother. 'You're right, Grandpa, I'm sorry, I am grateful you took me in when my own parents didn't want me.'

Beatrice glared at her husband. Theirs had been an arranged, loveless marriage and he liked to keep reminding her he was the king of his castle. She was not his queen, but had always been amenable, which was what he liked. She had long since accepted her lot and been grateful for the three children she had borne, two sons and a daughter, but as soon as they had become of age they had left, one by one. He had driven them away.

Herbert's dark, bushy eyebrows pulled together, a deep crease forming between them. 'Yes, yes, well so you should be.'

Herbert picked up his paper and lowered himself back into the chair. 'I'll not have it.'

Beatrice couldn't look at her beloved grandson. She knew she should be protecting him more. After all, she was the one that had defied her husband and brought him into this house, when he was just a small child.

3

Mr Leadbetter held his breath as he watched Victoria reach up to straighten several books that were leaning awkwardly on the shelves.

Victoria sighed. It seemed as though the books had lain undisturbed for years, as the particles of dust rose up in the air and drifted back down again. She coughed as they caught in the back of her throat, covering her mouth with her dust-smeared palm. Her mouth felt coated as she wiped her lips with the back of her hand.

'Miss Appleton.' Mr Leadbetter edged his way nearer to where Victoria was standing precariously on a stepladder.

Startled, Victoria gripped the edge of the wooden ladder that was leaning against the racking, laden with books of various shapes and sizes, before looking down at him.

Mr Leadbetter immediately averted his eyes, concentrating on the books at eye level. He instinctively swerved to miss a child that came running round the corner, clutching a book. 'Be careful, young man, you'll hurt someone.'

The boy looked sheepish. 'Sorry, sir, me ma's said she'd buy me a book.' He smiled, waving his book in the air. 'But only if I was quick, and I've spent ages with a lady who helped me to pick this one, *Treasure Island*.'

A smile crept across Mr Leadbetter's soft, wrinkled face as he took in the boy's dark ruffled hair, scuffed shoes and patched short trousers. 'I hope you enjoy it.'

'Oh I will, the lady read me some of it. She put on different voices for each person, even the pirates, and told me to do the same because then it will be fun for me.'

Mr Leadbetter beamed at the boy. Molly Cooper was back. 'Come back and let us know if you enjoyed it.'

'She's good she is, and really made me laugh. She's behind me somewhere, talking to someone, I fink, but me ma's waiting so I can't wait. Can you tell 'er I said fanks? She's the pretty lady up there.' The boy blushed and street urchin became an endearing child, as he giggled and disappeared around the corner.

Mr Leadbetter chuckled to himself, before turning his attention back to Victoria. 'I understand the van has pulled up out the back, so will you go down to the basement and check what books the driver has collected today. If they are in good condition, we might be able to get them straight onto the shelves.' He paused for a moment. 'As fast as we're selling them, we're getting more in and I suspect we must be running out of space to store them.'

Victoria frowned. 'Yes, sir.' She took a tenuous step backwards, to descend the ladder. 'I've never been in the basement.'

Mr Leadbetter stepped forward and wrapped his fingers around the side of the ladder. 'It's through the staff area; the door's on your left.' He watched her eyebrows furrow together and her eyes dart from left to right. There was no desire to admit his old bones wouldn't allow him to do strenuous work anymore. His frown gave way to a slight smile, which lifted the corner of his lips. 'Have you been in your own basement?'

'Yes, sir. Daisy and I have slept down there every night, since the war began. It's easier than to keep moving, every time the policeman cycles down our street, blowing his whistle and shouting "the Germans are coming.'

'That's true, and very sensible.' Mr Leadbetter frowned. 'Well, I suppose it's no different. It might be bigger, but other than that, it'll be the same.' He chuckled, almost to himself. 'Oh, and the fact it's full of books of course.'

Victoria nodded and finished stepping down off the ladder.

'As it's your first time, I could come down with you.'

'No, no, I need to do this.' Victoria forced a smile. 'It's the spiders and mice you might find in these places that bother me.'

Mr Leadbetter gave a hearty laugh. 'Would you like one of your partners in crime to go with you? Mrs Leybourne or Miss Cooper maybe.'

Victoria dusted her hands together. 'No, thank you, I can do this.' Turning on her heels, she walked towards the staff area.

She stood in front of the basement door for several minutes. Beads of perspiration formed on Victoria's face as she pushed her clammy hands down the sides of her skirt before hesitantly reaching for the door handle. The hinges of the basement door creaked as Victoria pulled it open for the third time in as many minutes, each time letting the door swing shut. Perhaps she should tell Mr Leadbetter she couldn't do this, but then where would that leave her? Was this going to be part of her daily routine now? She might lose her promotion and the extra money. She frowned as she mumbled, 'Look, it opens and shuts easily enough.' She fidgeted from one foot to the other. 'Come on you can do this, just run down there and do what you've got to do then run back up again. Easy.' Glancing around, she looked for something to prop open the door, but there was nothing heavy enough. Victoria stood, rooted to the spot; she peered into the darkness, searching for a light switch. A glow came from under the door at the bottom of the worn, cold and uninviting stone steps. She took a deep breath and began inching her way down into the darkness. The door slammed shut. Victoria gripped her chest as the sound like a trapped animal escaped from her. She ran back up the stairs as though the devil him-self was after her and pushed the door hard, it swung open with ease. She gasped for breath before mutter-ing to herself, 'I can do this, I'm a grown-up, I can do this.' Victoria turned and took a deep breath before gripping the handrail and taking another step into the basement. There was a mustiness, and damp hung in the air. There was a smell she couldn't pinpoint; fresh air hadn't blown down here for a long time. Stepping aside quickly, she just managed to avoid a large cobweb that had attached itself to the beams. She didn't know anyone who had ever ventured down these steps before, but why would she? Her position had always been in the payment booth. Victoria took a deep breath and shuddered as darkness wrapped itself like a cloak around her shoulders, sealing in the fear as panic rose in her chest. It occurred to her that she hadn't told anyone she was going into the base-ment of Foyles Bookstore. What if she never came out again? Over the years, she had heard many stories of people getting lost, not finding their way to the front of the shop and escaping into the street. There was even a rumour of someone dying amongst the many books that were stacked high on the rows of shelving, as well as teetering piles sitting on the floor, but no one ever mentioned the basement. Maybe she should have told someone. Would anyone look for her? *Pull yourself together, girl — Mr Leadbetter knows you're down here, even if nobody else does.* A creaking noise broke the silence. Victoria stood rigid on the step, clutching her skirt. Light drifted up the stairs. It could be a Frankenstein moment. Victoria almost scampered back up the stairs. A sound escaped from her; too much imagination that was her trouble.

'Vic.' A familiar voice called out from above.

Victoria sprung round, her anger automatically bubbling to the surface. Only one person would have the nerve to call her Vic. Friend or not she'd lost count of how many times over the years Molly had been told not to shorten her name, after all her parents had named her after the great Queen herself. She could hear the thud of the footsteps on the stairs, as they got nearer.

Slowly, a dim glow of yellow electric light began to chase away the darkness. 'Ah, you are down here.'

Victoria tried to compose herself and swallow her pride; her hand automatically rubbed the back of her neck. She took a deep breath, she was glad to have company. 'Yes, Molly, what is it?'

'Old Leadbetter said you might want help down here, so here I am.' Molly smiled. 'What's happened? You look quite worried, why didn't you put the light on?'

Victoria shook her head and forced a smile. 'Nothing, I couldn't find the light, and you startled me, that's all.

Well, apart from you calling me Vic, which you know I hate.'

Molly giggled. 'Sorry, ma'am, I forgot myself for a moment.'

'I don't know what it is about basements, but they are always creepy places.' Victoria looked towards the doorway. 'I'd hate to work down here. Imagine if the door got stuck and you couldn't get out. I remember that happening to me when I was little. I was banging and screaming for what seemed like ages before someone came.' She shuddered. 'It doesn't bear thinking about.'

Molly took Victoria's hand in hers. 'Come on, it's all right, we're grown-ups now and anyway you sleep in yours every night, so they can't be that scary.'

'I'm used to ours.' A thud travelled up towards them. Victoria grabbed Molly's arm. 'What's that noise? Do you think someone's down here?'

Laughter burst from Molly. 'Of course, Albert is. He does all the deliveries and collections. Haven't you met him before?'

Victoria shook her head as she stared wide-eyed at her friend.

Molly gently pulled her down the remaining steps. 'It's time you did. He's about a hundred and ten years old and he has a heart of gold.' She beamed, pushing open the creaking, heavy wooden door. 'He's like the grandpa I wish I had.'

Victoria followed Molly through the open door and mustiness hit the back of her throat. She wrinkled her nose before gasping as she looked over her shoulder, staring at the piles of books that stood on wall-to-wall counters and shelves. Her mouth dropped open and she quickly snapped it shut again. 'I have never seen so many books. I thought there were hundreds in the shop, but that's nothing to what is down here.'

Molly giggled. 'Isn't it wonderful? It's as though we've hit upon our own treasure chest.'

Victoria smiled. 'It was you that read *Treasure Island*, I knew it was.'

'Ooh argh captain.' Molly gave a mock salute. 'Albert, where are you hiding?' Coughing came from somewhere out of sight, so they tried to follow the sound. 'Albert?'

They stood, rooted to the spot, as a shuffling sound slowly got louder.

'Hello, ladies, to what do I owe this pleasure?' A short, stocky, grey-haired man was suddenly in front of them. He hobbled closer, his shoes dusting the floor as he moved.

'Hi, Albert, this is Miss Victoria Appleton.' Molly lifted her hand towards her mouth before whispering, 'She's just been promoted.' She dropped her hand and gave Albert a smile. 'We're here to see what books can go straight up to the shop.'

Albert stretched out his hand. 'Please to meet you, Miss Appleton.' He snatched it back when he saw how dusty it was and wiped it down the side of his grey trousers, which had seen better days. 'I'm nearly always down here, except when I'm delivering or collecting books.'

Victoria nodded. 'Please call me Victoria.' She looked around again. 'How do you find anything?'

Albert gave a deep throaty chuckle. 'I don't. The plan is to get them all in the shop as quickly as possible, so they can be sold. As Mr Leadbetter says, 'they won't sell in the basement.'

Victoria moved to pick up a large hardback book.

She stared at the ornate bandstand that stood central on the cover, against a perfect blue sky. 'I wonder what this is about? It looks lovely.'

Molly took the book from her hand and placed it back on the pile. 'Don't start looking at them or we'll both be in trouble. We need to decide what has to go in the shop, and what stays down here for a while.'

The cellar door snapped shut. Panic tightened around Victoria's chest. What if they couldn't get out again?

Molly glanced at Victoria. 'Stop worrying, we're with Albert.'

* * *

Mabel Atkins closed the door to her small room in the nurses' living quarters. She wrinkled her nose at the pungent smell of disinfectant and carbolic soap that greeted her in the narrow hallway. Time was running away from her; she should never have stopped to read her young brother's letter. A clock chimed in the distance. Mabel counted them in her head as she rushed down the stairs, almost slipping on one of the steps near the bottom. Eight times, the clock had chimed eight times. Perhaps she had miscounted and it was seven. Mabel shook her head. Who was she kidding? Not herself, that was for sure. She grabbed her thick, black wayward curls and tied them back off her face with an old shoelace. Loose grey strands fell down and framed her face. She tutted to herself, thinking she had more grey hair these days, than black. She was forty-five, and yet she felt like a naughty schoolgirl. She was going to be in trouble with Matron, of that there was no doubt. She stepped outside and gave an involuntary shiver as the cold air hit her, freezing the moisture on her lips. She looked up at the grey clouds that didn't appear to be moving, thankful the rain had stopped. She sighed. There was going to be more snow, before the day was over.

The large metal gates of Endell Street Military Hospital were open and ambulances stood silent in the courtyard. A couple of nurses stood chatting in the doorway. One of them yawned as Mabel approached them. 'It's been a busy night, Mabel, so prepare yourself. I think it's going to be a helluva day and Matron isn't in a very good mood.'

Mabel groaned. 'Thanks, Enid, that's all I need when I'm already late.' The two nurses stepped aside, to allow her to walk through. 'You look like you should be in bed.'

'And that's exactly where I'm going.' Enid laughed. 'After I've had my dinner, of course.'

Their laughter followed Mabel down the corridor, as she hurried along it. Her shoes had developed a squeak, which became more annoying with each step she took. The green walls at the hospital were plain, but vases of flowers gave it a welcoming feel. The large wards all had an abundance of natural light from the large windows on both sides of the rooms. The warm reds and blues of the bedcovers gave it a homely feel, along with the many pots filled with flowers. She opened the door to Catherine Ward and was greeted by the sister on duty.

'You're late, Atkins.'

Mabel gasped for breath and lowered her eyes. 'Yes, sorry, Sister, time has just run away with me this morning.'

Sister looked at her with a stony expression. 'Well,

make sure it doesn't happen again, otherwise your days of being a nursing orderly will be cut short, at this hospital at least.'

Mabel nodded and began unbuttoning her black winter coat. 'Yes, Sister, I'm sorry. It won't happen again.'

'Let's hope not.' The sister looked down at her paper. 'Don't take your coat off; it looks like you're expected on Joan of Arc Ward this morning. It's been a busy night so, as my father would have said, it's all hands on deck, I'm afraid.' She looked up at Mabel. 'Take the lift; it will be quicker than the stairs. They are waiting for you, and please remember what I've said.'

'Yes, Sister, thank you.' Mabel quickly turned away and headed for the door. Colour flooded her cheeks as the squeak of her shoes got louder. She couldn't help looking over her shoulder as she passed through the doorway. The lift was already stationary on the ground floor. She pulled open the grey heavy metal door, propping it open with her body while she opened the black metal grill, before stepping inside and closing it behind her. Mabel pressed the button for the second floor and the lift jerked into action. A minute later, she was stepping out of the lift and facing the doors to Joan of Arc Ward. As the lift door slammed shut behind her, she stepped forward and opened the ward doors. Antiseptic hung in the air. The groans from some of the patients reached her and she frowned, wondering what she could do to make the soldiers more comfortable. The ward had forty beds and a quick glance on both sides of the room told Mabel that each one was in use. Some of the men sat in chairs next to their beds, while others lay very still, under the covers.

Sister Williams marched towards Mabel. 'I see you've finally arrived, Atkins. I'd given up on you.'

Mabel lifted her chin slightly. 'Yes, I'm sorry, I went to Catherine Ward because that's where I was working yesterday, so I assumed — '

'You should never assume anything.' Sister Williams raised her eyebrows. 'Especially not with everything that is going on.'

'No, Sister.'

Sister Williams nodded. 'Right, I want you to work from bed twenty onwards. They will need the usual things done.' She glanced at Mabel. 'By usual, I mean blood pressure, temperature and dressings checked. Anything untoward, let me know.'

Mabel nodded as she slipped her arm out of her coat. 'I'll get started straight away.' She hung her coat on a stand and smoothed down her white overall, before picking up a stethoscope from the hooks by the desk and placing it in her pocket.

'Hello, Atkins.' The soldier in the nearest bed beamed at her. 'Yer know the best thing about being in 'ere is all the pretty nurses, well, that and not being shot at.'

Mabel smiled at the young man as she walked past; he wasn't much older than her young brother. 'Thank you, kind sir.'

★ ★ ★

Victoria glanced at Daisy across the oak breakfast table. A candle stood between them, the flame flickering as the draughts from the windows caught it. An uncut loaf stood to one side, neither of the girls wanting to cut into it. She took a sip from her luke-warm cup of tea and wrinkled her nose. 'Do you know what you've got ahead of you today?'

Daisy grimaced. She put down her slice of lightly buttered bread, wishing she'd cut a slice from the fresh loaf. 'Lily and I always seem to be on the women of the night look out.' She chuckled. 'Mind you, with all the young men gone, I'm surprised they're making enough money to live on.'

'That's true, it must be all the old men prowling the streets, while their wives are out at work.' Victoria giggled at the picture that had formed in her mind. 'Do you get to make many arrests?'

'No, we're not allowed to arrest anyone; only the men get to do that.' Daisy shook her head. 'I love it, but wouldn't mind being more than a show police-woman.'

'I suppose it's all about small steps.' Victoria shook her head. 'Before this war, you wouldn't have been able to do anything, except be in domestic service, married or a woman of the night.'

Daisy gave a wry smile and glanced across at her sister. 'Are you all right?'

'I'm thinking of volunteering at Endell Street Military Hospital in Covent Garden.' Victoria paused for a moment. 'I thought, even if I just sit and chat or read to an injured soldier, it could make a difference to them.'

Daisy nodded. 'I think that's a good idea; maybe I'll think about doing that as well.'

'There's another thing I've got to do.' Victoria gripped her hands together in her lap, the black folds of the material creeping up and covering her hands. 'Hopefully you'll help me . . .'

'Of course, what is it?'

'I think it's time we sorted through Ma and Pa's things. It's been seven years and I've not been in their room since it happened.'

Daisy frowned, before jumping up and running around the table. 'Of course.' She threw her arms around Victoria. 'It's going to be tough, but it's something we should have done years ago.'

Victoria patted the coarse cotton sleeve of Daisy's uniform, breathing in her floral perfume. 'Thank you. I can't pretend I'm looking forward to it, but as you say, we should have done it a long time ago.'

Daisy gave her sister an extra squeeze. 'It'll be all right, you'll see.' She stood up straight. 'I'm afraid I have to go, otherwise I'll be late.' Her flat shoes made no noise as she walked into the hall and grabbed her black winter coat. She did up her buttons and picked up her hat and scarf. 'See you later.'

'Take care.' With a sigh, Victoria waved Daisy off to work. There was a light flurry of snow. Victoria hoped it wouldn't settle; she didn't want to be slipping and sliding along Charing Cross Road to Foyles, or the hospital. Her sister didn't look back. She was huddled under a hat and scarf that Alice had knitted her. Only the click of the front door shutting could be heard above the grandfather clock ticking in the hall. A bong startled her. She looked round as another one rang out; six o'clock in the morning and it was still dark outside. Taking the couple of steps back to the dining table, her bare feet were silent as they walked over the tiled floor of the hall. She sat back down on the chair she had only recently vacated. The treasured letter she had carried around all the previous day was poking out of her skirt pocket. She and Daisy had pored over it together, after they had eaten dinner. Victoria pulled the envelope free and ran her hands over the creases. Her beloved brother was safe, thank goodness. The paper rustled as she pulled the one sheet out, laying it on the table. She stared down at the spidery handwriting.

Dear Victoria and Daisy,

Sorry it's been a while since I wrote a letter, I didn't mean to worry you. I've nothing new to report. As always I can't tell you where I am but it's a popular destination right now. It's not one I'd recommend for your holidays though, as it's a bit muddy and damp. I'd stick to Margate or Southend. Something tells me it won't be so busy or noisy. I love getting your letters, they cheer me up. I know you write every day but I don't always get them straight away and then I get a bundle delivered at once, which is great. Keep them coming because they do give me a lift. I hope you are both all right, we all share bits of news with each other so I know it's tough for you back home as well.

The rats seem to be leaving us alone, I think it's because there's not much food. It's bloody freezing here, sorry for swearing sis. We've had so much snow and rain we're wading in water. Most of us have got trench foot so I wouldn't say no to a parcel of socks to share around. It would be lovely to have dry feet again and a decent bed to sleep in. I don't think Charles and I thought this little adventure through when we signed up for it, and what's more I haven't met one French girl, how bad is that? Joking aside, I've asked for some leave. It's been a while so I must

42

be allowed to come home soon, so hopefully I might see you soon.

Love you both.

Stephen xx

Water splashed onto the paper. Victoria sniffed and wiped away her tears. She folded the paper in half and thrust it back inside the envelope. She tapped it on the table a couple of times before taking a deep breath and jumping up, scraping back her chair on the wooden floor. *It's time you sorted yourself out, girl. You keep talking about doing things for the war effort, sorting out this house, and yet nothing.* She shook her head angrily, remembering all the advice she was quick to dish out to Molly, and yet not following it herself. *First, I need to find some socks to send to Stephen.* She dropped the letter on the table and walked back into the hall. 'Then to Foyles Bookstore.' Victoria ran up the stairs, not noticing the groans from the age-ing wood. The closed door of her parents' bedroom stopped her in her tracks. Should she go in? It was time she plucked up the courage, but not today.

4

Victoria's feet ached as she flopped down on one of the four wooden chairs, around a small square table in the staff area at Foyles Bookstore. She leant back and closed her eyes for a moment. The dong of the staff cards being marked by the clock faded into background noise.

'Everything all right, Victoria?'

Victoria opened her eyes and glanced up at Alice. 'It's only tiredness.' She pulled herself upright and gave a wry smile. 'I was up early, having breakfast with Daisy. What with that and being on my feet all day, I feel worn out. I suspect flat shoes will be in order, from now on.'

Alice smiled. 'Are you enjoying your new position?'

'It's certainly different to what I'm used to. I had to go down into the basement the other day, which was a bit scary.'

Alice chuckled as she pulled out a chair and sat down next to her friend. 'You'll soon get used to it.' She tidied her black skirt around her legs and pulled at the bottom of her white blouse.

'I wouldn't want to be down there on my own; it's quite eerie. If that door slammed shut and got stuck, I'm sure no one would hear you screaming. I don't know how Albert does it.'

'You have an over-active imagination; it comes from reading too many books, especially as you sleep in your own basement every night.'

'Molly more or less said the same thing, but it's not

the same. I've got used to my basement, plus I always try and prop open the door when I'm down there on my own.' Victoria smiled, but her eyes stayed focused on Alice, as her fingers tweaked the white buttons at the bottom of her blouse, her body rigid with tension. 'You didn't mind me getting made up to Floor Manager, did you?' She paused. 'You know it's only temporary.'

Alice reached out and rubbed Victoria's arm. 'Of course not, silly; why would I?'

'I can think of several reasons, but the main one is that you have a lot more experience than I do.'

Alice shook her head. 'Trust me when I say I'm very happy for you. Now stop worrying and enjoy escaping from that payment booth.'

Relief spread across Victoria's face and she visibly relaxed.

Alice shook her head. 'You haven't been worrying about it, have you?'

'I'd be lying if I said no.' Victoria raised her eyebrows. 'The funny thing was, I thought Mr Leadbetter was either going to give me the sack or proposition me. I never for one minute thought he was going to promote me.'

Alice's laughter filled the air around them. 'I bet your face was a picture when he started talking to you.'

Victoria blushed. 'I just hope he didn't realise what was going on inside my head.'

They both leant back in their chairs and giggled.

Alice shook her head. 'It must feel strange to be able to move around the shop, without worrying if you are going to get into trouble for not being at your post.'

'You two sound like a couple of naughty schoolgirls.' Molly pulled out a chair, scraping it across the wooden floor.

'It's good to have you back, Molly.' Victoria looked across at her friend. 'Have you settled in again?'

'It's like I've never been away.' Molly chuckled to herself, as she began to unwrap her sandwiches, the greaseproof paper rustling as she unfolded it. 'I've promised Mr Leadbetter I will behave myself this time.' She looked up, giving them both a wry smile. 'I suppose I should be careful what I say, now we have management eating at the table with us.'

The girls laughed as one.

Victoria tried to look stern as she frowned at her friend. 'Don't you start, Molly Cooper.'

Alice beamed, as she looked from one to the other. 'It's just like old times.'

They sat in silence for a moment, as they each unwrapped their lunches. The chatter and laughter around them slowly grew as other members of staff came in, to clock off for lunch.

'I 'ave news.' A woman's shrill voice cut above the noise.

Everyone turned to stare at the woman standing in the doorway.

'Apparently, the newspapers are saying the Americans have joined the war. Let's 'ope that means it'll soon be over, eh.'

Cheering and clapping filled the room.

Alice turned back to her friends. 'I do hope they're right; it'll be good to have our menfolk home safe and sound.'

The girls nodded.

'It feels like it's been going on forever.' Molly sighed. 'There's so much tragedy around it, it's sometimes hard to remember what it was like before the war

46

started. That lovely day in Southend seems a lifetime ago, and yet it's less than three years. I remember the excitement at the thought of paddling in the sea and having an ice cream.'

Alice smiled. 'It was certainly a carefree bank holiday for us, with all the boys safe at home.'

Victoria frowned. 'Yes, when I think back, I thought I was carrying the weight of the world on my shoulders, trying to be a mother and father at sixteen to Daisy and Stephen. Then Ted disappearing when I needed him the most and, just when I thought it couldn't get any worse, Stephen enlisted without a word.' Sadness washed over her as she immediately remembered Ted's smile and laughter. She felt her heart was breaking all over again as she remembered how they had giggled their way hand in hand along Southend seafront, before she had lost her childhood to tragedy. The heat of the day meant they couldn't eat their ice creams quickly enough; memories of it running down the cone and on to her fingers made her smile. Afterwards Ted had whisked off his shoes and socks, rolled up his trouser legs and paddled at the water's edge. It hadn't taken her long to join him. She could still feel the sand and the salty water caressing her toes. Tears pricked at her eyes. How she longed for this war to be over and have him back with her.

Molly glanced over at her friends. 'That's true, but it also tells us we're all stronger than we think.' She sighed. 'But one thing I have learnt is that you can only deal with and worry about what's in front of you. None of us know what's around the corner, waiting to jump out at us. Just as well too; can you imagine it?'

Victoria glanced across at Alice and they both gave a wry smile.

Molly looked from one to the other. 'What?'

'See, it's happened again.' Victoria raised her eyebrows and stared at Molly, before quickly looking back at Alice. 'How do you think it works?'

She leant across and prodded Molly's hand. 'It feels so life-like.'

Alice giggled as confusion tripped across Molly's face.

'Sorry, Molly.' Victoria's smile belied her words. 'I know you've been through a lot since this awful war started, more than any of us sitting here, but it still throws me when you come out with your words of wisdom.'

Molly laughed. 'I don't know about that. We've all been through it in different ways, and we're all living on our memories of carefree times, but I'm glad I could make you both smile.'

Victoria lifted the corner of her bread, peering at the fish paste that she'd thinly spread that morning, with no butter to moisten it. 'I'm thinking of going to Endell Street after work, you know, the military hospital in Covent Garden.' She looked up at her friends' wide-eyed expressions, each holding their sandwiches in mid-air. 'No, Stephen isn't a patient there.' She paused for a moment, as her friends each took a bite of their lunch. 'I want to see if I can volunteer in some way, you know, read or sit and chat to the patients. I've heard only women work there, so maybe I can help in some small way. What do you think?'

Alice ran her tongue over her lips. 'I'm sure they are always grateful for any help they can get. My father is still going to St. Thomas's every day. I think the first time he went, it really left its mark on him.'

Molly placed her half-eaten giblet sandwich down

on the greaseproof paper. 'Would you like to train as a nurse?'

Victoria shook her head. 'I think I'm too squeamish for that, and anyway it's all about small steps. I thought I'd get there first, then maybe ask to do the training, but I don't want to waste everyone's time.'

Alice nodded. 'That makes sense. When I started doing the ambulance run at Victoria train station, it was scary. It took me a while to realise most of them want to see a friendly face and talk about normal things. I suppose they just want to forget what they've seen and heard.' She looked pensive for a moment. 'Prepare yourself, because some of them say some outlandish things, but it's just their humour.'

* * *

Tom stood outside the open gates of Endell Street Military Hospital. The cold wind licked his face and cut through his jacket, into his skin. His body shivered as he moved from one foot to the other, wriggling his toes inside his heavy boots in a bid to keep his feet warm. His breath made grey swirls in front of him, disappearing into the greyness of the sky, reminding him he could do with a cigarette. He pulled a box from his trouser pocket and opened it. He looked down at the cigarettes, lined up like soldiers on parade. He shook his head and closed the box again, pushing them back into his pocket. His sister didn't like him smoking. He looked at his wristwatch and, watching the hospital doorway, he wondered what time she finished work. He lifted his hands to his mouth and blew, before rubbing them together. Tom looked around him and sighed, before taking the decision to go inside the hospital. He rubbed his hands together again. 'She'll find me frozen if I wait out here for much longer.' He strode towards the door and yanked it open.

Reception was busy. Nursing staff dashed in and out, only stopping momentarily. Tom looked around and wondered at the wisdom of coming inside. A nurse glanced over at him, before looking back at her paperwork, writing something and handing it over to the receptionist. He turned to go back outside; he didn't want to be in the way.

'Can I help you?'

A woman's voice stopped him in his tracks. He turned around and saw the nurse walking towards him.

'Are you here to see someone?'

Tom smiled at her. 'I'm afraid I'm not here to see a patient.'

'Are you hurt?' The nurse frowned as her eyes wandered over him, looking for signs of injury. 'Do you need some medical attention?'

Colour crept up Tom's neck. 'No, I'm sorry . . . I should have waited outside, but that wind's bitter today . . . I'm here to meet my sister, before I get my train out of London, but I don't know what time she finishes work.'

The nurse eyed his khaki uniform, with two stripes on his sleeve. 'What's your sister's name?'

Tom shook his head. 'I don't want to get her into trouble.' He grinned. 'She'll make my life hell.'

A smile spread across the nurse's face. 'What's her name?'

'Mabel Atkins.'

'Ahh, yes, I know her.'

Tom frowned. 'That doesn't sound good.'

The nurse chuckled. 'I'm Sister Philips. I'll send someone to fetch Mabel and she can finish for the day; I'm sure we'll manage.' She turned and beckoned to a young nurse, who almost ran over to her. 'Please go to Joan of Arc Ward and fetch Nurse Atkins. Tell her she has a visitor and she can finish for the day.'

The young nurse nodded and sped off towards the lift.

Tom watched her go. 'Joan of Arc Ward? I thought all military hospital wards were given letters of the alphabet for names?'

Sister Philips replied, 'This hospital is run by women; even the doctors are women. I believe it's the only one of its kind, so the wards are named after women who are saints or holy.'

Tom nodded. 'That's quite something. I had no idea, although I've heard this hospital has got an excellent reputation.'

They both looked across reception, as the swish of the lift doors opening caught their attention. Mabel was tangled up in her coat, as she tried thrusting her arms inside her sleeves. Her face lit up at the sight of her brother and she almost ran towards him.

Sister Philips wanted to smile at the sight of Mabel fighting with her coat, but forced herself to look stern. 'Atkins, you know the rules, no running.'

'Yes, Sister, sorry.'

'Right, I'll let you get on with what's left of the day and I'll see you tomorrow, Atkins.'

Mabel nodded. 'Thank you, Sister, but I'll probably be back later. I suspect my brother doesn't have long.'

The sister gave a curt nod. 'Well, as it suits. I never say no to an extra pair of hands.' She cast her gaze towards Mabel's brother. 'Take care.'

Mabel watched the sister walk away, before turning her attention to Tom. She arched her eyebrows and grinned. 'Tom, how wonderful.' She took a step forward and wrapped her arms around him, ignoring the admiring looks they were getting. She squeezed him tight against her ample bosom, before pulling away. 'Let me look at you.'

Colour began to rise in Tom's neck, as he realised they were attracting attention. 'Come on. Let's find somewhere for a coffee and a chat. I don't have long.' He grabbed her warm hand and pulled her towards him and the hospital doorway.

Mabel thrust her hand under his arm and rested it against the coarse material of his uniform. They stepped forward as one. 'I got your letter, but I wasn't sure what time you'd get here.' She braced herself against the cold air, after the warmth of the hospital, as her brother opened the door. 'There's a small café near Covent Garden that I hear is very good.'

'That sounds fine.' Tom paused. 'I wanted to talk to you about John . . . '

'Is he all right?' Mabel's eyes widened with concern.

Tom squeezed his sister's arm. 'In all honesty, I don't know. Ma is doing her best, but you know what Pa's like, and I think his temper is getting worse.'

Mabel made a humourless sound. 'Is that even possible?'

Tom stared straight ahead, not wanting to admit what he feared they all knew anyway. 'He's always been a bully; I don't know how David could have left John with them.'

Mabel sighed. 'No, I think ordinarily he wouldn't

have done, after all he was the first of us to leave, but John's health is better because of the sea air. The London smog would have killed him. You may not remember but they never had the money to move to Brighton and David's work was here. Last I heard they were saving so they could move and have John live with them.'

'Yes, yes, I know that,' Tom snapped. 'What I don't understand is how he and Margaret haven't checked on him for, what, seven years. What's changed? After all, at least one of them used to visit every week. I even remember Victoria, Daisy and Stephen coming a couple of times. They're a lovely couple and no one knows better than David how bad Father can be, so to leave his son at his mercy seems unforgivable to me.'

Mabel nodded, as memories of their childhood began to flood her mind. She shook her head; now was not the time. 'I agree, it does look bad, but David must have his reasons.' She hesitated for a moment. 'Perhaps it's time to talk to him and find out what's going on with him, Margaret and the children.'

Tom smiled at his older sister, always wanting to see good in everyone. 'That's your call, you are the only one able to do that, as you're here in London.'

'The trouble is, I don't have an address for him. When I knocked I was told by a neighbour they had gone, otherwise I would have done it before now.'

Tom nodded. 'I suspect Ma probably has it.' He took a deep breath. 'I want you to do something while I'm away this time.'

Mabel looked up at him with wide eyes. Her lips tightened for a second; she knew what was coming.

'I wouldn't ask but — '

'You want me to visit from time to time, to keep an eye on John.'

Tom's mouth lifted in one corner. 'Not just John, but Ma as well. I know I'm asking a lot, but I'm really concerned, and it will be one less thing for me to be worrying about, while I'm up to my ankles in water and God knows what else.'

Mabel frowned and anxiety flitted across her face, before she quickly forced a smile. 'How can I refuse? There isn't anything I wouldn't do for you, and I definitely don't want you worrying about things back here.'

Tom frowned. 'I know I'm asking a lot.'

Mabel could feel the tears weren't far away. 'No, Tom, it's nothing compared to what you're doing. Please stay safe, and don't worry about Ma and John. I don't suppose you can tell me where you're going this time.'

Tom laughed. 'You do know that if I said, I'd have to kill you, in case you're a German spy.'

★ ★ ★

Shaftesbury Avenue was as busy as always. The street vendors were still out, selling their wares on their barrows, their voices vying for attention against each other and the cars spluttering along the road. The aroma of hot soup and potatoes followed Victoria down the street. Her tummy gurgled, reminding her she was hungry. She shook her head at an old lady holding out a small bunch of spring flowers. 'No thank you.'

Crossing the road at Seven Dials confused her, as always; so many streets to cross, but the walk from Foyles Bookshop in Charing Cross Road hadn't taken long. As Victoria stood at the edge of the pavement, she was suddenly back to the many times Ted had put her arm through his at this very spot, making sure they both got across the roads safely. The coarseness of his jacket sleeve under her soft fingers was imprinted on her memory along with the woody cologne he wore sparingly. They had spent many happy hours at Covent Garden watching and listening to the street performers and market traders. He will return to her. Her throat tightened with unspent tears, but she had to believe that. She had to hold on to her memories until that day came.

It wasn't long before Victoria was standing in front of the large metal gates at Endell Street Military Hospital. They looked forbidding as the early evening closed in. It would be dark when she left later. In the half-light, the old Victorian workhouse looked intimidating, as she stood near the scrolled ironwork on the gates. Victoria took a deep breath. *You don't have to go in*, a voice mumbled in her head. She pulled herself up to her full height and took a step forward. *Yes I do*.

Several nurses were chatting as they walked towards her.

'You all right, luvvie?'

Nurses nodded in her direction, waving and shouting goodnight to each other, as they walked past.

Victoria nodded.

'If you're here to visit someone, just go in; they won't bite you.' The nurse smiled kindly at Victoria. 'Do you need help with something?'

'No, thank you.' Victoria paused for a moment and looked up at the hospital. The bowed brickwork at the windows matched the curvature of the arched doorway, which dominated the front of the building.

The large courtyard had two ambulances parked to the right of it. Her stomach churned and nausea began to rise in her. Her head started to pound. Perhaps she shouldn't have come, but she couldn't stop the words from tumbling out. 'I'm here to visit some of the patients.'

The nurse's smile faded as she looked at her, quizzically. 'It's your first time, isn't it?'

Victoria nodded.

'Well, it's been busy in there today; actually, it is every day. We had several ambulances dropping off soldiers today, so just take care. Oh, and stick to the main ward or the sister will not be happy, the side rooms are off limits to volunteers.'

Victoria glanced at the nurse. 'Why?'

'The main reason is because those rooms are for patients with complications, who may not make it, and of course they don't want them catching infections.'

Victoria nodded.

'Don't feel sorry for the men, because they don't like that as a rule. Just see past their injuries and talk to them naturally.' The nurse patted Victoria's arm. 'They're happy to have someone else to chat to, other than us nurses, that is. You'll be all right, you'll see.'

'Thank you for your kindness.'

The nurse looked towards the hospital. 'We've all had to walk through those doors for the first time.' She turned back to Victoria. 'I'm sorry for my rudeness; all this information and I haven't introduced myself. I'm Mabel, at your service, ma'am.' She looked down at her uniform and chuckled. She stretched out her arms. 'I'm a nurse here.'

Victoria laughed. 'I think the uniform gave you

away, but it's lovely to meet you, Mabel. I'm Victoria. You must be cold, without a coat.'

'Yeah, I made the mistake of forgetting it earlier, but I only have to go to the nurses' home, which isn't far. I suspect we could be seeing a lot of each other.' Mabel studied the young girl in front of her. Her dark hair was just visible under a woollen hat and black winter coat. 'Have we met before?'

Victoria studied the older woman, trying to guess her age. Her salt and pepper hair was pulled back into a bun. Her forehead had worry lines etched into it. Her eyes, though shining bright, had a hint of sadness about them, like she imagined her own did. She shook her head. 'I don't think so.'

Mabel stared for a moment. 'I don't know; I don't often forget a face, and yours looks vaguely familiar. Never mind, if we have, it'll come to me.'

Victoria frowned. 'I'm sure I'd remember if we had, although I do talk to a lot of people, where I work.'

Mabel nodded. 'I expect you're right. Come on, I'll walk you in, otherwise you'll be trying to pluck up courage all night.' She laughed and turned to face the hospital. 'So where do you work?'

'Foyles Bookshop, on Charing Cross Road.'

Mabel thrust her arm in Victoria's and pulled her forward. They stepped forward in time with each other. 'You like your books then?'

'Yes, have you ever come to the shop?'

Mabel's laughter shrilled out. 'Definitely not.'

Victoria raised her eyebrows. 'You should, it's a brilliant shop with so many books. Rumour has it that people have got lost in there.'

'I'll bear that in mind.' Mabel pulled open the hospital door.

Victoria immediately squinted at the brightness of the electric light. Disinfectant and carbolic hung in the air, causing her to cough as she breathed it in. Her flat shoes were silent on the grey floor as she followed Mabel to the reception desk.

Mabel chuckled and looked round at Victoria. 'You'll get used to the light and smells in the hospital; soon you won't notice it at all. That's if you come back again.'

'I will.' Victoria knew she sounded more confident than she felt.

'Hhmm, we'll see.' Mabel looked back at the lady sitting behind the reception desk. 'Ivy, I'm delivering Victoria safely to you. She's here to visit patients. Can you arrange for someone to take her to the ward, then Sister can let her know who she needs to sit with.' She studied Ivy for a moment. 'Can you also ask someone to keep an extra eye on the corporal in the side room on Joan of Arc ward, I believe he's quite badly injured but he's also going to need some rehabilitation time so he's going to be here for a while.'

Ivy nodded. 'Stop worrying and get off home.' She gave Victoria a smile. 'Welcome to the mad house.'

Mabel giggled. 'Don't put her off before she's even started.' She turned to face Victoria. 'Take no notice of Ivy, she should have retired years ago.' She pulled a tongue out at the grey-haired woman behind the desk. 'Take care, Victoria. What you are about to do is hard and not for everyone, but it's also a great thing. Hopefully, I'll see you again.'

'Thank you.' Victoria watched Mabel walk towards the door, and out into the cold.

Ivy gave a little cough. 'Can I just take your full name, Victoria? It's only for our records.' Her lips curled. 'Matron is quite strict about knowing who is in here, both visitors and patients.'

Victoria smiled and leant forward a little. 'It's Appleton, Victoria Appleton.'

Ivy jotted the name down on her pad, before walking around her desk. 'Most of our patients are in a pretty bad way, so don't be surprised if you don't get much of a response from them.'

A shiver ran up Victoria's spine as she fell into step with Ivy. She forced a smile. 'Thank you for the warning.'

Ivy glanced across at her. 'I'm sure you'll be fine.'

Within minutes, they had climbed the stairs and were pushing open the doors to a room with beds on either side, for as far as the eye could see. The green walls were broken up by the daylight coming through the windows.

Small clipboards holding sheets of white paper hung near each neatly made bed. Some men were lying still and groans escaped into the air, while others were more upright. A bedside cabinet and a wooden chair, not dissimilar to the ones Victoria had at home, filled the space between each bed. There was no room for private conversation. Perhaps it would be safer to read books; she could read to two patients at once.

'Oh look, lads, a pretty young lady has just walked in; now that should brighten our days here.'

Ivy gave a mischievous smile and nudged Victoria with her elbow. 'Aww, come on now, it's not the first time I've been up to see you all.'

The ward came alive with laughter.

5

'Do you think we come here too much?' Molly asked, looking around the Regent Street restaurant. Nothing had changed in Monico's since they'd first had tea and cake there a few years ago. The strategically placed large potted palms had probably got taller. A grandfather clock chimed in the corner, partially covered by the fronds of the plants. The large mirrors along the walls gave the illusion that it was larger than it really was. The roman pillars and arches gave it an exotic feel.

Victoria ran her hands over the stiff white tablecloth. 'Definitely not. This is still my favourite place to come to eat, but I would like to have a proper meal one of these days; it always smells so good as it wafts past my nose.' She glanced over at the neighbouring table. 'Maybe one day.'

Molly laughed, pulling her royal blue skirt from around her legs and straightening the cuffs of her cream blouse. 'We haven't actually looked at the menu for a couple of years; goodness knows what meals they have on there to tempt us.'

'That's true; we always order the same thing,' said Alice. 'We've created our own tradition of tea and chocolate cake, regardless of good news or bad.' She turned to look at Victoria. 'Talking of which, how did you get on at Endell Street Hospital?'

Victoria's eyes lit up. 'It was a bit daunting, walking up to the large gates, and it's a huge building, but once I'd walked in, they were very welcoming. Well

60

actually, a nurse took me in, when she found me loitering around outside, trying to pluck up courage. Apparently, it's run by women who were active suffragettes before the war started. Anyway, it seems I can go whenever I want. I have to let them know I'm there and they will tell me which patient to sit with.' She lowered her eyes for a moment. 'The sister said that, unless someone wasn't expected to last the day, they would want me to only spend maybe an hour with each soldier. Apparently, not many of them get visitors, so it's about spreading the good cheer, so to speak.'

Alice nodded. 'That makes sense.' She paused, turning the wedding ring on her finger. 'I like to think if my brother, Charles, was in that situation, someone would be kind enough to spend time with him, and when I think about Robert, I want to believe he didn't die on his own.'

Molly reached out and rested her hand on top of Alice's, squeezing it tight. 'There are good people out there and we mustn't forget that.'

'That's why I want to do it, Alice. Your brother is still fighting, as is mine, and then there's Ted.' Victoria paused. 'I refuse to accept I won't see Ted again. I still love him and want someone to be by his side when he needs it.' A tear ran down her face and she quickly swiped it away.

Molly frowned. 'I know Ted's the love of your life but is there room in your heart for you to love anyone else?'

Victoria shook her head. 'I could never love anyone the way I love Ted.'

Alice took Victoria's hand and gently stroked it. 'There's nothing to say he won't come back to you.

61

Remember we have to have faith; it won't let us down.'

The waitress sidled up to the table, wearing the traditional long black dress, white frilly-bibbed apron and a white hat perched precariously on her black curls. She smiled as she placed the china tea service in front of them, before silently moving away.

'Let's talk about happier things.' Victoria glanced over at Molly. 'What's happening with your wedding plans?'

Molly pushed her blonde hair behind her ear. 'Nothing is happening — well actually, that isn't true, I'm getting nagged a lot.'

Victoria frowned. 'Who from, Andrew or your mother?'

Molly groaned. 'All of them.'

The waitress appeared, placing plates in front of them, with a large slice of chocolate cake on each.

Alice nodded. 'Thank you.'

The waitress smiled, before moving away from their table.

'Why are they nagging you?' Victoria picked up her cake fork. 'I thought you would have it all organised by now.'

Molly gave a humourless laugh. 'Victoria, I haven't organised anything, that's the problem, and what's more, I'm not going to.'

Alice raised her eyebrows, as she looked across at Victoria. 'Is the wedding off?'

'No, it's just not on.'

Victoria sighed. 'What is that supposed to mean?'

'I want both my parents to slow down, before they end up in an early grave. I wish they would stop working and move to the house they bought for me, but they're refusing to do it, so I've told me ma I'll not be getting married until they have.' Molly lifted her chin. 'Pa has offered the house and his savings to Andrew as a dowry; talk about old fashioned, and Andrew said no to it.'

Victoria reached out and clasped Molly's hand. 'Your father is only trying to do the right thing. I think it's quite sweet that he wants to do the traditional things.'

'I know, I know. It's hard work keep battling all the time, and no one seems to understand that I want to do the right thing by them.'

'Maybe you need to find a different way to solve the problem,' said Alice. 'I'm not saying I have the answers, but there must be another way of appealing to your father's sense of pride and duty.'

The three girls fell silent for a few minutes.

Alice grabbed Molly's arm. 'I know, why don't you tell him that if he moves into the house, it will still be yours, rather than him giving it to Andrew. Then, if anything happens, you would still have somewhere to live.' She beamed at her friends. 'It may not work, but I think it is definitely worth a try.'

Molly glanced across at Alice. 'You look like the cat that's got the cream.'

'That's because that's exactly how I feel.' Alice blushed, and her cheeks matched the dress she was wearing. 'I'm getting good at this stuff.' Laughter erupted around their table.

Victoria placed her hand on her chest, as she gasped for breath. The soft silky material of her pale blue blouse seeped between her fingers. 'In all seriousness, it is a good idea. When you think about it, your father has only ever wanted to look after you, even more so when he's no longer around, so I think that idea could work.'

Molly nodded. 'Maybe I'll try it; arguing isn't getting me anywhere.'

'That's true. And you don't want to keep Andrew waiting too long, especially as nothing has been straightforward between the two of you. I'm sorry, I should have asked how he is.'

Molly's face lit up. 'He's wonderful, and his burns from the munitions explosion are improving all the time, but he is urging me to set a date for our wedding.'

Alice gave Molly a sideways glance. 'Once the wedding is over with, you'll then be under pressure to produce grandchildren.'

Molly picked up her cake fork and let it balance on the end of her thumb. 'Hmmm, I'm not sure I'm ready for children yet.'

'I'd love another child. It would be good for Arthur to have a brother or sister.'

Victoria put down her fork. 'Is this your way of telling us something?'

Alice chuckled. 'No, but I would love it to happen again.' She took the lid off the teapot and began stirring vigorously. 'This tea will be cold if we don't drink it soon.' She replaced the lid and poured the dark brown liquid through the tea strainer, over the cups. 'You can add your own milk.'

Molly stabbed her fork into the end of the chocolate cake. 'So, Victoria, you mentioned a while ago about sorting out your parents' things. Have you decided when you are going to do it?'

Victoria let her fork clatter on to the tea plate. 'No . . . if I'm honest, I'm dreading it.'

Molly licked the crumbs from her lips and picked

up her teacup. 'That's understandable.' She took a sip of the lukewarm liquid. 'I'm sure I speak for Alice as well, when I say we can both come round and be with you when you do it. You're not on your own, you know.'

'I know, and I do appreciate that, but it's something I should do on my own.'

Alice licked the cake from around her teeth. 'You don't have to, though.'

Molly eyed Victoria. 'I don't think you'll start, if someone doesn't force you to, so I think, initially, we should be there, until you begin to go through some things.'

Victoria sighed. 'I'm ashamed to say I closed their bedroom door just after they died, and I've not opened it since.' Her eyes welled up. 'To be honest, I can't bring myself to go in there. I know it will smell of my mother, and I dread the memories that will come flooding back.'

Alice's eyes narrowed a little. 'We'll do it together, like we do everything.'

'Are you worried about what you'll find?' asked Molly.

Victoria could feel her throat tightening. 'Maybe — let's face it, it was seven years ago and I was only sixteen.' She paused. 'I didn't know them as an adult, so they could have secrets that might shock me.'

Molly shook her head. 'I'm sure there won't be anything you can't overcome, and we will be with you every step of the way, like you were for me. That's what friends are for.'

Victoria gave a watery smile. 'Yes, that's true, it's not like they would have been German spies or something.'

Molly laughed. 'Right, let's eat cake and drink our tea.' She smiled at Victoria. 'It was you who once said tea and cake solves everything.'

* * *

Molly shut the front door behind her, pulling her pink woollen gloves from the pockets of her winter coat. She glanced up at Alice as she pushed her hands inside them. 'I thought it might be warmer today; I nearly went for a lighter jacket.'

It was early, but Carlisle Street was already a hive of activity. Women wearing headscarves and aprons were cleaning windows and scrubbing doorsteps. They mopped their brows and stretched their aching backs as they nodded and shouted good morning to Molly and Alice. Water and soap suds trickled off steps and formed pools at the side of the road.

Both Molly and Alice shouted good morning to them, as they walked past.

'Don't overdo it,' Molly called out to them. 'It's too cold to be out here, scrubbing steps and cleaning windows.'

Mrs Taylor groaned at her neighbour. 'Trust me, after five minutes of scrubbing the front doorstep, you're sweating like a pig.'

Molly smiled. 'That I can believe.'

The girls walked on in silence. Molly looked back to watch the women doing their chores; some didn't look much older than her. They disappeared from view as they turned into Dean Street, heading towards New Oxford Street. 'It's only just occurred to me, you've come the long way round to go to Victoria's; you could have walked across Bedford Square from Bloomsbury Street. It would have probably only taken you five minutes, and been prettier, with the spring flowers out.'

Alice wrinkled her nose as she caught a waft of maltiness coming from the fermenting hops at the Horseshoe Brewery. 'I know, but I thought it might be better if we arrived together.'

Molly nodded. 'I wonder how Victoria is today.' She stepped behind Alice, allowing a suited gentleman to walk past. He lifted his bowler hat and nodded as he drew level with her.

Alice waited for Molly to join her. 'I expect the very thought of opening her parents' bedroom door has got her in a terrible state. She told me once that she hasn't been in there since just after the train crash, and that was only to leave things on the bed.'

Molly looked down at the pavement, and their feet stepping forward, in time with each other. 'I can't say I'm looking forward to it. Don't get me wrong, I wouldn't not help, but there's something not quite right about rifling through someone else's belongings.' She tightened her lips. 'The sooner we get to Percy Street and get started, the better.'

'You need to be patient, and don't tease her. Hopefully, Victoria won't be too bad, once we get started.'

'I'm not so sure about that; it's going to be a painful day for her, but unfortunately, it's long overdue.'

A car horn tooted. Both Alice and Molly looked in the direction it came from, but they couldn't see anything untoward.

Alice looked sideways at Molly. 'I know it is.'

'I know she said she wouldn't, but do you think she'll ever let go of Ted? After all she was devastated when he disappeared, I'm amazed she's still standing

67

what with him leaving shortly after losing her parents.' She glanced across at Alice. 'I'm sure if she made room in her heart she would find someone else to love, and more importantly, love her back, no matter what life throws at them.'

'I don't think she will ever move on from him — she has forgiven him because she loves him no matter what.'

Molly sighed. 'I know you're right, but the whole thing just makes me feel so sad.'

Alice pushed her hand through Molly's arm. 'I know, but we need to think of something good, to take her mind off things.'

'What? Why are you looking at me like that?' Molly chuckled. 'You're the good news person, so start thinking of something.'

Alice giggled as they weaved in and out of the stalls littering the pavement. 'I don't know about that. I've been listening to my grandfather moaning about some of the sport being stopped this summer; he'll miss his days out at the cricket, that's for sure. Anyway, you could potentially have some good news if you set your wedding date, instead of keeping us all waiting.'

'I haven't kept everyone waiting, as you put it.' Molly sighed. 'It's the only way I can get my parents to give up working and stop potentially killing themselves. After my father's scare, it's all I can think about, but they are so stubborn.'

'Ah, so that's where you get it from.' She shook her head at an old lady carrying small bunches of flowers in a basket.

'I'm not stubborn.' Molly looked across at Alice. 'All right, maybe a little, but they want us to get married and have children, so there's never going to be

68

a better time for me to get them to put themselves first.' She paused for a moment. 'Anyway, I did as you suggested and told them this morning they could live in the house in Percy Street. That way, my father doesn't have to worry about stopping work and losing the house that goes with the job. Andrew and I can live in his family home.'

'I must say, he's being very patient with you.'

'Andrew understands how important it is to me, and I think it's pretty fair to say that he thinks I'm stubborn too.' Molly giggled. 'So he's letting me go with it, for now.' Her voice dropped a little as she continued. 'I don't want to lose him though, so I do have to get my parents to agree to something, and quickly.'

Alice frowned. 'Has he said something then?'

'Oh no.' Molly sighed. 'But I'm not very good at this relationship malarkey, and don't want to make any more mistakes.'

Alice tucked her hand through Molly's arm. 'I think you'll be all right, Andrew is totally smitten with you.'

Molly blushed as she pulled on Alice's arm. She watched a man stretch out his hand to the people, as they rushed past him. He was invisible to them, as he sat on the cold grey pavement, his only leg huddled up close to his chest. His heavy coat was grubby and had seen better days. While his unshaven face was weather-worn, it also held a film of dust that filled the deep lines etched on it. Shaking her head, she undid her handbag and took out her purse.

'Spare me some change please,' the man repeated over and over again.

An old lady appeared, giving him a cup of tea and a sandwich. 'It's not much, but it'll help keep you warm and fill your belly for a while.'

The man grabbed it and bit hungrily into the bread. When he finally spoke, his voice was thick with emotion. 'Thank you, ma'am, thank you.'

A tear tripped down Alice's face.

Molly pulled out her handkerchief and sniffed into it, before dabbing at her eyes. She opened her purse and took out two silver coins.

Alice nodded and did the same.

The old woman glanced over at them. ''E's 'ere every day; there must be somewhere these injured soldiers can go.' She sighed. 'He can't work with his injuries, but I don't suppose he's alone in that.'

Molly bit down on her lip. Blood seeped into her mouth, leaving an iron taste on her tongue. She bent down next to the man. Despite the cold weather, there was a stench of sweat around him. 'Take this.' She placed her two silver half crowns on the palm of his grubby hand.

The man stopped chewing. His eyes widened and his mouth gaped open, as he stared down at the money. 'I can't take that; it wouldn't be right.'

'Let us worry about that.'

The man clenched his hand shut. 'Sorry.' He gave a wry smile. 'I was suddenly afraid you'd change your mind.'

Alice tapped Molly on the shoulder and passed her the two silver florins she was holding.

'Thank you, thank you, I can't say thank you enough.'

Molly stood up and smiled. 'It's the least we can do. I truly wish there was more.'

In silent agreement, Alice and Molly stopped at the edge of the pavement. Their arms linked, as they looked left and right, so they could cross Oxford

70

Street to walk along Rathbone Place.

Alice glanced at Molly. 'It's sad, isn't it? That man risked his life for us, and now look at him, begging on the street with nowhere to live.'

Molly nodded. 'I wonder if there's someone who can help him, maybe the Salvation Army, even if he only got a bath and a hot meal every day.'

Alice mumbled, 'It's shameful, treating him like that, and he can't be the only soldier in that position. It's terrible.'

'I can see why your cousin opened up a women's refuge; it's heartbreaking.' Molly paused. 'It brings home how my parents could have ended up, if it hadn't been for the kindness of the refuge they grew up in.' She tightened her lips for a moment. 'Perhaps I'll make some enquiries.'

The doors to The Old Queen's Head public house stood ajar, an old dog lay in the doorway, his sad eyes looking their way. A woman leant over the dog and shook an old rag into the air. The breeze carried the dust in their direction. 'Sorry, girls.' The woman disappeared again.

Alice waved her hand in front of her face as they crossed the road, threading their way through the cars chugging along Oxford Street. 'Anyway, you and Andrew have been through some scary times, so I think waiting to set a date won't throw him.'

'Let's hope not.' Molly gave her friend a sideways glance. 'Do you like being a wife and mother?'

'I love it. I don't spend as much time with my son as I would like.' Alice stared into the distance. 'When this war is over, Freddie and I will be looking for our own place, but at the moment, with driving the ambulance and being under the continual threat of bombs going off, it's good to go home and see that the family is safe. He's still in pain from his injuries, but happy to be back at the police station. At least he can keep an eye on Lily and Daisy.' Alice chuckled.

'Has the arguing stopped between Lily and your father?'

'I don't think they will ever be the best of friends. That sister of mine is quite headstrong, but joining the police has focused her, so things have calmed down. Also, father is more tolerant since he's been visiting the soldiers in St. Thomas'.'

Molly nodded. 'That's good. I wonder how Victoria got on at Endell Street Military Hospital last night. I think she was quite nervous about visiting the patients again.'

'Yes, it must be quite nerve-wracking; after all, what do you talk to them about? I told her to take some books to read to them. At least when I go to Victoria train station to collect the wounded, the conversation is often about where they are going and what's going to happen to them.' Alice smiled. 'Some of them like to do some harmless flirting, but I think that's what they hide behind.'

'I expect it was quite scary when you first did it on your own.'

Alice nodded. 'I was terrified, but I kept telling myself if it were my brothers in this situation, I would want someone to be nice to them. My mother was very good at it.'

Molly immediately thought about her own mother. 'Mothers put us to shame. You have to admire them; they have strength that none of us know about.'

Alice sidestepped a child that ran out in front of her. 'You were brave too, leaving what you knew at

Foyles, to work at the munitions factory.'

Molly shrugged her shoulders. 'I don't know whether I was brave or stupid, but at least I met Andrew and have a newfound respect for the work they do in those places.'

'Do you ever hear from Grace? I often wonder if she settled into working on the land.'

Molly's eyes lit up. 'She writes to me every week and is loving working outside; she's doing well. I think a stray dog has adopted her.' She laughed then paused for a moment. 'I don't think Grace will ever get over you saving her life. There aren't many letters it's not mentioned in.'

Alice smiled. 'You know, that's the best bit about what I do — '

'What, saving lives?'

'No, although that's obviously good as well, but I was thinking more about how we can make a difference to someone's life by the small things we do.' Alice looked across at Molly. 'You know, I can't count the number of soldiers I've taken to hospitals, or spoken to at the rest station at Victoria.'

Molly frowned. 'And yet you sound quite sad about it, when actually you should be proud of all the work you've done, especially having a small child as well.'

Alice tried to raise a smile but failed. 'That's just it, it's all getting too much. I'm so tired all the time, and it's Arthur that doesn't get my full attention. I've got to give up something and it's a difficult decision to make.'

'You're not ill though, are you?'

'No, just tired.'

Molly pondered for a moment. 'Now I'm not at the munitions factory, I've still to find something to do towards the war effort, so I could take over one of your jobs, although driving an ambulance might be more difficult for me than serving the soldiers at Victoria station.'

'Don't put yourself down, Molly. None of it's easy, in fact some of it is heart-wrenching.' She paused. 'I'll try and make a decision.'

Molly and Alice stood outside the black front door of Victoria's home in Percy Street, worry and dread etched on their faces.

'It's not going to get done with us gazing up at the front door.' Molly took a deep breath. 'Are we going in, or shall we walk away?'

Alice lifted her hand and grabbed the brass door-knocker, letting it drop with a heavy thud.

Molly silently watched her actions. 'I suppose that means we are definitely doing this.'

'It's what we came to do, and we have to be strong, for Victoria's sake.'

A curtain twitching at the house next door caught Molly's attention. 'Ooh, we're being watched.' She chuckled. 'She's spying on Victoria; do you think she's a German spy, or just nosey?'

A smile broke across Alice's face as she looked at the neighbour's house. The dark curtain immediately dropped back into place. 'You're terrible; if she is a spy, she's not a very good one.'

Giggles erupted from them both and the tension of the day ahead was momentarily forgotten. The creaking of the front door brought the laughter to an abrupt end.

Colour drained from Alice's face, as she stared at the man standing in front of them in police uni-form.

Molly gasped, but no words came out.

'Can I help you?' The officer's deep voice filtered through to the pair of them.

6

John stared down at his hands, clutching a piece of his puzzle in his lap. The knuckles were almost visible through his translucent skin. His bony fingers confirmed he was losing weight, as they twisted and turned the awkward shape he was holding.

Beatrice frowned as she gave him a sideways glance; if only the sun would come out, so they could go for a walk. She sighed. It felt like the rain lashing against the window hadn't stopped for weeks. She looked out at the grey afternoon, the wind moaning as it collided against the house. Beatrice knew that, if she stood up and looked out at the sea, the white foam crests of the waves would be roaring onto the pebbles and the golden sand would be buried under the crashing waves. 'I'll be glad when the summer comes.'

John jolted out of his daze and looked up from his puzzle. 'I believe this is summer, Grandma. You'd think there wasn't much more rain to come down.'

Beatrice raised her eyebrows as she looked across at him. 'Yes, well, it'll be good when we can sit in the yard, or on the sea front, and get some fresh air into our lungs.' She paused for a moment. 'You look very pale this morning; shall I fetch the doctor?'

John gave a humourless laugh. 'No, Grandma.' He hesitated, staring at the fragile lady he adored. 'Here's something I do want to do though.' He stared at the puzzle piece, while biting down on his lip.

Beatrice dropped the newspaper onto her lap, before whispering, 'What is it?'

76

'Oh nothing.' John shook his head. 'I'm sorry to disturb your reading. I know Grandpa will keep you busy, once he gets home from his club.'

'You are much more important to me than anything that is written in this paper.' It rustled as she straightened the pages and folded it shut. 'So tell me what's going on inside your head, because I know something is.'

John smiled. 'You know me too well.'

'So tell me.' A long silence followed Beatrice's words; she didn't take her eyes off him.

John took a deep breath. He closed his eyes and gasped, then immediately straightened his lips into a tense thin line, as pain gripped his chest. Experience told him it would gradually subside. He slowly opened his eyes to see his grandma staring at him with fear in her eyes. 'It's all right, Grandma, it's about time I learned not to take deep breaths.' He forced a smile, in a bid to reassure her. 'You do know you mean everything to me, don't you?'

Beatrice could feel the tears pricking at her eyes; she blinked quickly, before nodding. 'As you do to me too.'

'I want you to always remember that —'

'You're scaring me.' Beatrice pulled herself out of the armchair, the newspaper forgotten, as it fell to the floor.

It was John's turn to try and brush away the anxiety that had gripped him. 'I'm sorry, Grandma, there's nothing to be frightened about.' He paused, not taking his eyes off her. 'I believe my asthma is getting worse and I would like to see my mother and father. They haven't been to see me for years and I want to know why. Was it so terrible, the last time they were here?

77

I know there was an argument with Grandpa, but he seems to argue with everyone. Surely that wouldn't have kept them away, would it?'

A chime rang through the house. Beatrice breathed a sigh of relief. 'I'll just get that; I'm not expecting visitors, so goodness knows who it is.'

John watched her almost run from the room, the door slowly gliding shut behind her. Regret wrapped itself around him. He shouldn't have mentioned it; after all, she was stuck in the middle of everything that happened in this house. Laughter came from the hall, followed by heels clattering on the red and black tiles. He sighed; the moment was gone, but it was probably just as well. The sitting room door swung open. A smile quickly spread across John's face. 'Aunt Mabel.' He pressed his hands hard on to the arms of the chair and pushed himself up. 'How wonderful.'

Mabel took the couple of steps to him. 'Don't get up, John, and don't call me aunt.'

John gave a feeble laugh. 'I'm not strong, but surely I can give my aunt a cuddle.' He wrapped his thin arms around her. He could feel her arms tighten around him, her expert hands taking in his thinness, without a word being said. Instinctively, he knew the thick jumper would not stop her from knowing he was getting worse.

Beatrice beamed at them both. 'I'll go and put the kettle on. It's lovely to see you, Mabel, so we shall make this an occasion to have biscuits.' She chuckled as she left the room.

Mabel smiled after her mother; she had missed her more than she realised.

John watched his aunt, wondering what had prompted the visit after such a long time. 'It's lovely

78

to see you; it's been a while. It's grand to see you looking so well, London must suit you.'

Mabel smiled and gave a little curtsey. 'Why, thank you, kind sir.'

Laughter burst from them both.

'How are you managing, John?'

'Nothing changes here, as I'm sure you know, but what about you?' John waited, but the silence became unbearable.

Mabel looked away, her joy no longer visible. She blinked rapidly.

John grabbed her hand. 'How are you coping without Uncle Sid?'

'London keeps me busy and Endell Street Hospital is a great place to work. The doctors and nurses care so much for the injured soldiers.' Mabel paused. 'I miss him every day, but I know we will meet again, when my maker calls me to him.'

John squeezed her hand. 'It all seems so unfair. To survive on the front line and then cop it when the Germans bomb London —'

'Yes, well, we were daft to visit Greenwich when there's a war on, but he wanted to get away from here for a couple of days and have me all to himself.' Mabel took a deep breath. 'Anyway, enough about me, I want to know how you are?' She pulled up a chair to sit next to him.

'As I said, nothing changes.'

Mabel ran a critical eye over him. 'I disagree. You're quite pale, and I believe you are losing weight, so I'm guessing you're not eating properly.' She watched a flicker of something run across his face but wasn't sure what it was. 'I know you're stuck here with the grumpiest man in the world but you can write to me, or better still, talk to me now.'

John laughed. 'Yes, I do believe he is the grumpiest man in the world.' He paused to catch his breath. 'I've missed you; you always make me laugh.'

'So, how are you really doing?'

John brushed away imaginary fluff from his trousers. 'If I'm honest I think my asthma has moved on to something else, although I don't know what. I'm coughing up stuff, which is new.' He cast a glance in his aunt's direction. 'And I'm eating properly yet I'm still losing weight.' He looked down at his hands. 'I think my fingers look a bit misshapen, they seem to be swollen on the ends and around the knuckle. I'm also sweating more than I used to, that seems to have a particularly salty taste to it.'

Mabel's mouth dropped open for a moment before she put on her professional nurse's head again. 'Have you told anyone?'

'No, I don't want you to either. I'm tired of living like this.'

Mabel shook her head defiantly. 'You have to fight whatever it is, see a doctor. I have money saved, and we can use that to pay for any treatment you might need.'

'It's not what I want, and anyway I think it's gone beyond that.' He paused. 'I was just talking to Grandma about finding my parents. I want to know why they haven't been to see me for so long.'

Mabel felt her heart leap in her chest; he had caught her by surprise. 'You know they love you to bits, so they must have their reasons.' She stood up and paced around the room. 'I remember each time they visited, it broke their hearts to leave you, but they had to think of your welfare.'

John nodded. 'But they haven't been back for years, so I want to know why? Do they no longer have time or care about me?'

Mabel glared at her nephew. 'John Appleton, I shall wash your mouth out with soap if you continue talking like that. Your parents adore you, and don't you forget it.'

John's face contorted with rage. 'So where are they?'

* * *

Molly grabbed Alice's arm, as they both stared wide-eyed up at the policeman.

The man at the door frowned, glancing from one to the other. 'Are you ladies all right? You've both gone quite pale.'

'We're er . . . ' Molly struggled to speak.

Alice blinked rapidly as she looked across at Molly, and back to the policeman blocking the doorway. Memories of seven years previously jumped into her head, when she'd opened the same front door to a policeman. It was the dreadful day she met Freddie, who had brought news of the Stoats Nest train crash, which had killed Victoria's parents. The news had taken Victoria years to come to terms with and was a harrowing experience; not one Alice had wished to repeat, but the war dictated otherwise. Why was he here? Her mouth was dry, her tongue stuck to her lips as she tried to moisten them. 'We're here to see Victoria, we're . . . er . . . friends of hers.'

A woman's voice called out from inside the house. 'Who is it?'

The policeman looked over his shoulder into the hallway, but before he could speak, Daisy was standing

81

next to him.

Alice blinked quickly, trying to recover her equilibrium. 'Morning, Daisy. Sorry, when I saw the policeman, I thought you had received bad news.'

Daisy frowned for a moment. 'Oh, you mean Peter; no, he's a colleague that popped in for a cup of tea while walking his beat.' She looked from one to the other. 'I shouldn't have allowed him to answer the door, but I was upstairs changing into my uniform and didn't think about the consequences, which isn't very good for a policewoman. Let me introduce you properly.' She moved her arm between them. 'Constable Peter Albright, please meet Alice Leybourne and Molly Cooper.'

Everyone nodded to each other and Molly's ashen pallor began to recover.

Daisy continued with her introductions. 'These ladies are dear family friends. In fact, I would say they are more like sisters; Alice is Lily's sister and Sergeant Leybourne's wife.'

Alice pulled back her shoulders and lifted her chin. 'It's nice to meet you, Constable Albright.'

Daisy beamed at the girls. 'It's lovely to see you both; it's been ages. Come in. I'm sorry I worried you for a moment.' She stepped aside to allow them entry into the small hallway. 'I know I see Lily every day, but it's good to see you both looking so well.' She paused for a moment. 'Especially you, Molly; from what I hear, you've been through it lately, but you look well.'

Molly smiled. 'Thank you; it was a tough time, and not one I could have got through without Alice and your sister.'

Alice removed her gloves, thrusting them into her coat pocket. 'I know it's early, but we're here to see

Victoria.'

Daisy nodded. 'Of course, let me take your coats and then you can go into the sitting room. I'll let her know you're here.'

Alice and Molly undid the buttons of their heavy coats.

'Thank you, Daisy.' Molly removed her coat. 'I hope you are keeping well; have you heard from Stephen?'

Daisy took the coat, wrapping the coarse material over her arm while she waited for Alice's. 'He writes often; I'm not sure he always tells us what's going on, but he's still alive and we are grateful for that.'

Peter ran his hand up and down Daisy's back. Her cheeks suddenly had a rosy glow about them. She cleared her throat and took Alice's coat from her, before hanging them both on the coat stand. 'Go in and take a seat while I find Victoria. I think she's in the kitchen, so I'll put the kettle on while I'm there.'

Peter followed the girls into the sitting room.

Alice eyed the man sitting in the armchair opposite her. She wondered how old he was, twenty, maybe twenty-one. She sighed. He only looked about twelve; maybe that's why he hadn't enlisted, along with every other young man. 'Have you been a policeman long, Constable Albright?'

'No, ma'am, and please call me Peter.' He smiled, showing even white teeth. 'It must be coming up to a year.' He paused for a moment. 'I expect you are wondering why I haven't enlisted; everyone does.'

Alice fidgeted in her seat. 'Not at all, sir, it's none of my business.'

'Well, I like to get ahead and set the record straight, to stop further discussion after I've left the room — '

'I can assure you, Constable Albright, we are not

prone to discussing other people's business; I was just making polite conversation with you.'

Peter held up his hand. 'I'm sorry, Mrs Leybourne. I didn't mean to offend, but I'm used to people thinking I'm a coward, because I'm here, rather than in France or somewhere.'

Molly looked across at him. 'The problem is, Peter, we are not "people". As you've heard, we are very good friends of Victoria and Daisy, and have been through a lot together.'

Peter lowered his eyes for a moment, anxiety tripping across his young features. 'I'm sorry, we seem to have got off on the wrong foot. Can we start again please?'

The girls nodded as one.

'I have chosen to enter the police force, because the army rejected me, due to me having flat feet. I'm hoping it won't affect my job, because I love it.' Peter stood up and paced around the small room, gazing out of the window onto the busy street. Cars, chugging past the house, drowned people's voices out. 'I'm used to people calling me names, because they think I'm a coward. My ma's pleased that I couldn't go, but that's where it ends.'

Sympathy surged through Molly's veins, as she remembered Andrew keeping the white feather he had been given. 'Unfortunately, Peter, people make assumptions.'

He turned and looked at her. 'I know, and I understand that. Everyone is losing loved ones, so they look at me, but don't stop to ask. I feel I should wear a board, explaining why I'm still here.'

Alice nodded. 'But instead, you get in first.'

Peter walked over to the chair he had vacated earlier.

'I should have thought, instead of automatically thinking the usual; I know Sergeant Leybourne suffered terrible injuries.'

Alice sighed, before choosing her words carefully. 'This war is a terrible thing, tearing the country apart, as well as friends and neighbours.'

Heels could be heard clattering on the floor tiles in the hallway, drowning out the mumbled voices that followed. The sitting room door was pushed open.

'Good morning.' Victoria entered, carrying a silver tray of crockery.

Daisy shrugged her arms into a heavy black coat. 'I'm sorry I can't stay, but Peter and I have got to get to work.' She chuckled almost to herself. 'We don't want Sergeant Leybourne telling us off.'

Peter jumped out of his seat. 'It was lovely to meet you.' He bowed his head slightly.

'Likewise, Peter,' Molly and Alice chorused.

Victoria smiled at him, before glancing over at Daisy. 'Take care, the pair of you.'

'We will,' they both answered as one, laughing as they left the room.

Victoria shook her head at the thud of the front door closing, but her face was bright, her smile lighting it up.

Molly raised an eyebrow. 'Is this a romance in the making?'

Victoria picked up the heavy, white teapot. 'I don't know about that.'

Alice glanced at her friend. 'Then you must be the only one who doesn't. Daisy's cheeks went quite pink when he stroked her back.'

Teaspoons clattered against the china cups, as Victoria stirred the tea. 'I hope she does find love; let's face it, there aren't going to be many young men around, by the time this war is finished.'

The girls sat in silence for a few minutes, each clutching their cup of tea, while lost in thoughts about the future.

Molly sipped the hot brown liquid. The heat seared her top lip; she gasped and put the cup back on the matching floral saucer. 'This is very nice, but we're not here to drink tea and gossip all day, so why don't we take our drinks upstairs and get on with the job we're here to do?'

Alice nodded. 'That sounds like a good idea, if Victoria agrees.'

Victoria paled. 'Job, what job?'

Molly gazed at her friend's ashen face. 'We've come to help you sort out your parents' bedroom.'

The silence that followed was filled with tension.

Victoria stared down into her cup. 'I . . . er . . . I was going out.'

Molly stood up, placing her cup and saucer on the small side table. 'Is it urgent; do you have to go out?' She paused. 'We all know this isn't a job you want to do, but it has to be done; you can't go on like this. We're your friends and we're here to help; nothing else.'

Victoria slowly nodded her head.

Alice stood up and placed her arm around Victoria's shoulders. 'We know this is hard for you; that's why we're here.' She paused, watching the fear trample over her friend. 'We're like sisters, remember? Actually, we're better than sisters, if that's possible.'

Victoria lifted her watery eyes, to meet her friends' gaze. 'All right, let's get on with it.'

Victoria stood outside her parents' bedroom, with her hands clenched down by her side. She bit her bottom lip as she stared at the dark wooden door. It had been a while since she had closed it on the room, vowing never to open it again. Alice and Molly stood either side of her, waiting to see what was ahead of them.

Molly glanced at Alice, raising her eyebrows at her, urging her to move things along.

Alice shrugged.

Molly waited for a moment, before giving Alice another sideways look, but she was looking straight ahead. She sipped at her lukewarm tea. 'Are we going to do this, Victoria?'

Victoria's eyes were wide with fear.

Molly wrapped her arm around Victoria's shoulders. 'You can do this. We're here for you.'

Victoria looked from one of her friends to the other; she wanted to run, but her feet wouldn't move. She slowly put her hand into her black skirt pocket. Her fingers touched the bedroom door key, but they snatched away from the ice-cold metal. The door had been locked for a long time. As they got older, Daisy and Stephen had wanted to investigate what was behind the locked door, but Victoria had guarded the key with her life. It was never away from her.

Molly squeezed the top of Victoria's arm. 'Come on girl, you can do this.'

Victoria glanced over at Alice, who nodded at her. Her fingers slowly wrapped around the cold metal key; it burnt into her skin, but she could no longer hide from it. Pulling it free from the soft material that had held it tight away from prying eyes, she gazed down at it. Was she really going to do this?

Molly leant in and whispered, 'You can do this, Victoria, I know you can.'

Frightened eyes stared back at Molly. 'I don't know if I can.'

'Do you want me to unlock the door?'

Victoria shook her head and looked back down at the key. Without another word, she thrust it into the lock and tried to turn it. A grating noise filled the air. Victoria pressed harder, her face contorted, as she twisted the key inside the lock. Without warning, it suddenly moved. A loud grinding noise followed the movement and the door was suddenly unlocked.

Alice whispered, 'Well done, Victoria. I know this is hard for you, but it's the right thing to do.'

Without a word, Victoria twisted the door handle and pushed hard. The hinges screamed their objection, causing the girls to wince.

The three girls stood in silence, staring into the bedroom. The dust was visible from the landing. Layer upon layer covered everything in the room. There were no footprints on the wooden floorboards, or finger marks to show the dust had been disturbed on the chest of drawers. There was no evidence that anyone had entered this room for years.

Fear gripped Molly as she noticed the lacy cobwebs, visible around the ceiling and walls. There was clearly more than one spider in here. Her eyes darted around the room, looking for the spiders that had taken up residence, fleetingly wondering how many there could be.

Victoria spoke in a whisper. 'This is more than a little embarrassing.' She sighed, as colour gradually filled her ashen face. 'I should have come up and cleaned the room before today, but . . . '

Alice rubbed Victoria's back. 'None of that matters; we'll clean as we go, won't we, Molly?'

Molly eyed the cobwebs again. 'Of course.' She lowered her voice. 'It won't take us long.'

Victoria's gaze followed Molly's. 'Do you think there's spiders in there?'

'No, of course not,' Molly and Alice chorused unconvincingly.

Victoria frowned, before a nervous giggle escaped, as she looked at her friends. 'You know I hate spiders.'

Molly nudged her. 'Everyone hates spiders; they move so quickly, so we'll all be squealing together.'

'I now have a picture of us all screaming, as we run for the doorway.'

'Now that's quite possible.' Alice chuckled. 'But first, we have to go into the room, so we can run out again.'

'I can do this.' Victoria took the couple of steps into her parents' bedroom.

Alice and Molly followed her.

Molly looked around the room. 'I think we need my mother here; she'd have this room clean in no time.'

Victoria's mouth dropped open for moment. 'Are you serious?'

Molly smiled. 'No, of course not, but we need a broom, some rags and something to put the bedding in, so we can shake it outside. We can't start until the room has been cleaned; there's nowhere to sit, for a start.'

Alice looked around the once lovely room. The black coals were grey, with the layers of dust in the open fireplace. The ornate blue tiles that surrounded it had lost their sheen. The air was musty and stale perfume hung in the air. Alice walked over to the sash window, leaving her footprints in the dust. Turning the catch to unlock the wooden frame, she then pushed the stiff, unyielding window upwards. Nothing happened. She took a deep breath and tried again; slowly it began to give way and lift a little. Alice brushed off the dust that had fallen on her hands, expecting the early morning chill to immediately whoosh in and fill every corner of the room. She was pleased there was now warmth in the air. 'I don't very often say these words, but Molly's right, we do need to clean first and sort through everything afterwards.'

'I should have come in here before today.' Victoria's watery eyes moved to each of them in turn. 'I'm sorry, I just couldn't bring — '

'It's all right, we'll soon have it clean.' Molly placed her arm around Victoria's hunched shoulders.

Victoria sniffed, coughing as the dust hit her nose. 'My mother would be so ashamed of me, right now.'

'No.' Alice shook her head. 'I'm not having this; you have been through a lot and it's a wonder you are still here at all. Your parents loved you and they would understand how difficult it has been for you.'

Molly nodded. 'I think we need to busy ourselves; at least it will stop us thinking too much.' She looked up at the ceiling again. 'Particularly about death by spider.'

7

Daisy Appleton and Lily Taylor walked side by side along Charing Cross Road. The road was one of their favourites to walk along. The cars and trams trundled along, with grey smoke spluttering from the bottom of the vehicles. They had long since got used to the attention that their navy police uniforms attracted. Stallholders shouted their good mornings, as they strolled past. It was a warm, humid day, but grey clouds lurked in the distance, threatening to spoil it. People stopped to chat, as they made their way from shop to shop, only stopping to give the girls a smile or a curious look.

'Want some soup, luvvie?'

'No, thank you; maybe later.' Daisy smiled at the weatherworn old man, standing next to his barrow.

The man lifted his gnarled hand, saluting his acknowledgement.

'Alice seemed in a bit of a stew this morning.' Lily waved at a woman selling flowers. 'I don't know what's going on, but I suspect Molly and Victoria will be involved.'

Daisy straightened the belt of her jacket, the coarse material rough against her fingers. 'That's usually the case.'

'It's a good job we know they're law-abiding citizens. Imagine the embarrassment of them being placed in a cell at the station.' Lily paused for a moment. 'Oh my goodness, I'm turning into my father.' She pulled a face, as the realisation hit home. 'He went berserk

91

when I was brought home by a policeman, after the suffragette demonstration outside the Houses of Parliament. He said I was an embarrassment to him.'

'I expect he's proud of you now.' Daisy lowered her eyelashes and studied the cracks in the pavement for a moment. 'As far as the girls are concerned, I think you'll find it's Victoria, this time.'

Lily stopped short and looked at her friend's slender back as she stepped ahead. 'Is everything all right?'

Daisy stopped and looked back at Lily. 'I'll find out, when I get home.'

'I'm sorry, I didn't mean to pry; I'm just concerned.' Lily hesitated for a second, before stepping forward. 'I know you and I haven't been friends for years, like our sisters have, but I like to think we've got closer since this damned war started.'

'We spend an awful lot of time together and I like to think we are friends. This war confuses me a little, because it's taken the country's men away, and yet saved me from working in domestic service, which I hated.'

'I know what you mean. It's given me the freedom that my father would never have allowed, if it hadn't been for the good of the country.'

Daisy gave a humourless laugh. 'I don't think we appreciate our parents until they are no longer with us. You know, it's been seven years since mine died in that train derailment, and I'm frightened I'm going to forget who they really were.'

Lily rested her hand on Daisy's arm. 'You won't forget them; they are too important to you. Has something happened to make you worry about it?'

'I've caught Victoria staring at our parents' locked bedroom door a few times lately. She looks quite anxious but tries to push her fear away when she sees me. I can't help wondering if she's finally thinking of unlocking it. She hasn't said anything but I can't bring myself to offer to help. I think Victoria is going to be in bits, so it's better that Alice and Molly are there, instead of me.'

Lily nodded. 'They are true friends and I'm sure they'll help her through it, and I am here for you, as indeed we all are, should you need us.'

Daisy's sombre expression told Lily she should change the subject.

The girls parted as a little boy and girl rushed at them, both clutching a book.

Lily glanced across at her companion. 'So what's going on with you and Constable Peter Albright?'

Daisy giggled, colour creeping into her cheeks. 'Nothing is going on; we are just work colleagues, that's all.'

Lily gave a mischievous grin. 'Oh, so you have all your work colleagues pop in for a cup of tea, do you?'

'My goodness, gossip soon gets around. I'd ask who told you, but I suspect you wouldn't tell me. I know it wasn't Alice, because she and Molly only met him this morning, and you haven't seen her since then.'

'Was it a secret then?'

'No, it was just a cup of tea.' Daisy shook her head.

'I'm sorry, I'm just having fun with you. He told me at the station. I think he's sweet on you.'

Daisy kept looking ahead, but her blushing cheeks gave her away.

A young boy clutching a red apple came running towards them, swerving to miss the girls. Daisy stepped to the side and thrust her arm out. 'What's your hurry, young man?'

93

Lily took a step nearer to the youngster. 'What have you been up to?' She scowled at him. 'You're looking guilty of something.'

The boy tilted his head back and lifted his chin, before thrusting his arm behind his back. 'I ain't done nuffink.'

Daisy bit her lip, trying not to smile at the lad, as she took in his dirty trousers. His patched trouser legs swung around his ankles and his shirt hung out of the waistband. 'Has someone been pulling at your clothes?'

'No, I was just in an 'urry, that's all.'

Lily gave him her best policewoman stare, before walking around him. 'You know we've had complaints about a young lad stealing fruit from old Mr Wilson's stall.' She glanced down at the apple he was holding. 'That's not you, by any chance, is it?'

The lad spun round. 'No miss, it ain't.'

Daisy looked at Lily. 'Perhaps we should take him back and ask Mr Wilson if this young man is the culprit. If he is, we'll take him down to the police station and sit him in a cell, while we do the paperwork.'

'No, please don't; the apple ain't for me.' The boy looked crestfallen, as he stared at the fruit in his hand. 'It's for my sister. My pa's away fighting, and my ma's sick. I'm trying to look after us all, but since me ma ain't working, there's no money to buy food or anyfink.'

Lily immediately felt bad for trying to scare the young lad into not stealing again. 'How long has your ma been sick?'

The boy shrugged his shoulders. 'I dunno, a few days. She's burning up. My sister keeps putting a wet cloth on her forehead, but nuffink seems to work.'

Daisy laid a hand on the boy's shoulder. 'First we'll go and apologise to Mr Wilson; that poor man has to make a living too. Then we'll go and see your ma.'

'Ya mean, yer not going to take me down the station?'

Lily smiled. 'We'll see, come on.'

A portly policeman cycled past them, ringing his bell several times. 'The Germans are coming. Take cover, the Germans are coming.'

Daisy looked around them. 'Come on, we have to find a basement somewhere.' She moved to grab the boy's arm, but he moved in the opposite direction.

'Sorry, miss, I've got to get 'ome for me ma, otherwise they won't make it.' He started to run but stopped and looked round. 'I promise I'll speak to Mr Wilson, but I've got to get home for me ma.' He continued to run away from them.

'Come on, Lily; I think Victoria mentioned that Foyles has a basement, so let's see if we can go in there until it passes.'

★ ★ ★

A bicycle bell rang out through the air. Molly rushed to the open bedroom window, just as a policeman yelled out, 'The Germans are coming. Take cover, the Germans are coming.' The bell rang continually. Molly turned quickly to her friends. 'Come on, girls, we've got to get to the basement.'

Victoria turned towards the bedroom door. 'Don't worry about taking anything; the basement has biscuits and water, so we'll be safe there for a few hours. Come on, follow me.'

Alice and Molly followed Victoria out of the room

and ran down the stairs. Victoria opened the basement door, propping it open with a full coalscuttle. A damp musty smell, mingled with candle wax, rushed out to greet them. As the girls stared into the darkness, Victoria struck a match and lit a church candle that was kept on the nearby console table for such occasions. The small flame grew until it stood upright and the aroma of beeswax filled the space around them. They each gripped the banister and followed their friend down the stairs.

Victoria began to light the candles that were scattered around the basement. The flames flickered into existence in the chill that filled the room, casting shadows as they danced.

Molly moved the coalscuttle and closed the basement door, shutting out the natural daylight, with the exception of a thin slither, showing underneath it.

'No, Molly, leave it open.'

Molly raised her eyebrows but put the coalscuttle back where it was. 'I don't think having the door wide open will give you much protection if a bomb hits the house.'

Victoria turned away. 'I can't have it shut.'

Alice glanced at Molly, giving a slight shrug of her shoulders before turning back to look around her. 'You've made this very cosy, Victoria.' A couple of woollen shawls sat on a small armchair. A side table was stacked high with books. Two single beds were beside each other, quite close to the chairs.

Molly nodded. 'Yes, ours is still a basement with a couple of chairs in it, but this feels like it's part of your home, if you know what I mean.'

Victoria looked around her. 'Daisy and I have spent a lot of time down here in the last three years.

96

We decided early on to just sleep down here every night, so we had to make it a little bit cosy, otherwise it would have felt like going to prison every night.'

The girls chuckled at her words; they all knew Victoria wouldn't have a clue about the inside of a prison, nor indeed would any of them.

Victoria indicated to the chairs. 'Make yourself comfortable. You'll need the shawls, because it does get chilly down here.'

The girls wrapped the shawls around them and made themselves comfortable in the armchairs. They sat in silence for a few minutes, each wrapped up in their own thoughts.

Victoria looked from one to the other of her friends. 'I know nobody likes these bombings, but I find the daytime ones especially scary.' She paused for a moment. 'I'm never with Daisy when they happen, and I worry we won't see each other again.' She sucked in her breath. 'I hope she's safe. I can't think about Stephen and Ted facing this every day . . . I just worry so much. I wish Daisy wasn't putting herself at risk.'

Alice reached out and held Victoria's hand. 'I know, we feel like that about Lily; at least at night we are all with our families, at home. I worry what sort of world Arthur is going to grow up into; all this fighting, people dying, and for what?' She pulled her hand away and clenched it in her lap.

Molly sat in silence, wondering if her father was home to carry her gran down into the basement. A shiver ran down her back. She prayed her family would be safe. Perhaps it was time she set the date for her wedding, so at least her gran would see her walk down the aisle, even if she didn't live long enough to see great grandchildren. She would talk to Andrew, it was time to stop being stubborn, and forcing them into a life they didn't want.

Victoria glanced across at Molly. 'Are you all right, Molly?'

Molly forced a smile. 'Yes, just thinking about whether Gran managed to get down to the basement.' Victoria nodded.

'It is scary when you're not with them.'

Alice looked down at her hands, clenched in the folds of the floral apron. 'We have to stay positive and have faith, otherwise we'll go mad with worry.'

Molly sighed. 'I wonder how long we'll be stuck down here for.'

'Listen.' Victoria lifted her hand. A rumbling could be heard above them.

The room fell silent, as the noise got louder.

Molly whispered. 'I can't bear this; let's sing a song or talk about something that will lift us.'

Victoria frowned. 'Like what?'

'I don't know, but there must be tons of things.' Molly paused. 'What about Peter Albright; what do you think of him? He's obviously smitten with Daisy. Or we could talk about Arthur and how he's wrecking Alice's parents' home, now he's, what, two years old? We could talk about anything; it's got to be better than listening to that noise outside and wondering what awaits us.'

Alice nodded. 'You are quite right, Molly.' She smiled at her friend. 'So when are you going to set your wedding date?'

Molly giggled. 'I've just been thinking about that; I shall speak to Andrew later. Life's too short to be holding my family to ransom over a house. I have to let them live the life they want to live.' She looked down at her hands, clasped on her lap. 'I want what I think is best for them, but it's time I realised they want what's best for me too.' She sighed. 'Life's too short, so I should give them the wedding and grandchildren they want, while they are still alive to enjoy it.'

Victoria nodded. 'I'm sure Andrew will be pleased; he's been very patient with you.'

'I know; I'm a lucky woman. Anyway, I'm hoping you two will accompany me down the aisle, whenever it is.'

The girls beamed at each other. 'Of course.'

'I could have Arthur as a pageboy, but I don't know if I'm that brave. From what I can gather, trying to get a two-year-old to do what you want is almost impossible.'

Alice laughed. 'You're right there, so don't feel you have to, because it's not necessary. Have you seen much of Andrew's sister; it's Elizabeth, isn't it?'

'Yes, she's lovely, and so easy to get along with.' Molly looked wistful for a moment. 'She and Andrew are so close.'

Victoria fidgeted in her chair, pulling her shawl closer. 'It's good that they have each other.' She smiled over at Molly. 'And now you as well — I'm sure there won't be a dull moment.'

The girls laughed and Molly pulled a face at Victoria. 'I'm sure I don't know what you mean.'

★ ★ ★

Daisy and Lily stepped across the busy Charing Cross Road, weaving quickly between the cars coughing and spluttering along the road. Men, women and children raced down the street, to find shelter. Panic was plastered on every person's face, some looking up and searching the clouded sky. Children's cries filled the air, their fear tangible.

Daisy shouted out. 'Take cover everyone. Find a basement. Go into the shops and the underground stations. If you're near your home, get there quickly and head for the basement.'

Lily followed Daisy's lead. 'Don't panic, but please hurry.'

The girls ran up the road, repeating their words. The large white lettering of the Foyles Bookshop came into view. They passed it every day, but today there was more urgency to reach it. They could only hope there was room for them in the basement.

Daisy glanced up at the sky but couldn't see any aircraft. There was still time. 'These daytime bombings are frightening everyone; at least at night, you know you are with your loved ones.'

A little girl sobbed as she ran up to them and grabbed Lily's hand.

'What is it, little one, where's your ma?' Lily looked around at the people, some running, while others walked briskly in all directions.

The little girl sobbed.

Lily picked her up and held her close. 'It's all right, little one, we'll find your ma.' She raised her eyebrows at Daisy.

Daisy came across and rubbed the girl's back. 'Can you tell us your name?'

The child looked at them, before sniffing and wiping her hand across her face. 'Susan.' She sniffed.

Relief tripped across Daisy's features. 'Right, Susan, can you remember where you were when you last saw your ma?'

'I wasn't with me ma.' Susan sniffed again. 'My grandma was buying me a book, cos it's me birthday.' Her sobs grew louder again.

Lily pulled her close again. 'Everything's going to be all right, Susan. This will be like an adventure you read about in books.' She stroked the child's blonde hair, wishing she had more experience with children, other than her robust nephew, Arthur. 'So how old are you today?'

'Six.'

Daisy glanced up at the sky again.

Lily followed suit; was that rumblings she could hear. 'Six; you are a big girl. Perhaps we should sing happy birthday to you, but first we need to take cover.'

The girls walked quickly towards Foyles Bookshop. An elderly man, wearing a black suit, stood tall at the doorway, glancing upwards every couple of minutes, as he beckoned people to get inside the store. A grey-haired woman of tiny proportions came out of the shop, stopping to talk to him. She was sobbing and shaking her head.

'Susan, is that your grandma?' Lily sent up a quick prayer for it to be so. She quickened her pace. The man in the doorway of the bookshop pointed in their direction, waving at the girls to come over.

Susan's head popped up. 'Yes, yes it is.' A smile spread across her red, blotchy face.

Daisy and Lily gave a collective sigh of relief.

The man shouted, 'Come on in and someone will show you to the basement.'

The girls ran through the doorway, followed by the grey-haired woman. Susan held out her arms to her grandmother.

The lady held the child close and squeezed her tight. 'Thank you, so much. I was so frightened; I thought . . .' She looked across at the policewomen standing in front of her. 'Thank you, thank you so much.' She gave her granddaughter an extra squeeze. 'None of it matters now; you're safe.'

Susan giggled. 'Grandma, you're squeezing me so tight, I can't breathe.'

'Sorry, little one.'

The bolts were pulled across the shop door, jerking everyone's thoughts back to what was happening. 'Right, ladies, let's go down to the basement. I'm afraid it will be rather cramped down there, but at least everyone will be safe.' He led the way through to the back of the shop. There was no time to stop and look at the shelves of books that they passed. 'Forgive my rudeness; I haven't introduced myself.' He peered over his shoulder. 'I'm Mr Leadbetter, the floor manager of this wonderful bookshop.' He gave them a worried glance as he stood aside, for them to enter the basement. 'Please hold on to the handrail; we don't want any accidents.'

People's mumbled voices could be heard at the top of the stairs. The girls followed Susan and her grandma down into the basement, with Mr Leadbetter close behind them. He pulled the door shut with a bang. Lily gasped as she walked into the basement. It was not only crowded with people, but books as well, stacked high on every available shelf and counter. There was a mustiness that hung in the air, along with a calmness that everything was going to be all right. Some were leafing through books, while others were deeply engrossed.

Mr Leadbetter looked around, pleased he had

managed to get so many people in there, but more grateful that the child had been reunited with her grandma. He watched the girl looking at a picture book. 'These daytime bombings have made people even more fearful of losing loved ones; at least at night, most families would be together.'

Lily stared at the tall, upright man, catching the musky scent he was wearing. 'That's very true.' She licked her dry lips, wishing she could busy herself making a cup of tea, before she looked across at Daisy. They frowned at each other. No words were needed, as they knew they were both thinking about their own sisters, and whether they would be safe when this was all over with.

8

Victoria looked around her parents' bedroom. The green curtains fluttered at the window. The fresh air had cleared the musty smell that the three of them had faced earlier. Murmurs of conversations from the street filtered up to the bedroom, as the heat of the day lessened. Children's laughter drowned out everything around them. They were happy to be back out in the sunshine, unaware of the dangerous times they lived in. Victoria sent up a silent prayer, hoping that Stephen, Daisy and Ted were safe. She couldn't bear the thought of losing them too. She shook her head quickly before turning to Alice and Molly, smiling at the smudges on their faces. The colourful red and blue scarves Victoria had found earlier were wrapped around their heads, and aprons gave inadequate protection as they tried to protect their clothes. 'I couldn't have done this without your help; the pair of you haven't stopped, since arriving this morning, apart from our time in the basement. I can't thank you enough. It looks like a different room to the one we walked into earlier.'

Molly laughed. 'I've never worked so hard, not even at the munitions factory, but at least it hasn't killed me.' She glanced around the walls. 'And more importantly, there's been no death by spider, at least not yet.'

Alice wiped her hands down her apron. 'It's the first step. We can actually start going through things now, but we will have to be guided by you, Victoria;

104

what we're about to do is very personal to you and your family.'

Victoria's face paled. She took a deep breath. 'It needs to be done, though.'

Molly picked up a rag and ran it along the top of the chest of drawers. 'That's right; I know it's hard for you, but it will be a good job when it's done.' She stopped, only to pick up a photograph of Victoria's mother and father. Molly studied it for a moment, before turning to glance across at Victoria. 'Is that you, in your mother's arms?'

Victoria took the photograph from her friend. 'This should be where we can enjoy it every day. Ma always said it was my brother, so it must be Stephen. Mind you, to look at it, you would never know who it was. He's so young and wrapped up, he could be anybody.' She placed the silver-framed photograph back on the chest of drawers. 'To be honest, I don't know where to start.'

Alice looked around the room. The heavy, dark oak wardrobe dominated it, with a matching dressing table and chest of drawers. The dusty white crochet doilies stood on every surface possible, nestling under photographs, next to a blue floral jug and bowl, and a silver hairbrush set. 'Why don't we concentrate on removing the clothes? We could fold them up and place them on the bed, so you can decide whether you want to keep any of them. When you've done that, we can arrange for them to go to the Salvation Army. I'm sure someone could make use of them.'

Victoria gripped her hands tight, before giving a slight nod. 'It's a good place to start.'

Alice opened the wardrobe door and stared at the few clothes hanging there. She frowned; she had expected to see more but decided not to say anything. 'We'll need to check the pockets, just in case there's anything you want to keep.'

Molly peered over Alice's shoulder. 'Victoria, why don't you make us a cup of tea; it'll help take the dusty taste away, and I'll start on the drawers.'

Victoria took a step towards the doorway, before looking back over her shoulder. 'Thank you. If you do nothing else, I want you to know I appreciate everything you've done.' She paused as her eyes welled up. 'I'll go and make the tea.'

The stairs creaked as Victoria ran down them. Molly was immediately transported back to her first day at the munitions factory. *It's the stairs that give you away, every time.* She pulled open the top drawer of six and immediately frowned. 'It doesn't feel right to be going through someone's belongings.'

Alice stared into the wardrobe. 'I know what you mean, but we have to remember we're doing this for Victoria; she needs to move on, once and for all. Seven years is a long time.'

Molly shook her head. 'I know you're right, but it feels like I'm prying.' She pulled out several pretty floral scarves, folded them and placed them on the bed. Lacy handkerchiefs quickly followed these, with initials embroidered in one of the corners.

Alice removed a black dress from the wardrobe and felt inside the pockets that lay on the side seams, but they were empty. She removed the hanger, neatly folded the dress and placed it on the bed, before repeating the action on the next garment.

They both worked their way through the task they had undertaken to do, until the stairs creaked again and the rattling of crockery could be heard. Victoria

106

came in and placed the tray of tea things on top of the chest of drawers.

Victoria didn't say anything, but her eyes were drawn to the growing piles of clothes that were partially covering the bed. She sat on the edge of it and pulled a white blouse free from the neatly folded pile of clothing. Staring at it for a moment, she let her fingers rub the soft material, before lifting it to her face. Victoria buried her nose into the blouse and took a deep breath. There was a musty smell, but she could still catch the faint scent of lavender. She blinked rapidly, as memories filtered through, of her mother making small lavender bags, to place in the drawers and hang in the wardrobes.

Molly rested her hand on Victoria's arm. 'Have a look at what's there, and then you can keep whatever you'd like.'

'No, I don't think that's a good idea.' Victoria stood up and turned back to the crockery. 'You know me; I won't want to throw anything away. I shall just keep things like photos and trinkets, for now.' She picked up the teapot and began to pour the dark brown tea, the strainer catching the leaves as they tried to reach inside the cups.

Molly quickly looked away as sadness washed over her. She picked up a pale blue, woollen jumper, which unfolded slightly in her hand. There was something hard within its folds. Molly opened it and letters, tied with blue ribbon, fell on the floor. The clatter of the teapot landing on the silver tray made her jump. She looked up, but Victoria was already stooping to pick up the letters that had lain hidden until now.

Victoria slowly pulled at the end of the silk ribbon. The bow held tight; she hesitated, before tugging harder at the end. The ribbon gradually loosened. She lifted each individual envelope and there were at least a couple of dozen of them. She didn't recognise the handwriting on them. She stared at them for a moment. A sigh escaped. 'I shouldn't look at these now, otherwise I'll not get anything done.' She quickly re-tied the ribbon and placed them on the bed.

A thud from downstairs startled the three of them and they all looked towards the bedroom door.

'Hello, it's only me.' Daisy's voice rang through the house.

Victoria called out. 'We're upstairs.'

The groaning of the stair treads told the girls Daisy was running up them. 'You'll never guess what those Germans have done; it's terrible.' She gasped for breath, as she stood in the doorway. 'They've only gone and bombed a school in Poplar.'

★ ★ ★

Foyles Bookshop was as busy as ever, with children playing amongst the racks of books. Victoria watched them for a moment, smiling at the sound of their laughter, hoping their innocence wouldn't be snatched away from them. She reached up and straightened the books that were precariously balanced on a wooden shelf, close by. Dust clouded the air. Victoria glanced left and right. She needed to find a member of staff to run a duster over these books, before Mr Leadbetter found out.

Molly came bustling round the corner, her eyes fixed on a young woman who was talking animatedly to her, balancing a small child on her hip, while clutching two books in one hand and carrying her shopping bag in the other. 'It was lovely to meet you, and if you need help finding any books, then please come and see me.' Molly held up her arm. 'The payment booth is just over there.' She indicated to the right. 'But first you must go and see Mrs Leybourne, the lady standing behind the wooden counter over there. Give her the books and she will give you a bill payment slip to take to the booth. Once you've paid, you take your receipt back to Mrs Leybourne and she will give you the books.' Molly smiled. 'I know it sounds complicated, but unfortunately, only the lady in the booth is allowed to handle the customers' money.'

The lady chuckled. 'Don't worry. I have my sixpence ready. My husband will be so happy about getting another Sherlock Holmes book; he'll share it with the other soldiers, but not before he's read it.' She paused. Her eyes glazed over for a moment. 'He does enjoy Arthur Conan Doyle, although I can't say I've ever read one of his books.'

Molly glanced down at the cover. 'Maybe you should try reading it, before you send it to him.'

The woman glanced at Molly. 'No, this is my gift to him. It's the only pleasure he gets, stuck in trenches, practically knee-deep in water and God knows what else.' She frowned, before forcing a smile. 'Anyway, I get to read *The 39 Steps*, before I send it to him.'

Molly nodded. 'Well, I hope you and your husband enjoy them.'

'Thank you, and thank you so much for your help.' The lady walked towards Alice's counter, adjusting the child on her hip as she went.

Molly watched her walk away. She couldn't help wondering if she would ever be as strong as some of these young mothers, bringing up a family on their own.

'Molly.'

Molly jerked at the sound of her name. Her usual ready smile formed, as she watched Victoria wrinkling her nose. The books she'd straightened leaned heavily to one side. 'Yes, Miss Appleton, are you requiring my assistance?'

Victoria let her hands fall to her sides. The first few books fell flat, onto the shelf. She scowled at Molly. 'Don't you Miss Appleton me.'

'I'm sorry, I thought we had to call all managers by their full name and title.' Molly gave Victoria an innocent look, biting down on her lip, to stop laughter bubbling to the surface.

Victoria decided to ignore her friend's attempt at poking fun at her. 'Can you find one of the new girls and get them to come and dust these books, before Mr Leadbetter sees the state they're in.'

Molly bobbed her head. 'Yes, Miss Appleton, I shall do it straight away.' She turned to walk away, her shoulders the only give-away to the laughter that had finally erupted from her.

Victoria watched her for a moment, before shaking her head. A smile came readily to her lips; Molly might be a very good friend, but she was definitely a nightmare when it came to pushing the boundaries of what was acceptable.

Molly looked back over her shoulder. 'Are you stopping for lunch in a minute?'

Victoria glanced at the wristwatch her mother and father had given her the Christmas before they died. 'I'll see you there, after you've found someone to straighten this lot.'

Molly nodded and carried on down the aisle.

Victoria moved away from the books and immediately bumped into Mr Leadbetter. 'Sorry, sir, I should have been more careful.'

'Not at all, Miss Appleton, I was watching some children playing. I trust you were in a safe place when the Germans flew over, yesterday?'

'Yes, I took to the basement of my home, with Alice and Molly; we were down there for some time.'

Mr Leadbetter nodded. 'It's a shame you weren't here; we had all the customers in the basement. I could have done with your help then, although everybody stayed relatively calm.' He chuckled. 'But that might have been because we had two policewomen present. They reunited a little girl and her grandmother, so everyone was in good spirits.'

Victoria smiled. 'So I heard.' A thud behind her made her turn quickly.

One of the new girls was picking up a book she had dropped. 'Sorry.' She placed it back on the shelf and proceeded to tidy it up.

Mr Leadbetter raised his eyebrows.

Victoria returned her attention to Mr Leadbetter. 'From what I've been told, the two policewomen were Lily and Daisy — Alice's sister and mine.'

'I didn't realise. Well, they were very helpful and professional.'

Victoria sighed. 'Daisy told me last night that the Germans bombed a school in Poplar; those poor children must have been terrified.' She shook her head. 'I don't know if there were any deaths, but just the thought of it upsets me.'

Mr Leadbetter looked grim when he spoke again. 'I'll be glad when this damned war is over with. It's only the innocent that are suffering, whether it's on the front line, or at home. The daytime bombings mean that families are separated, and in some cases, like the school, people are not able to protect or comfort their loved ones when they die and have no means of finding out for some time.' He glanced across at Victoria. 'Sorry, I shouldn't be talking like that, but I've lost the understanding of what this war is all about, because killing children won't change anything.'

Without thinking, Victoria rested her hand on Mr Leadbetter's arm. The softness of his jacket sleeve surprised her, as did the thinness of his arm inside it. 'There's no need to apologise, Mr Leadbetter. My ma always used to say, "it's good to get things off your chest" and my experience tells me it certainly doesn't do any harm to share thoughts with people you trust.'

Mr Leadbetter nodded. 'You are very lucky to have good friends around you; it can be very lonely without them.'

'I couldn't agree more. The trouble is, we don't always appreciate what we have, until it is ripped away from us.' Victoria frowned as images of her parents and Ted immediately jumped into her mind.

Mr Leadbetter stared at her for a moment. He opened his mouth to say something but instead he gave her a curt nod and walked away.

Victoria couldn't help wondering what was bothering him. As she walked towards the staffroom, she realised she didn't know much about him at all.

Molly shouted out as Victoria stepped into the back of the shop. 'Ah good, you made it.'

'Yes, I've made it. What are you so excited about? You're like a child at Christmas.' Victoria let her gaze wander between Alice and Molly.

'Don't look at me,' said Alice. 'I have no idea what

it's all about.'

Molly giggled. 'We should be in Café Monico, really.'

Victoria laughed. 'Ooh, it's that important.' She pulled out a chair and sat down. 'Well come on, you know you're bursting to tell us.'

'I'm getting married.' She beamed and clapped her hands together. 'Can you believe it? We've actually set the date.'

Victoria got up from the table and swept her arms around her friend. 'I'm so excited; that's wonderful news.' She stepped over towards Alice and repeated her actions. 'I can't believe what a monumental day this has turned out to be.'

Alice grinned. 'I can't believe it either. I was beginning to think it was never going to happen.' She reached over and hugged Molly tight. 'So when will it be?'

'The August bank holiday weekend, so we need to make sure we can all get that day off work.' Molly clapped her hands together again. 'I can't believe it either.'

Victoria sat grinning at her friends. 'Does that mean your parents have agreed to move into Percy Street?'

'Yes, I think they are desperate for grandchildren.' Colour rose up Molly's neck. 'They said they would move, as soon as Andrew and I were married.'

Victoria reached out and clasped both of her friends' hands. 'I feel like I could burst with happiness; it's good to have something exciting to look forward to. I'm absolutely thrilled for you both.'

Molly picked up her paste sandwich and held it up high. 'To us, and a happy, healthy and peaceful future.'

The girls followed suit, before giggling uncontrol-
lably.

* * *

Daisy and Victoria sat in their parents' bedroom, on
the coarse rug. The newly lit oil lamps flickered, casting shadows around the room as the evening drew in.
The heavy wardrobe doors were wide open. A carved
wooden box sat in front of them. They looked at each
other for a moment.

Victoria gave a slight nod to her sister.

Daisy slowly lifted her hand and gripped the small
ornate key. She attempted to turn it in the lock. It
was stiff and unyielding, the mechanism grinding
together as she applied pressure, but suddenly it gave
way. Daisy let go of it, glancing down at the deep red
imprint of the key on her fingers.

Victoria stared at her sister's hand. 'Have you hurt
yourself?'

'No.' Daisy rubbed her fingers together. 'It was just
harder to open than I thought it was going to be, but
I suppose it hasn't been opened for years.'

'That's true.' With some trepidation, Victoria slowly
lifted the lid and peered inside. It had a mustiness
about it. 'It's papers of some sort.' She reached in and
grabbed a handful, as dust flew upwards and caught
in her throat. She coughed, frowning as she pulled
the papers free. 'They look like newspaper cuttings.'
Victoria placed them on the carpet, before pulling out
some more.

Daisy wrinkled her nose, then picked up the top one
and started reading it. She stopped halfway through,
to separate them all and lay them out, so they could

all be seen.

It didn't take long for the area around them to be covered with scraps of paper. The girls looked at each other, before staring back down at the scattering of paperwork and photographs.

Victoria was the first to break the silence. 'These cuttings must have been important, but they don't mean anything to me, nor do the pictures.' She picked up a small photograph and tilted it, to examine it closely.

Daisy picked up a cutting. 'This one's an obituary; it's an Appleton, so maybe it was Pa's father or grand-father. I don't know.' She studied it for a moment. 'It must have been his grandfather, because he was eighty-six when he died.'

Victoria's lips tightened. 'I don't remember meet-ing him, do you?'

Daisy shook her head and put the cutting back down on the rug.

'I can't decide if this is Ma and Pa in this wedding photograph. It's not their wedding, but I don't recog-nise anyone in it, or the place.' Victoria turned it over, before smiling at the words on it. 'We have a bit of a clue here.' She waved the photograph around. 'It says *Mabel and Sid's wedding, 14th June 1892.'*

Daisy smiled at her sister. 'But who are Mabel and Sid?'

Victoria shrugged. 'Heaven only knows, but they kept it, so it must have been important to them.'

Daisy frowned. 'Yes, but they didn't put it in a frame or show us, not that we remember anyway.'

'That's true.' Victoria looked around at the array of paperwork. 'What else do we have?'

'This is interesting, I think.' Daisy frowned, as she

reached for another cutting. 'I've only given it a quick read, but it's about a London doctor, who appears to be a specialist of some sort.' Her eyes scanned the paper. 'It looks like he was a heart and lung doctor.'

Victoria looked at her sister with troubled eyes. 'I'm sorry, I know I keep saying it, but none of this makes any sense.' She threw her arms wide. 'Why have they got an article about a doctor?'

It was Daisy's turn to shrug. 'Do you think one of us was ill, at some point?'

A groan escaped from Victoria. 'I wish I knew or remembered.'

Daisy clasped her sister's hand and gave it a squeeze. 'Hold on, with all the questions we've had, I almost forgot.' She moved a couple of papers, and a black book became visible. 'This might help.' She picked it up and passed it to Victoria. 'I say that, but I haven't opened it, so I don't know what's inside.'

Victoria took the soft, leather-bound book from her sister. She rested it on her legs and stared down at it, wondering what to do. She gave a sigh and picked it up again. 'I don't know if I can open it.'

Daisy's eyes were fixed on the book. Her voice was low when she finally spoke. 'I don't think we have any choice, if we're going to try and make sense of all this stuff.'

Victoria thrust the book at her sister. 'You do it, then.'

Daisy held it tight, turning it one way, then the other. 'All right.' She paused. 'Here goes.' She bent the cover and let the pages quickly flicker from one end to the other. 'It looks like a diary. Perhaps you're right, we shouldn't read someone else's private thoughts; it's not like a crime has been committed here.'

116

Victoria nodded her agreement.

Daisy looked around, her eyes wide with amazement, before placing the diary back on the floor. 'Are you sure these beautiful silk blouses were Ma's?' She stood up and pulled a cream and navy blouse free of the pile of clothes on the bed. 'I don't know much about these things, but this is so soft and silky, it must be expensive.' She held out the sleeve of the blouse. 'It doesn't look like it's been worn.'

Victoria squashed the material between her forefinger and thumb. 'I know, it doesn't make sense. They never had the money to buy expensive clothes. It's a bit confusing, isn't it?'

Daisy folded the blouse and placed it back on the bed. 'None of it makes sense.'

Victoria pushed herself upright. 'There are these, as well.' She bent down and pulled open the bottom drawer of the seven-drawer chest, revealing neatly folded baby clothes. 'Why did Ma keep these?'

Daisy reached in and pulled out a couple of knitted, pale blue baby jumpers.

Victoria picked up the letters that were on the bedside table. 'These were hidden inside a jumper.' She handed them to her sister. 'I haven't read them, mainly because it feels wrong to.'

Daisy nodded, as she reached out and looked at the stamped addressed envelopes. She looked up at the pile of clothes. 'I suddenly have a sense that we didn't really know Ma or Pa. Perhaps we should read them.'

'Maybe, or are you just being a policewoman, looking for a mystery where there isn't one.'

Daisy looked around the room; her eyes were drawn back to the blouse, and the letters she was holding. 'Do you not feel the same?'

Tension sat between them, as Victoria wrestled with her conscience. 'I don't want to invade their private lives.' She paused. 'But I suppose they won't know any different, will they?'

Daisy swung her arm around Victoria's slender shoulders. 'I don't think Ma would have kept secrets, unless it was to protect us, and we're no longer the children we were.'

9

Alice, Victoria and Molly stood in line, waiting to put their cards into the clocking in machine. Women in front of them chatted. Laughter could be heard further up the line, mingling with the ding of the clock, every time a card was inserted.

Victoria groaned. 'I don't feel like this today, I reckon it's going to be another hot one.'

Alice smiled. 'I know what you mean, but we'll be all right once we get started.'

'Mm.' Victoria looked over her shoulder at Alice. 'Daisy and I went through some more of my parents' things last night and we found newspaper cuttings and photographs of our mother and father, with people we didn't recognise. We couldn't even decide where they were taken.' Victoria placed her card in the slot and waited for the ding, before removing it.

Alice followed suit. 'Perhaps we should look at them, and then we might be able to work it out. Was there anything written on the back?'

'There was on one, but I didn't look at all of them.' Victoria raised her eyebrows. 'I clearly wasn't thinking properly, because that would have been an obvious thing to do, wouldn't it, especially as I looked at one of them.'

Molly shuffled forward, placing her card into the machine, as the others stepped aside. 'Don't be hard on yourself; sometimes when you're in a situation, you don't think clearly, as I know only too well.'

Victoria nodded. 'I can't go through things tonight,

because I must go to Endell Street Hospital. I've only done a couple of shifts, so I have a bit of catching up to do.'

Molly smiled. 'Well, it's voluntary work, so I don't suppose it matters, and you've had a lot going on.'

Victoria grimaced. 'Yes, but it's not very good. My pa used to say that you either do something whole-heartedly, or don't bother. Anyway, I want to do more.'

'Obviously that's good, but don't punish yourself.'

'My problems are nothing compared to what others are going through. I've got to stop feeling sorry for myself and just get on with things, although it's all rather confusing to me.' Victoria led the way out into the shop. 'I'll see you both at lunchtime.'

'Definitely,' Alice and Molly chorused.

The three girls went their separate ways.

Victoria did a walk around the store, and then headed for the basement. She liked to check Albert was all right down there; she guessed he very rarely saw anyone during the day, until she'd started venturing down there. She gripped the handrail. The palms of her hands became damp. She could see the glow of the light filtering under the door. *Come on, you can do this, and Albert will be pleased to see you.* She slowly lowered herself on to the next step. 'Albert, are you down here?' She waited a moment, before venturing further and calling out again. 'Albert?' Panic began to rise in her throat. What if he'd had a fall or collapsed? Victoria ran down the remaining steps and, without ceremony, pushed open the door. The creaking echoed back off the walls. 'Albert?' The door thudded shut behind her.

Albert looked up from the pile of books in front of him and gave a toothless smile. 'Hello, Miss Appleton.'

His smile faded as he took in her worried expression. 'Are yer all right?' He pulled an old wooden chair forward. 'Here, sit down a minute; yer don't look at all well.'

Victoria slumped down. 'Sorry, I was calling you and when you didn't answer, I thought something had happened.'

Albert chuckled. 'Nah, I'm just mutton, that's all.'

Victoria frowned. 'What?'

Albert roared with laughter. 'I don't know, you youngsters are losing yer 'eritage.' He took in her blank expression, before speaking again, slowly. 'Mutt and Jeff is cockney rhyming slang for deaf init, but it gets shortened to mutton these days.' He chuckled as she stared at him. 'So for example, you'd say to young Molly, "You'll 'ave to speak up, cos Albert's a bit mutton." One day, I'll give yer a lesson in it.' He watched her for a few seconds. 'Are yer feeling better now?'

'Yes, thank you.'

'Good. Now what can I do for yer, Miss Appleton?'

'Please call me Victoria.' She hesitated for a minute. 'I don't really want anything; I just came down to see if you were all right.'

'Ah, now that's mighty kind of yer, and I frightened the living daylights out of yer. Next time, can yer bring a brew wiv yer, only it saves me climbing the apples and pears.'

Victoria stared at him for a minute, repeating the words apples and pears under her breath a few times. 'Stairs.'

Albert chuckled. 'Yer learning, well done.'

Victoria beamed at the praise. 'I'll make sure I bring you a cuppa next time.' She looked around the basement. There wasn't a surface that didn't have a pile of books on it, including the floor. 'Don't you get lonely down here?'

'Nah, yer'll be surprised 'ow many people come down to say 'ello, and that's nice. I get to 'ear all the gossip too.'

Victoria laughed. 'There was I, thinking you probably got fed up down here.'

'What, wiv all these books?' Albert waved his arms around. 'Yer kidding, right.'

The basement door creaked open. 'Albert, I'm just gonna leave me shopping down 'ere, so mind you don't fall over it.'

Victoria took a step towards the door, but only in time to see it slowly closing. She looked back at Albert with raised eyebrows.

'They ain't doing no 'arm.' Albert shuffled from one foot to the other. 'It's always colder down 'ere, so it makes sense for the girls to leave their bits and pieces wiv me.' He smiled. 'No 'arm in it.'

Victoria picked up the bag. 'Does it happen every day?'

Albert lowered his eyes. 'No.'

Victoria tilted her head to one side, trying hard to look like a manager who had discovered something of great importance.

Albert looked at her, sheepishly. 'All right, I'm not a grass yer know, and I don't want them girls getting in to trouble, but it 'appens most days.'

Victoria's laughter bubbled to the surface. 'You're not in trouble, Albert, but just be careful you don't fall over them.' She looked around her. 'Perhaps we need to find somewhere safe to put the shopping bags, so there are no accidents.'

Albert busied himself, leafing through books, before

dusting the covers. Particles floated up, as they were disturbed. He cleared his throat. Stale tobacco and smoke wafted around him, with the dust. He picked up the next book and studied the cover for a moment. 'Someone's gonna love this, come Christmas.' He smiled, showing his pink gums where his teeth once stood, before turning the book to face Victoria.

The cover showed Father Christmas, with his long grey beard and wearing his red, fur-trimmed coat and hat, hanging a small doll above the fireplace. Victoria took the book, *The Life and Adventures of Santa Claus*, from Albert. Her smile came readily to her face, as she looked at the little girl, asleep in her bed, oblivious of her visitor. 'What a beautiful cover.'

The old man grinned. 'It's very Christmassy, that's for sure.'

Victoria opened the cover and read the first few lines of chapter one. 'I might buy this myself, when we get paid.' She flicked through the book, past something caught in the spine. She tried to turn the pages back but couldn't find the right place. Perhaps it had been a trick of the light. She shook her head, before handing the book back to Albert.

He picked up his duster and ran it over the cover. 'Would you like me to hang onto it down here, so nobody else buys it?' He didn't look up as he shook the book and flicked the pages. What looked like a postcard, fell onto the table.

'I thought I saw something tucked inside, but I couldn't find it again.' Victoria spoke with relief. 'I thought I'd imagined it.'

Albert picked it up and studied the seaside scene, before passing it to Victoria. She turned it over, but there was nothing written on the back, indicating who it might belong to. 'This must have been a keepsake, because it hasn't been written on.' She turned it back over. The black and white picture was of a pier with a pavilion. It could have been anywhere, yet it looked familiar to her. She held out the postcard for Albert to take.

'I don't want it; it'll just go in the bin. It's only the books I'm interested in, nuffing else.'

Victoria frowned as she looked down at it. 'I might hold on to it, then.'

Albert nodded. 'And the book?' He held the book up, for her to see.

'Oh yes, sorry, I'll definitely get that at the end of the week.' Victoria smiled at Albert. 'I couldn't do your job; I'd want to buy everything, or I'd sit here reading all day.' She chuckled to herself. 'They've chosen the right person for the job.'

Albert beamed at Victoria. 'Thank you, miss.'

Victoria blushed and quickly turned away. 'I suppose I should go back upstairs and do some work, before Mr Leadbetter comes looking for me.'

Albert had already moved on to dusting his next book. 'Very well, but don't forget the brew next time yer visit, and I'll save yer book for you.'

'Thank you.' Victoria took the couple of steps to the basement door. A smile came readily as she noticed a couple more shopping bags had been placed just inside the doorway, though she didn't recall hearing anyone. The door was ajar and Victoria pulled at it. The light from the basement lit the stairs. She ran up them, as quickly as she could, trying to remember to look ladylike in the process. Her breathing was heavy when she pushed open the door at the top, into the staff area.

Startled, Alice looked round. 'Thank goodness, I've been looking for you.'

Victoria's eyes widened, fear immediately gripping her, tying her stomach into knots. Her heart was pounding in her ears.

Alice shook her head. 'Sorry, it's a work thing, not family.'

'What is it?' The fear left Victoria, as quickly as it had taken hold. 'Has something happened? You never leave your counter, unless it's to go to lunch.' She looked around her, but there was no one to be seen, except them. She frowned. 'Is it Mr Leadbetter?'

'No, although I don't know where he is. One of the new ladies has been upset, this morning.' Alice paused. 'I don't want to get her into trouble, which is why I was looking for you, but she keeps leaving her station. If Mr Leadbetter finds out, she could end up losing her job, and from what I've heard, she needs the money.'

Victoria nodded; that was a worry she could most definitely relate to. 'Who is it?'

'Edith, the small dark-haired girl who works near Molly. It was her who told me, because she's covering for her every time she goes missing.' Alice paused. 'I hope she's all right.'

Victoria ran her damp hands down the sides of her black skirt and took a deep breath. 'I'll go and find her; wish me luck.'

Alice nodded. 'You don't need luck; you'll be fine. I'd better get back to work, before I end up in trouble.'

Victoria laughed. 'I've never heard of anything less likely to happen.'

The girls walked out of the staff area together, into the busy bookshop.

Victoria eyed a young red-eyed assistant walking towards them. She touched Alice's arm and gave a slight nod.

Alice followed Victoria's gaze and nodded back, before pacing back to her counter.

'Edith,' Victoria called out, waving to the young girl, who didn't look any older than Daisy.

Edith stopped in her tracks for a second.

Victoria beckoned her to come forward, forcing her best smile, to try and reassure the young girl.

Edith walked slowly towards her.

Victoria turned around and headed back to the staff area, peering over her shoulder to make sure Edith was following her. She pulled out two chairs. She looked round and Edith was close to tears. 'Come and take a seat. I don't wish to pry.' She paused, her mind jumping from one thing to another. 'But I can see you're upset and at Foyles we care for our staff, so if there is anything we . . . I can do, then I'm here for you.'

Tears flowed down Edith's face. An unladylike sniff filled the space between them.

Victoria placed her hand on Edith's. 'You . . . you haven't lost a loved one, have you?'

Edith shook her head vigorously, her brown curls swaying with the movement.

Victoria squeezed Edith's hand, wondering what it could be that would get her into such a state. 'Surely, whatever it is can't be that bad, can it?' Aware lunchtime was looming, she looked over her shoulder to make sure nobody was coming in. 'Is it something you can talk to your mother about?'

Edith gulped for air. 'No, she'd kill me.'

Realisation dawned on Victoria. How many times had she asked Molly, but did she dare to ask this young girl? She shook her head and took a deep breath. 'Are you pregnant?'

Edith nodded. 'I think so.' She swiped her fingers across her face. 'I don't know for sure, but I keep being sick.'

Victoria felt helpless to deal with this situation. 'Have you told the father?'

Edith shook her head and a fresh set of tears rolled down her cheeks. 'He's away fighting somewhere; I don't even know if he'll come back.'

Victoria wrapped her arms around Edith. Her shoulders shuddered under the embrace. 'You need to tell your mother; if you are pregnant, it's going to be obvious pretty soon, so you might as well get it over and done with.' She pulled back from Edith. 'Is there anyone who can be with you, when you tell her?'

No words came, just a shake of her head.

'Your mother may take the news better than you think.' Victoria paused. 'I could come with you, but it might make matters worse.'

Edith looked up. For a moment, hope was shining bright in her eyes, before her tears washed it away. 'I'm not giving my baby up, I'm not.'

Victoria pulled Edith in tight, trying to give her comfort. 'I think you need to go home and talk it out with your family.' She pulled away from the frail girl. 'We'll still be here tomorrow, and I promise I will not tell a soul, until you want me to.'

Edith nodded, once again wiping away the tear trails with her fingers.

Laughter erupted from the doorway. Victoria and Edith both sat in silence as they looked over, but no one was there.

'The staff will be coming in for lunch shortly.' Victoria glanced back to the doorway, before returning her attention back to Edith. 'Go on, get yourself home and we'll speak tomorrow, if you want to.'

Edith stood up. 'Thank you.'

* * *

It had been a busy day at Foyles, and Victoria wasn't sure her legs would hold her upright as she pushed a wooden trolley along Mary Ward at Endell Street Hospital. Her brows knitted together as she tried to remember when she'd last had a letter from Ted; the last one was worn from being taken out of the envelope so many times. Her daily letters weren't being returned to her, so that gave her hope everything was all right. She couldn't help wondering if he had changed his mind about her. The trolley wheels gave intermittent squeaks as they turned, bringing her mind back to the task at hand. Every available windowsill had a vase of flowers sitting on it. The colours brightened the ward, while the perfume mingled with disinfectant and antiseptic. There wasn't an empty bed to be had. She wondered how to approach the men lying so still in their beds, their white sheets still crisp, as though they hadn't moved all day. She heard groans from the far end of the ward. Could she get them interested in a newspaper or a book? The evening light was beginning to fade and lamps were slowly being switched on, casting shadows on the green walls. Nurses and doctors stopped at beds, examining the patients, giving words of encouragement to them, but mumbling to each other as they walked away. Victoria watched, in awe of what they were doing.

'Is everything all right here?'

Victoria jumped at the sister's voice, booming in her ears. 'Yes, ma'am.' Gripping the trolley, she pushed it forward, stopping at the foot of the next bed. Victoria cleared her throat and pushed her damp palms down the sides of her black skirt. When she finally found her voice, it was no more than a whisper. 'Can I interest you in a book or newspaper?'

The man in the bed turned his head to face her but said nothing.

She couldn't help staring at his short dark hair and pale unshaven features, against the white pillows.

'I know you're staring at me; have you never seen an injured man before?' He attempted to lift his arm but couldn't. 'Damn it.'

Opposite, a group of men cheered as they played cards, causing others to gather around the bed. The springs of the mattresses joined in, as the men bounced up and down in their excitement.

Their laughter gave Victoria courage. 'I . . . ' She pulled back her shoulders and lifted her chin. 'I'm sorry, I didn't mean to stare, and I just wanted to know whether you would like something to read.'

The man in the bed frowned. 'Are you talking to me?'

Victoria's lips tightened for a moment. 'Yes, I am, and I'm sure there's no reason to be so rude.'

'Isn't there?'

'Corporal Peters, I hope you're not frightening off our volunteers.'

Victoria turned around to see Mabel Atkins smiling. 'Don't mind him; his bark is much worse than his bite.'

'I know that voice; it's Atkins isn't it?' The man smiled and his whole face lit up.

'It is.'

'So where have you been all day?' His hand pulled at the bed sheet.

Victoria nodded to the nurse. She moved aside to give them some privacy, but Mabel rested her hand on Victoria's arm.

'I've been visiting my family, which was quite nice.'

'Huh, at least you have family to visit.' The soldier moved his head to one side.

Mabel grimaced. 'You're not looking for sympathy, are you, Peters?'

'What, from you? There's no chance of that happening.' His lips lifted in the corners, showing his smile wasn't very far away. 'So I've been lying here, pining for you, and you've been out enjoying the sunshine.'

Laughter burst from Mabel. 'Oh, I'm sure that's true. You men are such flirts.'

Victoria awkwardly tried to sidle away.

Mabel noticed Victoria stepping aside. 'Anyway, as much as it's lovely chatting to you, Corporal Peters, Victoria and I have work to do.'

The man in the bed chuckled. 'Coward.'

Mabel moved towards Victoria, whose colour had risen in her cheeks.

Victoria looked over towards Corporal Peters and back at Mabel. 'I'm so embarrassed. I didn't realise he was blind; no wonder he was angry with me.'

'Yes, well you should have checked his notes before offering him something to read, but I suppose you're new, so you weren't to know.' Mabel paused. 'I probably should have made you aware, or at least someone should have. The trouble is I've been caught up with the corporal in the side room — he's not in a good way and he insists there's no one we can contact. It's quite sad, everyone should have someone at times like this.' She shook her head. 'Anyway make sure you check, before going to individual beds. Might I suggest that, in future, you just call out in the direction of two or three beds at a time, so it's not aimed at one patient. That will go some way to preventing this from happening again.'

Victoria shook her head. 'I need to become more aware, and not stare. After all, I wouldn't like it if I was in their position.'

'That's true. It was lucky that Sister wasn't on the ward, or all hell would have broken loose, and both our heads would be on the chopping block. But what's done is done, so there's no point worrying about it. Corporal Peters is an angry man at the moment, but he's improving every day.' Mabel looked at Victoria. 'No one has told him yet, but I've heard said his sight might even come back over time, but they are not sure, so don't want to raise his hopes at this stage.'

'That would be wonderful news for him.'

Mabel frowned for a moment. 'I probably shouldn't have told you, so please don't repeat it; you'll get me shot.'

Loud laughter came from the men playing cards. Mabel smiled at them. 'Try to keep it down a little, boys. Remember, we're a hospital, and that means we have some people here that don't feel so good.'

An older man looked over at the girls. 'Sorry, nurse, we didn't mean to disturb anyone.'

Mabel walked over to them. 'It's not a problem; I'm glad you're having fun. Who's winning?'

The older man grinned. 'Jackson; he's got a great poker face.'

Another man lifted his head. 'Some would call it a face that had been hit with a frying pan, or perhaps I should say a poker.' Laughter erupted from everyone within earshot.

Mabel chuckled as she walked back towards Victoria. 'They are all good men. What you probably need to remember is that they will all deal with their injuries in a different way.'

Victoria nodded. 'I've a lot to learn.'

'Don't be hard on yourself, it will come with time and experience.' Mabel smiled at the young girl in front of her.

'You're very good with the men, quite relaxed and not intimidated by them.'

'I'm a lot older than you, luvvie, so as much as I hate to say it, it probably means I've a helluva lot more experience of being in this sort of situation. Also, I have a nephew who's been sick since he was a baby.' She smiled. 'Maybe that's why I became a nurse — that and my husband dying last year, when the Germans bombed Greenwich.' She sighed and shook her head. 'Nursing has put a roof over my head.'

Victoria was suddenly swamped with her emotions of seven years ago and could feel the tears pricking at the back of her eyes. 'I'm so sorry. I didn't realise. You seem so happy all the time.'

Mabel forced a smile. 'Nobody wants to be around someone who's miserable all the time, and look around you. These men are so brave, it puts what we are going through into insignificance.'

Victoria nodded, as she looked around her. 'That's true, but when something happens, you can't help the way it affects you.' She looked down at the floor. 'I was devastated when my parents died unexpectedly.

It's taken me seven years to pluck up the courage to go through their things, and that was only with the help of my friends and my sister.'

10

Victoria turned the key in the front door, before looking round at Molly and Alice. 'Thank you for coming round again, especially straight from work.'

Molly smiled. 'As long as there's a brew going, I'm happy.'

The girls laughed as they stepped inside and the door thudded shut behind them.

'I noticed young Edith wasn't in today.' Alice took off her lightweight, summer jacket and glanced across at Victoria. 'Is she all right? I was quite concerned about her yesterday.'

'So was I.' Molly removed her jacket. 'I tried talking to her but she just kept crying, so all I could do was cover her work every time she disappeared. I hope she's all right.'

Victoria was aware that both her friends were staring at her. 'Look.' She sighed. 'If you're waiting for me to tell you other people's private problems, you're in for a long wait.'

Molly stuck out her bottom lip. 'I ask you, what's the point of having a manager for a friend, if you don't get to hear something you shouldn't?'

Victoria glared at Molly. 'Don't start; you wouldn't like me to tell other people your personal problems, would you?'

'But we're not other people. Alice and I are your friends, doesn't that make a difference? Does Mr Leadbetter know she isn't in work?'

'No and no. Now will you please stop asking me

questions.' Victoria could feel the anxiety wrapping itself around her. 'I'm hoping she'll be back before Mr Leadbetter notices.'

Molly turned to Alice for support. After all, she had started this conversation.

'Victoria's right, it's none of our business and we shouldn't be putting her in this predicament — although you're taking a bit of a risk with Mr Leadbetter.' She turned and hung her jacket on the coat stand before continuing. 'It's lovely and cool in here. I've been so hot today. Perhaps we should go straight upstairs, otherwise we'll be sitting around chatting for ages, and won't get anything done.'

Victoria knew Alice was right but couldn't bring herself to think about it. She forced a smile. 'I expect you're right; we do like to chatter. How do you both feel about getting started, while I put the kettle on and make a cup of tea?' She glanced at Molly, waiting for her to make a comment, but nothing came.

Alice nodded. 'That sounds good to me.'

The girls ran up the stairs, leaving the creaking and groaning of the treads in their wake. The bedroom door was ajar and they pushed it wide open. The room had a fresh smell about it, now all the dust was gone.

Alice walked straight over and unlocked the sash window, pushing it open a little. Warm air rushed in and the curtains gave a little dance as it touched them. 'The window really needs to be opened every day, because it's quite stiff and hard to push up. I think it might loosen, with use.'

Molly chuckled. 'Hark at you; when did you become so grown up?'

Alice laughed. 'I don't know; it's crept up on me.'

The girls looked around the room. The bed was

covered with folded clothes from the wardrobe and the chest of drawers.

'I've only emptied one drawer, but there seems to be an awful lot of stuff here.' Molly paused. 'It's going to be difficult for Victoria to decide what to do with it all.'

Alice nodded her agreement and went back to the wardrobe she was clearing. 'There are some beautiful dresses and expensive men's shirts here; too good to just throw away, that's for certain.'

Molly glanced into the wardrobe. 'I didn't think they were that well off, not that I knew them very well, at least not in the same way you did.'

Alice reached out and rubbed her fingers and thumb on the sleeve of a white shirt. 'I'm not sure I knew them well. You have to remember, I wasn't very old myself when they died, so I wouldn't have been privy to the way they lived their lives.' She scrunched the material of the shirt in her hand and let go, but there were no creases. 'I think this shirt is made of silk.'

The clattering of china told them Victoria was close by. She stepped into the room with a tray, heavy with crockery, teapot and a milk jug. 'Good job none of you take sugar, because I'm out of it.' Victoria placed the tray on top of the chest of drawers and gave a sigh.

Alice looked over at her. 'I was just saying to Molly how these clothes look too nice and expensive to just throw away.'

A puzzled look crept over Victoria's features. 'I don't have any memories of them wearing expensive clothes, not that I would have necessarily known they were expensive.' She walked over to the wardrobe as Alice pulled out the man's shirt. 'Hmm, perhaps it was Pa's Sunday best, not that I remember him wearing it to church, but then why would I?'

'Well, you probably wouldn't, but some of the clothes are too good to just throw away, so you'd better get your thinking cap on.' Alice took the shirt off the coat hanger and began folding it.

Victoria glanced across at the clothes covering the bed. 'Perhaps I should sort them into piles, to go to different places.'

Alice touched a couple of the dresses on the bed. 'Maybe some of them could be altered or unpicked to make outfits for you and Daisy, or for Molly's wedding.' She hesitated. 'I don't know I just thought it's a shame to just get rid of them.'

Molly nodded. 'And, don't forget there are people that have lost everything, and not that long ago either.'

'Of course, they are both excellent ideas.' Victoria sighed. 'I was thinking of the poor, but with that munitions explosion, families lost everything.'

'Yes, Grace was lucky Andrew's sister was so generous with her clothes, albeit they all needed altering. I don't know what we would have done without her, at the time.'

Victoria hugged Molly. 'It was a terrible time. I'm annoyed at myself, because having witnessed the devastation and destruction, those families should be at the forefront of my mind.'

Alice walked over to the tea tray. 'Don't be hard on yourself, Victoria. What you are doing here is tough for you to deal with and we'll make sure it all goes to the people that need it.' She lifted the lid off the teapot and stirred the dark liquid. 'Right, who wants tea?' The crockery clattered, as the china cups were put onto the matching saucers, followed by teaspoons.

Molly smiled. 'I think it's safe to say we all do.'

Victoria lifted her eyes from the spectacle of the bed, hidden under the clothes. 'Is Grace still doing well, with her land work?'

Molly chuckled. 'She still loves it. Going by her weekly letters, she sounds so happy. It's clear that her reading and writing has improved, no end.' Molly took the cup of tea from Alice. 'I might send her some books, because I'm not sure how often she gets out to the shops. Also, it's always lovely to get a present in the post, or otherwise actually.'

The girls laughed at Molly's ramblings.

★ ★ ★

'So has Constable Albright asked you out yet?' Lily chuckled as Daisy's face flushed with colour.

'No, I've told you, we're just friends.'

Lily grinned. 'Is that why he gazes at you from across the police station?'

'He doesn't,' Daisy snapped, but she forced a smile at a woman passing by. She squinted as they turned the corner, into the bustle of New Oxford Street. 'I'm hot already today; it's going to be a scorcher.'

Lily ran her fingers around the neck of her collar. 'We could do with a summer and winter uniform.'

Daisy grinned. 'Perhaps we should put it forward as a suggestion for next year.'

'That would go down well.' Lily scanned the stall-holders, as they walked past, smiling and nodding as they caught her eye. The waft of hot soup and jacket potatoes followed them down the street. The aroma of fresh bread made her stomach gurgle with hunger. 'I love this street but hate it all at the same time.'

'What?'

'I love the atmosphere of the stallholders and people going about their business, but the smell of hot food always makes me feel so hungry, even when I know I can't be.'

Daisy laughed. 'You are funny.'

'I'm serious.' Lily chuckled. 'If we were allowed to eat while we walked, I'd be huge.'

'No you wouldn't.' Daisy frowned. 'I was thinking, maybe we should check on Mr Wilson today, to see if that young lad . . . ' She caught Lily's puzzled expression. 'You know, the one that stole the apple, the day we went into Foyles' basement.'

'Aah, yes, I remember.'

'I wondered if the lad kept his word and went back to talk to Mr Wilson.'

'That's a good idea.' Lily's mouth straightened for a moment. 'I wonder what happened to his ma; I hope she got well. It's a shame we never got his address, because we could have called on her and maybe organised a doctor.'

Daisy nodded. 'If he was stealing food, I don't think they could have afforded a doctor or medicine.'

'I know, but I'm sure, between us, we could have offered some help. I'd have collected money from everyone back at the station, if need be.' Lily paused. 'It's so unfair that people can't afford hospitals and doctors, yet the country is spending millions on bombs and guns.'

Daisy grinned at her friend. 'Let's hope we get the vote, when this is over and done with.'

They walked along in silence for a few minutes, watching everyone rushing to get to their places of work, some stopping to buy sandwiches or hot food

139

from a vendor. The sellers' voices rang out, each competing to be heard over the other, with the cars coughing and spluttering along. Two young boys ran towards a horse and cart, parked outside a public house, giggling as they asked a man if they could stroke the horse's neck. The man gave a toothless grin, nodded and produced a carrot from his pocket. Daisy smiled as she watched him break it in two, so they could each feed the horse.

Lily cleared her throat. 'So, how's sorting out your parents' room going?'

Daisy groaned. 'There's so much stuff. I can see why Victoria never wanted to do it.'

Lily nodded. 'It must be difficult for you both, even knowing where to start.'

'The clothes that were in the wardrobe are now strewn all over the bed, and I know that's nothing in itself, but Lily, some of it looks very expensive. We can't understand it, because most of the clothes we don't remember them ever wearing. They were never rich, so where did they come from?'

'Perhaps they were gifts. Our cousin, Emily, always buys Alice and me expensive perfume for our birthday or Christmas, so maybe they had their own Emily.'

Daisy frowned, her eyes darting from side to side. 'They could have, I suppose, but we just don't remember anyone like that, or actually any relatives at all. It's not as though anyone has come visiting since they died, so I find it hard to believe there was anyone like that.'

'That's true, I suppose.' Lily paused. 'Maybe the clothes were what they owned before they had children. My father has always said we bled him dry, well, us girls did.'

Daisy cast Lily a sideways glance. 'How are things at home now?'

Lily laughed. 'Surprisingly good since Alice lost her temper with him; he almost seems a reformed character.' She smiled. 'I think he was totally shocked at Alice, whereas he always expected some lip from me.'

Raised voices caught the girls' attention. They both looked along the street and saw two men pointing and yelling at each other. Without a word, they quickened their pace.

Lily was the first to reach them. 'What's going on?'

Children stared up at the men as they walked past, clutching their mothers' hands.

The weather-worn, grey-haired burly man looked at the policewomen standing next to him. He waved his hand at them. 'Aww, nothing to concern yourselves about.'

Lily felt the hairs on the back of her neck stand on end. 'I think we should be the judge of that, don't you?'

Daisy stepped nearer. 'You're yelling at each other on the street and children are frightened as they walk past you. So, I repeat the question, what's going on here?'

The younger, thinner man only looked about twelve, close up. He fidgeted from one foot to the other. 'It's nothing. We're sorry; we just got carried away. It won't happen again.'

Lily eyed them both suspiciously. 'It's enough that we have to fight the Germans, without us all fighting each other as well.'

The burly man sighed. 'We weren't fighting; we were just talking, that's all.'

'Really, well, we heard you down the other end of

the street.'

Daisy tried to hide the smile that was threatening to break through, at Lily's exaggeration of where they were when they heard the yelling.

The burly man tightened his lips for a second. 'Look, I just wanted to know why he hadn't enlisted, when everyone else had, that's all.'

'Ahh, that old chestnut.' Daisy shook her head. 'And pray tell us, why does he have to explain himself to you, or anyone else come to that? If the powers that be are happy enough with why he's not being shot at, then it should be good enough for you.'

Lily sucked in her breath as she tried to hold in her shock at Daisy's words. In her own way, was she secretly defending Peter Albright?

The burly man leant back, as though he was preparing for Daisy to slap his face. He didn't take his eyes off her, as he growled back at her. 'I suppose, with all our children gone, you don't like to think others are shirking off.'

Lily took a step nearer. 'You must understand, a lot of men want to do their bit, but for health reasons they can't, and it doesn't help anyone for them to be bullied about it.'

The burly man nodded and turned to the young lad. 'Sorry, mate.' He stretched out his arm for a handshake and the young lad accepted it.

The girls nodded. Lily put her hand over theirs. 'Well done; have a good day and enjoy the sunshine, while you can.'

The girls slowly walked away. Daisy looked over her shoulder a couple of times.

'That was a bit of a bouncer, wasn't it?'

Daisy frowned. 'What?'

Lily giggled. 'Sorry, it's a cricketing term; you'll have to blame my grandfather for that one. Did that hit a nerve with you? I wondered if you were defending Peter.'

'Of course not.' Daisy studied the ground in front of her. 'I just get sick of hearing about it.'

★ ★ ★

Victoria studied the inside of her mother's heavy oak wardrobe before placing her cup and saucer back on to the tray. 'Alice, can you see what that is, at the bottom? It looks like a chest, or box of some sort.'

Alice leant in and reached down, grabbing the side handle of the dark wooden chest. 'I don't know what's inside, but it's heavy.' She took a deep breath and yanked at the handle, pulling it out.

The three girls stood staring at it for a while. A layer of dust covered the top of it and Alice's fingers had left their mark.

Molly didn't take her eyes off the box. She wrinkled her nose and sneezed, as the dust began to settle around her. Pulling a white cotton handkerchief from her skirt pocket, she delicately brushed it across the end of her nose. 'It looks more than a wooden box; with the black studded metal strips, it's how I imagine a sea chest would look.'

Victoria reluctantly moved her gaze away from the box and started to rummage amongst the clothes on the bed, before finally pulling an apron free. She wrapped part of it around her hand and brushed it over the top of the box.

Alice hadn't taken her eyes off the box and watched Victoria moving the dust to one end. 'Shall I go and

143

find a dustpan and brush? It might be easier.'

Victoria shook her head, but kept her eyes peeled on the box. She couldn't recall ever having seen it before, but why would it have been hidden away like that? She stooped and pushed hard on the edges of the box, but it didn't open.

Molly rested her hand on Victoria's arm. 'It looks like there's a lock.'

Victoria threw her arms down by her side. 'Well, where's the key? Why isn't it sitting in the lock? Do you think my mother had it on her, when she died?'

Alice shrugged. 'I don't think so, and anyway, the police brought all their belongings to you, remember.'

Victoria nodded, staying silent for a moment. 'Then the key must be here, somewhere.'

Molly glanced at Alice and whispered, 'I'm sure we'll come across it as we sort through the drawers and everything. You just have to be patient.'

'I know. It just feels important that I open the chest.' Victoria paused for a moment. 'I wonder where it came from. I'm sure I've never seen it before.'

Alice hugged her friend. 'Come on, Victoria, the best thing will be to keep working, then we might come across the key.'

Molly turned away and carried on opening drawers, emptying the contents onto the bed. She was careful to press down on everything she lifted out, in case anything was wrapped inside the many socks, nightdresses, cardigans and underwear, but there was nothing. Molly sighed as she pulled open yet another drawer. All this made her realise she had to sort through her things, before she got married to Andrew. She gave a small gasp when she peered into the drawer. 'Victoria.'

144

Victoria and Alice looked up and took the step towards Molly, who hadn't moved. They both looked down at the same time.

'Oh my goodness.' Victoria grabbed Alice's arm. The drawer was full of children's clothes, little boy's clothes. 'They must be Stephen's, but why would they keep them?' Victoria lifted up a pair of very small blue trousers. 'They are so tiny.' She noticed something wrapped in paper and bent down to pick it up. She placed it on the bed, carefully unfolding the paper. 'Look.' She peered back at the girls. 'It's a baby's christening gown.'

Alice and Molly looked at each other for a second. Molly stepped nearer. 'It looks beautiful; there's some quite intricate embroidery work.' She patted Victoria's back. 'I think my ma kept my christening gown. I'll ask her and we can compare them and see who had the best, me or you.' She did her best to sound light-hearted, but wasn't convinced she had pulled it off.

Victoria stared hard at the delicate material that had been wrapped up so carefully. 'I don't know what to do with it, with any of it.'

Alice took a step towards Victoria. 'You should talk to Daisy. It doesn't have to be your decision, alone.'

Molly didn't take her eyes off the outfit. 'You should keep it, for when you have children.'

A strange noise escaped from Victoria. 'Oh yes, because that's likely to happen, isn't it?'

Alice glared at Molly.

'Look, Victoria, I know all this is upsetting.' Molly waved her arms around the room. 'I really do, but don't start feeling sorry for yourself about the future. It hasn't happened yet, and it's yours for the making.

Ted will return, or you'll meet someone else, but it'll be when you least expect it. Look at me and Andrew.'

Victoria sighed. That was the problem — she didn't want anyone else, but Ted seemed to have stopped writing. Maybe she wouldn't have any choice in the matter. She began wrapping the gown back in the paper. 'I'll speak to Daisy; she might want to keep it.'

Alice returned to the drawer that the christening gown had been in; it was a shame to disturb the tiny items of clothing. 'I understand why they would have kept that gown, but I wonder why your parents kept these?'

'Who knows?' Victoria turned to Alice. 'I remember them as being practical; fun, but practical.' She looked back at the bed. 'Some of their clothes look expensive as well. It doesn't make sense.'

11

Victoria had been speaking to a customer, helping her to find a particular book. The lady hadn't understood what order they were in on the shelves. She must remember to talk to Mr Leadbetter about her concerns. The books were in publisher order, and not many people would know how to make sense of that.

Mr Leadbetter had been watching his new protégé going about her business. She could easily take over once he retired, and was very good with customers, both old and young alike. 'Everything all right, Miss Appleton?'

Victoria smiled, even though he still scared her a little. 'Yes, sir.' She peered over her shoulder, watching the customer she had just been chatting to. 'I have had customers come up to me unable to find the books they are looking for. They don't understand our system on the shelves.'

Mr Leadbetter bristled; was she criticising his beloved bookshop? 'Did you explain that everything was in publisher order?'

Victoria nodded. 'I did, sir, but each has come back and said they didn't know who it was published by. They barely know who has written the book.'

Mr Leadbetter tightened his lips and stared down the aisle and at the books crammed on the shelving. 'I suppose I can see that could be a problem.'

Victoria followed his gaze. 'I think, in the beginning, it probably wasn't, but now we have so many books, it's proving to be so.'

Mr Leadbetter puffed out his chest. 'I don't think it's affecting sales, so it can't be that much of a problem. In fact, they may well be finding other books to read, while they're looking.'

Victoria chuckled. 'That could well be true, sir. I just thought I'd mention it.'

Mr Leadbetter hitched his thumb into his waistcoat pocket. 'Are you enjoying being on the shop floor?'

'I am, sir. Thank you for giving me the opportunity; I do appreciate it.'

Mr Leadbetter nodded. 'I've been meaning to talk to you about the young girl that works near Miss Cooper.'

Victoria's heart pounded in her chest. 'Yes, sir.'

Mr Leadbetter kept his eyes fixed on her. 'I haven't seen her today, have you?'

'I'm not sure which young girl you mean, sir.'

Mr Leadbetter chuckled to himself; this young lady would go far in life. 'I believe she was a little upset, when she was last in.'

'Oh, you mean Edith.' Victoria clasped her sweaty palms together, wondering how vague she could get away with being. 'I understand she had received some bad news, sir.'

'Oh, I hope it's not family troubles.'

'I think so, sir. I hope you don't mind, but I sent her home to see her mother. I was hoping she'd feel better today and come to work. I'm sorry if I made a mistake.'

Mr Leadbetter pulled his fob watch from his waistcoat, flicking the gold lid open. 'It sounds to me as though you did the right thing; I hope everything is all right.' He pressed the lid down and returned the watch to his pocket. 'I don't know where this morning

148

has gone to; it'll soon be lunchtime.'

Victoria breathed a sigh of relief. 'If you don't need me here, sir, I thought I'd go and check on Albert, before lunch.'

Mr Leadbetter laughed. 'I hear you and he have had some strange conversations together.'

Victoria looked up and straightened a book that was hanging precariously off the shelf. 'If you mean the conversation we had about his cockney rhyming slang, then you would be correct. I don't know what he's talking about sometimes, but I feel I should keep an eye on him, being down in the basement by himself.'

'From what I hear, he's not on his own for very long down there; good job he works while he chatters.' Mr Leadbetter turned to walk towards the open doors of the shop. 'Don't forget to have your lunch break, though.'

'No, sir, I won't.' Victoria watched him walk away, glad he hadn't told her off for sending Edith home, although she hadn't told him the whole truth. She frowned as she made her way to the basement, hoping she had done the right thing. Pulling open the door between the staff area and the basement sent the usual shiver down her spine. Victoria shook her head; she should be used to going down these stairs by now, but the usual fear of being stuck down them jumped into her head. *Stop it.* Before she could think another thought, she ran down the stairs and pushed open the basement door. The heavy wood creaked under her hands.

Albert looked up. 'Hello, Miss Appleton.'

Victoria smiled at the old man. 'Good morning, Albert.'

'I take it yer must be getting over yer fear of coming down 'ere now, being one of my regular visitors these days.'

'Who said I was frightened of coming down here?'

Albert grinned. 'No one did, but every time yer come down 'ere, yer look like the devil himself is after yer.'

'I'm trying to be braver, but the thought of being locked in here frightens me.' Victoria looked down at the grey floor. 'It sounds idiotic when I say it out loud; I'm a grown woman.'

Albert shook his head. 'Don't worry yerself about it.' He beamed at Victoria. 'There's many a woman that would like to be stuck down 'ere wiv me, I can tell yer.'

Victoria giggled. 'I'm sure that's true, Albert.'

Albert picked up his piece of rag and began wiping the book in front of him. 'How yer doing, anyway? 'Ave yer 'eard 'ow young Edith is doing?'

Victoria frowned. 'How do you know about Edith?'

'I told yer, not much gets past me.'

'I never realised people gossiped so much.' Victoria picked up a book and stared at the black and white cover. 'I don't think I'll read this.' She looked at Albert. '*The Magician*, by W. Somerset Maugham; it looks a little creepy.' She put the book down again.

'I've still got yer other one saved for yer.' Albert nodded towards the corner of the table.

'I know, I haven't forgotten.'

Albert fixed his gaze on her. 'So, what's 'appening then?'

'Nothing much.' Victoria flicked through *The Magician.*

Albert dropped his rag on to the table. 'Well, yer

don't 'ave to tell me, but I will say this, yer look a little sad, if yer ask me.'

Victoria's eyes widened. 'Sad?'

'Yep, sad, it's in yer eyes.' He paused, not taking his eyes off her. 'Yer know, my dear old ma, God rest her soul, used to say the eyes are the window to the soul, and I reckon she was right.'

Victoria sighed. 'I've been going through my parents' things and it's just upsetting, that's all.'

'Aye, it would be.' Albert picked up his rag again. 'It was a big thing yer did after they died, looking after yer bruvver and sister.'

Victoria opened her mouth to ask how he knew about that, but then his words 'not much gets past me' bounced into her mind. 'I've come across photographs my parents are in, but I don't know who the other people are or where they were taken.'

Albert could feel his throat tightening. He coughed. 'Sorry, the dust gets on my chest from time to time.'

Victoria nodded. 'You need to take care, perhaps pop out and get some fresh air.'

Albert remained silent for a moment. 'Yer should bring some of the photographs in, and I'll take a look. I probably won't know, but old Leadbetter might. He's quite travelled, yer know.'

Victoria's eyes lit up. 'I'm open to any help I can get, thank you. I've brought a couple in today, so maybe I'll pop down with them later.' She brushed her hands together. 'I suppose I had better get on; I don't want to get the sack.'

Albert nodded as he watched her walk towards the door. 'Take care now.'

* * *

151

Victoria stood hidden between two aisles of books, watching Alice smile at a customer, before handing over the bill payment slip. It was strange, watching someone else doing the job she had done for years. Things were changing. Alice had a family of her own and would, no doubt have her own home before long. Molly would be next. She watched Molly stroll towards Alice; they stood talking for a moment. Victoria wanted to go over and see what they were nattering about, but something held her back. Molly's laughter could be heard around the shop, and she quickly clamped her hand across her mouth. Victoria couldn't take her eyes off her friends. As they leant into each other, all smiles and laughter had disappeared. She turned and moved from her hiding place, quickly straightening the shelves around her. She couldn't give up, though. Would she always be the single aunt? Would she become a crazy cat lady? Would she just become a sad and lonely old woman? Going through her parents' things had churned her up, and she hadn't heard from Ted for weeks. Tears pricked at her eyes. He might be no more, but how would she know?

'Miss Appleton.'

Victoria blinked rapidly and forced her best customer friendly smile, before she turned round. Her eyes widened and her smile faded. 'Edith, my goodness, how are you?'

Edith gave a tentative smile. 'I'm not too bad, thank you.'

'At least your ma hasn't killed you. I take it you've told her?'

Edith laughed. 'Yes, I've told her and, yes, she went mad and told me I was stupid for getting myself into

152

this situation.'

Victoria nodded, holding onto the thought that Edith was smiling.

'Anyway, when she eventually calmed down, she gave me a cuddle.' A tear tripped down her cheek. 'So I'm not being shipped off anywhere to have it, or getting the baby adopted. Me ma says I should hold my head up high and we'll get through it together.'

Victoria stepped forward and wrapped her arms around Edith. 'I'm so happy it's turned out well. Your ma sounds like a wonderful mother, so you should trust her and the love she has for you.'

Edith stepped back and looked up at her manager. 'I can't help feeling I've disappointed her, though. I don't think it's the future she had hoped I'd have.'

'Of course it isn't.' Victoria frowned. 'But you must understand, all our futures could be whipped away at any time, so none of that matters. Your ma just wants you to be happy, and to have an easier life than she's had.'

'That's more or less what she said.'

'See, I said your ma sounded like a wonderful woman.'

Edith giggled. 'If it's all right, I would like to come back to work tomorrow. I need the money more than ever, now.'

'Of course, just come in at the usual time.'

'Thank you, and thank you for listening to me ramble on, and for giving me the courage to speak to me ma.'

Victoria smiled, before bending her head slightly. 'You're most welcome. Now get yourself off and enjoy what's left of your day.'

Edith nodded, before turning around and heading

towards the shop door, seemingly oblivious of the hard task ahead of her.

Victoria shrugged; it had turned out well, and that was all that mattered at this time. She turned to look back at Alice and Molly, but Alice was serving customers and Molly was nowhere to be seen.

'Excuse me.'

Victoria looked around at the woman's voice. 'Yes, madam, can I help you?'

The young woman twisted her hands in front of her. 'You work 'ere right, only I'm looking for a book.'

Victoria smiled. 'I do and it sounds like you've come to the right shop. Foyles must have at least one copy of everything that has ever been printed.'

The woman breathed a sigh of relief. She pulled a scrap of paper from her long, grey skirt and handed it to Victoria. 'It's not for me, it's a present for me bruvver. He's away fighting and I wanted to send 'im summink.'

Using only her fingertips, Victoria pulled apart the edges of the tea-stained paper. 'It says *Man of Property* by John Galsworthy. Hmm, I don't suppose you know who published it, do you?'

The woman shrugged. 'No, and I wouldn't know where to start looking. I've never seen so many books in one place.'

Victoria saw Mr Leadbetter striding towards her. 'Mr Leadbetter, I have a quandary.'

Mr Leadbetter smiled graciously at the customer, before looking back at Victoria. 'What is it?'

'This lady would like to buy *Man of Property* by John Galsworthy, but I don't know who published it.'

'Hmm.' Mr Leadbetter rubbed his hand over his

154

chin. 'I have a feeling we did have a copy under Grosset and Dunlap, but I'm not sure it's still there.'

Victoria stared, in awe of his knowledge. 'Thank you, sir. I'll go and have a look.'

'Allow me; you go and have your lunch.' Mr Leadbetter smiled at the customer. 'Come madam, I do love a challenge, and if it's not there, you can leave it with me and come back tomorrow.'

The young woman beamed up at him as she turned and followed him. She stopped and looked over her shoulder. 'Thank you for your help, miss.'

Victoria smiled. The woman looked tiny, as she walked next to Mr Leadbetter.

'Are you ready for lunch, Miss Appleton?'

Victoria chuckled; she'd know that voice anywhere. 'Thank you, Miss Cooper, I was just on my way.' She turned and beamed at her friend.

'Come on then, Alice has got a table for us.'

The pair of them walked into the staff area together.

Alice looked up as they walked towards her. She had made them a cup of tea each. 'How are you getting on today, Victoria? We haven't had time to chat.'

Molly chimed in. 'It's been a busy day, as always.'

Victoria looked at her friends for a moment, before taking a postcard out of her skirt pocket. 'This fell out of a book that Albert was getting ready to bring up to the shop, the other day.' She placed the card down on the table.

Molly stared down at the black and white picture. 'Why are you carrying it around with you?'

Victoria twisted it around, so she could see it better. 'I feel like I should know where it is; it looks familiar and yet I can't place it. Do either of you have any ideas?'

155

They both shook their heads.

Alice picked it up, to study it closer. 'It's obviously the seaside, but other than that, I don't know.' She placed it back in the centre of the round table.

The girls sat in silence, each staring at it.

Alice picked it up again. 'If you want, I can take it home and ask my grandfather; he might know.'

Victoria smiled. 'If you could ask him, that would be good, because I'm not getting anywhere by myself and yet I can't seem to let it go.'

Alice nodded and placed the postcard in her pocket.

Molly bit into her fish paste sandwich. 'You know, we haven't been to Café Monico for a while. It's a visit that's long overdue.'

Alice nodded. 'The trouble is, between work, driving the ambulance and going round Victoria's, I'm not seeing very much of Freddie and Arthur at the moment. They'll start to wonder who I am, soon.'

Victoria rested her hand on Alice's arm. 'Oh my goodness, I'm so sorry. I've been so wrapped up in my own problems, I didn't give anything, or anyone else a thought. How bad am I?'

Alice laughed and patted Victoria's hand. 'I'm sorry. I didn't mean to make you feel bad. I was just saying there is a lot of call on my time. Freddie totally understands me helping you, but I'm not sure he'd understand me gallivanting to Monico's.'

Molly nodded. 'Well, I understand that, but it does mean I can't give you my news.' She giggled, as she enjoyed tormenting her friends.

Victoria looked across at Molly. 'What news?'

With a sparkle in her eye, Molly put her sandwich back onto its wrapper. 'I told you, I can't tell you.'

Alice and Molly followed Victoria into the hallway of her home in Percy Street.

'It's lovely and cool in here.' Alice fanned her hand in front of her face. 'I swear June is getting hotter, with each day that goes by.'

Molly nodded. 'But we shouldn't moan, because autumn will be here before we know it, and then we'll be complaining about that.'

Victoria noticed a layer of dust sitting on the console table. She picked up the church candle, revealing the clear ring, where it had stood; evidence that no housework had been done for over a week.

Molly touched her arm. 'Don't worry about it, Victoria. It's not like you haven't been busy.'

Alice sniffed the air. 'Is that beeswax I can smell?'

Daisy stepped into the hall, her slippers silent on the tiled floor. 'Now that's a shame.'

Victoria jumped at the sound of her sister's voice. She turned around to see her, with a scarf wrapped around her head and an overall covering her clothes. A rag hung out of her pocket and she was carrying a tin of polish.

Daisy smiled at Victoria's confusion. 'I was hoping to get the house tidied before you got home.' She glanced across at the girls. 'I thought it was time I showed I was an adult, but it's taken me ages to find the stuff I need to clean with.'

Laughter burst from all three girls.

Daisy looked confused, as she scanned across the three friends. 'What?'

Alice was the first to catch her breath. 'It's brave of you to admit you didn't know where anything was kept, especially as you've been in domestic service.'

Daisy giggled. 'Yes, well, I think my sister has protected me from everyday things, and it's time I did my bit.'

Victoria beamed at her sister. 'Thank you, Daisy; it's all appreciated.'

Daisy looked over her shoulder, and back again. 'Oh, I'm not doing it by myself. I've roped Lily into helping me.'

'Oh my goodness.' Alice squealed with laughter. 'Don't let Father know, otherwise he'll get rid of Mrs Headley.'

'What's all the noise about?' Lily was suddenly in front of them, dressed in the same uniform as Daisy.

Alice shook her head and smiled. 'I never thought I'd see the day.'

Lily chuckled. 'If I find out you've told anyone about this, there'll be trouble.'

Molly laughed at Lily's indignation. 'I think your secret is safe, because apart from Freddie, everyone else she would tell is already here.'

Lily smiled. 'I suppose we'll be the topic of conversation between the three of you for a while.'

Victoria stepped forward and threw her arms around the two girls. 'Only in a good way. What you were trying to do was wonderful, and I don't think we should hold you up.' She gave them a squeeze, before stepping back. 'Right, who wants tea?'

Daisy's eyes sparkled. 'The kettle is already on, so I'll make it.'

Victoria looked at her sister. 'You are spoiling me.' She turned and looked at her friends. 'We might as well go straight upstairs.' She looked back at Daisy and Lily. 'Thank you, both of you, I'm so lucky to be surrounded by such wonderful people.'

Molly sniffed. 'Come on, before you have us all in tears — and Alice needs to see Arthur, before the little mite forgets who she is.'

The three of them ran up the stairs, which creaked and groaned under them. Victoria led the way into her parents' bedroom. A groan escaped, as she looked around the room. 'I think this looks worse than it did, before we started.'

The girls nodded.

Alice moved some clothing on the bed and perched down on the edge of it. 'I think you need to start making some decisions about what to do with some of this stuff, because we're running out of space.'

Victoria glanced around. 'You're right. I need to sit down with Daisy and talk about it all.'

Molly stepped forward. 'Right, we need to get on, because tomorrow I would like us to go to Monico's, as I'm suffering with chocolate cake withdrawal symptoms.'

'You clearly have something you want to tell us, so just say it.' Victoria paused, waiting for a clue of what it was. 'It's either the wedding date, or you're pregnant.'

Molly smiled but didn't bite. 'Tradition is important, and we started it so it should continue.' She winked at Victoria. 'It may not be anything except the urge to have a piece of their chocolate cake, but you need to exercise some patience to find out.'

Alice laughed. 'Right, we'll go tomorrow, but let's try and get everything out of here tonight.'

The girls nodded and moved to different items of furniture, pulling things free.

Victoria bent down to pick up one of her father's

ties, which had fallen and was lying half under the bed. She cast a glance under there and gasped at the sight of another ornate box. She got down on all fours and pulled the box free. She lifted the lid, her mouth dropping open as she stared into it. When she finally found her voice, it was barely audible. 'Look . . . look at this.'

The girls looked round.

'What is it Vic?' Molly frowned, as she noticed the colour draining away from her friend.

'Look . . . ' Victoria fell back and knelt in front of the box. 'Where has all this come from?'

Alice and Molly stepped around the bed and peered inside the box.

'Oh my goodness.' Molly gasped. 'Is that all that's in there?'

'I . . . I don't know.' Victoria lifted her hand to delve inside but stopped halfway. 'Where has it all come from?'

Alice rested her hand on Victoria's shoulders. 'Maybe it was their savings.'

'Savings?' Victoria spluttered. 'Hadn't they heard of banks?'

Molly sat down on the floor next to the box. 'Is there anything else in there?'

Victoria jumped up. 'I don't know and I can't look.' Tears began to stream down her face. 'We could barely afford to eat at times, yet this box of money was sitting up here all this time.'

Molly looked up from the box and wanted to give her friend sympathy, but knew that wouldn't work. 'If we had done this earlier, you would have discovered it sooner, and then you would have had money to buy food.' She could feel the tears pushing to get out. She blinked quickly; now was not the time. 'You need to stop being angry, and check if there is anything else in this box, other than money.'

Victoria glared at Molly.

Molly lifted her chin. 'It's no good you glaring at me. You know I'm right, just like you were right when you told me to be myself.' Molly pushed her arms out wide. 'This is me, being myself with my best friends.' Silence hung in the air, gripped in the tension that was sparking between the two girls. 'Take it or leave it, but I'm taking your advice, Victoria.'

Victoria fell to her knees. 'Trust you to take the bit of advice that suits you, at this given time.' She forced a weak smile. 'I hate it when my words of wisdom are used against me.'

Alice smiled. 'We can't always see what's staring us in the face; that's why we need good friends that will tell us as it is.'

Victoria nodded.

The clatter of crockery mingled with the creaking stairs.

Daisy came in, beaming from ear to ear. 'Tea is finally here, girls.' She placed the tray down and Lily followed her into the room, carrying a small plate of biscuits.

Daisy started pouring the tea. 'How's it going?'

Lily glanced over at the girls and then nudged her friend's arm.

'Careful.' Daisy didn't look up. 'I almost spilt the tea everywhere.'

Lily nudged her again and raised her eyebrows. An exasperated sigh escaped from her. 'Daisy, for a police officer, your observation skills leave a lot to be desired.'

'What, I'm —'

'Look.'

Daisy finally glanced over at her sister. 'You've been crying.' She took the couple of steps to place an arm around Victoria's shoulders. 'What is it? What's happened?'

12

Alice, Victoria and Molly ambled along Regent Street, heading for the pyramid sign of Café Monico. Their luxury of tea and chocolate cake was long overdue. The heat of the day was subsiding. Ladies still had their parasols up, to protect them from the heat of the July sun. The girls bobbed and weaved, avoiding getting their hats caught in the spokes as they walked past.

Alice smiled at her friends. 'It would be easy to forget there was a war on, on a day like today. Doesn't it make you want to paddle in the sea?'

Molly giggled. 'I so enjoyed it at Southend, that bank holiday, before this awful war started and changed our lives forever.'

Victoria nodded, clasping her handbag tight; it contained precious cargo. She had made herself wait to read Stephen's letter. That would be much later, when she was at home with Daisy. 'The nearest we have to that is the Thames, and I wouldn't fancy dipping my toes in there.'

The two adjacent pyramid signs of the Café Monico were just ahead. People were milling around outside, having heated discussions about the war. Molly pushed open the wooden doors to Monico's and was immediately transported back to another time and place. She had forgotten how grand it was inside. The arched mirrors on the wall gave the illusion of space, while the white roman pillars gave it grandeur. The panelled ceiling was edged with scrolled mouldings and large potted palms were placed around the room. A waitress appeared to glide towards them, dressed in a floor length, black dress with a pristine white apron tied around her waist, while the frilled straps rested easily on her slim shoulders.

Alice smiled at the waitress. 'Can we have a table for three please?'

The young girl nodded. 'If you'd like to follow me.'

As they were shown to a table, their heels clattered on the tiled floor, blending in with the constant buzz of conversation around the room.

'I love this place.' Victoria looked around her. 'Although I still don't like seeing myself in the arched mirrors.'

Molly raised her voice a little. 'It's obviously still a popular place; the war doesn't appear to have touched it.'

The waitress pulled out the first chair, for one of them to use. Victoria quickly claimed the seat. 'I'll take this one, because I can't see myself from here.'

Alice and Molly laughed at her.

Molly pulled out the chair opposite her. 'I think you get worse.'

With a sigh, Alice also sat down. 'Ahh, this is nice. You're right, Molly, it has been a while.'

Victoria studied Alice for a moment. 'You look tired and that's my fault, keeping you busy at my house, most evenings.' She paused. 'I'm sorry. I tend to forget you have your own family.'

Alice chuckled. 'I wouldn't have it any other way. Anyway, I don't think that has anything to do with it. I've been feeling exhausted for quite some time.'

Molly listened to the exchange and nodded. 'You said, a while ago, you were thinking of giving up some of the war work, because you were tired. Have you done that?'

The waitress stepped towards them but hovered in the background.

Alice shook her head and indicated to the waitress that they were ready to order. 'Is it the usual, girls?' Alice smiled at them. 'Or are we going to pretend we might have something else?'

Molly giggled. 'Well, for me it's the usual, but Victoria likes to think about it first.'

Victoria pulled a face at Molly, before smiling at Alice. 'It's the usual.'

Alice laughed at them both. Molly was right; this had been long overdue. She looked up at the waitress. 'Can we have a pot of tea and your finest chocolate cake, for three please.'

Molly glanced around her, as the waitress walked away. 'This is lovely; it feels like it's been ages since we were last here.'

Victoria followed Molly's gaze. 'It is, and with everything that's going on, I'd forgotten how lovely it is.'

Molly stared at Victoria for a moment. 'You've always had a sadness about you, although I thought at one time you were happier, but now I'm not so sure.' She paused for a second. 'Is that because of your parents' things?'

Victoria gave a weak smile. 'There's so much I don't understand.' She lowered her eyes. 'I feel like I didn't know them at all.'

The girls glanced at each other. Molly swallowed hard. 'They were still the same people. They just had belongings that you, as a child, didn't know about.'

'Molly's right.' Alice clasped Victoria's hand. 'Oh,

I almost forgot, my grandfather thought the picture postcard looked like Brighton, but he wasn't sure. I'll try and remember to bring it back tomorrow.'

'Brighton?' Victoria gave Alice a pensive look. 'It doesn't mean anything to me. At least, I don't remember going there, so I'm probably getting carried away with everything.'

'Did you empty the box you found last night? Did it only contain money?'

Victoria looked up at them. 'I didn't look at everything, but there was a small box with what looked like a lock of baby's hair in it, as well as a tooth. Their marriage certificate and a few other certificates were there too. I only looked at two of them and assumed the rest were our birth certificates. There was a tiny baby's rattle as well, but it was mainly money. Oh, and a bible.'

Alice nodded. 'It sounds like it was a keepsake box. I have one for Arthur.'

Victoria sighed. 'I haven't counted the money; I can't bring myself to do it.'

Molly whispered across the table. 'Perhaps Daisy can do it for you.'

Victoria nodded. 'I just don't understand it all. I have a bad feeling about it. It's like there's a family secret, but I don't know what it is.'

Alice shook her head. 'Your parents adored you all, you know that, so if there is a secret, there'll be a good reason for it. They weren't bad people.'

Victoria took a deep breath and nodded. 'Anyway, enough of that, I've just got to be ruthless and clear it all out.' She forced a smile and looked across at her friends.

The waitress appeared with the tea and chocolate

166

cake, carefully laying out the place settings in front of each girl.

Molly looked down at the slice on her plate. 'Thank goodness the war hasn't hit Monico's.'

The girls laughed and each picked up their cake forks.

Victoria glanced at the china teapot. 'Who's going to be mother and pour the tea?'

Molly didn't look up. Her eyes were fixed on the decadent cake that was calling out to her. 'Not me, I'm diving straight in.' She stabbed the fork into the light chocolate sponge.

Alice laughed. 'Well, I guess that'll be me again, then.' She let her gaze flick between her two friends, waiting for the penny to drop.

There was a clatter of cutlery hitting crockery, just before Molly looked up. 'What?'

Victoria's mouth dropped open slightly. 'Are you — '

'Yes.' Alice giggled at them. 'You should see your faces.'

'Gosh.' Molly beamed. 'Arthur is going to have a little brother or sister.' Victoria grinned. 'When?' She held up her hand and counted on her fingers, before bubbling with laughter. 'Is it going to be a Christmas baby?'

'If it is and it's a girl, you'll have to call her Holly.' Molly laughed.

'Or Noel if it's a boy,' Victoria offered.

Alice laughed at them both. 'I don't think it will be a Christmas baby, but if it is, it will just have a normal name.'

Molly picked up her fork again. 'That's a shame, but I suppose you could have a biblical name.'

Alice nodded.

Molly looked pensive for a moment. 'Maybe David; he was a great king and killed Goliath.'

'David's a good name.' Alice smiled at her friends. 'I'm quite excited, because Freddie will be with me this time, so I won't have the worry of whether he's safe or not.'

Victoria nodded. 'Yes, that's good, but I can't believe you kept it a secret from us.'

Alice's lips tightened. 'It just never seemed the right time to tell you. There's been a lot going on.'

'I've been too wrapped up in myself, otherwise I'm sure I would have noticed.' Victoria looked over at Molly. 'And to think I thought it was you, not Alice, who wanted to give us some news.'

Molly put down her fork again. 'You know, I don't think I'm meant to eat this cake.' She stared at it, before looking up and letting out a sigh. 'Well, I wanted us to go shopping together for my wedding, but with everything that's been going on, I'm not so sure now.'

Victoria smiled. 'Don't be ridiculous; you only have one wedding. Well, at least, that's what we all hope.'

Alice frowned. 'What about your mother, won't she want to go with you? We shouldn't tread on her toes.'

Molly nodded. 'I thought I'd go out with her over the weekend, while Pa's at home to look after gran, just to get a feel for what she likes. I want to buy her and gran an outfit, but I know she'll want to be frugal about it, so I thought if I went separately, it would keep our arguments between us. I can go out again and have fun with you two.'

Victoria picked up her fork. 'It sounds like you've thought it through.'

Molly smiled. 'I haven't got much time, so if we can make it the weekend after next, that'll be good. Maybe we'll go to Selfridges first.'

Victoria dropped her fork and beamed, as she clapped her hands together. 'We haven't had a good shopping trip for ages.'

★ ★ ★

Endell Street Military Hospital seemed quieter than usual, although the nurses were as busy as ever. Victoria carried an armful of newspapers, quietly offering them to soldiers as she walked down the ward. It was six o'clock in the evening, but the heat of the day was still strong. Beads of perspiration formed on her forehead, as the papers weighed heavily on her arms. She fleetingly wondered how the boys on the street corners managed to hold so many, and take money at the same time.

'Come on, lads, help a girl out and take a newspaper off her.'

Victoria spun round on her heels, to see Nurse Atkins following her.

'It's no good you whispering, girl. You've got to shout for all you're worth and pretend you're one of the lads selling papers on the street corners.'

Colour flooded Victoria's cheeks.

'Come on, they won't bite, well at least most of them won't.' Mabel frowned at Victoria's obvious discomfort.

Victoria gave an anxious look up and down the ward, before taking a deep breath. 'Come on you men, take some of these newspapers off my hands. You'd be helping me out, of that there's no doubt.'

Some of the men cheered and clapped. There was a chorus of 'I'll take one' from around the room.

Mabel patted her on the back. 'That's a girl, I said you could do it, didn't I?'

'Get your paper now, before they all go!' Victoria shouted, before her courage left her. 'Winston Churchill is home from the frontline and back in politics. He's been appointed Minister of Munitions.' She gave a little laugh. 'I don't know whether that's a good thing, or not.'

Another nurse spoke, as she walked past Victoria. 'It all takes a bit of getting used to.'

Victoria nodded.

Corporal Peters shouted out, 'You'll have to read it to me, Atkins.'

Mabel laughed. 'Good try, Peters. Victoria can do that, if you want her to.'

'Oh, you got better things to do than read to me then, have you, Atkins?'

Mabel took a step nearer to his bed. 'No, not better, just other things.' She paused. 'Stop trying to make me feel bad, when you know I have patients to bathe, dressings and bedding to change. You'll get me shot, at this rate.'

'Sorry, Atkins, I just get so bored lying here.' Corporal Peters fidgeted in the bed.

Mabel glanced across at Victoria, before turning her attention back to Peters. 'Well, you don't have to be lying there, feeling sorry for yourself. You could get out of bed, for a start. Sit in a chair and feel sorry for yourself, if that's what you want to do, or here's a thought, talk to the poor bloke in the next bed. You don't have to be able to see to do that.'

Victoria gasped, holding her breath, waiting for the

170

anger that was surely going to come Mabel's way.

There was silence between them for a moment, before laughter burst from Peters. 'Try not to be too nice to me.'

Atkins shook her head and lowered her tone, when she finally spoke. 'Nice won't get you back on your feet, or feeling like you can cope as a man.'

Tension filled the silence between them. Mabel turned back to Victoria. 'Right, I can't stand here chatting all day. I have loads to do, and as my Sid would have said, Sister will have my guts for garters, if I don't get a move on.' Mabel turned and paced it to the other end of the ward.

Victoria couldn't help smiling, as she watched her stopping at beds along the way. She had to learn to chat to the men more, and not be frightened about what she said. After all, most of them just wanted company. She watched Mabel go into the side room and hoped the corporal was improving.

'Victoria.' Corporal Peters' voice jolted her back to her task at hand. 'Victoria, are you still there?' He sniffed. 'I think you are, because I can smell your perfume. I don't know what it smells of.' He sniffed again. 'It could be spring flowers maybe, who knows, but it's a lovely smell.'

'I'm still here, Corporal Peters.' Victoria cleared her throat. 'Is there anything I can do for you?'

Corporal Peters laughed. 'If your perfume is anything to go by, I'm sure there's a lot you can do for me.'

Victoria felt the heat rising in her cheeks, and a nervous giggle escaped. 'Shall I rephrase what I said —'

'No, that won't be necessary, I'm just playing with you.' Peters paused. 'You sound so young and timid.'

Victoria pushed back her shoulders and pulled herself up tall. 'I'm not as timid as you may think.'

Peters laughed. 'I don't think any woman is.'

Victoria smiled. 'I think you could have a point there; anyway, I must get on.'

'No wait.' Peters stopped and listened hard. 'I want you to help me get out of bed, and onto the chair.'

Victoria frowned as she looked along the ward. All the nurses were busy with patients. Would she get into trouble if she helped move him? After all, she wasn't a nurse.

Peters snapped at her. 'Are you going to help me, or not?'

Fear ran across Victoria's pale complexion, as she looked back at him. 'I'm not a nurse, so I don't think I'm allowed to.'

Peters laughed. 'There's nothing wrong with me except I'm blind, so I'm sure you can guide me to a chair.'

Victoria nodded. She blushed when she realised he couldn't see her nodding. Taking a deep breath, she moved nearer to the bed. 'All right, I'll help you, but you will have to guide me, because I've never done anything like this before.'

Peters smiled in her direction. 'Ahh, what can go wrong?'

Victoria couldn't help thinking those words were tempting fate. She tentatively stretched out her arm and her fingertips touched his arm, so he knew she was there.

Peters laughed. 'Don't be frightened girl; I won't bite. I'm probably old enough to be your father.'

Victoria pulled back the blankets and sheet, clasping his thin arm in her hand. 'Are you ready for this?'

172

'You have very soft hands.'

Victoria whispered, 'Thank you.'

Peters' eyes, blank of expression, stared at her. 'Are your father or brother away fighting?'

'My brother is; we write to each other regularly.' Victoria paused, wondering how much to tell this man. 'My parents died in a train crash, several years ago, before the war started.'

Peters' tone dropped. 'I'm sorry to hear that. You don't sound very old, so you must have been quite young to lose both your parents.'

'I was sixteen, but it's in the past. It's hard, but we have to move on and deal with what's in front of us now.' As the words came out, Victoria realised it was time she practised what she preached. 'Life goes on, you know, whether you like it or not. I have a friend who's getting married next month, and another one who's expecting her second child.'

Peters tilted his head slightly. 'And yet I sense you feel you haven't moved on.'

Victoria laughed. 'I am meant to be getting you out of bed, so your life can move on.'

'All right, don't let go, and you'll have to give me instructions of where to go.'

'This will be interesting.' Victoria looked across at the chair and back at Peters, before she let go of his arm and stepped aside. 'All right, swing your legs off the bed.'

Peters looked down at his legs. 'You know, I'm a little bit scared.'

'You are?' Victoria gave a nervous giggle. 'Do you know how many times I say left, when I mean right? Of course you don't, but it's more times than I care to admit to.'

Peters laughed. 'Now you tell me.' He immediately swung his legs out of bed, his feet dangling several inches off the floor.

Victoria clasped his arm again. 'Right, shuffle yourself forward a bit, so you are still on the bed, but at the very edge.'

Without saying a word, Peters did as she asked.

'Excellent, right give me your hand and slowly lower yourself, so one foot is on the ground.'

Peters again followed her instructions.

Victoria held his hand in a vice like grip, as he was suddenly standing on two feet. She breathed a sigh of relief.

Peters laughed. 'Were you holding your breath?'

'Not knowingly, but yes, I think I was.' She glanced over at the chair. 'Right, I think you need to take about two small steps in an off-right direction.'

'What does that mean, "off-right"?'

Victoria hesitated for a moment. 'Well, it's sort of straight but it isn't.' She giggled. 'I told you I'd be rubbish at this.'

'You're not rubbish, but you're keeping it interesting, I'll say that for you.'

Victoria shook her head. 'Take one step forward and then another, slightly to the right.'

Peters did as she asked and could feel the hard wood of the chair's legs against his own.

'Now you need to turn.' Victoria let go of his arm but kept her hand hovering nearby. 'And it doesn't matter which way, because I'll make sure you're in line with the chair.'

Peters slowly took the tentative steps to turn around.

Victoria didn't take her eyes off him. When he had finished moving, she pulled the chair in line with his legs.

'I can feel the chair, so does that mean I can sit down?'

Victoria held onto his arm with one hand and the chair with the other. 'Yes, you can now sit down.'

Peters gradually lowered himself onto the chair, smiling as he finally sat on the seat. 'We did it.' He laughed.

Victoria relaxed her shoulders as she smiled too. 'We did.' She clasped his hand with hers and squeezed it. 'Well done, you should be proud.

You've taken the first difficult step to moving on.' She immediately thought of her parents' bedroom. *And so have I.*

Peters nodded, as he beamed from ear to ear. 'Thank you.'

* * *

John sat on the wooden bench staring out at the deep blue sea, watching the white-tipped waves gradually lose their force, to roll in and move amongst the pebbles. Pools of water settled between the many shapes and colours, leaving a shine on each of the stones. John smiled as he remembered coming down to the beach as a child, collecting and polishing the more unusual stones and smuggling them into the house, because his grandfather would moan about him bringing them home. His grandmother had encouraged him to hide them in his bedroom, where his grandfather would never go. John sighed; he had been stronger then, at least that was how he remembered it.

Many people were in various states of undress, sitting in deck chairs or lying on towels. Women wore large hats, to protect themselves from the sun. Children paddled at the water's edge, screaming with joy every time a wave crashed into their legs.

He sighed and closed his eyes for a moment, enjoying the warmth of the sun, which was energising his body. He knew he was growing weaker with each passing day, and wondered how much of his young life he had left. He tried to take a deep breath, enjoying the salty smell of the sea and committing it to memory, but his body started to convulse with coughing. He took a large white handkerchief from his trouser pocket and held it to his mouth. He knew, without looking, that it had blood on it; the taste of it filled his mouth. He shivered as though it was the middle of winter, instead of a warm summer's day.

'Are you all right, John?'

John squinted, as he looked along the footpath at his grandmother, walking towards him, carrying two mugs of tea. 'Yes, Gran, I'm just enjoying the sea.'

'Look.' Beatrice beamed. 'The man who owns the café isn't in today, so Mavis gave me a couple of mugs of tea and a slice of Madeira cake for us to share.'

John laughed at his grandmother's obvious delight. 'That was very kind of her.'

'Yes, especially as they are quite busy in there.'

John took the mug of tea from her outstretched hand and stood it on the ground, next to his feet.

'Make sure you don't kick it over, we might not get another treat like this again.'

'Don't worry, Gran, I'll take care.'

Beatrice lifted the mug to her lips, the steam clouding her vision, as she sipped the strong brown liquid. She put the mug down, as John had done before her, pulling a white folded napkin from her lightweight,

176

lavender jacket pocket. She slowly peeled away the layers, to reveal a yellow sponge. She carefully broke it in half and offered the cake to her grandson.

John smiled. 'I can't resist a piece of cake; it looks delicious.' He picked it up and hungrily bit into it. 'Hmm, it tastes as good as it looks.' He licked his lips, before popping the final piece into his mouth.

Beatrice laughed, as she broke off a small piece of cake. 'Isn't it a beautiful day? I know we haven't walked far from the house, but I'm glad we ventured outside.'

John nodded. 'Me too, it's been a long time since I felt the warmth of the sun on my face.' He looked over at his grandmother, who was smiling at something she could see on the beach. John guessed it was the squealing children at the water's edge. He picked up his mug, taking a mouthful of the warm liquid, removing the last of the cake crumbs from around his teeth. 'Gran, you know I've never wanted to be a problem for you, don't you?'

Beatrice frowned, but kept her eyes focused on the children having fun. 'You have never been a problem to me, John. You have only ever brought joy into my life. I would hope you'd know that.' She popped the last few crumbs of the cake into her mouth and folded the napkin into a small square, returning it to her pocket. 'That was very enjoyable.'

John gave a faint smile; he had been brought up to always take his rubbish home and never drop paper, or anything else, on the ground. 'Gran, while we are out of the house and away from Grandpa, I wanted to talk to you about my parents.'

Beatrice looked at him through hooded eyes. 'What did you want to know?'

John reached out and grabbed her soft wrinkled hand in his. 'I don't want to hurt you or open up old wounds. I love you too much to want to hurt you on purpose.'

Beatrice forced a smile as she looked at him. She knew the time was getting closer. She knew their time together had all been borrowed, and she would do anything to make her grandson happy, in whatever time was left. 'I know, and I love you too.' She took a deep breath, before looking back out to where the blue of the sea met the lighter blue of the sky.

A girl ran past, screaming and giggling, accidentally flicking water at them as she went, at the same time as a young woman chased her along the footpath.

John watched the woman scoop the girl up into her arms. He enjoyed the shrieking that came from her being caught.

Beatrice closed her eyes, sending up a silent prayer for God to give her the strength from somewhere, to be able to answer all his questions honestly. 'What is it you want to know?'

John frowned. 'They haven't been to see me, since before the war started. In fact, I believe it was a few years before that —'

'It's been just over seven years.' Beatrice could feel the tears pricking at her eyes.

John stared at her for a moment, before gazing out to sea. 'That's even worse than I thought, I was thinking it had been about five or six years.' His voice became almost a whisper. 'There was I, blaming the war. I've read how London has been bombed, and just thought . . . '

'I don't know . . . I haven't heard anything from them, since they last visited.'

'I'm sorry, Gran, I didn't realise . . . I'm sorry.' John squeezed her hand in his. 'Is there any way we can contact them?'

Beatrice made a strangled sound. 'Your grandfather won't allow it.'

Anger swept up John's features and took hold. 'Won't allow it? Won't allow it? Who the hell does he think he is? These are my parents. Don't I have a right to know, before I meet my maker, why they haven't been down to see me, or is it because of Grandpa? He seems to drive everyone away.'

A tear tripped over Beatrice's lashes and rolled down to her lips.

'I'm sorry, Gran, perhaps I'm more like him than I realise.' He paused; unable to look at her he stared at the children playing amongst the pebbles. 'I don't think I'm long for this world. I'm coughing up blood and stuff as well as losing weight.' John sighed and shook his head. 'I just need some answers, that's all.'

13

Molly squealed as she squeezed Alice's arm. 'I can't believe I'm actually going wedding dress shopping.' She pulled at her high-collared blouse, adjusting it around her neck, and the way it sat on the wide belt around her waist.

Alice and Victoria laughed.

'Stop fidgeting.' Alice tapped her hand.

Molly gave a nervous giggle. 'Sorry.'

'I know you're nervous, but you look lovely. That copper-coloured dress really suits you.'

'Thank you; my gran embroidered the collar.'

Victoria nodded. 'She certainly has a way with a sewing needle, and a great eye for detail.'

Molly's lips tightened a little. 'I think her eyesight is failing, although she wouldn't tell anyone.'

Alice glanced across at Molly. 'All the more reason to make sure you walk down the aisle sooner, rather than later.'

The girls fell silent as they fell into step with each other. The sun was already high in the sky when the three girls were nearing Selfridges, on New Oxford Street. The street traders were out in force with their baskets and barrows. Every few minutes, voices would shout out, to sell fruit and vegetables. Freshly baked bread stood on wooden trays, adding to the aroma of hot food and coffee, which followed the girls down the street. Old ladies carried baskets of flowers, enticing the passers-by to smell, and hopefully buy, a bunch.

Victoria swerved to miss a grim-faced woman,

scowling down at a little boy she was pulling along the road. 'It's about time. I was beginning to think you were never going to do it.'

Molly looked back at Victoria, who quickened her step to catch up. 'To be honest, I've been wrestling with my conscience about even wearing a proper wedding dress and veil, or whether I should just buy a white two-piece suit and a hat.'

'But it's your wedding day. Haven't you dreamt of the big white dress, with a long flowing veil, since you were a child?'

Molly frowned. 'Of course I have, but I'm no longer a child, and there's a war on.'

Victoria shook her head. 'Yes, I know that, but you only get married once and you don't want to look back on it with regret.'

'I'm excited to be looking at them, and shall wait and see what we find, but the day isn't just about a dress.'

Victoria looked at Molly, and then Alice. 'Well, that told me, didn't it?'

Molly let go of Alice's arm and stepped towards the large window of Selfridges. 'I'm sorry, Victoria, I don't want to spoil today, because I've so been looking forward to it, but I suppose what I'm trying to say is, if Ted suddenly came home and said let's get married, would you worry about whether you had the dress of your childhood dreams?'

Victoria didn't stop to think about it. 'Of course I wouldn't, but you do have time, and now money, on your side, so I don't understand why you wouldn't want it.'

Molly sighed and gave a little laugh. 'I don't know either.' She paused for a moment. 'I think seeing people lose everything at the munitions factory explosion, made me realise life isn't just about status and money. It's about friendship and family, and I think my money could be better spent supporting people who have nothing or sending parcels to our men on the frontline.'

Alice's mouth dropped open slightly, as she looked across at Victoria.

Victoria smiled. 'Well, I think you've put me to shame.'

'I'm sorry, I didn't mean to. And anyway, when was today ever meant to be serious about what we spend our money on?' She tucked her arm in Victoria's. 'Come on, we're going to have fun, and if you are really good, I'll buy you a crepe and a coffee later. Now that would be money well spent.' A smile slowly spread across her face, as they took the few steps to one of the many grand wooden doorways and entered the world of Selfridges.

Victoria gasped. 'I don't think I've been in here before.' She looked around her. 'If I had, I'm sure I'd remember.' The shop assistants, dressed in black skirts and white blouses, looked professional and yet gentle, with a hint of a smile on their lips and not a hair out of place, as they served their customers. She looked around at the many sparkling glass cabinets. 'I wonder whose job it is to remove all the finger marks from all that glass. I don't envy them, that's for sure.'

Molly laughed, as she took in the chatter around the shop. 'I had the same thoughts at Christmas; it must be an awful job to do.'

Alice chuckled. 'Hark at you two. When did you become so grown up that the first thing you think of when you walk into this magnificent shop is who cleans the glass? When did we stop being young women, wanting to go out and just have a good time?'

'I think it sneaked up on us, when we weren't looking.' Molly giggled. 'But we should go to the theatre or something, soon.'

Alice nodded. 'I'm not sure we can fit it into our busy lives at the moment.' The chink of coins dropping into the tills could be heard, above the rustling of paper, as the assistants wrapped the many purchases being made. 'Still, we've plenty of time to worry about that. We have a wedding dress to buy.' She grabbed Molly's hand, pulling her towards the sign, to find out where they needed to go.

A few minutes later, the three of them were staring at tall mannequins, each standing on a wooden block, wearing a different style of wedding dress.

Molly's eyes widened, as they roamed from one dress to another. From calf to ankle length, fitted to ballroom, long sleeved or short, there was so much choice. Then there were the veils, practically any length, and as plain or fancy as you like. This was going to be difficult.

Victoria gazed around her. 'We could be here for some time.'

Molly pulled her eyes towards her friends. 'Perhaps we should eat first.'

Alice and Victoria burst out laughing.

'What?'

Alice nodded at Victoria and they took an arm each, pulling Molly towards a hanging rail of wedding dresses. Alice used her best mother voice, the one she used when Arthur played up. 'You're not going home until we've chosen your dress, otherwise this wedding just isn't going to take place.'

Victoria took a step nearer to the dress rail, unaware that an assistant was walking towards them. She pulled back a dress to get a better look at it, before wrinkling her nose and letting the white material fall back into position. 'Andrew strikes me as being a very patient man, but even he will have his breaking point, so don't keep him waiting any longer than you already have.'

Molly frowned, as she turned one way, then another. 'I haven't told you yet, but it's going to be a very small affair; it doesn't feel right to be frivolous at the moment. Andrew and I have only invited our closest family and friends, so I just want something pretty, but practical.'

The elegant assistant stood to one side of the girls, carefully eyeing the three of them. 'Can I be of any assistance, ladies?'

The three of them looked across at her. Colour flooded Molly's cheeks.

The assistant stepped towards Molly. 'Are you the bride?'

Molly nodded, but stayed rooted to the spot, as anxiety tripped across her face.

Victoria stepped back and stood next to Molly, squeezing her hand. 'We want today to be fun and special; it's no less than Molly deserves. She's a good person, with a good heart.'

The assistant smiled at the three of them. 'Of course; picking your wedding dress should always be a special moment, and we at Selfridges pride ourselves on making it just so.'

Alice nodded. 'I'm afraid we don't really know what type of dress we're looking for.'

Molly cleared her throat. 'It has to be something

184

simple and not too fussy. We'll also need dresses for my friends here, so I'm afraid we'll all have to agree on the style.'

Victoria glanced at Molly. 'We could make our dresses from the ones at home, that will save money.'

Molly shook her head. 'I do think we should alter the dresses but we don't have time to do it for my wedding.'

The assistant beamed at Molly. 'You've come to the right place then.'

'You probably also need to know that I want something that looks good, but I don't want to spend the earth on it.' Molly gasped. 'Oh God, I'm turning into my mother.'

The girls burst into laughter, while the assistant tried to hide her confusion.

'No, I'm not,' Molly spluttered. 'I'd just rather buy books with my money.'

★ ★ ★

Ted Marsden lay still in his hospital bed. When he slept he could forget what was happening to him. His dreams were in colour and so real but every morning he woke up confused and his grief hit him all over again. Every day was the same; he had to live with the imposed silence and his demons in this room. His world was dark now. There was no light or shade, and there was definitely no colour. The smell of the toast seemed heightened as it mingled with the overpowering antiseptic and disinfectant that oozed from within the walls. His blindness meant he was unable to reach for his toast or the cup of tea that was placed nearby without knocking it over, but then he had no reason to eat or drink. He had no reason to live anymore.

His hand touched the soft bandage that covered his eyes and most of his face before slowly moving down to rub his nose. He turned his head towards the muffled laughter and voices creeping through the closed door of his side room, those soldiers were happy to be home but he wished he'd died with his friends on the battlefield. He had no future; he was destined to be alone and unable to work. His blindness was disorientating. He didn't want to be that person waving his hand around trying to grab things; he didn't want to feel unable to cope with the different noises and smells that appeared to be assaulting him from every direction, while always trying to guess what they are.

Ted sighed. He had nothing to offer Victoria; there was no future for them so there was no future for him. Tears pricked at his eyes. Ignoring the pain that took his breath away, he squeezed them tight as memories of Victoria immediately jumped into his mind. The many times they had sat together holding hands in Hyde Park watching the world go by. They had been happy to just be in each other's company, but he was never again going to see the blueness of the sky or the vivid colours of the flowers in the park, and more importantly he was never again going to see the beauty of the girl he loved or watch her wonderful face light up when she laughed. Anger surged through him, he had thrown away seven years of being with her, all because he wasn't able to cope with her grief and new responsibilities. It hadn't taken him long to realise he had been a selfish coward; he'd had plenty of time to reflect and regret his actions but there had been no going back. He had left it too late. His mind cast back to when he'd finally plucked up the courage to write and ask for her forgiveness. The bombing and rifle fire had stopped and left an eerie silence around him in the trench he had been standing in, only occasionally broken by the murmurs of conversation amongst the men. Ted had seen many things no man should witness and he knew he was living on borrowed time. He didn't want to die without letting the love of his life know he regretted his actions and wished he could turn back time, but knew that wasn't possible. His hand had been shaking when he wrote to Victoria. Looking down at the letter, he'd wondered if she would be able to read the spidery writing that was crunched together on the page. Tears had mingled with the dirt on his face and blotted the paper. Ted had begged for forgiveness, pleaded the case for the shallow young man he had been. Victoria's reply had given him hope for the future, should he survive, but now that had been ripped away again, this time through no fault of his own. He slammed his hand down on to the bed-covers, the vibration of the thud travelled along the bed. His fingers clenched into a tight fist until his nails burnt into his skin.

There was a knock on the door. Ted ignored it. The last thing he wanted was another nurse trying to jolly him along.

The click of the door told him it had opened. The footsteps across the room drowned out his thoughts.

'Morning, I'm Atkins, your nurse for today.' Mabel picked up the board that had the patient notes clipped to them.

Ted flinched at the unexpected voice; he turned his head trying to work out its direction. The rustling of paper mingled with other noises he didn't recognise, some he wasn't sure he'd heard before.

'How are you feeling today, Corporal Marsden?'

Silence sat between them.

Mabel stared at the bandaged face of the patient. 'It's a lovely day, it was already warm when I came in this morning.' She returned the board to the end of the bed. 'Are you going to try and eat your breakfast today.'

Corporal Marsden didn't move or make a sound.

Mabel stared at his face before lowering her gaze to his chest, watching his breathing rhythm to see if he was asleep or worse, unconscious. 'It's no good you starving yourself, you'll never get better if you don't eat or drink.'

The thud of her footsteps told him she was on the move.

'Overall, the doctors are pleased with your progress.'

Ted's hearing was sharper than ever and he recognised the forced smile in her voice.

'We'll probably remove the bandage from around your ribs today but I'll check with the doctor first. The doctors were lucky to save your leg. All the cuts and bruises have healed nicely.' She walked around the bed. 'I think they are happy with the stomach wound as well. It's lucky you were a strong and healthy man before you were injured.'

He flinched as she expertly placed her fingers on his wrist.

Mabel gently placed his arm back on the bed. 'I'm going to take your temperature in a minute, just to make sure everything's all right. Then I'll pass you your tea and a slice of toast.'

Ted moved his head slightly to the sound of her

voice.

Mabel tapped her feet on the floor. 'Are you sure there's no one I can contact to let them know you're in hospital?' She frowned. 'Can you at least say something so I know you can hear me?'

Ted sucked in his breath. 'I don't know how many times I have to say it, there's no one.'

Mabel smiled. 'I find that hard to believe, a good-looking man like you, there must be someone.' She stood up. 'Someone must be missing you, you've been in here for a few months now.' She walked over to the door pulling it open.

The noise from outside the room invaded his ears. Was that machinery he could hear amongst the voices interspersed with groans and laughter?

'You think about it, I'll be back shortly.'

The door thud shut. Silence enveloped him and once again he was left with his own thoughts, thoughts he didn't want. How he wished Victoria was with him but he had to let her go. Let her think he was dead so she could find the love she deserved with someone else.

★ ★ ★

Victoria yawned, as she dragged her feet along Charing Cross Road. The early morning mist still hung in the air, causing it to feel damp underfoot. Dogs could be heard barking nearby.

'We worked hard last night.' Daisy smiled as she stepped alongside her sister.

'Yes, we did, but what with that, and a day's shopping with Molly and Alice, I'm tired this morning.'

'It sounds as though the shopping was successful

and fun.'

'It was. Maybe we should have a day out shopping, or lunch together?'

'That would be good.' Daisy frowned. 'Perhaps packing the clothes into bags last night was too much.'

Victoria yawned again. 'I know it was a longer job but we were right to separate the clothes we could alter.'

'It made sense to do that, I just don't want you overdoing it, that's all.'

Victoria gave a faint smile. 'Are you trying to mother me?'

Daisy laughed. 'That'll be the day. I'm just trying to look out for you, as you do me. We're both grown up now.' She glanced across and smiled at Victoria. 'I'm no longer the petulant child I once was, at least I hope I'm not, so you've got to stop feeling as though you have to carry these burdens on your own.' Daisy chuckled. 'I'm a responsible adult. I'm a police-woman.'

Victoria stopped and threw her arms around her sister. 'You are, and I'm very proud of you, as I know our mother and father would be.'

Daisy squeezed her sister tight, before pulling away. 'You now have a determination about you; it's not something I have seen before.'

Victoria shook her head. 'You know, Alice is right, when you see the injured soldiers; it puts your own problems into perspective. Me moping around about our family things isn't going to change anything.' She sighed. 'I told a corporal that, whether we liked it or not, life goes on, and I realised I had to move on or get left behind. The truth is, I don't want to get left behind. Alice is expecting her second child and Molly is arranging her wedding for next month, but I'm still where I was seven years ago.'

Daisy thrust her arm under Victoria's. 'No, you're not, we're not as poor as we were then.' She glanced across at her sister. 'Don't think Stephen and I didn't know you were selling and pawning things, to make ends meet. We've all done a lot of growing up since then, and please remember, I may be your little sister, but I'm an adult who can share your worries and concerns.'

Victoria looked at her sister through watery eyes. 'I don't know what to say. I tried hard to protect you and Stephen, but I was young myself and didn't know what I was doing. I should have tackled the bedroom years ago.'

'Don't punish yourself. You're a great sister and we're moving ahead in leaps and bounds now, so that's all that matters. I'll get Peter to help me take those bags somewhere, like the Salvation Army.'

Victoria nodded. 'Are you sweet on him?'

Daisy blushed.

Victoria laughed. 'You don't have to say anything; your colour says it all.'

Daisy squeezed the thin cotton material of Victoria's jacket. 'Do you mind?'

'Of course I don't. Why would I?'

Daisy shrugged.

Victoria looked down at the pavement, fleetingly wondering why the ants didn't drown when it was wet; maybe they did. Someone jolted her arm. 'Sorry,' the man shouted as he sped past her.

Daisy looked over her shoulder. 'Are you all right? Everyone's in such a hurry these days.'

'You don't have to worry about me, I'm good. As

for Peter, I just want you to be happy, that's all.' She stopped and looked ahead. The large black and white Foyles Bookstore sign could be seen from where they were. 'I have chosen to wait for Ted, even though he's not writing to me anymore. If I'm honest, it's hard.' She paused. 'Mainly because I don't know whether or not he'll come back from the front and even if he does, it doesn't look like he'll want me so there's no prospects of love, marriage or children happening for me, but that's the decision I've made.'

Daisy frowned. 'You do know it's not only Ted's decision, don't you? You're not the same person you were seven years ago; a lot has happened since then.'

Victoria nodded. 'I know, but I still feel it's the right decision to wait and see how everything goes. If it's in God's plan for me, it will happen, and if it isn't, then something else will happen instead.'

Daisy nodded. 'He'll be lucky to have you, but don't think he's your only chance of happiness. You're a lovely, kind person and anybody that has you in their life is very fortunate.'

Victoria laughed. 'Stop it, you're embarrassing me.'

'That may well be, but I meant every word of it.' She looked up and saw men and women milling outside Foyles. 'It looks like you're in for another busy day.'

Victoria followed her eye line. 'I prefer to be busy, as the time flies by. What about you, do you know what you've got ahead of you?'

'Lily and I will just walk the streets, showing a presence for anyone who needs to talk to us, or to stop any problems developing further. A few days ago, we caught a young lad who'd pinched an apple for his sister. Their mother was ill, so couldn't work. We were going to take him back to the stall-holder, but there was a police shout that the Germans were coming, so we let him go. He did promise to go and talk to Mr Wilson, but we don't know if he did or not, so I'd like to see if the lad has kept his word.'

Victoria shook her head. 'It must be hard for the children who are left to fend for themselves like that. I suppose we were lucky we were that much older, when we were left on our own.'

Daisy nodded. 'I just hope his mother didn't fall prey to this flu epidemic that's going around. Lily and I wanted to go and see her, and maybe get a doctor, but we didn't know where she lived.'

Victoria gasped. 'Oh my goodness, if you find them and they are on their own, bring them home with you.'

Daisy laughed. 'I'm not sure it's as simple as that, and anyway, I may never see them again.' She looked at her sister, scowling into the sun that was breaking through the clouds. 'If it's any consolation, I'm going to look for him, but I do think he's one of life's survivors.'

Victoria squinted as she looked up at the Foyles Bookstore. 'Let's hope so. I'd better get in, before Mr Leadbetter sacks me.'

Daisy nodded. 'He seemed really nice when he ushered us down to the basement.'

Victoria laughed. 'He is.' She stepped forward and hugged her sister. 'Stay safe.'

Daisy squeezed her back. 'I will, and you.'

At the sound of raised voices coming from inside the shop, the girls pulled back from each other. They both ran towards the doorway.

Victoria stopped in her tracks, but Daisy pushed forward, gasping when she saw the man sprawled out on the floor.

'Give the man some room.' Daisy looked up at her sister, who was quite ashen. 'Sit down Victoria, before you fall down.'

Victoria didn't take her eyes off the man on the floor.

Gradually, the murmurs of staff and customers that had wandered in to see what was going on invaded her numbed mind.

'Do you think he'll be all right?'

'I saw it; he dropped like a stone.'

People moved in closer, to get a better look.

Victoria gripped her hands tight, as her body began to tremble. She sniffed and closed her eyes for a moment. Floral perfumes, mingled with carbolic soap, were overpowering and nausea began to rise from her stomach. It wouldn't be the same at Foyles without him. He was the face of Foyles Bookshop. She had to do something. A voice shouted out. 'No, this isn't what Mr Leadbetter would want; this shop is his life.' She felt everyone's eyes on her and looked up, only then realising it had been her voice. She clapped her hands together. 'Come on everyone, the shop is open in a few minutes, so please get to your posts.'

Daisy leant over the man and pressed her ear against his chest for a few minutes. She ran her hands down his arms and legs, before pushing him on his side and quickly unbuttoning her uniform jacket. Removing her arms, getting tangled in the jacket in the process, she rolled it up and put it under the man's head.

Victoria cleared her throat, but her voice was barely a whisper when she spoke. 'Is he going to be all right?'

Daisy didn't take her eyes off him. 'I think so.'

Victoria looked around her, to see if Alice was in

yet; at least she'd had some training, driving an ambulance, but there was no sign of her. She knelt down beside Mr Leadbetter, touching his forehead, which was warm. He looked grey. 'Do you think we should get an ambulance for him?'

'What's going on?' Alice's voice carried through the people that were still hanging around, waiting to see if the man in the suit was going to be all right. She gasped. 'Mr Leadbetter, what happened?' Alice immediately fell to her knees, expertly finding his pulse at the base of his thumb.

Victoria held her breath as Alice looked at her watch from time to time.

Mr Leadbetter groaned.

'What happened? Did he faint?'

Victoria shook her head. 'I don't know. Daisy and I were outside, when we heard a noise. We rushed in, but he was already out cold. Daisy turned him on his side.'

Daisy looked startled at the sound of her name. 'I only did it in case he was sick.' She looked down at Mr Leadbetter. 'I ran my hands down his arms and legs first, but couldn't feel anything broken, so I assumed he must have fainted.'

Alice nodded. She loosened his tie from around his neck, pulling it down so she could undo his shirt button. 'Victoria, can you get a small glass of water.'

Victoria stood up, looking down at the man that had come to mean a lot to her. He groaned.

Alice looked up at her friend. 'It looks like he's coming round, so we'll let him sip it and see how he goes.'

Victoria gave him a last look, before running to the back of the shop, swerving to miss customers and their children. She turned the three-pronged tap to the right and water gushed out, spraying her and everything in sight. Victoria quickly twisted it to the left, to turn it down again. Her heart was racing, as she mumbled to herself, 'Stop rushing and you'll get it done much quicker in the long run.' Placing a cup under the cold water, she let it half fill, before turning it off again and rushing back into the shop, unaware of the splash marks on her blouse and skirt. When Victoria reached them, Mr Leadbetter was sitting propped up against Daisy. His skin was still grey.

Alice reached out for the cup. 'Take a sip of this cold water.'

Mr Leadbetter did as he was bid and swallowed a few sips of the water. 'It's all right, folks, there's nothing to see, just an old man fainting, nothing more.' As the people began to disperse, he looked at the girls. 'I think I need to move from here, so business can continue.'

Victoria watched him grimace, as he tried to move. 'You gave us quite a scare, sir. What happened? Do you need a doctor?'

Mr Leadbetter gave a faint laugh. 'I'm sorry; I didn't mean to frighten you all. I think I just fainted. To be honest, I don't really remember.' He paused, looking at their concerned faces. 'I'm all right; I expect it was just the heat.'

'What's happened?' Molly came rushing from around the bookshelves.

'Have you just got in, Miss Cooper?'

'No, sir.' Molly looked indignant for a second, before her features relaxed a little. 'I was upstairs working and someone said you'd collapsed, so I naturally came down to see if I could do something.'

Mr Leadbetter smiled, as he looked at the concerned faces staring down at him. 'I'll be all right, but if someone could just help me up off this floor, that would be good. This old body of mine can't manage to get up from down here, these days.'

The girls all held out their hands, to support him up under the arms.

Daisy eyed him, as he strained to lift his body. 'Go careful, sir, just in case you've hurt yourself falling.'

As Mr Leadbetter moved his legs, Victoria saw him wince. 'I think we need to get him to a doctor, or a hospital.'

Mr Leadbetter raised his eyebrows and growled at Victoria. 'Going to a hospital would cost me a small fortune.'

Victoria stood her ground. 'That may well be, sir, but you may have hurt yourself, so I think you should be looked at.' She looked over at Alice. 'Can you at least drive him home?'

Alice looked confused. 'In what?'

'In the Foyles van, I'm sure Mr Leadbetter can't live far away, as he's here all the time.'

Alice nodded.

Mr Leadbetter frowned. 'I don't suppose there's any point in me objecting, is there?'

Victoria smiled. 'Absolutely not, and I don't want you coming back tomorrow, if you're still unwell.' She chuckled. 'It's so disruptive, this kind of drama.'

Mr Leadbetter shook his head. 'I've created a monster.' He couldn't resist a smile at her words.

Victoria chuckled. 'Don't worry, sir; the bookshop will be safe in my hands. You've taught me well.'

14

Molly glanced over at Victoria. 'You must have frightened old Leadbetter, because he didn't come in today. I hope he's all right.'

Alice looked over at her friends. 'He promised me he would see a doctor. Hopefully, he's just been overdoing it and some rest will see him return to Foyles in good spirits.'

'I hope so. He's a good man; a little bit scary, but he has a heart of gold.'

Alice and Molly nodded at Victoria's words.

Molly leaned in a little, examining the dark circles under Victoria's eyes. 'You look tired.' She pulled back again. 'I know we've been extraordinarily busy here today, but that's nothing new. Are you missing Mr Leadbetter?'

Victoria smiled. 'I have been busier, running up and down stairs, and it's not a wonder he needed help to manage the shop. I don't think I ever realised how big it was, until I went up the stairs for about the fifth time in a couple of hours.' She picked up her tea and sipped the hot liquid, burning her top lip and tongue. 'I'm glad the day is over, and the shop is shut.'

Molly chuckled. 'And yet here we are, sitting in the staff area, sipping tea, like we have nowhere to go.'

Victoria clasped her cup tight. 'I do appreciate you staying with me; it's a bit spooky in here, once the shop has shut and everyone has gone home.'

Alice clasped her hands around her cup. 'It's not a problem, although I'll have to get home soon.'

'Of course.' Victoria squirmed on her chair. 'Are you having the sickness that you had with Arthur?'

Alice eyed Victoria, wondering what was really going on with her, and why she had wanted them to stay after Foyles had closed. 'No, thankfully.'

Molly beamed. 'Perhaps it's a girl then.' She looked across at Victoria. 'We'll be able to take her clothes shopping.' She clapped her hands together, with excitement.

Alice looked down at her rounded tummy. 'Yes, well, I feel like I'm getting bigger with every passing second.' She chuckled, rubbing a protective hand over her baby bump. 'And you'll probably both have your own children by then.'

Victoria forced a smile. 'I think Molly may have, but I wouldn't count on me having any anytime soon.'

Alice couldn't stop the worry showing on her face. 'What is really bothering you tonight, Victoria? This isn't just about locking up, is it?'

Victoria put down her cup, staring into it, as though the answers she was looking for were about to float to the top. She sighed and looked up, to find her friends staring at her, silently waiting.

The clock ticked away the seconds and the minutes, but no one noticed. They sat very still, waiting for Victoria to let them know what was bothering her.

'All right, I took a good look inside that keepsake box, you know, the one with all the money in it, and before you ask, no, I haven't counted it.' Victoria paused, searching for the words to move forward. 'At the bottom of the box were some certificates.'

Molly held up her hand, to stop Victoria. 'What sort of certificates?'

'My parents' marriage certificate and our birth

certificates.'

Alice nodded. 'That's a good find, right?'

Victoria's stomach was doing somersaults; nausea and dizziness came from nowhere. She took a deep breath and sipped her tea, before continuing. 'There was also another birth certificate, for someone I've never heard of.'

'What? Whose?' the girls yelled as one.

'I haven't mentioned this to Daisy yet, so it's not to be repeated.'

'No, we promise, don't we, Molly?'

'Of course, of course; just tell us.'

Victoria sighed. 'My parents are down as being the mother and father to a John Appleton.'

The girls sat in silence, letting their gaze flick between Victoria and each other.

Victoria moved her hands to her lap and twisted the black skirt material between her fingers. 'And according to the birth certificate, he's a year younger than Stephen.'

The three of them sat in silence.

Molly was the first to break it. 'So where is he?'

Victoria shrugged. 'I've never seen or heard of him before, at least not to my knowledge.'

Molly rested her head in her hands, for a moment.

Alice frowned. 'Perhaps he died when you were young.'

Victoria nodded. 'I thought that too.'

Molly looked up, her eyes widening, as the answer filled her head. 'That would explain all the baby boy's clothes in the drawer, and the christening gown.' She tilted her head to one side. 'Well, maybe not the christening gown, because everyone tends to keep them, anyway.'

200

Victoria nodded. 'But there's no death certificate in the box, so that implies he's still alive.'

'So that brings me back to my question, where is he?'

Again Victoria shrugged. 'I don't know where to begin to look, and does he want to be found? What I don't understand is, why I don't know anything about him.'

Molly stood up and wrapped her arms around Victoria, her rose perfume mingling with Molly's jasmine scent. 'We'll figure it out.' She pulled back. 'Maybe we could get the two policewomen on to it.'

Panic ran across Victoria's face. 'Daisy doesn't know she could have a younger brother yet, so don't go mentioning it to her or Lily.'

Alice reached across the small round table. 'It's all right. Everything is going to be all right. I promise I won't say anything.'

Molly sat back down. 'I certainly won't, either. For one thing, I never see them, unless one of you is with them.'

Victoria closed her eyes and tried to calm herself. 'I've also wondered if that money was meant for John, especially as it was in the same box. If my parents were still alive, I wouldn't ever have known about it, or him.'

Alice frowned at her friend. 'Please try to hold on to the fact that your parents adored you all, and they wouldn't have kept a brother or sister from you without good reason.'

Victoria's eyes suddenly snapped open and anger was about to be fired in Alice's direction.

'I . . . I admit, I don't know what those reasons could possibly be.' Alice looked to Molly, for support.

'Look, Victoria.' Molly hit her hand on the table. 'It's no good taking it out on us. I know you're hurt, angry and probably lots of other things, but if your parents hadn't died, I don't doubt it would have all been explained to you in due course, but they did and now all we can try and do is find him, so you get to know the truth.'

Alice gave an enthusiastic nod. 'Look, why don't we come round tomorrow? We can talk about all of this and look at the photographs, certificates and whatever else there is, and try and put the pieces together.'

Molly reached out and stroked Victoria's arm. 'It sounds like a good plan of action.'

Victoria gave a wry smile. 'You're right. I'm sorry. You're both good friends; I couldn't ask for better, but Molly, you should be organising your wedding. It's not very far away now.'

Molly giggled. 'That's true, but we've all got our dresses, and the rest I've left to the grown-ups.'

Laughter broke out around the table.

★ ★ ★

Victoria stood in the doorway of her parents' bedroom. Her grey skirt complemented the soft pink blouse, with its bow tied loosely at the neckline. She pulled at the soft material tails of the bow, remembering it was one of the last things they had bought her. She stared inside the room, wishing she'd never started clearing it out. It felt like her life had been turned upside down, and there was no one to ask the many questions, which kept her awake every night. How could she have a brother and not know about him? What did that say about her parents — they

202

were good people, weren't they? It begged the question, what other secrets did they have?

The bed that had been strewn with clothes was now covered in paperwork and photographs. Daisy had been true to her word and got Peter to help her with the bags of clothing, which they'd separated and given to several good causes. Victoria wandered over and perched on the edge of the bed. 'Ma, Pa, I don't understand why I don't know about John. Is he alive or dead?' She stood up and walked over to the sash window, undoing the catch and pushing it up. The heat of the evening took her breath away and people's voices carried in the air, as they walked past the house. Children could be heard playing war games and pretending to shoot each other, while arguing about who was German and who was British. 'If John's alive, where is he? How do I find him? You've got to help me, please, before I go mad and have to be locked away in a sanatorium.' Victoria shook her head and a small smile hovered on her lips. *I think that time has already come.*

The chimes of the doorbell echoed from the hallway. Victoria ran down the creaking stairs and pulled open the front door, to see the smiling faces of her friends. She stepped aside. 'Come in; the kettle's just boiled.'

Alice nodded. 'Lovely, shall we go up?'

'Of course. Is everything all right, only you look tired?'

Molly followed Alice into the hall and Victoria shut the door with a thud.

Alice sighed. 'Yes, I am a little, but everything is good.'

The three of them climbed the stairs, ignoring the

usual creaks. They entered the bedroom and gasped at the double bed.

Molly whispered. 'Oh my.'

Alice stared at it all. 'No wonder you don't know where to start.'

Victoria followed their gazes. 'It looks worse than it is.' Her slippers made no sound, as she stepped nearer the bed. 'I've tried to put things into piles.' She picked up a stack. 'For example, these are the ones I would expect to find, like their marriage certificate and our birth certificates.' She placed the items back on the bed and picked up another lot of paperwork. 'These are things I don't really know what to do with. John's birth certificate is here, along with a couple of small books that look like diaries, but I haven't had a chance to read them. There are also a couple of newspaper clippings, but I'm not sure what they are doing here.'

Molly looked pensive, as her eyes scanned the items on the bed. 'And don't forget the photos.'

Victoria nodded, as she picked up the framed photograph of her parents, holding her brother as a baby. She stared at it for a moment. 'I wonder if this was . . . John, not Stephen . . . ' She looked pensive. 'If it is, it means they wanted to tell us, but probably didn't know how.'

The girls stood in silence, watching the array of emotions trample over Victoria.

Victoria tore her gaze away and looked over at them. 'It would also explain why it was in their room, and not downstairs.'

Alice reached out her hand. 'Can I have a look at it, please?'

Victoria nodded, silently handing it over.

Alice studied it, moving nearer to the window, to have a closer look. 'I was trying to see if I could find a clue as to where the photograph was taken, but other than by the seaside, I can't see anything at all.'

'I know; I've looked at it a hundred times, trying to figure it out.'

Molly walked to the window and peered over Alice's shoulder. 'If it's close to London, then there are only so many seaside places it could be.'

Alice looked up. 'Molly's right. I can't imagine they would have travelled for hours, with a small baby.'

Molly picked up another photograph from the bed. 'Ahh, I think this is the wedding photograph you looked at, when we were sorting things out. That dress your ma's wearing reminds me of one Alice took out of the wardrobe.'

Victoria looked over. 'Maybe those clothes are what they kept for best, especially once they started saving their money in that chest. I really don't know, but then, I have no idea who the other people are either.' She sighed. 'There's too many questions and not enough answers.

Molly turned it over, to remind herself who it was. *Mabel and Sid's wedding day 14th June 1892.*

'These newspaper clippings are another thing I don't understand, why were they kept?' Victoria flicked through them. 'One is an obituary of a man, that I can only assume is my grandfather, or uncle, maybe. Then I have one of a doctor and his pioneering research on breathing disorders.' Victoria flopped down on the edge of the bed. 'It doesn't matter how much I look at it all, none of it makes sense.'

Molly stared at the clippings in Victoria's hand. 'We need to look at it as a puzzle, because it's all here for a reason. We just don't know what that is at the moment — well, apart from the fact they clearly loved John and wanted to keep him close.' She looked up at her friends. 'Perhaps we need to think about why he wouldn't be living here, in the first place.' She shook her head. 'We need Daisy and Lily here.'

Alice picked up one of the small diaries and looked over at Victoria. 'May I?'

'I have no secrets from you two. Feel free to examine it all. I just want to try and figure out what has happened to John.'

Alice flicked through the pages, scanning the spidery handwriting. A smile crept across her face. 'Ahh, your ma's written about you three.' She turned the page. 'It's obvious she loves you all very much,'

'I think we already knew that, Alice.' Molly picked up the baby photograph again. 'Maybe he was sick.'

Victoria looked down at her hands. 'That thought had crossed my mind, mainly because of the clippings of the doctor, but that could mean I should just leave things alone. He's probably dead by now, bearing in mind the clipping was about pioneering work the doctor was doing.'

Molly walked over and stroked Victoria's back. 'Either way, you still want to know, don't you?'

'Sometimes I do, but sometimes I don't, after all, no one contacted me when my parents died. There was no family rushing forward, to help us through it.' A lonely tear ran down her cheek. She suddenly jumped up, brushing her fingers across her face. 'I've got to stop this; otherwise I'm never going to find out, or sort this mess out. Maybe I should just walk away from it all, I'm tired of worrying about everything. There's Stephen, Ted and now John, I just can't do it anymore.'

★ ★ ★

Victoria stood to one side of the entrance to Endell Street Hospital, finding a little shade, as she watched the ambulances queuing up. The medical staff were rushing inside, carrying wounded men on stretchers, to reappear minutes later without their patients.

'Everything all right, Victoria? You look very pale.'

Victoria jerked round, to see Alice standing there. Her pregnancy was beginning to show through her uniform, which was smeared with blood. Once again, she wondered how Alice did it. 'What are you doing here?' she mumbled, as she turned to look back at the injured men, watching the walking wounded hobble through the doorway. 'I thought you normally went to Charing Cross or St Thomas's Hospital.'

Alice frowned. 'I do, but I was told to bring them here, today.' She stepped forward, so she was standing next to her friend. 'In case you're wondering, I haven't seen Stephen here.'

Victoria shook her head. 'Stephen writes to me and Daisy nearly every week, to let us know he's safe, and we do the same.' Her body became rigid and she blinked rapidly, to stop the tears from falling. 'It's Ted. I haven't heard from him in weeks.'

Alice slipped her arm around her friend's shoulder. 'Stay positive; you've given him something to live for, so he'll get home, if he can.'

Victoria cast her haunted eyes towards her friend. 'The trouble is, I'd never know if something had happened to him. We're not married, and I'm not family.'

Alice tightened her grip on Victoria. She had no words of wisdom to pass on.

'Is everything all right here?'

Guilt swarmed in on Alice, as she dropped her arm from her friend's shoulder. Both girls looked round at the pristinely turned out nurse.

Victoria straightened her shoulders. 'Yes, Nurse Atkins.'

'Are you on your way in, or out?'

Victoria jutted out her chin. 'I'm just coming in now. I'm sorry, if I'm late.'

Nurse Atkins looked at the young girl's pasty complexion. She still couldn't lift the feeling that they had met before, and yet she didn't remember where or when. 'You're not late, but that's because you're a volunteer.' She frowned in their direction. 'I could do with some help though; we seem to have a lot of new patients.' She turned to the ambulance driver. 'Have you been to this hospital before, only I don't recognise you?'

Alice stepped forward. 'No, I haven't. I'm Alice Leybourne. Victoria and I are good friends; in fact, I'd say we were like sisters.'

Mabel nodded. 'Well, we certainly all need good friends and family, especially at this time.'

Victoria nodded. 'I'd better go in. It sounds like it's going to be busy.'

Alice hugged her friend. 'I'll see you in the morning. Don't be late; we can't keep the groom waiting.'

'No.' Victoria smiled. 'We certainly need to make sure she gets to the church. You know what Molly's like.'

They all giggled and Alice waved goodbye to them both. 'It was lovely to meet you, Nurse Atkins.'

208

Mabel lifted her hand, just in time to see Alice climb into the driver's seat of the ambulance. They both watched her back up and drive out of the hospital grounds.

'Victoria, let's get out of this heat.' Mabel adjusted her cap and stepped further back, inside the doorway. 'You'll be working with me, on Joan of Arc Ward. We're pretty thin on the ground today, so I might have you doing more than arranging flowers and delivering newspapers.'

Victoria opened her mouth to speak, but Mabel raised her hand.

'I know that's important too. I know it's all about patient welfare, but first, we have to save their lives, otherwise there's no welfare to worry about.' She turned away, not waiting for an answer. 'Follow me.'

Victoria did as she was bid. The corridors were full of men, sitting on chairs. Everywhere she looked, the once deep red blood was now brown, congealed and cracked by the heat, on bandages and uniforms. The stench of dust, mingled with vomit, hung in the air. Men on trollies groaned, as waves of agony grabbed them. When she finally drew her eyes away, her voice was barely a whisper. 'I don't know what I can do to help?'

Mabel looked at her, wondering how good she would be in this critical situation; she had no choice but to find out. 'Just try and watch what I do, then follow my instructions, without fail, and to the letter of the law.'

Victoria nodded.

Mabel pushed open the door to the ward and it quickly became clear to Victoria that the new patients had to be cleaned up and put into vacant beds. Mabel

209

marched down the ward and Victoria trotted behind her. She stopped at the foot of a bed, all made up with clean bedding. 'Now, what I want you to do is help the soldiers get undressed, and if that means cutting them out of the uniform, then so be it. Those that need surgery straight away have already gone downstairs, and the doctors are already working on them; I get the impression there are going to be a few amputations, this time.'

Victoria gave Mabel a confused look. 'I don't know what an amputation is.'

Mabel stared at her for a few seconds. 'It's where a limb has to be removed, you know, an arm or a leg. The doctors here are getting a very good reputation for doing them successfully. Anyway, I want you to do the best you can at removing the old bandages, clean the area with an antiseptic to stop any infections from forming, and then get some clean bandages to cover the wound again.'

Panic ran across Victoria's face. 'I've never done anything like that before. What if I mess up?'

Mabel relaxed a little. 'You won't; it's no different to looking after children who have fallen over.' She frowned. 'It's just a little more serious, and anyway, I watched you with Corporal Peters; you're a natural. Just make sure you hide your own worry, about the wound and the sight of blood. Make sure you try to reassure them. They might act tough, but they're all frightened and have seen some terrible things, by the time they get here.'

Victoria nodded, knowing this was going to be a baptism of fire. She took a deep breath. Well, she wanted to know whether she would make a good nurse or not, and there was no time like the present.

15

The girls had spent the morning together, at Carlisle Street, getting Molly ready for her big day. She had shown no sign of nerves as she had giggled her way through the morning. Molly had refused to worry about how hot it was going to be. She had just kept repeating with a huge smile, 'It's August and it's my wedding day.'

Victoria and Alice had tears in their eyes when Molly appeared in all her finery with her mother.

Victoria had pushed away any doubts about her own wedding day and dabbed her handkerchief at her eyes. 'You look beautiful.'

Her father and grandmother had gasped with pride and wonder, as she had come down the stairs in her wedding dress. Molly wore her grandmother's gold locket around her neck, which her father had gifted to her, promising to guard it with her life.

Victoria stood alone now, staring down the narrow aisle of the church. She couldn't help wondering why Alice had been giving her strange glances all morning; were they sympathy looks? Then Alice had whispered that she wanted to speak to her later, when they were on their own. Victoria shook her head, hoping it wasn't for more 'your time will come' talks. She caught a glimpse of Andrew, nervously looking around at the few guests he and Molly had invited to their big day. He had been a patient man, and Victoria told herself she too had to be patient. Her eyes welled up. She prayed every day that Ted would write to say he was well. She wouldn't — couldn't — allow herself to think about any other outcome. One day, she would walk down this aisle, but not as a bridesmaid. Even if it wasn't with Ted, surely there was someone out there for her to love, and who could love her back. Molly had been right; she didn't need all the splendour. She just needed the man that she loved, to return home to her. It had been a long time to wait, but she would keep the faith and it would all turn out right for her, too. Victoria glanced around the church, and at its stained-glass windows. It was an intimate place, with seating for no more than two hundred people. The altar was small and the aisle narrow, but Molly had loved this church when Alice and Freddie had got married there, nearly three years ago. She smiled, as she remembered that day, when her brother had come home so unexpectedly. All her anger, of him enlisting at sixteen, had evaporated when she saw him.

Andrew turned to the woman by his side. 'It won't be long now.'

Elizabeth smiled. 'Nervous?'

A sound escaped from him, like a cat in distress. 'I just hope Molly turns up; she's a little unpredictable, that one.'

'She will. No one has ever been loved more, on either side, and she's just what you need.'

He grinned at his sister. 'Thanks for being my best man.'

Elizabeth flushed with colour. 'It's an honour to be asked, if not unusual, being a woman.' She giggled. 'I suppose I should have taken you out last night and got you drunk, on your last night of freedom.'

Andrew smiled and wrapped his arm around his sister, careful not to crush her pale blue dress. 'Yeah, that sounds like something I would do, and I wouldn't want anyone else standing next to me, on one of the most important days of my life.'

Molly's mother, Charlotte, walked through the church doorway, dabbing at her forehead with a lace handkerchief, as she stood in the cool vestibule, glad to be out of the midday heat. She gazed down the aisle at Andrew waiting patiently for her daughter. A smile played on her lips as she remembered Molly trying to avoid him, but he never gave up and he was a good match for her high-spirited, independent daughter. The dark oak door was pushed back, against the grey stone of the church wall. She lifted her hand to check her hair, patting the plaited bun at the back of her head. She was thankful Daisy had come round with Victoria that morning. She ran her hands down her sage green, tulip-style dress, under the matching jacket, smoothing out the non-existent creases, enjoying the softness of the fabric against her skin. Lily guided Molly's grandmother, Sophie, into the church entrance. Jack escorted Molly through the doorway. Victoria turned and tweaked at Molly's blonde hair and long veil, while Alice straightened the bottom of it, across the floor.

Molly had chosen a calf-length, white wedding dress. The white underskirt was covered in layers of lace, while the long sleeves tightened at the wrists. The bodice was covered with detailed embroidered lace, with a white sash under it. The veil was a perfect match for the dress and was held in place with the orange blossom her mother loved so much.

Molly took a deep breath, before giving a nervous laugh. 'Stop worrying, it's all good, he'll think I've changed my mind if I don't hurry up.'

'Molly, you look wonderful.' Charlotte beamed, her eyes welling up. 'I'm glad you decided to carry your gran's bible, instead of flowers. You've always been your own person, and I want you to know that I'm very proud of you, even though I don't always show it.'

Molly blinked quickly. 'I love you, Ma.'

Sophie looked at her through watery eyes. 'Be happy. Andrew is a good man.' She leant forward, giving her granddaughter a kiss on the cheek. 'You will never know how much you are loved by all of us, and I'm thrilled to see this happy day.' She turned as quickly as she could, to lean on Lily.

Molly's tears pricked at her eyelids. She reached out and grasped her gran's hand. 'Thank you.'

Sophie nodded. 'Let's go, Lily, or the wedding will probably be over before I've made it to my seat at the speed I walk, and I need to make the most of this beautiful silver-grey gown.'

Lily chuckled. 'We have plenty of time, so no rushing please.'

Charlotte lifted her hand, to touch the soft skin of her daughter's cheek. 'Ready?'

Molly nodded, catching her mother's lily of the valley scent she had used sparingly, that morning.

With Victoria's help, Charlotte gently pulled a short layer of the veil over her daughter's face. She beamed at her daughter. 'You look beautiful. Andrew's a lucky man.' Tears filled her eyes.

They all stood motionless for a moment. Jack cleared his throat, while straightening his blue tie, and the blue cufflinks on his white shirt.

Molly closed her eyes, stopping her own tears from falling. 'Thank you,' she whispered, opening them again.

Charlotte leant towards Jack and kissed his cheek, before turning on her heels and stepping forward. Her shoes clattered on the stone floor, as she walked towards the front pew. She nodded towards Alice's family and Daisy, before taking her seat, next to her mother.

The priest stepped forward and the chords of the pipe organ filled the air. The congregation stood up as one, and with Alice leading the way, the two bridesmaids slowly walked down the aisle, in single file, towards the waiting priest, in step with each other and Mendelssohn's 'Wedding March'. The white lace and pale pink satin underlay of the column dresses swished around their calves, and their white shoes clipped, with every step they took. The bridesmaids each carried a small, round posy of fresh cut flowers, made up of white and pink roses and baby's breath.

Molly stood in the vestibule with her father, gazing up at him. 'I hope I don't make a fool of myself, by tripping up or something.'

Jack looked adoringly at his daughter. 'No matter what, I will always be here to catch you.' He paused, tucking his daughter's hand under his arm. 'I suppose this is it, time for me to give you away.' His eyes became watery. 'You look beautiful. I am so proud of you, and all that you stand for. You are beautiful, inside and out.'

'Thank you, Pa; please remember my family and friends are everything to me.' She blinked quickly. 'We need to go, before I'm the first bride to walk towards her groom, blubbering her eyes out.'

Jack laughed and squeezed her hand. 'Ready?'

Molly nodded, and they stepped forward together,

in line with the bridesmaids. One hand gripped her father's arm, while the other carried her grand mother's worn and well-thumbed bible.

Charlotte stood, proudly watching her daughter and husband, as they followed the girls towards the altar.

Andrew clutched his hand in front of him; the knuckles were white, as the bone tried to break free of his skin.

Victoria nodded and beamed at him and Elizabeth, as she followed Alice along the front pew, past Mrs Cooper.

Molly and her father finally drew level with Andrew. 'You look beautiful, Molly. You're making me the happiest man alive, today.'

Her eyes lit up and she smiled back at him. 'Then, we are making each other happy today.'

The priest cleared his throat and nodded at the pair of them.

They nodded back, in unison.

'Dearly beloved, we are gathered here today . . . '

* * *

The Foyles Bookshop door had been closed on the last customer. The shop was cooler for having shut out the sunshine that had shone relentlessly, through the open doorway.

Victoria grinned up at Mr Leadbetter. 'It's been lovely to have you back, sir, but I hope you haven't been overdoing it today.'

'Don't worry, Miss Appleton, I think my age is catching up with me.' Mr Leadbetter gave a faint smile, running his fingers around the inside of his stiff, white collar. 'But I understand you managed very well, without me.'

'That's very kind of you to say, but I think the girls will tell you otherwise.' Victoria giggled. 'I made Alice and Molly stay with me, after the staff had gone home. We checked the shop together; it's very spooky when there's no one in here and you hear all kinds of noises, that you don't hear during the day.'

Mr Leadbetter chuckled. 'I know what you mean.' He paused as he looked around at the loaded shelves. 'It's almost as though the shop is settling down for the night, the groans of the floor and the stairs letting you know they're worn out from the busy day they've had, but you soon get used to it.'

'You make the shop sound like a living and breathing thing.'

'I suppose that is how I see it.' Mr Leadbetter found himself straightening a book, on a shelf within arm's reach. 'I once found a man wandering around upstairs; he couldn't find his way out of the store.' He roared with laughter. 'He frightened the life out of me. It's a wonder I survived the night.'

Victoria's eyes widened. 'Oh my goodness, I probably would have screamed the place down. I expect you have so many stories you could tell.'

Mr Leadbetter's eyes sparkled. 'Indeed I do, Miss Appleton. Indeed I do.'

Alice waddled over towards Victoria. 'Good evening, Mr Leadbetter, I haven't had a chance to ask you how you are now. I expect this first day back has been tiring for you.'

'I am well, Mrs Leybourne. Thank you for asking, and I should also thank you for driving me home, when I embarrassed myself.'

217

Alice shook her head. 'It was not an embarrassment, sir; we were all genuinely concerned for your welfare.' She eyed him sheepishly. 'It's not for me to tell you what to do, but you clearly still look a bit peaky. You need to make sure you get as much rest as you can, for the time being, at least.'

Mr Leadbetter frowned. 'I appreciate your kind thoughts, Mrs Leybourne. I think it was just the heat, but if not, I have Miss Appleton to lighten the load for me.'

Alice smiled. 'We were all quite concerned for you, sir, but it's good to have you back.'

Mr Leadbetter nodded. 'I'm expecting Miss Cooper, or perhaps I should say Mrs Greenwood, back tomorrow. Is that right?'

The girls grinned. 'Yes, sir,' they chorused as one.

Mr Leadbetter smiled at them both.

Alice glanced at Victoria. 'Are you ready to go?'

Victoria nodded.

The girls both looked up at their manager, speaking in unison. 'Goodnight, Mr Leadbetter.'

Mr Leadbetter pulled the shop door open and stood aside. 'Take care, ladies, and I'll see you tomorrow.' The girls nodded, stepping out into the late afternoon sunshine, and the busy Charing Cross Road. The door thudded shut behind them.

Victoria frowned. 'I hope Mr Leadbetter is going to be all right.'

Alice looked back at the closed door. 'The trouble is, he's not getting any younger.'

They stepped forward, each lost in thought, as they weaved in and out of people rushing to go about their business, some stopping at stalls to buy drinks and snacks. A grey-haired man rushed past them, clutching

218

a pound note high in the sky. Curiosity got the better of them and they turned to see what was so urgent, but the man was just handing over his money to a flower seller.

Victoria smiled. 'Someone's in for a treat tonight.'

Alice laughed. 'They certainly are.' She tucked her hand under Victoria's arm. 'I've been wanting to talk to you today. In fact, I wanted to talk to you yesterday, but with the wedding and everything, I didn't get a chance.'

Victoria gave a wistful smile. 'Wasn't it a lovely day? I think Molly got it just right. She looked beautiful and it was clear for all to see how much Andrew loves her. She's a very lucky woman to find such love.'

Alice lost her concentration for a moment. 'It was lovely. I couldn't agree more, it was a beautiful day all round. Mr and Mrs Cooper looked so happy and proud. Going inside that church reminded me of my own wedding to Freddie.'

Victoria nodded. 'Wasn't it wonderful that Elizabeth was her brother's best man, or should I say woman? They are so close, I'm pleased Andrew broke with tradition. I was so happy for them.' Victoria momentarily stepped off the pavement, to avoid a child running towards her. 'Mrs Cooper was telling me Andrew had booked the Savoy Hotel for their wedding night, as a surprise for Molly. She would have been thrilled. She was always saying how she'd like to go inside that hotel, or even better, spend a night there, but she couldn't afford it.' She beamed at Alice. 'Isn't that wonderful?'

Alice couldn't help laughing at Victoria's joy. 'It is wonderful. Molly looked beautiful and there was no doubt about how much she loved Andrew; it shone from her soul.'

'It did. I'm so happy for them both, and Mr and Mrs Cooper, it's all worked out in the end.'

Alice nodded. 'It was a good day all round and she will be full of it tomorrow.'

'That she will, and rightly so.' Victoria smiled. 'I won't get any work out of her tomorrow, that's for sure.'

The girls giggled as they stepped across Sutton Street and headed towards Oxford Street.

Alice glanced down at the pavement, for a moment. 'Look, I want to talk to you about something. In fact, I wanted to talk to you yesterday, but the opportunity didn't arise.'

Victoria stayed silent, staring ahead, waiting to hear what was so important that Alice had kept giving her strange looks yesterday.

Alice frowned. 'Please don't think it's anything bad.' She looked left and right along Oxford Street, before dragging Victoria across the road.

Victoria turned to her friend. 'What is it, for goodness' sake? I knew something was bothering you yesterday, but I guessed it was because I am the last person to get married, and let's face it, it's not going to happen anytime soon. I haven't even got a boyfriend; in fact, Daisy is likely to get married before me. I know everyone thinks I'll be the dried-up spinster, left on the shelf.'

Alice stopped in her tracks. 'What?' The person behind collided into her. Alice turned. 'Sorry.' She took a step forward, to catch up with Victoria. 'I don't understand. Am I that bad, that you thought I was going to give you the "it'll be your turn soon" speech?' Anger spots filled her cheeks. 'I thought we knew each other better than that.' She stepped past Victoria, shaking her head as she went.

Victoria reached out and grabbed Alice's arm. 'Wait, I'm sorry. I shouldn't have said those things, I need to stop and think before letting my emotions run away with me. I'm sorry for speaking out of turn, it's not fair on you or Molly. It's just I know everyone thinks I'm going to be an old maid, and they're probably right, because I've had thoughts about being a crazy cat lady and always being the aunt and not the mother.'

Alice turned to face her friend. 'If you end up being a crazy cat lady or "an old maid", you do. Time will tell, but I'm not the one to say that to you. You're a lovely person and any man would be lucky to have you on their arm, let alone as a wife.' The anger spots began to fade. 'I've been on the end of your tongue before. Remember the pawn tickets? You don't think I'm brave enough to risk that again, do you?'

Victoria gave a wry smile. 'I was wrong then, as well.'

Alice shook her head. 'We were both wrong then, but I don't think I'm wrong this time.' She paused. 'Do you want to hear what I've been busting to tell you, since I left you at Endell Street Hospital.'

Victoria took a deep breath. 'All right.' She stepped nearer to her friend and placed her hand under Alice's arm, as they walked forward together.

'I want you to understand that what I'm about to say is a bit of a long shot.'

Victoria tutted. 'Will you please just say it and get it over and done with?'

'All right.' Alice took a breath. 'When we were talking at the hospital, you introduced me to Nurse

Atkins — didn't you once say her name was Mabel?' She gave Victoria an expectant look, waiting for the penny to drop.

Victoria gave her a blank expression. 'I know that, but — '

'No buts. Do you know whether Mabel Atkins was ever married? She clearly isn't now, because she's a nurse, but there's a war going on, so she might have been, and his name might have been Sid.' Alice stopped, looking like the cat that had got the cream.

Victoria stopped, yanking at Alice's arm. Realisation suddenly spread across her face. 'Her husband was called Sid. I remember her telling me he died when the Germans dropped some bombs on Greenwich; at least, I think that's what she said.' She paused. 'Do you really think it's possible she knew my parents?'

* * *

Victoria had forgotten that, when she left Foyles with Alice, she was meant to be walking towards Endell Street, but at least it had given her time to pick up the photograph. She gripped her handbag strap tight, her fingernails digging into the palm of her hand, leaving red welts when she released her grip a little. Without a thought, Victoria turned right, onto Tottenham Court Road. The summer heat made the daily odour of the spent hops from the Horseshoe Brewery overpowering. The stench hung in the evening air, but her mind was too full of Mabel and Sid to notice. How did Mabel know her parents, and why hadn't she said anything? Should she ask her, maybe show her the wedding photograph? Of course, it might not be her at all. She fought the urge to take it out of her bag and

222

have another look. She didn't have time to dawdle; she was going to be late.

An old lady shouted out as Victoria trotted past her stall. 'Buy some flowers, luvvie; they're fresh.'

Victoria peered over her shoulder. 'Sorry, I'm already late.' She carried on striding up New Oxford Street, beads of perspiration forming on her forehead, as she weaved past the many barrows and sellers that were still out, trying to sell their wares.

'Come on ladies and gents, don't make me take 'ome this food. I'll only get into trouble wiv the wife.'

Victoria smiled as she sped past and turned right into High Holborn. Thank goodness it wasn't a long walk to Endell Street. She pulled her handkerchief out of her skirt pocket and dabbed at her face, guessing it was probably crimson in colour. It wasn't long before she turned left and saw the large open gates to the hospital. Victoria stopped to catch her breath; she still hadn't worked out whether to speak to Mabel about her parents or not. A horn beeped behind her. She jumped out of the way, having been oblivious to the fact she was blocking ambulances coming to the hospital. A voice shouted in her head. *Come on, snap out of it, either you talk to Mabel about it, or you don't; it's pretty simple.* Victoria shook her head and pulled back her shoulders. She didn't have time for this.

The receptionist saw Victoria as soon as she walked through the door. The hospital was still bright, with the late evening sunshine beaming through the windows, and vases full of cut flowers were placed on every available space. 'Evening, Victoria, Mabel was looking for you earlier; I think you're meant to be working with her, on Joan of Arc Ward again.'

Victoria nodded, forcing herself to smile. 'I think

I've only ever worked with Mabel, since I've been coming here.'

The lady laughed. 'That's because, where possible, they like the volunteers to report to the same nurse. It helps you to get to know the staff, and the patients' needs, better.'

Victoria nodded. 'Thank you, that explains it.'

A young nurse came rushing in, who Victoria didn't recognise, trying desperately not to run. 'Sorry, Elsie, I'm late and I hope the sister doesn't notice. Where am I meant to be?'

Elsie smiled. 'St Catherine's, but you're too late. Sister has already been asking if I've seen you.'

The nurse groaned, lifting her eyes heavenward.

'I told her I thought I saw you going into the ladies' room.'

The nurse smiled. 'You're a darling, Elsie.' She ran towards the staircase and disappeared from view.

Elsie chuckled. 'One day she'll get shot, or I will, for covering up for her.'

Victoria nodded, as her gaze followed where the nurse had been. She wondered who the nurse was. 'I suppose I'd better get going as well.' She climbed the stairs, one at a time, perspiration trickling down the side of her face, as she pulled open the door to the ward. The sun cast its shadows and rays of light through the many windows, giving a warm feeling. The vases of flowers, along with the many books and newspapers scattered around, helped to give it a homely feel.

'Ahh, Victoria, you made it — excellent.' Mabel beamed.

As she stepped into the ward, the smell of antiseptic threw itself at Victoria. Closing her eyes and clutching the door handle, she took some deep breaths.

224

'Are you all right?' Mabel rushed forward, grabbing a wooden chair on her way. 'Here, sit down.'

Victoria did as she was instructed and closed her eyes.

Mabel rested her hand on the young volunteer's forehead. 'You feel quite warm and look very hot. It could quite easily be the weather; have you been rushing?'

Victoria took a breath and opened her eyes, staring straight at Mabel, wondering again who she was to her parents.

Mabel frowned. 'Don't rush to stand up. I don't want you passing out on me.'

Victoria jerked, as Mabel's voice filtered through the fog in her head. 'This is embarrassing. I'm all right, honestly.' She stared at the many beds in the ward. 'You have enough to do, with the real patients.' She stood up. 'I'll be all right in a moment; it's probably just the heat.'

Mabel stared at her, but then shook her head.

Victoria's eyes widened. 'What?'

Mabel opened her mouth to speak, but then shut it again.

Victoria didn't take her eyes off the nurse. 'What is it?'

Mabel took a step away. 'It's nothing.' The spell was broken. 'We have the usual stuff to be done this evening, but there are a couple of patients that have lost their sight, so you could always read to them, whether it's a newspaper or a book.'

Victoria nodded. 'Is there anyone in particular you have in mind?'

'We have a patient that has been moved on to the general ward from a side room, because he's particularly depressed. Apparently, he has no one so we need to lift his spirits as best we can. At the moment, he doesn't want us anywhere near him, so you'll have your work cut out, but I saw you with Corporal Peters, so I think you'll be all right. Don't take any notice of him if he's rude to you. They nearly all go through that phase, but I think it's guilt, because they've survived and their friends haven't.' She turned, to see the concern on Victoria's face. 'Do you think you're up to it?'

Victoria met her gaze. 'I'd be lying if I didn't say I was frightened, or maybe worried is a better word, but if I can help in any small way, then that's what I'm here for.'

Mabel smiled and patted her on the arm. 'I knew you would want to help. His face is quite heavily bandaged at the moment, so there's nothing on show for you to get squeamish about.'

Victoria pulled back her shoulders and took a deep breath. 'Right, I've got better since I've been coming here, so where is he?'

Mabel moved towards the desk in the corner of the ward and picked up a piece of paper that was covered in scribbles. 'He's right down the other end, in bed twenty-five, and please don't forget he's totally blind at the moment.' She looked at Victoria. 'He'll only have the sound of your voice to go by, so it's important to try and keep it as happy as you can, without making him angry.'

Victoria nodded. 'I'll do my best. What's his name?'

Mabel looked back down at the paper she was holding. 'Corporal Edward Marsden.'

16

Victoria's eyes fluttered open. They took a moment to focus. Mabel was frowning down at her, holding a glass of water. The floor was cold against her legs. Victoria ran her tongue against her lips; her mouth felt dry.

'Here, sip this.' Mabel propped Victoria's head up and held the glass to her lips.'

The cold water splashed against Victoria's mouth and tongue. She closed her eyes, welcoming the cool relief.

Mabel thumbed away a dribble that was running down Victoria's chin. 'Are you all right?' She waited a few seconds for a reply, but nothing came. 'You're very pale. Does anything hurt?'

Victoria shook her head. 'What . . . what happened?'

Mabel put the glass on the floor and rested the palm of her hand against Victoria's forehead. 'I don't know.' She paused. 'One minute, I was talking to you about Corporal Marsden, and the next, you were out cold on the floor.'

Victoria gasped, closing her eyes, as she remembered. Was that why he hadn't written — because he'd lost his sight? There must be some mistake. Surely he would have got someone else to write and tell her he was alive.

'I think, maybe you should go home; you've no colour in your cheeks at all.' Mabel put her arm around Victoria's shoulders. 'Here, let me help you into a chair.'

Victoria took Mabel's helping hand and perched on the edge of the chair for a moment, to gather herself. She stood up. 'I'll be all right. I've come to help, and that's what I shall do.' She smoothed down her skirt, patted the bun at the base of her neck and took a deep breath. 'Bed twenty-five, Corporal Edward Marsden.' She pulled her shoulders back and slowly began walking towards the other end of the ward. Victoria could feel Mabel's eyes boring into her back, but nothing else mattered, apart from making it to the end of the ward. Silently, she counted the beds, nodding her hellos to the soldiers, as she went past them. She stopped, two beds away from bed number twenty-five. The patient was still, most of his face hardly visible because of the bandages. She stared at him for a moment. Would he recognise her voice? Her smell? Should she tell him her name . . . and if she didn't, who would she say she was? She shook her head, wondering why life was so complicated. The photograph in her handbag came to the forefront of her mind; she hadn't spoken to Mabel about it. Ted had caught her unawares. The photograph wasn't important; in fact, nothing else mattered. She stared at the bed, as his legs moved under the covers. What was she going to say to him? Could she lie and pretend to be someone else?

The patient in bed twenty-five fidgeted for a moment, before moving his head at an angle. 'Is someone there?'

Victoria stepped forward, clearing her throat, but her voice came out barely louder than a whisper. 'Yes, I've come to sit and chat, or read to you.'

'Don't bother; you're wasting your time. Go and look after some other poor lad that needs your help.'

Victoria stared at him for a moment. From what she could see, his face looked weathered, and bristles had spiked through, forming a beard. Was this the man she fell in love with when she was sixteen, and he was twenty-one? They were going to take on the world, until her world had been turned upside down, and now his world was spiralling out of control.

A brusque voice interrupted her meanderings. 'I may not be able to see, but I know you're still there. I can feel you staring at me.'

Victoria took a deep breath. 'I am still here.' She paused. 'To be honest, I'm wondering what to do with you.'

'Hah.' Corporal Marsden turned his head away from her.

Victoria gasped; even in his blindness, he didn't want to look at her. 'Well, you can throw your tantrums and shout at me as much as you want, but I'm not going anywhere.'

He lay in his bed in silence.

Victoria pulled up a chair, seeing him flinch as it scraped along the floor. She sat herself down. Panic took hold, as she wondered what she was going to talk to him about. Silence sat between them. 'So, where have you been? I mean . . . '

'Not on me 'olidays, that's for sure.'

Victoria was grateful he couldn't see the colour rising up her neck. 'Corporal Marsden, I'm a new recruit at all this stuff, so I'd appreciate it if you showed me a little patience, because I'm not as stupid as I sound.'

'Really?' he quipped.

Victoria took a deep breath and counted to three. 'Is this how you treated the soldiers under your command? The lads that had enlisted because they wanted to do the right thing and defend their country's honour, and then there's the lads that enlisted at sixteen, because they thought it was an adventure. Did you not care what happened to them? Were you not patient with them, when they got scared, and experienced things that no person should?' She paused to catch her breath.

Ted Marsden stayed silent.

Victoria glared at him. 'If you didn't care about them, then you are right to treat yourself in the same manner, but if you did, then you should allow yourself to care about you and your future. If you don't care about you, who else will?'

Tension sat between them, and Victoria immediately felt guilty for giving him such a hard time. Perhaps this wasn't the job for her. 'Would you like a cup of tea, or something?'

Silence.

'Maybe a biscuit? If I can find some.'

Corporal Marsden clenched his hands into a fist, on top of his bedclothes. 'What I want is to be left alone, but you don't seem to understand that.'

Victoria chuckled. 'I will leave you in a minute, but please understand, I will be back tomorrow, and the day after, and the day after that, so you'd better start trying to be nice to me. Otherwise, I shall continue to make your life a misery, more than it already is.'

'You have no idea what I've been through, or what I've lost.' Ted Marsden waved his hand in the air. 'Or any of the soldiers that are here, so don't try to make out you do.'

'I wouldn't dream of it.' Victoria lowered her tone, to a little over a whisper. 'That wasn't what I was trying to do, nor would I ever.' She hesitated. 'I was trying to get a reaction from you.'

'Well, you certainly got that.'

Victoria lowered her eyes. Had she made a mistake in trying to push him too quickly? Would he hate her forever, when he realised who she was?

★ ★ ★

'Sorry I'm late, Mr Leadbetter.' Victoria rushed through the bookstore, to clock in for work, unaware of Alice's eyes following her. She put her handbag down on a chair and whisked her card out of the wooden slot, thrusting it into the clocking in machine. She shook her head. Half an hour late; she'd feel that in her pay packet.

'Is everything all right, Miss Appleton?' Mr Leadbetter stood in the doorway. 'You haven't ever been this late before, and actually, you haven't been late to work for some time now.'

Victoria pushed her card back into the wooden slot. 'I'm sorry, I'm afraid I didn't sleep very well last night, and then couldn't get up this morning.'

Mr Leadbetter nodded. 'If you need to talk because you're worrying about things, er, particularly work, then please feel free to find me.' He half turned to walk away, but stopped and looked back at her. 'I'm afraid, when it comes to matters of the heart, then I'm not very good, but I know you have your friends here and you're very good at supporting each other.' He shifted from one foot to the other, before walking away.

Victoria smiled to herself; she couldn't ever imagine confiding in Mr Leadbetter. She ran her hands down her black skirt and straightened her white blouse,

231

while stepping forward into the shop and immediately colliding with Alice.

'Is everything all right, Victoria? Molly and I were worried when you didn't come in this morning. Did you speak to Mabel about the photograph last night?'

Victoria shook her head. 'No, I forgot about it.'

Alice raised her eyebrows. 'Forgot? How could you forget? It's all you've talked about for weeks.'

'Look, now's not the time. I'm already late for work, and you'll get into trouble, being away from your counter.'

Alice smiled. 'Actually, Mr Leadbetter sent me in to see if everything was all right.'

Victoria could feel the hairs on the back of her neck stand on end. 'Well, he had no right. I'm sure if I have a problem I wish to discuss, I can talk about it without making it a big issue.'

Alice stared at her for a moment. The dark rings under her eyes, and the pale complexion, told their own story. Victoria's waspish comments added to the feeling that something was definitely wrong. Alice had seen this before and knew, without a doubt, she had to speak to Molly. Victoria hadn't ever been very good at sharing her problems, as she knew only too well.

Alice stepped aside, allowing Victoria to walk past her, into the shop. 'Molly and I are here for you, whatever the problem.'

Victoria peered over her shoulder at Alice, gave a slight nod, then carried on walking.

Alice sighed; she wanted to go and find Molly, but she knew they would both end up in trouble. It would have to wait until lunchtime. She pulled back her shoulders, her hand automatically cradling her small baby bump, as she went back to her counter.

Victoria wandered aimlessly around the shop, automatically nodding and saying hello to customers. She had momentarily thought about going down to the basement and having a chat with Albert, but had quickly decided that wasn't a good idea. Her mind was full of Ted, and what a mess she had made of things at the hospital. She hadn't thought it through; the situation had completely caught her off guard. There were no excuses. It wasn't a good start to learning about him all over again. He probably hated her, so any future she had hoped for with him, was lost. The best she could hope for was friendship. She had to find a better way of getting him to talk. She had tossed and turned all night, trying to figure it out, muffling her tears in her pillow, in a bid to not wake up Daisy. There was nothing she could come up with, that would make things right.

Molly startled Victoria, when she bumped into her while striding between the tall racks of books. 'Ahh, Victoria, are you ready for lunch?'

Victoria's lips tightened a little. 'I'm not sure I have time for lunch today.'

Molly thrust her hand under her friend's arm. 'Hmm, well I think you should at least stop for a cup of tea.' Molly pulled her along with her. 'It's no good fighting it; you were the one that told us tea made everything all right, remember? You also told me off for not sharing my problems with you. You need to know we are not letting it go, mainly because we care about you, and the last time you didn't confide in us, you and Alice had a terrible argument, leaving me in charge.' Molly laughed. 'And you of all people should know, that's never a good thing.'

With Molly's laughter, Victoria's face lifted. 'All

right, I'm coming.'

They walked into the staff area together, where Alice already had three cups of tea sitting on the table. 'Victoria, did you bring some lunch with you?'

Victoria frowned at her.

'I'm only asking, because when you had a lot going on before, you hardly ever brought your lunch with you.' Alice dropped her wrapped sandwiches onto the table. 'You can always share mine.'

Molly smiled. 'Or mine.'

Alice watched Molly undo the paper. The rustling broke the silence between them and revealed thin slices of crusty bread. 'It's good to have you back, Molly. Did you enjoy your wedding day?'

Colour flushed Molly's cheeks. 'I loved it, and it was lovely for you both to be a part of it. Apparently, my gran hasn't stopped talking about it.' She gave a wistful look. 'I now wish I hadn't kept Andrew waiting for so long, and the Savoy Hotel was every bit as grand as I thought it would be. He thoroughly spoilt me.'

Victoria smiled. 'I must say, you look very happy, so it must agree with you.'

'I am, and this weekend I'm moving my things into his home in Bury Street.' Molly paused. 'I think it will be a little strange at first, but Andrew has plans for us to decorate it, so it's not all in his parents' taste, not that there is anything wrong with it, it's just . . . '

'It's not yours.' Alice smiled.

Molly nodded. 'I didn't say anything to him about it, though; it was his suggestion.' She went quiet for a moment.

Victoria rested her hand on her friend's. 'What is it?'

Molly sighed and glanced at them both. 'He's been

offered his old job back, at the bank. Well, actually, it's a promotion.'

Alice frowned. 'That's a good thing, isn't it?'

'Probably; it's just that I know he hated working there before and only did it to please his father.' Molly looked down at her untouched sandwich. 'Andrew said things have changed.' She giggled. 'He tells me he's a married man now, so he can't afford to take risks with our livelihood, especially if we are going to have a family.'

Alice pushed her sandwich paper towards Victoria, before picking up a quarter of the paste sandwich. 'If Freddie is anything to go by, I'd say you've got to let them make those decisions; personally, I wouldn't get involved in it.'

Molly nodded, before looking up at Victoria. 'So what is it?' She also pushed her sandwich paper towards her friend. 'What's happened for you to look like you've seen a ghost? Did you ask that nurse about the photograph? Alice was telling me this morning, how her name is the same as the one on the back of it; sounds like it could be the breakthrough you were looking for.'

Victoria closed her eyes and took a couple of breaths. When she opened them again, her friends were both staring at her.

Molly didn't take her eyes off Victoria. 'Well, come on, you're quick to be impatient with me, so let's have it. Did you speak to her about it, or not?'

'No.' Victoria wrung her hands in her lap.

Molly shook her head. 'I don't understand; why not? I thought this was something you needed to know.'

Victoria puffed out her chest. 'I went to volunteer at the hospital last night . . . '

Molly tutted. 'We know that, but what happened, and why didn't you ask her?'

When she finally spoke, Victoria's voice was barely audible. 'Ted is a patient there.'

'Is he all right?' the girls cried.

'He's blind.'

Molly and Alice gasped as one.

Victoria stared hard at the table.

Molly shook her head and reached out to rest her hand on Victoria's arm. 'But you still love him, don't you?'

Victoria nodded. 'It was a shock, I wasn't expecting to see him in the hospital at all, never mind like that.'

Alice rested her hand on Victoria's arm. 'Well, at least you know he's alive, and from what I hear, that hospital does some great work.'

Molly's face lit up. 'That's wonderful to know he's alive and safe, isn't it?' Her gaze flitted between her two friends before settling on Victoria. 'I know he's probably quite badly injured, but you must have been excited to see each other after all this time.' She fidgeted in her seat as she realised her bad choice of words. 'Well, I know he can't actually see you, but he must have been pleased you were there.'

Silence sat between them.

Molly gave an exasperated sigh. 'Does it change things? Him being blind I mean, is it permanent?' She tilted her head to one side. 'Remember, love conquers all.'

Victoria could feel her throat tightening. 'Yes, but it takes two and he's told the hospital there's no one he wants to be contacted.'

Alice and Molly quickly glanced at each other.

Alice squeezed Victoria's arm. 'I expect there's a

reason, he's probably frightened.'

Molly nodded. 'Alice is right, you just need to talk to him, hold him, let him know nothing has changed for you.'

Victoria lowered her head and shrugged her shoulders. 'There's more to it than that.'

★ ★ ★

The sister began to thumb through some papers. 'Good evening, Victoria, I don't seem to have you on my list as working tonight.'

'I . . . I'm not, I . . . I just thought I could help out on Joan of Arc Ward, as they have a couple of patients that have lost their eyesight.'

'Hmm, they can be tricky patients, because they wonder how they're going to survive. You know, get a job and look after their family. To be honest, I don't know what's worse for them. Mind you, I feel for all of them; to lose an arm or a leg must be awful too.' The sister looked up. 'Well, I never turn down a volunteer. I believe Nurse Atkins is up there, but if not, you know what to do. Just tread carefully with them; they have all been through so much already.'

Victoria wanted to say that conversation was a day too late, but she wasn't brave enough to make any comment at all. Instead, she nodded and made her way to the ward. She pushed open the heavy doors.

Mabel looked up from her desk, where she was scribbling her notes. 'Hello, Victoria, I wasn't expecting you this evening.'

'I wanted to come along tonight, to chat to Corporal Marsden, to try and keep up the work we did yesterday.' She craned her neck to see down the ward, but there were too many nurses and patients in the way. A raucous laughter reached Victoria and Mabel.

Mabel glanced in the direction it came from. 'Keep it down, boys.'

'Sorry, Atkins, old Dickie here is telling one of his stories.' The men laughed again, but it was followed by shushing, from the same group.

Mabel smiled. 'It's good to hear the laughter, but I've just got to make sure they don't get too carried away.'

Victoria nodded. 'How has Corporal Marsden been today? Has there been any improvement, after last night?'

'None that I can tell.' Mabel looked at some notes on the desk. 'He's not really talking to anybody at the moment.'

'Is he allowed out of bed?'

Mabel chuckled. 'You are feeling brave, but I don't see any reason why not. Just be prepared to have your head bitten off.'

Victoria nodded and proceeded to stride down the ward. Ted Marsden didn't look like he'd moved since she was there the previous evening. An untouched plate of food stood on the bed tray. Frowning at the congealed gravy over the pie and mash potato, she fought the urge to wrap her arms around him. To let him know she would always look after him, love him, until she took her last breath. 'I see you're still feeling sorry for yourself.' She reached out and rattled the tray. 'You know, some children are starving because they have no parents to provide food for them, but you are so wrapped up in yourself, you couldn't even be bothered to donate it to someone.'

Ted Marsden sighed but said nothing.

Victoria pulled up a chair, wanting to clasp his hand in hers so he could feel her love for him. She shook her head before taking a deep breath. 'You can sit there in silence if you like, in fact, it's probably preferable for me. I can just carry on chatting about potential food shortages, and the fear that women and children have lived in since 1914, and people dying because they've been in the wrong place when a bomb was dropped.'

Ted Marsden turned his head, to face her.

Victoria could picture him scowling underneath the bandages.

'Your nursing skills stink. Whatever happened to sympathy?'

'Ah, so it's sympathy you're after.' Victoria scowled. 'Well, I can tell you that my nursing skills stink, because I'm not a nurse. I'm a volunteer.' She held her arms up in front of her. 'Yes, I know it's hard to believe, but I've volunteered to come here and receive your insults.'

'I might have known,' Ted muttered. 'That's just my luck.'

Victoria wanted to shake him, but remained in her chair and sat on her hands, just in case she was tempted. 'What? Do you think you're unlucky?'

Ted remained silent.

'Right, so it's just a "woe is me" comment is it? I can tell you, lots of men have died, bodies haven't been found and families have been distraught, just at the sight of the telegram boy. You're here, alive, and your life is still ahead of you. It may not be how you thought it was going to be, but I can tell you, that's the same for all of us. You have to decide whether you are going to lie in bed, wallowing in self-pity all day, or try and make something of your life.'

'That's just it, I don't want to be alive, I've lost everything. I have no future. Is that clear enough for you?'

Victoria's voice softened. 'That's just it, you haven't lost everything, and you just have to reach out.' She paused. The silence hung heavy between them. 'There must be someone.'

'Just leave me alone.'

'I will, but I'll be back tomorrow, and the day after, so it's up to you.' Victoria stood up and pushed the chair to one side. 'Goodnight, Corporal Marsden.'

Victoria didn't wait to see if he responded. She'd been hard on him, but it broke her heart to see him lying so lifeless in his bed. It was with a heavy heart that she strode away from Ted, wondering if she had built him up in her mind to be someone he wasn't. Was he not the romantic hero she remembered, and was heartbroken about having lost, for the last seven years? She stopped to straighten the bed covers on an empty bed, before picking up a glass vase from the windowsill and peering into it; the flowers needed more water. She examined the different flowers at close quarters, recognising only the roses and lilies, as she pulled off the dead leaves, careful not to drop them on the floor.

Mabel watched her. 'They were beautiful when they arrived.'

Victoria nodded. 'I think they might be all right for a few more days, if I top the water up.' She chuckled. 'Not that I'm an expert. I don't know what most of them are.'

Mabel watched her for a few seconds. 'How was Corporal Marsden?'

Victoria's lips tightened. 'He's still not talking,

240

except to tell me I'm not a very good nurse.'

Mabel laughed. 'I take it you were a little bit rough with him, then.'

'I'm afraid so.' Victoria turned to look at her. 'Probably too rough, but I thought if I was too sympathetic, he wouldn't move on.' She paused, her mind in turmoil. 'Having said that, I think I've probably made matters worse instead of better, so he's probably right.'

Mabel shook her head. 'Being a nurse isn't all about being sympathetic, but about trying to make them better, physically and mentally. Give it a couple of days and we'll soon know if your words of wisdom got through.' She strode towards her desk.

Clutching the vase, Victoria trotted behind her. She cleared her throat. 'There's just one other thing.'

'Hmm, what is it?'

'I want to show you something.' Victoria caught up, placing the vase on the desk. 'I'll just get it out of my handbag.'

Victoria opened the clip of her handbag and pulled out the small black and white photograph. 'I found this photograph at home.' She paused, not sure whether to continue or not, thrusting it at Mabel, before she could change her mind.

Mabel took the photograph and stared at it for what felt like a long time, before Victoria spoke again.

'It has names on the back, and I wondered if it was you and your husband, Sid.'

Mabel didn't take her eyes off the photograph. 'Where did you get this?'

'It was at home. Is it your wedding?'

Mabel nodded. 'I don't understand why you have it at your home.'

Victoria felt a glimmer of hope rise inside her, only

to be chased away by the fear of what she might find out. She wiped her damp palms down the sides of her skirt. 'So . . . so you know these others in the picture?'

Mabel frowned, but didn't look up. 'Of course I do, they were at my wedding, but I don't understand why you have it. How have you come by it?'

Victoria stared at Mabel. It was now or never. 'It belongs to my parents.'

Mabel eyed Victoria for a few minutes, before she handed her back the photograph. 'Of course, your parents; it all makes sense now. How is that brother of mine? You can tell him from me, it's about time he visited his son.'

Victoria's eyes widened. 'You mean John?'

'Who else? He's quite poorly with his asthma, although I think it's developed into something else.'

A young nurse came running towards them. 'Nurse Atkins.'

Mabel glanced towards the nurse, and back to Victoria before scowling down at the photograph. 'I can't believe they've just abandoned him like that. I worry about him and my mother.'

The young nurse's words tumbled over each other, as she got nearer to them. 'I'm so sorry, but Nurse Atkins, you're needed by Sister. It's urgent.'

Mabel shook her head and sighed before passing the photograph back to Victoria. She turned away to follow the young nurse.

Victoria called out, desperate not to let the moment go. 'Wait.'

Mabel stopped and peered over her shoulder, giving her niece a tearful look.

Victoria's voice was barely audible when she spoke. 'I need to know where he is.'

'Brighton, of course, with my mother and father.'

Without another word, the two nurses trotted down the ward. Victoria held her breath. Was it Ted? She shook her head. Was Nurse Atkins really her aunt?

17

As she leant across Alice's wooden counter in Foyles, Molly clutched an old rag in her hand. There were another ten minutes before Mr Leadbetter would open the shop doors to its customers. Alice moved her bill payment pad and pen from one spot to another.

Molly peered over her shoulder. 'So this Nurse Atkins is your father's sister, your aunt?'

Victoria picked up a wooden chair and settled it nearer to Alice's counter. 'Here, sit down, while you can. I swear you're bigger this time than you were with Arthur. What are you, six months into your pregnancy?'

Alice lowered herself slowly. 'Yes, and I must admit I feel huge.' She laughed. 'This will be you soon, Molly.'

Molly immediately flushed with colour.

Victoria patted her hair back. "Yes, I suppose she must be my aunt, but what's more worrying is that I don't think she knows my mother and father died in the train derailment at Stoats Nest.'

Alice frowned. 'But why would she? You didn't tell anybody, because you didn't know there was another part of the family.'

Molly nodded. 'That's true.'

Victoria's gaze flicked from side to side. 'Apparently, John is in Brighton with Mabel's mother.' She raised her eyebrows. 'My grandmother. But why haven't they written to ask why they haven't visited or sent money?' Her eyes widened and a look of horror

244

trampled across her face. 'Do you think that's what all that money was for? Oh my goodness, he could be out on the streets, if no one has been paying for his keep.'

A deep cough came from behind them and Molly automatically flicked her rag across the countertop. 'That's better. I don't mind cleaning it every morning, for you Alice, especially in your condition.'

Victoria couldn't look at either of the girls, for fear of the bubbling laughter spilling out from inside her. She stood up straight, giving a small nod. 'You just need to take it easy, Alice. Remember, you haven't got that long to go now.'

Mr Leadbetter cleared his throat.

Alice kept her eyes fixed firmly on the floor. Molly and Victoria turned around at the same time.

Molly twisted the rag in her hands. 'Good morning, sir, how are you feeling today?'

Victoria thought she saw a glint of a sparkle in his eyes.

'I'm very well, Miss, er, I should say Mrs Greenwood. Is everything all right here?'

'Oh yes.' Molly gave her best smile. 'We were just making sure Alice wasn't overdoing it, in her condition, sir.' She absently swooshed the rag in front of her.

'Excellent.' Mr Leadbetter gave a wry smile. 'But please forgive me if I don't trust you three when you're huddled together; it usually means something is amiss.'

Molly giggled. 'Charming, sir, and me a reformed character as well.' She turned to walk away but looked back at them. 'I would like to stop for a chat, sir, but I have to get to my counter before the doors open.' Her shoulders were shaking as she walked away.

Mr Leadbetter chuckled as he watched her. 'It's good to see marriage hasn't changed Mrs Greenwood.' He turned back to Victoria. 'I don't think Albert is feeling too good today, so can you keep an eye on him for me.' He glanced across at Alice. 'And please do sit down if you need to. I don't mind, as long as the customers can see you are here to serve.'

Alice nodded. 'Don't worry, sir, I'll be fine.'

Mr Leadbetter nodded as he walked away.

Victoria turned to Alice. 'That was close. Molly does make me laugh; I couldn't look at either of you, for fear of bursting.'

'I know what you mean.'

Victoria moved the bill payment pad and pen nearer to Alice. 'I'd better go and see what's wrong with Albert. I hope he's all right.' As she turned away, she heard the bolts on the shop doors being pulled across. 'If anyone's looking for me, I'm in the basement.'

A few minutes later, Victoria, trying not to spill the mug of tea, pushed open the heavy basement door, the creaking signalling her arrival. As the door slowly swung shut, the noise was repeated. 'I think we should see about getting something done about this door.'

Albert chuckled. 'Good morning, Miss Appleton, you know me, a bit mutton, so it lets me know when I'm being visited.'

Victoria couldn't resist smiling at the old man as he dusted and checked the books. 'Morning, Albert, so it's your own personal alarm, then.'

Albert stopped work and looked over at her. 'Well done for remembering, the trouble and strife back 'ome, says I should stop trying to teach you youngsters, but I tell 'er it's your 'eritage, and cockney slang should never be forgotten.' He raised an eyebrow as he watched Victoria's concentration.

'Trouble and strife, wife.' She beamed, placing the mug of tea in front of Albert.

Albert nodded. 'Yer a quick learner.' He looked down at the pile of books in front of him. 'Thanks for the brew, always appreciated.'

Victoria smiled. 'Mr Leadbetter tells me you're not feeling too good today. Is there anything I can get you?'

'Nah, he's just fussing.' Albert moved the stack of books to one side and pulled another pile in front of him. 'I'll tell yer what though, these books are never-ending. 'Ere, while I fink of it, I still 'ave yer book 'ere.'

Victoria frowned. 'Book? What book?'

Albert stretched up to a shelf and grabbed it. He chuckled. 'It's the one yer liked the cover of, cos it 'ad Father Christmas on it.' He turned it so she could see.

'Oh my goodness, I'm so sorry, I totally forgot about it.' Victoria took it from him. *The Life and Adventures of Santa Claus*. She ran her hand over it. 'It is a beautiful cover. I'll take it up with me and get Alice to write me out a bill payment. With Christmas just a few months away, I don't want to risk someone else buying it.'

Albert laughed. 'You girls and yer fishhooks.'

'Hooks, books.'

'That's right; yer learning.'

Victoria watched him working for a second, before pulling herself up on to the counter. 'I should really get back to work.'

Albert looked over at her. 'What's the matter wiv yer, girl?'

'Have you got any family, Albert?'

247

'Nah, just me and the wife.' Albert's eyes narrowed a little. 'I 'ear yer've only got yer bruvver and sister.' He picked up a piece of rag. 'There ain't no secrets 'ere, yer know. By all accounts, yer've 'ad a lot to deal wiv, in yer young life.'

'Well, it seems I might 'ave . . . have family I didn't know about.'

Albert stopped what he was doing and stared at Victoria. 'That's a good find, ain't it?'

Victoria stared down at the book she was holding. 'I don't know. I suppose it must be, but I don't understand why I didn't know about them already.'

'Don't fink bad of yer ma and pa; they were probably trying to protect yer.'

Victoria nodded. 'Protect us from what? That's what I don't understand.'

Albert shrugged. 'Who knows, but I tell yer one fing, they'll 'ave only done what they thought was right at the time.'

Victoria jumped off the counter and wrapped her arms around him. 'Thank you, Albert.'

Albert flushed with colour and shook Victoria away. 'Aww, come on, yer don't 'ave to fank me. In fact, I ain't done anything.'

Victoria smiled. 'I'm thanking you for your words of wisdom, and for reminding me we all do what we think is right at the time, even if we get things totally wrong.'

'Just yer take care.'

'And you, Albert, and you.'

* * *

The candles danced in the shadows of the basement, in the house in Percy Street.

Daisy's eyes widened and her mouth dropped open, as she stared at Victoria for what felt like an eternity, but in reality was only a few seconds. 'So . . . so you're saying we have an aunt, grandparents and a brother we didn't know we had?' The flame from the candle, on the small table between them, flickered as Daisy blew out her breath. She stared at Victoria for a moment, before her eyes darted left and right, searching for memories of this family. 'I don't understand how that can be, I have no memory of them; none at all.'

Victoria paced around a small area of the basement. 'I know, I have no memory of them either, but there must be a reason why Ma and Pa didn't tell us.'

Daisy clenched her skirt. 'But you were sixteen when they died seven years ago.' Daisy shook her head as disbelief ran across her face. 'And all this time, we've struggled, you've struggled, while we've had a family we didn't know existed.'

Victoria slumped down in the small armchair, searching for words of wisdom, but none came. 'I know it's hard to understand, especially as we are so close.'

Daisy lifted her head slightly. 'They must have had an argument of some sort, because no one has been in touch since they died, have they?'

Victoria shook her head. 'No, I just keep telling myself they wouldn't have kept it a secret to hurt us, but it does mean we've lost seven years that we'll never get back again.' Tears pricked at her eyes. 'I can't think about not talking to you for seven years, so you'd think it must be an argument, but that would

249

be a hell of an argument.'

Daisy nodded. She leant forward and squeezed Victoria's hand. 'Don't worry, that would never happen, no matter what.'

Victoria gave a watery smile, before opening her mouth to speak, but a rumbling noise above them stopped her. She looked at the clock. Eight o'clock. They had been down there since they'd had the police warning just over an hour ago; it would be dark outside. As the noise got louder, the girls both looked up to the ceiling, reaching out for each other. Victoria wrapped her arms around her sister. 'Daisy, no matter what happens tonight, or in the future, know that you and Stephen are everything to me, and I've always tried to do my best for you both.'

Daisy eyes shone in the dim light as she squeezed her sister.

The floor shuddered and dust fell from the ceiling. The girls jerked as a noise, not unlike a huge thunderclap, vibrated against the walls of the house. The windows rattled. Something crashed to the floor.

The girls gazed at each other, fear written on their faces.

Victoria looked up at the ceiling again, just as the dust showered down on them. 'If this is it — '

'I love you,' they both said in unison, clutching on to each other, their tears mingling with the dust that had settled on their faces, and in their hair.

The rumbling from above gradually faded and they loosened their hold on each other.

Victoria looked around the basement. The dust had settled everywhere. They would have to change the sheets, before they went to bed. Not even their glasses of water had escaped it.

Daisy started to shake. 'Do . . . do you think we still have a home upstairs, or are we buried in here?'

Victoria shook her head, trying to hide the fear that was running down her spine. 'No, we wouldn't be trapped down here for long. Alice and Molly would have the search parties digging us out.' She forced a smile, trying to reassure herself and Daisy. 'As indeed, I expect, would Peter.'

'Huh, I wouldn't rely on Peter; he seems to have a roaming eye. One of the men told me he'd asked someone else out.' Daisy stood up, wiping away the dust and tears that were now smeared across her face.

'Really, well that's his loss. Remember what you said to me,' Victoria said. 'Don't settle for second best, because any man would be lucky to have you.'

Daisy smiled. 'Are you sure that was me? It sounds too wise to be something I would have said.'

'Well, it probably isn't exactly what you said, but the sentiment is the same. You are beautiful, inside and out, so just remember that.'

Daisy nodded. She stood up and brushed down her skirt. 'Shall we be brave and see if we can get out?'

'All right.' Victoria took a step forward and stopped again, grabbing Daisy's arm. 'That explosion sounded really close. If it didn't get us, then it may have hit near Alice's home, in Bloomsbury Street.' She ran forward to the stairs. 'Come on, they may need our help.' In her haste, she tripped and fell up a couple of steps, grazing her shin. She sucked in her breath and held it tight for a few seconds.

Daisy tried to pull her hand away. 'Let me have a look.'

Victoria shook her head. 'No, we don't have time for that. Alice is pregnant, and there's little Arthur.'

Tears coursed down Victoria's cheeks.

'Don't get upset, they'll be all right.' Daisy stepped past Victoria, to the basement door. 'If I try to open this, are you ready?'

'No, wait, we'll do it together.' Victoria stood to her feet and hobbled up the stairs, to her sister. 'We're in this together.'

Daisy gave a wry smile as Victoria rested her hand on hers, to turn the doorknob. 'All right, on the count of three.'

Victoria bit down on her lip and nodded.

'One . . . ' Daisy shouted out. 'Two . . . three . . . '

They both turned the knob and pushed hard, almost falling over each other as the door swung open.

It took Victoria a minute to realise the hysterical laughter she could hear was her own and Daisy's. They spontaneously wrapped their arms around each other. 'Oh my goodness, we're still here.' Victoria squeezed her sister hard, looking for the confirmation. 'We're all right.' The laughter and relief disappeared as quickly as it had arrived. 'If it didn't get us, who did it get?'

Daisy and Victoria ran to the front door, swinging it wide open. Their neighbours were doing the same.

A deep voice carried down the street. 'Is everyone all right?'

Victoria coughed as the smoke and dust hit the back of her throat, along with an acrid smell of burning.

Daisy shouted back to the neighbour. 'We're safe, thank you.'

Other neighbours followed suit.

Victoria reached inside and grabbed a couple of scarves, to wrap around their mouths. She passed one to Daisy and wrapped the other around her neck, pulling part of it over her nose and mouth. 'Come on.

252

The bombs didn't get us, but I need to know whether Alice and her family are safe.' She pulled the front door shut.

Daisy followed her sister's actions and the pair of them half ran along Percy Street.

By the time they were crossing Bedford Square, towards Bloomsbury Street, Victoria's eyes were stinging, and she was gasping for breath under her scarf.

A boy on a bicycle sped past them, shouting at the top of his voice. 'It's over. The Germans have gone.'

Relief spread through Victoria when she saw the houses were still standing, but the smoke was thicker.

Daisy pulled down her scarf. 'They don't look like they've been hit.' She quickly looked around her, but couldn't see anything in the darkness. It now had an eerie stillness about it, despite several front doors opening.

Victoria nodded, her voice barely audible behind the scarf. 'The stench of burning is stronger around here, so something close by has obviously been hit.'

Daisy coughed, just the once at first, but then again.

Victoria patted her on the back, but the hacking continued as Daisy gasped for breath. 'Come, put the scarf in front of your mouth and let's give Alice a knock. We'll get you a drink of water.'

Daisy pulled the scarf up, coughing into the thin material. This was quickly followed by a wheezing noise, coming from her chest. She wiped her hands over her eyes.

With one arm firmly fixed around her sister, Victoria lifted the door-knocker and let it drop again with a thud. 'I hope Alice is all right and the shock hasn't sent her into having her baby early.'

Daisy made a little undistinguishable noise, behind

253

the scarf. 'I'm sure babies are stronger than we all think.'

Victoria smiled. 'Well, we are about to find out.'

'Victoria.'

Victoria and Daisy automatically turned away from Alice's front door, to face the direction of the voice. Victoria yanked the scarf away from her mouth. 'Molly, thank goodness.'

Molly threw herself at Victoria, wrapping her arms around both her and Daisy. 'Thank God you're safe. We felt the ground vibrate at Carlisle Street. Pa said he hadn't felt that since the munitions factory explosion, so I had to come to see if you and Alice were all right.'

Victoria tried to steady her breathing. 'Thank goodness your parents and gran are all right. Have you been home to check on Andrew?'

Molly shook her head. 'I don't know about the house, but Andrew was with me. As soon as the policeman sounded the alarm, we almost ran from Bury Street to Ma's.' She gave a nervous laugh. 'And I can tell you, I'm really not meant to be running. By the time we got there, I needed the hospital.'

The girls chuckled, as they started to become calmer.

Molly continued. 'Anyway, I've left Andrew helping to get Gran up from the basement. It's too much for Pa, these days.'

The creaking of the lock caught their attention and they all turned, as the front door swung open.

'Thank goodness, Mrs Headley. We've just come to see if everyone's all right.'

Daisy held the scarf tight to her mouth, as she cleared her throat.

Victoria lowered her arm around her sister. 'Is it possible to get some water for Daisy? Something seems to have caught in her throat.'

The housekeeper smiled and stepped aside. 'Of course, come in. Alice is fretting about you as well, so she'll be very happy to see you all. It's been all Mrs Taylor can do, to keep her daughter in the house. What with that, and worrying about her own parents in Russell Square, I'm sure you will be a happy diversion, for a few minutes at least.'

Victoria's relief was short lived. Her face paled as she stepped inside the house. 'I forgot about Mr and Mrs Gettin; Alice and her mother must be worried sick.'

'Victoria.' Alice's anxious voice travelled into the hallway. 'Is that you I can hear?'

Mrs Headley gave a faint smile. 'Go through, before she comes running out to check.'

Molly nodded. 'Thank you, Mrs Headley. Alice is all right, isn't she?'

'She would be, if she could only stop worrying about everyone.'

Molly frowned. 'The noise must have frightened Arthur.'

Mrs Headley chuckled. 'Little Arthur slept through the whole thing, bless him. He's such a joy.'

'I thought it was you.' Alice startled the four of them in the hall.

Mrs Headley clicked the door shut. 'I'll put the kettle on and get a glass of water.'

Alice nodded. 'Thank you, Mrs Headley, come through to the sitting room. I've been worried sick about you all.'

Daisy lowered her scarf. 'Thank you, Mrs Headley.'

255

The three of them followed Alice into the large sitting room. 'Take a seat.'

Victoria looked around the room. 'Where is everyone?'

'Freddie, Lily and my father have gone to Russell Square, to make sure our grandparents are safe.' Alice wrung her hands in front of her. 'I keep telling myself that last time this happened, Lily and I practically ran round there, only to find them sweeping glass and stones off the street, with their neighbours.' She gave a faint humourless laugh. 'I just wish I knew what was going on, though.'

Molly stood next to a chair, gripping her hands. 'Would you like me to run round there? I can come straight back, with a full report on what's happening. Then you, Victoria and Daisy can stay and look after each other. You all look a little pale.'

Victoria looked over her shoulder and studied Molly. 'Actually, so do you. I expect it's the shock and worry.'

Alice perched on the edge of a chair. 'Thank you, Molly. I do appreciate your offer, but I think we should just wait, as they'll probably be back soon.' She paused as Mrs Headley came into the room, carrying the tray of tea things and a glass of water. 'Thank you, Mrs Headley; don't worry, I'll pour the tea.'

'Yes, ma'am.' Mrs Headley picked up the glass of water and gave it to Daisy.'

'Thank you.' Daisy sipped the water, thankful to clear the dust and smoke from her mouth.

The housekeeper hovered for a moment. 'Shall I take a cup of tea up to Mrs Taylor?'

Alice nodded. 'If you don't mind, it would be good to check on her.'

Mrs Headley nodded, before leaving the room.

'Ma is having a lie down. Since Robert died, she has found the war increasingly difficult to deal with,' Alice murmured.

Victoria's gaze became blurry. 'Shall we go, so you can sit with her? The explosion sounded so near, but we didn't know what direction it had come from, so I only wanted to know that you and your family were safe. Mrs Headley told us Arthur slept through it all, which is amazing in itself.'

'Yes, there was me thinking we were about to meet our maker, and Arthur was totally unconcerned about it. I'm thankful it didn't bother him though.' Alice walked over to the tray of crockery and began putting cups on saucers, the teaspoons clattering, as she moved things around. 'I know exactly what you mean. I had to promise them all I wouldn't leave the house, otherwise they wouldn't have gone to Russell Square, and Ma wouldn't have had a lie down.' She picked up the heavy china teapot and began pouring the hot brown liquid into the cups, momentarily looking at her friends. 'I'm glad you're all here.' She sighed as she carried on pouring the tea. 'Now I just have to wait for Freddie and Lily to return.'

18

'Morning Alice, you look as tired as I feel.' Victoria forced a laugh, as she met her friend at the corner of Bedford Avenue. 'Ready for another busy day at Foyles?'

Alice groaned as she fell into line with her friend. 'It was a long night.' She pulled her collar up, to protect her neck from the chill of the early morning breeze. A couple of dogs barked in the distance, and another joined in their conversation.

'I had trouble sleeping, when I got home from yours, but I'm so pleased we all stayed with you.'

'Yes, I didn't expect it to be nearly midnight when they got home, but at least they had good news. That's two lucky escapes they've had.'

Victoria nodded. 'From what Freddie was saying last night, I think the owner of the Bedford Hotel feels he had a luckier one.'

Alice raised her eyebrows. 'I know. What did he say? The bomb created a crater, at least four-feet deep, right outside the hotel. You don't get any closer than that, without it being your time.'

Victoria gazed down at the pavement. 'Mind you, it sounds like quite a few people died, and several were injured. It's frightening, isn't it?' Victoria thrust her hands inside her coat pocket. 'Wasn't it Southampton Row that was bombed last time?'

'Yes, and Bedford Place, there was glass and debris everywhere. That's when Lily and I ran round to Russell Square, to check that everyone was all right.'

Victoria sighed. 'It makes you wonder when it will ever end.'

They stopped dead in their tracks, as they noticed a crowd of people gathering at Oxford Circus. Cars spluttered, filling the air with exhaust fumes, while they were stuck in a queue behind the horses and carts, making their deliveries around London.

'Looks like something's going on here.' Victoria craned her neck, one way, then another, but she couldn't see past the crowd.

A woman in the crowd spoke to an older person, standing next to her. 'That's another one. I don't know 'ow many bombs were dropped on us last night, but them Germans must really want to get us.'

The older woman nodded. 'I 'ear one went off outside Charing Cross 'ospital, yer know, the one in the Strand.'

The woman shook her head. 'Now that's bad. Ain't them poor people got enough to worry about?'

Alice and Victoria stared, wide-eyed, at each other. 'Good job you weren't driving that ambulance last night, otherwise it could have been you.'

Alice glanced back at the women chatting.

'Another woman told me one went off by a tram, killing the driver and two of his passengers. It's just not safe anymore.'

The older woman nodded. 'I was told by my neighbour that the safest place was to go down into an underground station, but my old legs can't manage all them stairs. I'm too old for all that malarkey.'

Victoria tucked her arm in Alice's and guided her around the growing crowd of people. 'Come on, we need to get to work. It's going to be a long day, but at least we know the people we love are safe.' Thoughts

259

of Stephen immediately jumped into her head, but she shook them away and concentrated on looking after Alice. 'You know, Constable Peter Albright apparently has a wandering eye.' Victoria looked disdainfully at Alice. 'He won't find anyone as good as my Daisy.'

Alice chuckled. 'You sound like a real mother.'

Anger spots appeared on Victoria's cheeks. 'Well, who does he think he is?'

Stepping on to the road, Alice made room for an elderly man to pass her. His gnarled fingers pulled a cigarette from his thin lips, as he blew out a plume of smoke and nodded at her. Alice gave a faint smile, before turning back to Victoria. 'Is Daisy broken-hearted?'

Victoria shrugged. 'I haven't had a chance to talk to her about it, because she only told me last night, and then we were being bombed, so it all got forgotten. To be honest, I don't believe they've been out much together, outside of work that is, but I think she still took a shine to him.'

Alice nodded. 'It might not be anything, other than jealousy and malicious gossip.'

'Maybe, but he doesn't want to knock on my door until he decides what he wants, because my Daisy is better than that.'

The traders were already out with their loaded barrows, each vying to sell their wares, yelling to grab the attention of the passers-by. The wonderful smell of hot pea soup, mingled with the aroma of hot coffee, followed Alice and Victoria along the road. 'Ladies, how about a lovely cup of hot soup? It'll set you up for the day, or there's always a lovely brew of tea or coffee.'

The girls shook their heads.

Trams and cars trundled along Charing Cross Road, spitting and coughing out smoke. An old lady stepped forward, with a small bunch of lavender. 'It's good for drying out and leaving in your chest of drawers. It'll make your clothes smell lovely and fresh, dearie.'

'Maybe another day.' Victoria smiled as she walked past, before turning to Alice. 'I could spend all my wages on the way to work.'

Alice laughed. 'Everyone is trying to make ends meet.'

'Oh, before I forget, I'm going to the hospital straight from work, so don't wait for me.'

Alice squinted. 'Is that wise, when you're so tired?'

Victoria looked straight ahead. 'Probably not, but I want to check on Ted and speak to Mabel, or maybe I should say Aunt Mabel, about my father.'

Alice nodded. 'Just don't overdo it. None of us are very good when we're tired. It was a long evening last night, and no doubt it will be another busy day today.'

As the large white lettering of the Foyles Bookshop came into view, a boy brushed past Victoria, as he ran down the road.

He glanced over his shoulder. 'Sorry, miss.'

Victoria looked back and smiled at the boy.

He turned and just managed to swerve at the last minute, to avoid colliding with someone else.

Victoria shook her head. 'I don't know what he's running from, or to.'

They both watched Mr Leadbetter, mingling with customers outside the shop, straightening the books on the racks. He stopped, looking up and down Charing Cross Road, before turning to talk to a customer.

Alice frowned at Victoria. 'We're not late, are we?'

Victoria shrugged. 'I don't know, but after last

night, they're lucky we're here at all, especially with you being pregnant.'

Mr Leadbetter watched the girls approach and smiled in their direction. His eyes gave away the anxiety that he was doing his best to hide. 'Thank goodness you are both safe. Mrs Greenwood isn't in yet, and I've been quite worried about you all.'

'Molly is alive and well, Mr Leadbetter. At least, she was when she left us, just before midnight.' Victoria paused. 'I'm sorry if we're late, but there are more people about, looking at the damage the Germans caused last night, and we had a late night. We thought a bomb had gone off at Russell Square, where Alice's grandparents live, but it was in Southampton Row. By all accounts, it killed and injured a lot of people.'

Mr Leadbetter nodded. 'I'm just thankful you are all safe.'

Molly came rushing down the road, clutching her handbag, as it swung violently at her side. 'I'm so sorry I'm late, sir. I had trouble getting out of bed this morning.'

Mr Leadbetter pulled his fob watch out of his waistcoat pocket and pressed the gold button on the side. The lid flicked up and he stared down at it. 'You still have two minutes before you are officially late.' He laughed. 'You'd better get yourselves clocked in; I'd hate for you all to lose money. I'll stand at your counter, Mrs Leybourne, and you can take your time to get yourselves together.'

Alice flushed with colour. 'Thank you, sir, I won't be long.'

'Go on, all of you.'

They all moved forward at the same time, before Victoria stopped and turned to Mr Leadbetter. 'Sir, is Albert in?'

Mr Leadbetter smiled. 'Indeed, he is. It will take more than the Germans to stop him trying to teach the world cockney rhyming slang.'

Victoria beamed and made her way inside the shop.

★ ★ ★

Victoria held the bunch of flowers in her arms, as she walked onto Joan of Arc Ward. She no longer noticed the strong smell of disinfectant and antiseptic. A nurse smiled as she approached her. 'They look beautiful; love the colours of the roses.'

'Thank you, I bought them off a barrow, on my way in.' Victoria lowered her head into the flowers. 'The lilies smell lovely.' She sized up the bunch. 'I think I'll need a few vases to separate them into.'

The nurse led her to a cupboard and pulled out a couple of china vases covered with painted yellow daffodils. 'I always think these look too beautiful to use, but after the bombings, I think we could all do with cheering up.'

'Nurse.'

Victoria peered over her shoulder, before looking back at the nurse. 'Thank you. I'll get them in water and then I can do what's ever needed to help.'

'Nurse.'

The nurse nodded and walked over to the patient.

Victoria finished putting the flowers in water, hoping that would revive the blooms. She picked up the vases, placing them on windowsills, on each side of the ward. Glancing around, there was no sign of Mabel so any conversation about her parents would have to wait. The ward seemed quite subdued, after

263

the laughter of the previous visits. She walked along, nodding to patients as she went. Victoria stopped at bed twenty-five. Her heart lurched in her chest. Ted was still in the same position he had been in since she had first discovered him. 'Good evening, Corporal Marsden.'

As always, silence stood between them.

'I think I probably owe you an apology, for being so hard on you.'

Ted turned his head in her direction. 'Why?' He paused. 'Do you feel sorry for me?'

It was Victoria's turn to be silent, as she searched for words.

'Or is it because you had a taste of it last night?'

All the love Victoria felt for him was washed away by the anger that surged through her veins. 'No, and I'll have you know it's not the first time. I know we haven't seen the horrendous things you have, but we are going through it in a different way, worrying about whether our men are safe, looking out for loved ones, hoping they will come home safe and sound, even though we know they won't be the same person anymore. Let alone all the women that have taken on the men's work, even though most of them only thought we were good enough for the kitchen and the bedroom before the war, so don't belittle what's happening here.'

Ted lowered his voice, as he returned to his usual position. 'That told me.'

'I'm sorry, but you seem to bring out the worst in me.'

'Huh, no kidding.' Ted's lips lifted in the corners for a moment.

'I obviously need to work on my bedside manner.

I was told to be careful how I spoke to you, because you were depressed, which I do understand, but you have to try and help yourself a little. I'm not saying all the problems will magically disappear, but you could be kind to yourself, and those around you. You do know that by lying here and not talking to anyone, you're only punishing yourself, don't you? Everyone just avoids you, when you could be part of the group that are laughing and joking, about some daft things I grant you, but laughter is the best cure. You should try it, because whatever has happened to you isn't going away. You just have to learn to live with it.'

Ted growled. 'That's easy for you to say.'

Victoria sighed and straightened his bedding. 'It's always easier to say than do, but you have to understand that you can't do it on your own. You need family and friends, or some kind soul who is happy to help when you need it.'

Ted stayed silent.

Victoria could feel her heart pounding in her chest. 'You should try talking about what's going on inside your head.' She took a step away from the bed. 'Trust me, I know about feeling low. I was lucky enough to have good friends that have helped me to help myself, but you're not doing yourself any favours lying in that dark hole . . . '

'Have you finished?'

Victoria nodded, then remembered he couldn't see her. 'I'm sorry. I didn't mean to go on, but in my clumsy way, I'm trying to help you. I'll leave you in peace from now on.'

'I have no one, Miss Know-it-all.'

'Everyone has someone,' Victoria whispered. 'It's about whether you choose to confide in them or not.'

Ted's lips straightened and a pulse could be seen throbbing in his neck. 'There was once but I blew it and now . . . well, now it's just too late.'

'It's never too late. What about your family, or someone who wrote to you while you were away?' Victoria held her breath, as the tension grew between them.

'There's no one.'

Victoria felt the tears pricking at her eyes, as her failure and exhaustion engulfed her. She needed to escape, before she made a complete fool of herself. Ted didn't want or need her. She looked around for Mabel, but she was nowhere to be seen. She stopped a nurse who was carrying a bundle of bandages. 'I'm sorry, I won't keep you, but I'm looking for Nurse Atkins. Is she not in today?'

The nurse looked around her. 'I'm sure she was in earlier.' She paused, as she looked from bed to bed. 'Oh no, I remember someone said she'd received bad news about her brother, so has gone back to have a lie down.'

Victoria slowly nodded as she whispered, 'Thank you.'

'Are you all right?' The nurse grabbed a bandage, as it nearly slipped over her arm.

Victoria nodded. Her mind was in a whirlwind. Was the bad news about John? *No, he's not Mabel's brother, he's yours, well, maybe.* So as well as her own father, Mabel must have another brother. Her mind searched to remember all the paperwork she had found. If only she had read her mother's diary, but that had seemed too intrusive at the time.

The nurse watched Victoria for a few seconds, then carried on to the end of the ward, trying to keep the bandages close to her body.

Victoria paced along the street towards the butcher's and saw Daisy queuing outside. They had been out of the house for hours, but she was thankful for the half a loaf she had managed to get.

Daisy frowned as she looked up and down the street. Victoria waved.

Daisy smiled and ran towards her. 'I persuaded the butcher to give me six sausages, and that took some doing, I can tell you.'

Victoria shook her head. 'Perhaps we should marry a butcher and a baker; none of them look like they're starving, and their prices have shot up. I got half a loaf; not much, but if we're careful, it'll last a couple of days.'

Daisy looped her hand under Victoria's arm. 'Are you all right? You've been preoccupied lately. Is there anything you want to share?'

'No, at least not yet, I'm more interested in you and Constable Albright.'

Daisy laughed. 'There's nothing to tell. We didn't really go out together, other than with work, so he is free to do what he wants.'

'Hmm, stupid man, he won't find anyone better than you.'

'Don't be hard on him. We still get on very well, and I'd like it to stay that way.'

Victoria eyed her. 'Are you soft on him then? I don't want you getting hurt.'

Daisy squeezed Victoria's arm, under the thick woollen coat. 'Don't worry about me, I'm a grown-up now.'

Victoria laughed. 'That doesn't stop me worrying

or wanting to protect you.'

Daisy pulled on Victoria's arm. 'Hold on, that's Mr Wilson's barrow and I've been meaning to catch up with him. Do you mind if we just stop for a moment?'

Victoria shook her head.

They walked over towards Mr Wilson, standing back as he took some coins from a customer.

'Thank you, don't forget we're 'ere every day.'

The customer nodded, before walking away.

'Mr Wilson.'

Mr Wilson beamed. 'Daisy. 'Ello girl, what can I do for you?'

'I've been meaning to come and see you. You may not remember, it was a few weeks ago, maybe months, but I wanted to find out whether the lad that stole the fruit came back, to at least apologise to you. We came across him, but we were then told to take cover because we were about to be bombed, so Lily and I ended up in the basement of Foyles Bookshop instead.'

'That's all right. Yer shouldn't worry yerself over a bit of fruit, not with everything else that's going on.'

Daisy watched Victoria peering at the fruit and vegetables on the barrow, before looking back at Mr Wilson. 'That's very kind of you to say so, but I'd like to know if he kept his word, because we were bringing him back to you, before we were all told to take cover. He was telling us about his sick mother, but I never got an address off him.'

Mr Wilson chuckled. 'Yer needn't 'ave been worrying yerself all this time. The young lad did come back to see me.' Mr Wilson picked up some mud-covered potatoes and placed them in a metal bowl. 'He was very sorry and offered to work off the price, because he 'ad no money. Well, I'm a real softie, though don't tell anyone cos I 'ave an image to protect.' He roared with laughter. 'Anyway, I gave 'im a job and I tell yer what, 'e's a great little worker.' He turned his attention to Victoria. 'Is this young lady wiv you?'

Daisy smiled. 'Yes, it looks like she's eyeing up your vegetables.'

Mr Wilson moved across to Victoria. ''Ere, give us yer bag and I'll put these potatoes in it, if yer don't mind a bit of dirt, that is?'

Victoria looked around, before she realised he was talking to her. 'How much are they?'

'Yer can 'ave 'em on me, yer look like yer need feeding up. I'll even chuck in a couple of carrots.' He picked up the orange vegetables. 'They ain't up to much, so don't 'ang about cooking 'em.'

'No, Mr Wilson, I can't let you do that.' Daisy moved nearer. 'It's your living that you're giving away.'

'Aww, a few spuds ain't gonna make any difference.'

Victoria glanced at Daisy, unsure what to do.

Daisy nodded.

Victoria handed over her shopping bag to Mr Wilson, who kept adding two of everything on his stall.

Daisy shook her head. 'I don't mean to sound ungrateful, but don't forget we have to carry that bag.'

Mr Wilson laughed. 'I 'ad forgotten, but it's just my way of saying thank you for checking up on me.'

It was Daisy's turn to laugh. 'There's no need to thank me, I wanted to see if I was right to have had faith in the lad.' She hesitated for a moment. 'Is his mother well now?'

Victoria sensed her sister was holding her breath, so she prayed it would be so.

'Yes, she is.' Mr Wilson offered the bag, over the top of the stall. 'So yer can stop yer worrying.'

Daisy gasped. 'Thank goodness.' She grabbed the bag handles. 'My, we might have to share the load here, Victoria. Thanks again, Mr Wilson.'

The girls took a handle each and proceeded to walk along Oxford Street. The cars were edging along the road. People moved in and out of shops, some were queuing outside, for food. Arguments were breaking out, as someone tried to jump the queue. The shortages were taking a hold.

Victoria wondered how much longer the traders would have enough to sell on their barrows. London wouldn't be the same without them shouting out every day.

Victoria sighed. 'There's something I haven't told you.'

Daisy raised her eyebrows, as she looked over at her sister. 'Wait, I need to change hands.' They put the bag down and swapped sides, before picking it up again. 'What is it? Should I be worried? Is it Stephen?'

Victoria stared hard at the ground in front of her. They both stepped forward. 'It's nothing for you to worry about.' She sighed. 'Ted is a patient at Endell Street Hospital.'

Daisy stared at her sister. Her mouth opened, and then closed again.

'You don't have to say anything, in fact there's nothing to say.' Victoria shook her head. 'At the moment, he can't see, but I don't know whether that's permanent or not.' Pain flicked across her face. 'But he's claiming he has no one in his life who can look after him, family or otherwise.'

They both stopped outside their house, dropping the bag on the footpath. Victoria stared at the front door, wondering why her life was in such a mess.

Without a word, Daisy pulled the string through the letterbox, until a key was revealed. 'Come inside,' Daisy commanded her sister.

Victoria did as she was told. She bent down to pick up a letter that was sitting on the hall mat.

'After all the letters and parcels you've sent him.' Daisy pushed the door closed. 'My God, how many times does that man have to hurt you? You are worth ten of him?'

'He doesn't mean to hurt me.' Victoria gave a humourless laugh. 'He doesn't know it's me he's talking to. He's depressed.' She turned the envelope over in her hand. It was addressed to their father. Who could be writing to him, after all these years?

19

Victoria clutched her father's letter in her hand. Red blotches appeared on her cheeks. She screwed the letter up for the second time that day. She marched along Bloomsbury Street, her mind in a whirl. What had the letter said? She didn't need to read it again. It was cold, and to the point.

Dear David,

I regret to inform you that I have received a telegram to say your brother, Tom, has died on the front line. Apparently, he died a hero.

Yours sincerely,

Mr Herbert Appleton

She had no idea about this man, who was obviously her grandfather, or why he was writing now, after all these years, but she had examined the envelope closely and noticed the Brighton postmark. Mabel had told her John was in Brighton. Maybe he was just trying to do the right thing, but was it really the way to tell someone their brother had died? Maybe that's why her parents had kept them away from them. The photograph jumped into her mind, of her parents by the seafront. Had that been taken at Brighton? Her mind just kept going round and round, but she was determined to get to the bottom of it once and for all.

Victoria stood at the pavement's edge, fidgeting and ready to run across New Oxford Street. She undid the black buttons and pulled her coat apart, as heat covered her body. The chill of the October early evening was lost on her, as she fanned her face with her hand. Victoria took a couple of deep breaths, trying to calm herself, but coughed as exhaust fumes hit the back of her throat. Deciding not to wait, she stepped out into the road. Car horns sounded and people shouted at her, but she kept going, waving at the car and tram drivers. She stormed along Shaftesbury Avenue until she reached Endell Street, where she stopped and glared up at the big metal gates at the front of the hospital. Mabel held the key to helping her sort it all out and Victoria was determined that she was going to get to the bottom of this so-called family of her father's. She walked through the open gates and stood by the doors, trying to decide whether to go in or go back home again, and what to tell Mabel? Should she tell her about the money and the fancy clothes?

'Hello, Victoria, are you going in to see Corporal Marsden?'

Victoria jumped at the sound of Mabel's voice. She turned to see her walking towards her. Victoria pulled her shoulders back and stuck out her chin. 'No.' Victoria hesitated before continuing. 'No, I've come to see you.'

Mabel looked amazed. 'Me?'

'Yes. I understand you had bad news about your brother yesterday and I wanted to pass on my condolences.' Victoria closed her eyes for a second.

Mabel stared at her. 'And?'

Victoria's eyes shot open. 'And . . . er . . . 'She pulled the letter from her coat pocket. 'My father received

273

this today.' She quietly waited for Mabel to reply, but there was nothing but silence for a few minutes.

Mabel stared at her. 'Am I supposed to know what that is?'

Victoria could feel the rage bubbling inside her. 'It's a short, cold letter from his father, I'm assuming your father, telling him his brother is dead.'

Mabel's colour drained away. 'Where is your father? I know he probably won't want to speak to any of us, but he needs to know about John. I just can't believe he would abandon his son for, what, seven years? I'm sorry, but it's disgraceful and I can only blame your mother, because my brother would never have willingly done that.'

The hospital door swung open and two nurses came out, chatting to each other.

Victoria and Mabel both nodded and stepped aside, to let them pass.

'My mother was one of the kindest people I know, and there was no way she would have kept my father from seeing a child. I don't understand why you think she was capable of such a thing?'

'Was? You said was.'

Victoria stayed silent as the tears threatened to spill over.

Mabel took a deep breath. 'Look, Victoria, maybe we should start again. I never knew your last name was Appleton, but it does explain why you've always looked familiar to me.'

Victoria stayed silent, gripping her hands together.

Mabel stared at the young women standing in front of her. 'I came to Percy Street several years ago, looking for my brother. I knocked on the door and waited for several minutes. I knocked many times, but there

274

was no answer.' Mabel paused, before giving a big sigh. 'A neighbour came out and told me that Mr and Mrs Appleton were not around anymore. Thinking about it now, it was you I saw walking towards me that day. That's probably why you've always looked familiar but I hadn't seen you for years and was only thinking about finding my brother.'

Victoria mumbled. 'I don't remember you.'

'No, well, I didn't wait around.' Mabel stared down at the ground. 'There was no point.' She looked up again, as colour flushed her cheeks. 'I didn't know where to go from there and Sid told me to just leave well alone. After all, my brother knew where his parents and his son lived, if he wanted to get in touch.' Her eyes sparked with defiance, waiting for Victoria to challenge her. 'I must admit, Sid was right about that.'

Victoria wrapped her arms around her waist. 'So, I know they live in Brighton, but I don't know the address. Can you give it to me?'

Mabel shrugged. 'Your father has it, or isn't he speaking to you either? I must admit, he was always the big brother I adored and wanted to live up to, but now I'm not so sure. Why would anyone want to be as stubborn as he's been over the last few years?'

Victoria pulled herself upright. 'He hasn't been being stubborn —'

'What? I don't know how you can say that, when he's ignored his son, your brother. His son is —'

'My parents are dead. They died seven years ago.'

* * *

275

Alice and Molly stared at Victoria's back, as they stood in the queue to clock into work. She had looked ashen and maudlin when she came in, just as she did a few years ago.

Molly tilted her head at Alice and lowered her tone. 'Go on, she'll take it from you, whereas I'll just get a tongue lashing.'

Alice tightened her lips. 'No.'

Victoria turned to face them. 'What are you two whispering about?' She raised her eyebrows.

Alice quickly shook her head. 'Nothing very important.'

Molly raised her eyebrows. 'I wanted Alice to talk to you, find out what's wrong. We haven't seen you look this pale for a while.'

'Really.' Victoria turned back to face the front. The queue slowly shuffled forward. The dinging of the clock rang out every couple of seconds, as each member of staff inserted their card and pulled it out again. Victoria followed suit, before stepping aside to allow Molly to do the same. 'If you must know, I had an argument with Mabel. She wanted to see my mother and father, and I'm afraid I left her reeling from the fact that they are no longer here, but in my defence, she was being horrid about them.'

Alice looked up from the clock. 'But if she didn't know they were . . . er . . . dead, she would think bad things about them, wouldn't she?'

Victoria looked shame-faced. 'I suppose . . . but I couldn't just let her moan about them.'

'Miss Appleton.' Mr Leadbetter stood in the door-way, his stern face giving nothing away. 'There's someone asking to see you urgently.'

Victoria grabbed the girls' arms, as fear and panic

snatched away her breath. The three of them didn't move. Colour drained from Molly's face. Victoria gave Alice a fearful look. She looked deathly. Victoria knew they were all thinking the same thing: Stephen.

Mr Leadbetter beckoned Victoria to come forward. 'Come.'

The three of them automatically stepped forward as one.

Molly squeezed Victoria's hand. 'Do you want us to come with you?'

Victoria nodded. 'Is that all right, Mr Leadbetter?'

He shook his head and tightened his lips. 'I wouldn't have expected anything else from the three of you.' He turned and walked back into the shop.

Victoria took a deep breath, causing a weight to sit heavily on her chest. She turned and looked at her friends, determined not to cry, especially here in the bookshop. She lifted her chin; after all, she was a manager now. 'Well, let's get this over and done with.'

The three of them walked slowly into the bookshop. People were milling around, looking at the shelves of books, some reading where they stood. Victoria wanted to laugh when she saw a lady smelling a novel. They should offer her a job.

'Sorry, girls.' Albert brushed past them, with an armful of books. 'No one's bin down to collect the mountain of books I've got down there, and I've got to make room for the next lot.'

Alice forced a smile. 'Leave them on my counter, Albert, and I'll sort them out.'

Victoria tried to gather herself together, reminding herself of the message she had given to Ted at the hospital. Life goes on, regardless. 'Sorry, Albert, standards are slipping. I'll get someone to come down

277

for them. I certainly don't want you carrying them up and down stairs.'

Albert looked at Victoria for the first time; he adjusted his hold on the books. 'Yer don't look too good this morning. Is there anyfink I can do for yer?'

Victoria's throat tightened. 'No, thank you, I'll be all right. Now go and put those books down, before you do yourself some damage.'

A woman's voice called out. 'Victoria.'

Victoria jerked round. She knew that voice. Mabel stood in front of her. The dark lines under her red, bloodshot eyes emphasised her pale skin. She looked different out of her nurse's uniform. Her black coat was undone and merged with her plain black, high necked dress, which she wore longer than Victoria and the girls normally did. 'Mabel? I thought it was . . . '

'Hello, Mabel, I'm Molly, one of Victoria's close friends and I believe you've already met Alice.'

Mabel gave them both a slight nod, but only took her eyes off Victoria for a couple of seconds. 'Victoria, you look like you've slept as badly as I have. We need to sit down and talk.'

Molly squinted at Mabel and took a step closer to Victoria.

Victoria hesitated, wondering if she should confess that it was Ted who had kept her awake all night. Should she have been honest and told him who she was? Would he have been kinder to her, if he'd known? Was he really still the man of her dreams, or had she been holding a candle for all those years, for someone who never really existed, except in her head? The questions had kept coming all night. She had tossed and turned. There were no tears, just endless questions with no answers.

Mabel's voice broke through her turmoil. 'Victoria, please.'

'I can't do it now, I'm at work.' Victoria knew she had to take the olive branch being offered, if she was ever going to put all the uncertainty behind her.

As relief spread across her face, Mabel gave a faint smile. 'The thing is, I'm going to Brighton this morning and I wondered if you would like to come with me, to meet your grandparents and brother.'

Victoria's eyes widened, as she realised this was the day she could meet her father's family, her family. Should she go? Should Daisy go with them? Her excitement was quickly chased away. Victoria wrung her hands in front of her. Fear trampled down her back. She could feel the heat filling her face. 'Even if I wanted to, I can't just leave work.'

Molly glanced from Mabel to Victoria. 'You could always tell Mr Leadbetter you don't feel well.'

Alice nodded. 'Or tell him there's a family problem. Neither is too far from the truth.'

Victoria looked at her friends, making no attempt to hide the fear that had a tight grip on her insides. Her voice was barely a whisper. 'I always thought that, when I found anything out, we would be together.'

Alice wrapped her arm around her friend's shoulders and pulled her close. She pulled away and looked Mabel squarely in the eye. 'Will you look after Victoria? She's been through a lot in her young life, much more than she should have.'

'Of course I will. She's family.'

Molly nodded. 'You need to know we'll not stand by and let you, or anyone else, family or not, hurt Victoria.'

Mabel nodded. 'She's lucky to have you both as

279

friends.'

Victoria gave a faint smile. 'They are more than friends, Mabel. They are like sisters to me.'

* * *

Mabel's footsteps slowed as she stared out to where Brighton's grey, murky sky met the dark uninviting sea. The foam-crested waves crashed on to the beach, leaving seaweed in their wake, the foam fading as it quickly rolled back to where it had come from. There was no gentleness today, like there was when the blue sky merged with the coastline in the distance, with the sun blazing down. It had been a long time since she had paddled in the calm waters, or enjoyed watching the sea rippling onto the pebbles that formed the beach. There were no children squealing as they chased the waves or gulls perching, ready to swoop on picnics.

Mabel tightened the scarf around her neck and tugged her collar a little higher. She stopped walking and kept her eyes forward. 'I'm so sorry I... we didn't know about David and Margaret.' She let her gaze look at Victoria's tense features, as she also stared out to sea. 'The last time I saw my brother, he and Margaret were looking at houses before going back to London to talk to you, Daisy and Stephen about moving to Brighton so John could live with you again. He was so excited about having all his children together again, but the family never heard from them again. It never occurred to us they had died in the train derailment at Stoats Nest, as we thought they were getting an earlier train.' Mabel sighed. 'I expect they walked along the beach first. David loved the fresh sea air, even in January. When he had things to think about, it was always where he could be found.' She shook her head. 'It never occurred to us that he was on that train.'

Victoria could feel the tears pricking at her eyes. The wind grabbed her scarf, swirling it around her face. She grabbed the end and tucked it inside her coat. 'Why did you think he hadn't come back to see John? After all, you said yourself that you looked up to him and you couldn't believe he would ignore any child of his?'

'If I'm to be honest, I thought it was probably something to do with you. If I remember rightly, you were just sixteen the last time I saw him. I assumed life had got difficult for your parents in some way.'

Victoria stood in silence for a moment. 'Is that why we didn't know about John before now, because I was difficult to be around?'

Mabel pulled her hand out of her coat pocket and thrust it under Victoria's arm, pulling her nearer. 'No, that was definitely not the case.' Mabel gazed out to sea for a few minutes, before sighing. 'I believe David wanted to keep you away from my father, because he's such an angry man. I remember him locking you in the basement for answering him back. I'm not sure how old you were at the time but you were only young.'

Victoria's brows drew together and her hand shot up to cover her mouth as she gasped.

'Your father thought you were outside playing and he was furious when he found out. He said he wouldn't bring any of you to visit again.'

Victoria shook her head. 'But why would he do that to a child? I don't understand.'

281

Mabel grunted. 'I've been asking questions like that all my life. The only answer I have managed to come up with is he comes from a different time.' She paused, staring at the water crashing on to the pebbles on the beach. 'His own father was very strict; my mother says he ruled with an iron fist. I think he wanted him to become a solicitor, or something, but my father didn't achieve it. In fact, I believe he had several jobs but none of them lived up to his father's expectations. Consequently, his life was made a misery. Mind you, I'm not sure that's an excuse for all that he's done, but I suppose he knows no different.' She sighed. 'That's the only reason I have been able to come up with. I don't know much about his life because he never talks about it.'

Victoria tightened her lips for a moment. 'It all sounds quite sad, doesn't it?'

Mabel glanced over at Victoria. 'It does but it doesn't take away from the fact he has a malicious tongue, which has done a lot of damage to the family over the years. There's a reason why we all left as soon as we were able to. My mother won't hear a bad word said about him and she does her best to protect John from him, but she's getting older and I think the roles have reversed.'

Victoria nodded. 'She must really love him then.'

Laughter erupted from Mabel. 'If she does, I truly don't understand it.'

'But as you say they come from different times.' Victoria pursed her lips. 'Maybe she knows why he's the way he is and doesn't think you'd all understand or she just wants to keep his secrets for him.'

Mabel laughed. 'And Tom always said I was the one that saw good in everyone.'

'Trust me when I say without my friends I don't think I would have survived my parents dying.'

Mabel nodded. 'John is quite ill now, I think his asthma has developed into something more but he won't go to the doctor so I'm not sure how much longer he will be able to cope with my father.' She paused, guilt oozing from her. 'When Sid died I should have come home again, to protect them more, but I acted selfishly. I just couldn't face it.'

Victoria felt the cold in her heart melt a little. They had all been through so much. 'Don't punish yourself. I'm here now and, hopefully, I'll be able to bring Daisy and Stephen down to meet John and our grandparents.' Victoria let her gaze wander up the beach. 'I can understand why my father liked to come here to think; there's something about it that brings clarity.'

Mabel laughed. 'You are definitely your father's daughter. That's exactly what he would have said.'

'That makes me very happy. I found a photo at home, with my parents holding a baby. I always thought it was Stephen, but they were in front of the sea, so now, I assume it was John.'

Mabel nodded. 'Without seeing the photograph, I can't be certain, but you're probably right. You know, they never wanted to leave John, it broke their hearts but the sea air was good for him.' She paused. 'You know one of them used to visit every week, mostly David.'

Victoria let out a sigh. 'We always thought he was at work all the time. Daisy and I, with the help of my friends, have been trying to piece everything together over the last few months, but we didn't know where the photograph was taken, or why John was not living in London.'

Mabel took a deep breath. 'It's a shame you didn't go through your parents' things seven years ago, or that I didn't persevere with knocking on your front door. There's been a lot of wasted time, that can never be given back to us all.'

They stood in silence.

'You say John may not be around for much longer; is he in hospital?'

'No, he probably should be, but he won't go, and my father won't pay.'

Victoria turned to face Mabel. 'I found a box of money when I was going through my parents' things. Do you think that was what they were saving for?'

Mabel nodded. 'Quite possibly, or the house they wanted to buy down here.'

Victoria frowned. 'Then that's what it shall be used for. They would want him to get the best possible care they could give him.' She paused. 'I need to speak to him.'

Mabel smiled at her newfound niece. 'You are so like your father. He would be proud of you, I'm sure.'

Colour flooded Victoria's cheeks. 'I don't know about that, but it's important I do what I can to help John. I know they would want me to do that, as indeed would my brother and sister.' She looked across the road at the houses facing the beach, all in different states of repair. 'Do they live far from here?'

'No, but I can't pretend I'm not a little nervous about this.' Mabel hesitated. 'I can't promise my father won't be at home. I didn't think this through when I came to Foyles this morning.'

Victoria squinted, as she looked up the road. 'Let's get it over and done with.' Her mouth felt dry. She licked her lips, removing the salty residue that the

284

wind had carried in from the sea.

They walked along the road in silence. Victoria could hear and feel her heart pounding in her chest. Her palms felt damp inside her coat pockets.

Mabel pulled Victoria to a standstill. 'This is it.'

They stood there for a few seconds.

Victoria stared up at the imposing house. Her throat felt tight. Panic took hold, and she was fighting for breath.

Mabel watched Victoria's conflict run across her pale features. 'Are you all right? Are you sure you want to do this?'

Victoria nodded. 'I can do this, I know I can.'

Mabel knocked on the door. 'I don't have a key. My father insisted I handed it back, when I left home.'

The door opened a little, to reveal a petite, grey-haired lady peering out at them both. Her face lit up. 'Mabel, how wonderful.' She stepped back, to allow them to enter into the hall.

Mabel stepped through the doorway. 'Hello, Ma, it's freezing out there.' She wrapped her arms around her mother and kissed her cheeks. 'How's John?'

Mabel's mother lowered her eyes. 'He's not good, he's very despondent.' She looked up and stared at Victoria.

'Sorry, Ma, this is — '

'Victoria, I'd know that face anywhere.' She stepped forward and wrapped her arms around Victoria. 'It's so wonderful to have you in my home. David, my son, your father, used to send me photographs of the three of you, but then they just stopped, which I didn't understand.'

Mabel stood behind her mother. 'Ma, let the poor girl get through the door.'

Beatrice giggled. 'Sorry, come in and I'll shut the front door.'

'What's all the commotion out there?'

At the sound of the deep voice, Victoria saw the two women stiffen.

'What's going on here?' An elderly man, dressed in a black three-piece suit, stood between them and the sitting room.

'Grandma, are you all right?'

Victoria's gaze immediately shifted to the direction of the feeble male voice. She looked at Mabel. 'Is that John?'

Before Mabel could answer, her father stepped forward and eyed her up and down. 'So, looking at you, I take it you're my eldest son's daughter.' He frowned and his face contorted with rage. 'Mabel had no business bringing you here, and you are not welcome, so please leave.'

There was no surprise on Mabel's face, as she addressed her father. 'Pa, John and Victoria have a right to meet each other. They are brother and sister.'

'Not under my roof, they don't. That time has long passed.' He strode to the front door and pulled it open. The wind immediately rushed in, filling every nook and cranny. 'You haven't bothered with him or us for years and your parents certainly haven't. Today, you turn up, uninvited, as if you have a right to be here. Now get out.'

Victoria stood rigid, tension etched on her face. 'But I — '

'I'm not interested in your excuses.' Herbert's knuckles whitened as he gripped the door handle. 'I've heard it all before, from your father.'

Mabel's hands were clenched tight, in front of

her. 'Pa — '

'Herbert,' Beatrice stepped forward. 'Let her stay, please.'

Herbert scowled at Victoria. 'Get out, now.'

Mabel's face was red with anger. 'Pa — '

'Leave it, Mabel. At least I now know why my father didn't bring me, or my sister and brother to Brighton anymore.' Victoria stepped forward and hugged her grandmother. Her vision became blurry. 'Maybe there will be another time.'

She turned towards Mabel, to thank her for everything, but her grandfather grabbed her arm and steered her towards the door. 'Get out and never come back. I'm surprised your father allowed you to come.' He pushed Victoria out, slamming the door shut.

'Pa, David and Margaret are dead.'

Mabel's voice carried through the wooden door. Victoria stood there for a moment, listening for voices, but there was nothing. She lifted her hand to knock on the door, but then thought better of it. She turned to walk away, holding back her tears until she was out of sight.

20

'Victoria.'

Anger surged through Victoria as she marched along Oxford Street, not seeing the usual traders, smiling at people walking by, while shouting out to sell their wares.

'Victoria.'

Something told Victoria she should have stayed and had the argument with her grandfather. After all, John was her brother, and Mabel had said he didn't have very long. She was sure she would regret that. She needed to speak to Daisy; after all, John was her brother too. Victoria sighed. She should've taken Daisy with her, but she was stubborn and hadn't stopped to think.

'Get your papers 'ere, just one penny,' a young boy yelled out, from a shop doorway. 'Read 'ow we're winning the war. Give me a penny an I'll give yer a paper. Come on ladies and gents, don't make me carry these papers all day. They're blooming heavy.'

Victoria stopped and watched the boy hand out a few newspapers, before taking the pennies offered. He looked frozen, in his ankle length trousers and scuffed out shoes. His jacket was open; it didn't look like it would meet in the middle. There were always people worse off than her. She carried on down Oxford Street. It was just like any other day.

The boy shouted out again, his voice following her down the street. 'Get yer news 'ere. Not only 'as Passchendale and Palestine been won, but the tanks are moving in too.'

Victoria wondered where Stephen was. She hadn't heard from him for a few weeks. Had he been killed at Passchendale? She shook her head, trying to shake away the devil sitting on her shoulder. *No, I'm not listening. He's all right. I know he is. I am not going to lose my faith; I'm not, I'm not.*

Victoria thought about the hospital steam train that had pulled into Victoria station the same time as hers. The two trains had filled the air with grey smoke. She wanted to stay and see if Stephen was among the injured, but she hadn't wanted to stare, so with her head down, Victoria had made her way to the end of the platform, wondering what she should do about John and Ted. She shook her head, wondering why life had to be so difficult. Was she the reason? Had she created all these problems?

'Victoria.'

Victoria turned to look in the direction of the woman's voice, searching the faces of the shoppers milling around.

Daisy's smile quickly faded when she saw her sister's grey pallor. 'Thank goodness. Your hearing must be going, I've been calling you for ages. I thought you were working at Foyles today.'

Victoria nodded. 'I was, but it's a long story.'

Daisy tucked her hand under her sister's arm. 'I have all the time in the world. Oh my goodness, you didn't get the sack, did you?'

Victoria grimaced. 'No, it's much worse than that.'

Daisy frowned. 'It can't be as bad as you think.' She squeezed her sister's arm, under the soft, thick wool of the winter coat. 'Let's go home and make a pot of tea, things always look better when you've had a cuppa.'

They both turned into Rathbone Place and headed towards Percy Street.

'Tell me, what is it?' Daisy glanced across at Victoria. 'It must be quite big, for you to miss a day at Foyles.'

Victoria shook her head. 'I've been foolish, that's all.'

Daisy frowned. 'Whatever it is has kept you occupied all the way along Oxford Street, because I kept calling you, and you didn't so much as look round. Come on, tell me. Is it Stephen or Ted?'

Victoria shook her head, again before taking a deep breath. 'I went to Brighton.'

'Brighton?' Daisy's voice went up an octave. 'Whatever for, especially in this weather, it's November. Why would anyone go to Brighton, when it's so cold?'

Victoria gave a faint sneer at her own words being repeated back from when her parents went in January, seven years ago, and never came home again. 'Mabel came to find me in Foyles this morning, and asked me to go with her to Brighton.' She gave Daisy a sideways glance, as they turned right, into Percy Street. 'The intention was to meet John, not that he knew I was coming.' She sighed. 'But it never happened.'

Daisy pulled the string through the letterbox and grabbed the key on the end of it. 'I don't know why you're bothering with it all. If Ma and Pa had wanted us to know, they would have told us when we were growing up, but they didn't. We should respect their reasons, whatever they were.'

'Don't you want to meet John?' Disbelief shone from Victoria's eyes. 'Doesn't it bother you that we have a brother we didn't know we had?'

Daisy turned to look at Victoria. 'No, not really. Everyone has their secrets, and he's no doubt had quite a good life in Brighton, otherwise we would have heard all about it before. It's not like they didn't know where we lived, is it?' She unbuttoned her coat and slipped her arms out of the sleeves. 'No one cared when Ma and Pa died. I don't remember anyone rushing to help us then. It was you that kept us all together. I know there were days when you didn't eat, so we could. I know you had a big argument with Alice, when she tried to help us.'

Victoria stepped inside and let the wind slam the door shut behind her. 'What makes you think you know so much?'

Daisy hung her coat on the peg, before glancing in her direction. 'Lily told me.' She gave a little giggle. 'That's how she got me to sign up for the police. She sold it on the grounds of more money and no domestic service.'

Victoria shook her head, before speaking in a low tone. 'I thought you would want the same things as I do, I thought you would want to make John part of our family. He's your brother.'

Daisy's face suddenly contorted with rage. 'Not if it means losing my sister to another family.' She turned and fled from the room. Her footsteps thudded on the stairs, each step creaking its objection.

Victoria stood rooted to the spot. 'What? I don't understand what just happened here.' She slowly lowered herself onto a chair.

The bedroom door thudded shut. Daisy's words repeated themselves in Victoria's mind, over and over again. So much for protecting her brother and sister. The burdens of the people she cared about

291

caved in on her. She covered her face with her hands and sobbed.

* * *

Victoria had dragged herself to Endell Street Hospital. She stood in the middle of Joan of Arc Ward and looked around her, wondering what she was doing there. She should have been at home talking to Daisy, but she had stayed locked in her room and wasn't answering the door. Victoria's eyes were bloodshot and sore from crying, and she hoped no one would ask her if she was all right. The lights were already on in the hospital, casting their shadows on the walls. The lighter summer evenings had long gone. There was no sign of Mabel, so did that mean something had happened to John? Had Mabel argued with her parents, or was she avoiding her because she was embarrassed by the whole situation? Victoria watched a nurse bending over a patient, changing a dressing. She was tempted to go over and ask after Mabel, but it could just be her day off. She pushed the wooden trolley, the wheels squeaking along the floor, towards the end of the next bed. 'I have some fresh water for you.' She put the full jug and clean glass on the bedside table.

The man looked up from his newspaper. 'Thank you.'

Victoria nodded and returned to the trolley. She noticed that some of the patients she had come to recognise were no longer on the ward. Corporal Peters was one of them. The laughter had temporarily left the ward, being replaced by the groans of fear and pain.

292

She had left Ted's water jug until the end. 'Good evening, Corporal Marsden.' A smile pulled at the corners of her mouth. 'I'm so pleased to see you out of bed. How are you feeling today?'

Ted moved his head in the direction of her voice. 'There's no change. I'm just sitting, instead of lying.' He gave a little smile. 'But you don't sound your usually fiery self. What's happened?'

'Nothing, it's just tiredness.' Victoria hesitated, before continuing. 'To you, it might be just sitting instead of lying, but to me, it's a major step forward.'

Ted laughed. 'How do you know I haven't just got out of bed to stop you from nagging me?'

Victoria chuckled. 'It doesn't matter why you got out of bed; you did, and that is all that I care about.' She perched on the edge of the bed. 'The next few steps will be getting you to feed yourself and mix with other patients, which will involve moving around the ward.'

Ted groaned. 'Blimey, there's no end to it. I thought you'd be pleased to see me out of bed, and then you'd stop going on at me.'

Victoria shook her head, but then remembered he couldn't see her. 'I want you to be prepared for when you have to leave the hospital.' She hesitated again, before continuing. 'I spoke to one of the nurses, and the doctors don't think you'll be permanently blind, but you'll have limited vision, so you won't be going back to the frontline.'

Ted's mouth straightened. 'I know. They told me that a couple of weeks ago, but they weren't sure, one way or the other.'

Victoria frowned. 'I thought I was giving you good news.'

Ted shook his head. 'It doesn't change anything, if I can't work.'

'You don't know that yet. You need to wait and see what vision you get back.'

Ted sat quietly for a couple of minutes.

Victoria clenched her hands in her lap, wondering if she had any words of wisdom to impart.

'You shouldn't waste your time on me; I'm not a very nice person.'

'It doesn't matter to me whether you're a nice person or not. I'm here to do what I can to help, and if nagging works, then so be it. Everyone has been through a lot since this so-called Great War started, even us at home.'

'I know, I'm sorry.' Ted paused. 'That's what I mean, I'm a mean person, and it's not the war that's made me like that, although it probably hasn't helped.'

Victoria opened her mouth to speak but closed it again. It was time for her to just listen.

'I had a girlfriend once and I ran away when she needed me the most.' Ted's hands were clenched in front of him. 'What kind of man does that?'

Victoria wanted to tell him he didn't have to talk about it, but something held her tongue.

'Her parents had died in a train crash and I just couldn't handle it, so I ran, like a coward.' Ted cleared his throat. 'I joined the army, before the war started, thinking I could forget her, but I couldn't.'

With Ted's unexpected confession came guilt. It wrapped itself around Victoria, and held her tight. She should tell him who she was, but he had already started talking again.

'I've written to her and she has forgiven me, or at least she says she has.'

Victoria licked her dry lips and cleared her throat. 'You don't have to talk to me about this.'

Ted continued as if she hadn't spoken, his voice a gravelly whisper. 'And I'd hoped we could start again when this war was over, but I've ruined things again, because now I have nothing to offer her.'

Victoria's throat tightened, as she fought the tears that wanted to escape. 'Have you asked her?'

'No.'

Victoria took a couple of breaths. 'Don't you think you should?' She stared at Ted. He looked vulnerable, sitting in the chair. He was almost skeletal, to how she remembered him. 'It's not your decision to make. If you love her, then you should let her decide.'

Ted jutted out his chin. 'I don't want her to marry me out of sympathy.'

Victoria's chin dropped; he had been going to propose. 'Then you need to fight for yourself, and what you want.'

Ted tilted his head. 'Is that what you do?'

Victoria gave a humourless laugh. 'No, despite giving similar advice to my friends, it's easier to say than to do.'

Ted nodded. 'Well, maybe it's time we both started fighting back.'

Victoria stared at the man she had spent so much of her life loving from a distance. 'I think you're right. No more feeling sorry for ourselves, which means I have another trip to make to Brighton.'

'Brighton? Is that where you come from?'

Victoria forced a smile. 'No, but it seems my father did, so I have a brother to officially meet.'

'It's strange that you haven't met him before.'

Victoria groaned, before giving a little laugh. 'That's

295

a long story that I will tell you some other time.'

Ted sat in silence for a few minutes.

Victoria stared at him. 'Are you all right? Did I say something wrong?'

'No. No, your laugh just reminded me of another time and place.'

'I'm sorry, I should tell you . . . '

'Tell me what?'

Victoria's courage took cover. 'Nothing.'

'Well.' Ted beamed. 'I hope it goes well, but if not, give them what for. It will be their loss, not yours.'

Victoria pushed herself off the edge of the bed, forcing a laugh. 'I will, and I'll let you know how I get on.' She leant forward and touched his hand. Butterflies immediately started fluttering around her stomach as Ted's fingers wrapped around her hand. There was no doubt in her mind she still loved him, but would he forgive her for not telling him who she really was? Her voice dropped to a whisper. 'I'll see you tomorrow.'

'I shall look forward to it.'

Victoria pulled her hand away and, without a backward glance, pushed the empty trolley to the other end of the ward. Was he looking forward to seeing a stranger instead of her?

A few minutes later, Victoria was pulling her coat over her grey dress, and walking out the door. She hadn't worked for as long as she would have liked, but three or four hours was better than not doing anything. At least, that's what she told herself as she left the hospital.

'At last!' Molly chimed. 'Victoria, we've been looking everywhere for you.'

Alice smiled. 'Well, not everywhere. We went to your home, but there was no answer.' Alice frowned

296

at Victoria. 'Although you had left the front door key on the outside of the door, so we pushed the string through the letterbox.'

Victoria groaned. 'I left in a hurry.' She looked at her friends. 'It's too cold for you to be out looking for me, especially you Alice.

'My mother's convinced I'll give birth soon so she doesn't want me leaving the house. I'm having difficulty getting in and out of chairs these days.' Alice looked down at her feet. 'Not that I can see them, but my ankles are swollen most days.'

'Edith's also quite a size now.' Molly grabbed Victoria's arm. 'But never mind all that. How did it go in Brighton?'

Victoria took a deep breath. 'It was horrendous. Mabel and I got on really well; we managed to clear the air a little, before we reached the family home. But once we were there, my grandfather threw me out, so I never met John.'

The girls gasped.

'When I told Daisy about going to Brighton, she got angry and flew upstairs sobbing, mumbling something about losing me to another family. I haven't heard from Stephen for weeks, so I don't know what has happened to him and I can't bring myself to think about it. I came here to see if Mabel was back, so I could ask how it went after I left, but she isn't working tonight, so I'm none the wiser.' Victoria's voice dropped to a whisper. 'I've made such a mess of things, and what's more, I keep making a mess of things. Ted has just been talking to me about me, and I'm too scared to tell him who I am, in case I lose him again.'

Alice and Molly looked at each other and nodded.

Molly squeezed her friend's arm. 'If anywhere was open, this would be a tea and cake moment, but I think it's too late for that, so we'll just have to go home and have tea. What was it you told me once, "tea solves everything", or something like that?'

Victoria grimaced. 'I've made such a mess of everything.'

Alice stroked Victoria's back. 'No you haven't; they just don't understand that you were trying to protect them, and yourself, from being hurt all over again.'

Molly sighed. 'We need to go back to Brighton and tell your grandfather what day of the week it is.'

A chorus of laughter came from the girls.

'Who do you think we are?' Victoria spluttered, in between gulps of air. 'Some gangster, in a film? I think we're more like Charlie Chaplin.'

The three girls roared.

Molly giggled. 'I actually prefer the three musketeers.'

'It's good to hear you laughing, Victoria, despite your bad day.' Alice paused. 'I don't want to let you down, but I'm not sure Freddie will approve of me going to Brighton, in my condition.'

'Definitely not,' Molly and Victoria said as one.

Victoria bit her bottom lip. 'Look, I appreciate you both wanting to support me in the fight ahead, but I think it's important I speak to Daisy and get her to come with me.'

The girls both nodded.

'The thing is, I don't want Daisy thinking she's losing a family, instead of gaining one.' Victoria paused. 'In reality, Daisy and Stephen are the most important people in my life.'

'Oh thanks.' Molly chuckled. 'There was I thinking

it was me, for both of you. In all seriousness, you know we'll support you, whatever you choose to do.' Molly leant into Victoria slightly. 'And don't worry about Ted; you can't have messed up as much as I did with Andrew.'

The girls laughed, as they walked down the road arm in arm.

★ ★ ★

Victoria and Daisy walked down the hill from Brighton train station and stood in almost the same spot on the seafront as Victoria had done with Mabel. She and Daisy stared out at the grey, murky sky, meeting the darkness of the sea. They both stood and watched the waves crashing in on the pebbled beach, leaving water trapped amongst the stones.

Victoria was mesmerised by the sea and licked the saltiness from her lips. 'It doesn't look very inviting, and yet I could watch it all day.'

Daisy nodded. 'Victoria, you were very quiet on the train. Are you worried about what we are about to do?'

Victoria stared straight ahead, her hands clenched together in front of her, wondering about the wisdom of what they were about to do.

Daisy gave a small sigh. 'I should have said earlier, on the train, but . . . ' She shrugged. 'Thank you for persuading me to come with you, and I'm sorry I acted in such a childish manner yesterday.'

Victoria glanced at her sister. 'None of that matters, Daisy. We're sisters and nothing will ever come between us, but that doesn't mean there isn't room for one more, does it?'

299

'No, it doesn't.'

'Anyway, it's probably my fault for not including you more.'

Daisy shook her head. 'I could have offered to do more, perhaps even use the police resources, but I didn't. If I'm honest, I was hoping you would give up looking.' Colour rose in her cheeks. 'I was so worried about losing you to another family.' She paused, and then opened her mouth to say more but changed her mind.

'The trouble is Daisy, in my head, it's not another family. It's our family.' She smiled across at her sister. 'And for the record, I'm glad you didn't use police resources, because the last thing I need is my little sister in prison. It doesn't bear thinking about.'

Daisy chuckled. 'You are funny, and you don't even realise it.'

Victoria looked back at the sea. 'Well, this isn't about blame, this is about keeping the family together.' Drops of rain started to hit the path. 'We should come here again in the summer, perhaps walk along to the pier and the pavilion, maybe have an ice cream.'

Daisy smiled, as she looked further along the sea-front. 'I expect it looks totally different with the blue sky meeting the sea, and the sun beating down.'

Victoria took a deep breath. 'It's time we went. You need to know our grandfather wants nothing to do with us, so it could get rather unpleasant. Are you ready for this?'

Daisy thrust her arm under Victoria's. 'We're in this together and I don't want you to ever feel you can't rely on me.'

Victoria's vision became blurry. She blinked rapidly. 'We've been through a lot and I'm thankful we have had good friends to get us through some of it.'

Daisy nodded. 'And it's time I was added to that list of people. Please don't ever feel you can't discuss things with me again.'

Victoria smiled. 'It should be me saying that to you.'

Daisy squeezed Victoria's arm. 'Come on, let's get this over and done with.' She pushed back her shoulders and lifted her chin. 'No one is going to stop us from meeting our brother. I don't care who they are.'

Victoria's stomach churned, as they both walked purposefully along the seafront and got nearer to the house. She forced a smile to her lips, trying to hide her worry. 'It's the grand-looking house with the black door and sash windows.'

Daisy frowned. 'They all look pretty grand to me.'

'Yes, I suppose it was a silly thing to say.' They took another couple of steps and Victoria stopped, taking a deep breath. 'This is it.' She took the lead and walked up to the front door, not wanting to think about what was ahead of them. Victoria lifted the door-knocker, which thudded back down, when she let go of it. She pulled herself upright, determined to fight for her brother, whether he wanted it or not.

The door opened.

Victoria breathed a sigh of relief to see her grandmother's petite frame. 'Hello, Grandma.' Victoria stepped aside. 'I thought you might like to meet my sister, Daisy.'

Daisy nodded.

Beatrice beamed and stepped to one side. 'Come in.' She stretched out her arms, enveloping them both in a hug, belying her age and size. 'I'm so pleased you came back. Mabel is still here.' She paused and stepped out on to the doorstep, before looking up and down the street. 'My husband, your grandfather, isn't in at the moment and, hopefully, he will be gone a while.' Beatrice stepped back though the doorway, closing the front door behind her.

'Ma, who are you talking to?'

Victoria looked in the direction of the voice.

Mabel stood in the sitting room doorway. She stepped forward, with outstretched arms. 'Thank goodness you came back.' She pulled Victoria into a bear hug. 'I'm so sorry about my father.'

Victoria pulled a letter from the pocket of her coat. 'He sent my father a letter, a very brief and cold letter at that, telling him his brother had died in action.'

Behind her, Beatrice gave a sob. Daisy immediately wrapped her arm around her grandmother.

'Come; let's sit down before we all fall down, particularly Ma. It's been a hard few days.' Mabel turned and led the way into the sitting room.

Daisy gasped. The room was twice the size of theirs, in Percy Street. There were gold-coloured curtains and a matching fringed pelmet at the windows. The large cushions on the sofa matched and contrasted with the brown and gold pattern in the carpet.

Beatrice indicated towards the sofa. 'Sit down and I'll make you some tea.'

Victoria rested her hand on her grandmother's arm. 'No, please, I don't know how long we have to talk, so I would like us to make the most of it, while we can.'

Beatrice nodded and sat down on one of the leather wingback chairs.

Victoria looked from her gran to Mabel and back again. 'I don't want to appear rude, but can we see John?'

Beatrice nodded.

Mabel stood up. 'Wait, before we go along to John's room, there are a few things you need to know.'

Beatrice sat back down again.

Victoria and Daisy looked at each other, before Victoria spoke in almost a whisper. 'What is it?'

Mabel took a step towards the window, staring out at the grey sea, thrashing on the beach. 'John isn't at all well.' She sighed and turned back to the girls. 'We called a doctor out to see him yesterday and they want to run some tests but he definitely has more wrong with him than asthma. The doctor mentioned something about reading an article about salt and vitamin loss in the body and he thought it would explain some of John's symptoms especially as he now coughs up stuff quite a lot.' She looked back out at the sea. 'He recommended John lay on his front and one of us repeatedly bangs on his back to try to clear his chest a little but we have to do it every day, maybe twice a day. I've seen that done before with children, but never with an adult, but hopefully it should help bring up whatever is sitting on his chest and ultimately give him some comfort.

Beatrice sniffed. 'I think John has only kept going, because he wanted and hoped he would see his London family again. He couldn't, doesn't, understand why your father never returned to see him again.' She paused. 'And I've never had the answers for him, although he knows all about you all.'

Victoria shook her head. 'It's all such a mess. If I'd been braver seven years ago, and cleared out my parents' room, I would have discovered about John earlier. I'm so sorry.'

Daisy wrapped her arm around her sister. 'It's no one's fault and there's nothing to be gained by blaming yourself.'

Victoria gave a watery smile. 'I think that could be said for all of us. We just need to do what we can for John and bring him peace.'

Mabel nodded. 'He's in a deep sleep at the moment; well, we are unclear whether he's asleep or unconscious. All we know is he's been asleep for a few hours and doesn't stir when we go in and check on him.' She paused. 'If it's anything to go by his breathing sounds calm so that's a good sign.'

Victoria's eyes widened. 'Can we still see him, maybe talk to him?'

Beatrice nodded. When she spoke, her voice sounded frail, and older than when she had opened the front door. 'I'm not convinced he'll hear you, and I shouldn't think he'll answer you, but you never know.'

Victoria looked over at her aunt, and then at her gran. 'I know, but my friend Molly's husband was unconscious after an explosion, and they told her to talk to him. They said they didn't know if it would help, but equally, it wouldn't do any harm.'

Mabel stretched out her arm to her nieces. 'There's nothing to lose, but he's frightfully thin.'

Victoria and Daisy stood up. They gripped each other's hands and followed Mabel along the hall, to a room at the back of the house.

Mabel looked back at the girls and waited for the go-ahead to open the door.

Victoria nodded and the door was sprung free of its lock. The room was in darkness and John was barely visible in the bed, which was in the centre of the large room. A couple of armchairs were situated by the window, with a small table between them.

Mabel stepped forward and pulled the green and

gold curtains open a little; shafts of grey light immediately broke up the darkness.

Victoria looked over at the ashen colour of the thin man, lying in the bed. She wanted to get nearer, but hesitated. He looked unwell but, contrarily, at peace as well. 'Hello, John.' She stepped nearer the bed. 'It's lovely to finally meet you. We're your sisters. I'm Victoria and this is Daisy.'

Daisy stepped forward, tears rolling down her cheeks. 'Hello, John.'

Mabel stepped over to her mother and guided her out of the room, leaving the girls alone with their brother.

The girls pulled up a chair each and sat down, close to the bed. Victoria held his bony fingers in hers. 'Let me tell you a little about myself, then Daisy can do the same.' She looked anxiously at Daisy, then back at John. He was lying so still that she fleetingly wondered if he had already passed, but then his finger twitched in her hand, giving her some comfort that the time hadn't yet come. 'Let's see, where shall I start? I work in Foyles Bookshop. It's on Charing Cross Road, and I love it. I love being surrounded by books, whereas Daisy is a police officer. She walks the streets of London, but I'll let her tell you about her work. Apparently, I've been to Brighton before but I don't remember it, so when I came the other day with Mabel, it was like the first time.' She chuckled. 'Oops, I should say Aunt Mabel, but I think I might be coming again, now I have a brother that lives here.' She paused, stroking the translucent skin across his knuckles. 'Maybe, when you come round, you can tell us about you, and what you get up to here in Brighton.' A tear ran down her cheek.

'Hello, John, I'm Daisy.'

Victoria's head jerked round to face the closed door, as she became aware of muffled voices. He was back.

21

The sound of glass hitting the floor was quickly followed by a thud.

Victoria stood up. 'You stay here, Daisy, and keep talking to John. You never know, he might be able to hear us.'

Beatrice's voice sounded along the hallway. 'No, Herbert, I'm not going to allow you to do this any longer. You've torn this family apart.'

Victoria opened the bedroom door. The atmosphere was tense. Her stomach churned. Should she go and confront him? She knew she wouldn't get to see John again, but she couldn't leave her gran and Mabel to deal with him. She stepped through the doorway, shutting the door quietly behind her. She tiptoed along the hall, not wanting to disturb the raised voices coming from the sitting room.

'You need help, Father.' Mabel's feeble voice could just be heard in the hallway. 'You're just a tyrant and a bully.'

'Am I, indeed? Well you can always leave, and not come back.' Herbert growled. 'This is my house, and I will not have you dictate who comes and goes, do you understand?'

'This is Ma's home too, as well as John's, and they are entitled to have visitors.'

'Mabel, leave it.' Beatrice's voice was thin and broken. 'It doesn't matter.'

Victoria quickened her pace. A glass vase was lying shattered in the hallway. Flowers lay in the pool of water that was spreading its tendrils out towards the stairs. She dropped her handkerchief onto the tiled floor, in a futile bid to stop it spreading further. Victoria stood in the doorway, watching the three of them. Sadness enveloped her, as she noticed the redness forming on the side of her grandmother's face.

'It does matter, Ma; how am I meant to leave you here, if he can so easily raise a hand to you?'

Victoria took a deep breath. 'Excuse me, I don't mean to interrupt, but there are pieces of broken glass and water on the floor in the hall, so please be careful if any of you go out there.'

Mr Appleton turned and glared at Victoria.

Colour rose up into Victoria's cheeks, as she felt everyone's eyes on her. She hadn't thought this through. 'Mr Appleton, or should I say Grandfather.' Victoria pulled herself up and straightened her shoulders. 'If you have any problems with my sister and me visiting our brother, then you should be taking it out on us, not an elderly woman, who you would blow over as easily as a feather. Surely that's no match for your manliness.' She paused, as she took in his jaw dropping open. 'What's the matter, are you used to people giving in to your tantrums? I mean no disrespect to you, sir, but you are nothing to me, so other than showing respect to the elderly, which is what I was brought up to do by my parents, I have no allegiance to you at all.'

Herbert's eyes blazed with rage. 'How dare you? You come uninvited into my house and cause all this trouble. You are your father's daughter, all right.'

'You are right on both counts. I did come into this house uninvited, which was very rude of me, and I extend my apologies for that.'

Herbert nodded. 'At least you admit that much.'

'However, I know you would have not allowed us to visit, had you known we were coming.'

Herbert's face contorted with rage.

'And as for your second comment, about me being my father's daughter.' Victoria smiled. 'I'm sorry; I'm not smiling at your anger. I'm smiling at the compliment you have just given me. I'm proud to be given that title; there was no man fairer, or more loving, to his wife and children. I'm afraid, sir, if you didn't get on with him, then I think you need to look to yourself, and I might add, even if my father had stepped out of line with you, does that mean you have to be so unforgiving as to not allow his children to meet the family they didn't know existed? If that is so, you are indeed a cruel man. You should ask yourself, is it a coincidence that no one, other than your long-suffering wife, wants to live with you?'

Herbert took a step nearer to Victoria and lifted his arm. 'Well, I've a good mind to — '

'To what, sir, strike me; is that how you deal with problems?' Victoria's eyes widened. 'I can tell you that my father never lifted a hand to anybody, so he was a better man than you'll ever be.'

Daisy stood in the doorway and coughed.

Victoria spun round on her heels and stretched out her arm, pulling Daisy into the room. 'This, sir, is your other granddaughter, Daisy. She's a police-woman.' She turned to her sister. 'Is John all right?'

Daisy didn't take her eyes off her grandfather, as she shrugged. 'I'm not an expert, but I don't think there's any change from when we went in there.'

Victoria turned back to her grandfather. 'You know, this isn't actually about you, and I'm not going to allow you to play God with our lives. It's about John and his needs.' Her voice softened. 'I understand he's been at a loss to understand why our father and mother haven't been to see him. I don't know if he can hear us or not, but I want to bring him some peace; even more so, if this is the only time I get to spend with him.'

'Herbert, leave them to it.' Beatrice's soft voice filled the vacuum between them. 'It's time to move on. Look at the people in this room. Apart from John, there is no one else. Thanks to the war, our family is getting smaller every day. We should be pulling together. It's your stubbornness that has prevented us from knowing about David and Margaret's train accident. I know I have a part to play in that, I should have defied you, but that is my regret. Now, poor John thinks his parents didn't love him, how do you think that makes him feel? We should have been there for all of our grandchildren, but instead, Victoria has shouldered a lot of responsibility, from a very young age.'

Daisy hugged her sister. 'And done a very good job, at that.'

Victoria stared at the man standing in front of her, seeing for the first time an old man, trying to protect his way of life, in the only way he knew how. She stepped forward and put her arms around him. 'It's never too late.' He didn't return the hug, but she squeezed him tight, before stepping away. 'We haven't come to break up a family. We came to find one.' She turned around, took Daisy's arm and walked back to John's room.

★ ★ ★

310

Alice gingerly lowered herself onto the wooden chair, at the white-clothed table inside the Monico Café. 'I feel like a barrel, sitting here.'

Molly giggled. 'You're definitely bigger than last time. It's a good job it's not the summer, because you'd block out the sunshine.'

A smile played on Victoria's lips, as she breathed in the strong aroma of coffee, infused with the hot food being carried to the surrounding tables. 'You're terrible, Molly; you wait until your turn comes.'

Molly looked contrite for a few seconds. 'Oh I'm sorry, I was only playing.' She patted Alice's hand. 'You look well, but I definitely think you're going to have a big baby.'

Victoria slapped Molly's hand with the menu. 'I'm surprised you're still coming to work, Alice. It must be due any time now.'

Alice groaned. 'I wish it was, but I think I have at least a month to go yet. Thank goodness I've at least started my Christmas shopping.'

Molly smiled. 'I've started mine too.'

Alice fidgeted in the chair, dragging the pristine tablecloth with her. 'I'm sorry.' She straightened it. 'So dare I ask, Victoria, what's happening about your brother? And Molly, what's happening about your parents moving to Percy Street?'

Molly laughed. 'Gosh, so many questions. You go first, Victoria.'

Victoria stared down at the silver cutlery shining up at them. 'You first, your answer will probably be much quicker than mine. In fact, I think asking Lloyd George about the war ending would probably be a quicker conversation.'

Molly frowned, but quickly followed it with a shrug

of her shoulders. 'I don't really have much to say, except they're promising me they will move, as soon as Christmas is over with.'

Alice smiled. 'Well that's good; it's only a few weeks away.'

'Yeah.' Molly laughed. 'To be honest, I'll believe it when it happens. Andrew, bless him, has me ma picking out colours for all the rooms. He says he'll get it painted and tidied up before they move in, but once again, me ma thinks it's all a waste of money.' She shook her head. 'I've told her, if she doesn't pick anything, I'll do it, and then she'll be stuck with something she'll probably hate.' Molly laughed. 'I've left me gran working on her.'

Alice straightened her knife and fork. 'I expect she'll pick something in the end. Your ma has a strong spirit, but your gran's is stronger.'

Molly laughed. 'That's true.' She glanced at Victoria. 'Come on spit it out. Something has been bothering you, all day.'

The waitress glided over to their table. 'Are you ready to order?'

Molly quickly looked at the girls, then back to the waitress. 'Three teas and three slices of your finest chocolate cake please.'

The waitress nodded, before turning away, straightening her black dress and the full white apron.

Molly watched her move amongst the tables, brushing against the large leaves of the potted ferns. 'They always come to the table when we're about to get into it.' She glanced around her. 'I know we've said it before, but you wouldn't know there was a war on, when you come here. It seems to be untouched by it. Even the large mirrors are shining, and crack-free. I wonder how they do it?'

Alice followed Molly's gaze. 'I know what you mean; it's not that far from the bomb that went off at Oxford Circus, but you would never know it.'

Molly turned back to Victoria. 'Now, Vic, remember what you told me, tea solves everything, so whatever is weighing heavily on your shoulders is about to disappear.'

Alice sat looking from one friend to the other. 'My goodness, things must be bad.'

Molly ran her hands over the tablecloth, not taking her eyes off Victoria. 'I know, it's like a measuring stick of badness, isn't it?'

Alice nodded. 'And there was nothing, nothing at all, not even a look.'

Molly kept a straight face. 'We might have to call a doctor out.'

Victoria glanced from one to the other. 'What on earth are you two on about?'

Molly roared with laughter. 'You, of course.'

'What about me?'

Molly shook her head. 'I called you Vic, and for the first time in goodness knows how many years, you didn't go mad at me. In fact, you didn't even acknowledge it.'

'I didn't even notice.'

'That's exactly what we're talking about,' said Alice. 'So come on, what is it? We know you got to see John, but you haven't given us any details, and clearly something is bothering you.'

Molly and Alice both sighed, as the waitress appeared with the three slices of chocolate cake and the pot of tea. The girls sat in silence, as she put the teacups on their matching blue, floral china saucers

313

and dropped silver spoons next to them. The heavy teapot was placed in the centre of the table, and the cake in front of each of them. The waitress nodded at them and turned to walk away.

'You look terrible, Victoria. In fact, I haven't seen you look this bad since the war started.' Molly gasped. 'It's not Stephen, is it?'

They waited for a few minutes, but Victoria sat staring at her cake.

Molly let out an exasperated sigh. 'Now look, Victoria, if this was me, which it was not that long ago, you'd be reading me the riot act and not allowing it to continue, so now it's my turn, if you don't start practising what you preach. I'm not having it.' She paused. 'Unless something has happened to Stephen, in which case, carry on, and I'm sorry.'

Victoria had the urge to laugh out loud, but she knew it wouldn't have been a humorous sound. She glanced up at Alice and Molly. 'Stephen is missing, but as far as I know he's alive. At least, I haven't had a telegram to say otherwise. I'm not allowing myself to think that he isn't. He'll turn up, when I least expect it.' She forced a laugh. 'As for John, well I don't know whether I'll get to see him again. When Daisy and I went to Brighton, he was unconscious so I'm just preparing myself for the worst.'

Molly grabbed Victoria's hand. 'Did you talk to him, like Elizabeth and I did Andrew? I'm convinced he knew we were there.'

'Yes, we did, and Mabel took over after we left.' Victoria sighed. 'So you never know.'

Alice studied Victoria's pale features. 'And your grandparents?'

Victoria groaned. 'My grandmother welcomed us

314

with open arms, but my grandfather was the complete opposite. We definitely won't be welcome in that house again.'

Alice gave Victoria a sideways glance, as she took the lid off the teapot and began stirring the dark brown liquid. 'Did you argue with him? I have to say, having been on the end of your tongue when you're not happy, you probably caught him by surprise.'

Victoria gave a faint smile. 'I know you're thinking about the pawn tickets, but I can tell you, I think I showed him respect — but I couldn't stand by and let him bully us, or my grandmother.'

Molly clapped her hands together and gave a beaming smile. 'And here was I, wondering what we could be celebrating with this slice of cake. There it is — standing up to men, or women, but mainly men who wish to keep women in their place.'

Alice and Victoria giggled.

Alice poured the tea and added the milk. 'You're mad, do you know that?'

Molly chuckled, as she picked up her cup and held it out to the centre of the table. 'I have a toast, well actually, it's two really.' Alice and Victoria eyed each other with suspicion, but followed suit. 'To the safety of our loved ones, at home or away, but this toast is for women everywhere. We're all stronger than we think.'

The women on the next table started clapping. 'Well said.'

Molly's face turned a lovely shade of red, as she turned to them. 'Thank you.'

Victoria giggled. 'You'll be standing for prime minister, next.'

★ ★ ★

Victoria carefully followed Molly down the steps, into the basement at Foyles. The damp, musty smell became stronger as they went further down the stairs.

Molly pushed the basement door open and stepped in, careful not to knock over the shopping bags that were propping each other up. 'Morning, Albert.' She craned her neck to look beyond the shelving, stacked high with books. 'You're not hiding from us, are you?'

Victoria held the door, as she moved inside the basement. Shaking her head, but without a word, she moved the bags away from the doorway. She needed to have a word, before someone broke their neck on them. It was evident that Albert wasn't policing them.

Albert appeared from behind some racking, stacked with books. 'Of course I ain't. I'm not six, yer know.'

Victoria let out a little chuckle. 'Thank goodness.' She let the door slide shut behind her. 'I was a little worried, when you didn't answer straight away.'

Albert grunted. 'There's no need to worry yourselves, I'm sure.'

Molly jumped up on to the table. 'What's wrong, Albert? I normally come down here when I want a laugh, but you don't seem up to laughing this morning.'

'Nah, I'm all right, I just 'ate Christmas.' Albert gave them a sheepish look. 'I always 'ave done, but now there's only me and the wife, cos who knows where me sons are, fighting somewhere on some foreign bloody soil, no doubt.'

Victoria fought the urge to give Albert a hug. 'I know what you mean; Christmas doesn't have the same excitement or appeal, since the boys went off to war. It feels wrong to be celebrating it.' She paused. 'I remember everyone saying how they'd be home for

Christmas in 1914, and here we are looking for some decorations to bring in some Christmas cheer in 1917, with them still not back.' She shook her head, and then wrinkled her nose. 'I don't remember this damp smell, last time I came down. Has the rain got in? I don't want you getting ill.'

Albert gave a small smile. 'Yer like me muvver.' He picked up a book and gave it a flick through, before putting it on top of a pile of others. 'I've told Mr Lead-better; it's only a small crack, but I've plugged it wiv newspaper at the moment.'

Molly nodded. 'That's good. We're here to take up the Christmas baubles for the shop window, so any ideas where we can find them?'

'Ooh blimey.' Albert stopped what he was doing and looked around the basement. 'Where did we put them, when they were brought down 'ere, in January.' He tapped his bony finger against his pursed lips. 'Hmm, they may be in a cupboard at the back.' He shuffled a little way along the aisle, between the racking, before turning to face the girls. 'Come on, yer allowed further than the table.'

Molly jumped down and followed Victoria.

Victoria gasped as she looked around her. 'I never realised all of the basement was full of books. We're never going to sell all of these; we have no room for them in the shop, for one thing. How many do you think are down here?'

Albert chuckled. 'I 'ave no idea, thousands I expect. I just know it's a never-ending job, cos more come in every day.' He turned to glance at them. 'But that's a good fing for us, ain't it?'

Molly nodded. 'It certainly is.'

'Maybe I'll ask if we can send some to the soldiers

on the front line. After all, someone should be read-ing them,' said Victoria.

Molly grinned. 'That's so true, Victoria. It's a waste, having all these books hidden away, depriving read-ers from enjoying them. I think I'll send some books to Grace for Christmas, and maybe some colourful ribbon to tie back her hair.'

Victoria giggled at Molly's excitement.

Albert pulled at the large wooden doors. They were stiff and unyielding. He placed the palm of one hand flat against one of the doors, while pulling hard on the other. The creaking sound told them it was on the brink of opening. When the door suddenly pulled free, Albert lost his balance and stepped back on to Victoria's foot. 'Sorry.' He looked round at her. 'Are yer all right? It caught me out, it did.'

Victoria forced a smile, trying to hide the pain of her throbbing foot. 'I'm fine, but I have to say, you're heavier than you look.'

Molly rubbed Victoria's arm, as she stepped for-ward to study the contents of the cupboard. She pulled boxes forward and opened the flaps, to look inside. She dipped her hand in and moved a couple of things around. 'This one looks like it's full of paper chains, and it looks like there may be a couple of glass baubles at the bottom.'

Albert stepped back. 'Well, I'll leave you girls to it, but don't leave a mess behind you for me to tidy up.'

Victoria stepped forward. 'Look at this.' She pulled out some ruby red cloth. 'We could hang this in the window, with some candles and baubles.'

Molly brushed her hands together, before reaching out to touch the silky material. 'It's beautiful; too nice for a window, but it would be a shame not to use it.'

She glanced across at Victoria. 'When you said candles, I trust you don't intend to light them, this being a shop full of paper.'

Victoria laughed. 'Of course not, silly, I just thought it might look Christmassy.'

Molly nodded. 'We could buy some green ribbon, to tie around some books or something.'

'That's a good idea.' Victoria's eyes lit up, as the excitement took hold. 'Why don't we see what's in these boxes, that we can use? Then we can make a list of what else is needed.'

They spent the next hour pulling out paper chains, some too tired and crumpled to be used, while others were torn beyond repair. There were long strings of beads, and strands of tinsel, that could be added to the Christmas window display.

22

Victoria walked on to the ward, her bag full of twigs and colourful ribbon. She gasped. The ceiling had paper chains hanging from one side of the ward to the other. There were chains looped against the walls. Baubles hung on ribbon, off the light fittings. Women stood in the corner singing 'Silent Night'. Christmas had arrived early at Endell Street Hospital. The men joined in with the singing, some more muted than others.

'It looks beautiful, doesn't it?'

Victoria jumped at the woman's voice, behind her. She turned to see a young nurse, looking up at the decorations hanging from the ceiling. 'It is beautiful, I . . . I wasn't expecting it at all.' Victoria held up her bag. 'I've been to the park to collect twigs.' Colour flooded her cheeks. 'I thought I'd tie some red and green ribbon around them and put them in a vase, but it doesn't matter, I can put them in the Foyles Bookshop window tomorrow. They won't go to waste.' She gazed around her. 'This looks beautiful.'

The nurse followed Victoria's gaze. 'It is.' She looked back at Victoria. 'The twigs are a good idea; it's up to you whether you use them here, or at Foyles.'

Victoria nodded and put the bag down. She loosened her scarf from around her neck and undid the buttons of her coat.

The nurse looked down at some paperwork on the nearby desk, before looking back at Victoria. 'Are you the one that's been helping Corporal Marsden, in bed twenty-five?'

Victoria nodded.

'Well, you'll be pleased to know, things appear to have moved forward for him.'

Victoria took off her coat and hung it up. 'Really.'

The nurse smiled. 'He's had his bandages removed today, and it seems he has some vision there, so everyone was absolutely thrilled with that news.'

Victoria was swamped with excitement, her face beaming, as she took in the news. 'That's wonderful.' Anxiety immediately trampled on her excitement. She wrapped her arms around herself. 'Do . . . do you know how much he can see?'

The smile faded from the nurse's face, as she studied Victoria. 'Do you want to sit down? You look very pale and I don't want you passing out.'

Victoria shook her head, fidgeting from one foot to the other. 'I'm fine; it's just he was convinced he was never going to be able to see again, so it must have been a shock for him.'

The nurse laughed. 'I think it was a shock for him, but he's very happy about it, and that's putting it mildly.'

Victoria forced a smile. 'How much can he see? I mean, does he have his full sight back?'

The nurse shook her head. 'No, he doesn't. He can only see blurred shapes and colours at the moment, but the doctors are convinced it's a good sign. He could have full sight eventually, or as good as.'

'That's wonderful news.' Victoria smiled, but fear ran down her spine. Shaking her head, she couldn't help but wonder how she always managed to make a mess of things.

'I'll speak to you later.' The nurse picked up a metal

tray. 'I have some dressings to change.'

Victoria watched her march down the ward, but her mind was full of what she could do about Ted. What had she told Molly, when she was going through her own anxieties about Andrew? Be honest, ask the questions and stop running away from the love you feel. The urge to giggle hysterically bubbled inside her. Hah, she was no different to Molly, she owed her friend an apology. It was easier to say, than to do. *Well, Victoria, it's time to practise what you preach.* She pulled back her shoulders and walked slowly down the ward.

'Hello, beautiful.' A soldier smiled as she came up to his bed.

'Hello, sir, I suspect you're feeling better today?'

The soldier laughed, and with trepidation, Victoria carried on to bed twenty-five. She slowed down and watched Ted from a safe distance, sitting in his chair. He looked different without the bandages wrapped around his head. His face was more tanned and weatherworn than she had first realised, and his dark hair looked longer. She had no idea what she was going to say, but she knew she had to be honest with him. He looked deep in thought. Was he thinking about his future? Did it include her? Or was he thinking of all the soldiers that had been injured or killed beside him, on the front line. Her thoughts immediately went to Stephen. She shook her head; she would not let the devil into her mind. Her brother had to be alive; he just had to be. She stepped forward to bed twenty-five. 'Hello, Corporal.'

Ted smiled. 'Hello, I recognise your voice. I've missed you telling me off.'

Victoria laughed. 'It was meant to encourage you to think positive and get out of bed.' She patted down the edge of the bed. 'Since I've been coming here, I've realised I wouldn't make a very good nurse. Anyway, I hear it's good news.'

Ted smiled. 'Yes, they think I'll get my sight back, which means I can start thinking about the future again.'

Victoria clenched her hands against her white overall. 'Good, that probably means I need to move on to another unsuspecting soldier.'

'No, wait.' Ted reached out to touch Victoria's arm, but missed it. He slammed his hand down on his leg.

'Stop it, be patient. It will all come together, you'll see.' Victoria reached out and held Ted's hand, giving it a squeeze. She moved to pull away, but he clasped it tight with his own.

'I want you to do something for me.'

Victoria leant forward. 'What?'

'I want you to contact someone for me; her name's Victoria.' Ted let go of Victoria's hand and felt his way to a drawer in his bedside table. 'She's the love of my life, but I've never been there for her.' He opened the drawer and pulled out several letters.

Victoria recognised her handwriting.

Ted tried to grab some more, but dropped a couple on the floor. 'I've tried to keep all her letters.' He waved them around, as evidence. 'I messed up once, several years ago, and when I say messed up, I mean really messed up, but I can't do it again.' He paused and pulled the envelopes up to his nose. 'I swear I can still smell her on these.' He dropped his arms, allowing the letters to fall onto his lap. 'Please help me find her. I should have done it before, instead of being a coward.'

Victoria felt the tears pricking her eyes. 'You weren't

a coward. You were just frightened, which was understandable.'

Ted shook his head. 'She lives in Percy Street; will
you tell Victoria I'm here?'

*Now. Now. A voice shouted in her head. Come clean tell
him you've been through this journey with him, and love
him more than ever,* but her voice stayed silent.

'I'm sorry, I shouldn't have asked you.'

Tension sat between them for a few minutes. Victoria wrung her hands on her lap. Ted was older than
she remembered, but then it was seven years ago.
They had all been through tough times, albeit in different ways.

Victoria took a deep breath. 'Look, there's something I need to tell you.'

*   *   *

Molly stood outside Foyles Bookshop in Charing
Cross Road, staring at the Christmas display she and
Victoria had put together the previous day, oblivious
to the cars spluttering along the road and the cart-
wheels squelching along the street. There had been a
light flurry of snow overnight, which the wheels had
turned to slush, but it sat untouched on the window
ledge, framing the window display. They had kept to
the traditional Christmas colours, with baubles hanging from every available space, glinting in the lights
hanging from the ceiling. Some hung, rather precariously, from the paper chains loop. The window display
was at odds with the dull grey day.

'You and Miss Appleton did a good job; it was probably time we updated some of the decorations.'

Molly looked over her shoulder and smiled. 'Thank

324

you, Mr Leadbetter; you did wonders, getting hold of the Christmas tree. It does give the window that extra special feel, and you can smell the pine inside the shop. It was most enjoyable decorating it, and we tried to make the best of what we had.'

'I like the books under the tree, tied with red and green ribbons. The idea of giving books for Christmas has to be a good thing. The candles remind everyone it's a religious festival, but we just need to remember not to light them, otherwise we'll all go up in smoke.'

Molly giggled, as she scanned the display for improvements. 'I'm sure no one would be that silly, Mr Leadbetter, not even me. I noticed, when we were looking at the Christmas decorations, that there was a Father Christmas outfit in the cupboard.'

'If you're going to ask me to dress up as Father Christmas, then I'm afraid the answer is no.' Mr Leadbetter chuckled. 'I haven't done that for a few years; in fact, I forgot that outfit was in there.'

'Well, it looked in very good condition.' She paused and bit her bottom lip, before looking up at her manager. 'If you have no desire to do it, can I ask my husband, Andrew? He could set up in the children's section, and we could give each child the gift of reading a good book.'

Mr Leadbetter thought for a moment. 'Why not? I'm sure the owners will agree to it.' He chuckled. 'After all, we have more books than we could sell, even if we were here for a hundred years.'

Molly beamed up at him, flinging her arms around him.

'I'm sorry I'm late, Mr Leadbetter.' Victoria rushed forward, almost colliding with Molly, as she stepped back.

Molly and Mr Leadbetter swung round at the same time and eyed her flushed face, on this cold morning. 'Is everything all right?' They spoke as one.

Mr Leadbetter glanced from Victoria to Molly.

Molly looked sheepishly at Mr Leadbetter, before lowering her eyes, to scan the snow-covered pavement. 'Sorry, sir.'

He returned his attention back to Victoria. 'Are you all right?'

Victoria gasped; thick grey clouds of her breath filled the air between them. 'Alice, Mrs Leybourne, has gone into labour, sir.'

Molly jumped up and down on the spot, clapping her hands. 'Oh goodness, it won't be long then, before we know whether little Arthur has a brother or a sister.'

Mr Leadbetter smiled. 'I can see I'm not going to get much out of you two today.' He pulled out his fob watch and pressed the small gold button on the side, to allow the lid to flip open. 'I take it Mrs Leybourne isn't on her own.'

Victoria shook her head. 'No, sir, she has all her family with her this time, and of course Mrs Headley, the housekeeper, who is a godsend and part of the family.'

Mr Leadbetter shut the lid of his watch and tucked it back into his waistcoat pocket. 'Well, if we're not too busy today, you can both go at lunchtime, but first, I need to see how things go.'

Molly grabbed Victoria's hand and squeezed it. 'It's a shame Alice couldn't have hung on for a couple of weeks; it would have been a Christmas baby. I wonder what they'll call it.'

Victoria laughed, doing her best to ignore the

wanting she had, to be married with children. 'We'll know soon enough.' She pulled open a shopping bag. 'I picked up some twigs to help decorate the hospital, but they have no need for them, so I wondered if we could use them; perhaps tie some ribbon around a few branches.'

Molly turned back to the window display. 'That's an excellent idea. Don't they decorate the hospital, then?'

Victoria raised her eyebrows. 'The wards look magnificent, so beautiful, and they had carol singers singing my favourite hymn, "Silent Night".'

Mr Leadbetter smiled, as he turned his back on the girls. 'Come on you two, otherwise you'll be going home before you've even started.' He peered over his shoulder at them. 'I wouldn't like to say which was my favourite carol. I do like "Once in Royal David's City" and "O Come All Ye Faithful", oh and mustn't forget "Hark The Herald Angels Sing".' He chuckled. 'As I said, I would find it hard to pick just one.'

Victoria and Molly followed Mr Leadbetter into the shop, each stamping the snow off their shoes.

'Mr Leadbetter, sir,' Victoria bit down on her bottom lip, for a second, 'I wondered whether it would be possible to donate some of the books as presents to the soldiers, either on the front line or at some of the London hospitals.' Her words jumped over themselves, to escape. 'Only, some of the men have nothing, and it might lift their spirits a little.'

Mr Leadbetter roared with laughter. 'You two have been busy thinking up ways to spread good cheer.' He shook his head, as his laughter gradually subsided. 'It's a lovely idea; I think the hospitals will be easier for us to do, at this late stage. I'll speak to the owners,

327

but I feel sure they will agree to it.'

Victoria beamed. 'Thank you, sir. I feel sure it will make a difference to them.'

Molly nodded. 'That's a great idea. Shall we start gathering some books together, and maybe after work, we could wrap them, ready for delivery.'

Mr Leadbetter replied, 'I admire your enthusiasm, but I think there will be too many to wrap.'

Victoria was thankful that, in the excitement, Molly hadn't noticed how tired she looked, or asked why she had gone round to Alice's home, before work. Victoria had tossed and turned all night, going over her conversation with Ted the previous evening. She groaned. It took two to have a conversation, but he had been silent the whole time she had been confessing to not saying who she was from the beginning. Even when she had tried to explain that she was there to help him, still he remained silent, and if he'd known it was her, she felt sure he would have had her removed. Exhaustion came over her in waves, and she still had the day to get through.

'Miss Appleton?' A small, thin lady marched over to Victoria.

Victoria turned and forced her best customer smile to her lips. 'Yes, can I help you?'

'Thank goodness.' The lady took a breath. 'I just wanted to come in and thank you, admittedly a little late, for talking some sense into my Edith.'

'Ahh, you're Edith's mother. How is she?'

The lady beamed. 'Well, that's why I'm here; she's now a mother, and I'm a grandmother to a beautiful little girl.'

Without thinking, Victoria wrapped her arms around the woman and squeezed her tight. 'That's wonderful news. Is Edith all right?'

Edith's mother smiled. 'She's a natural. I'm so proud of her, although I don't know how we'll manage with another mouth to feed, but we don't need to worry about that, just yet.'

Victoria shook her head. 'I wouldn't let worry spoil what you have, right now; something will turn up. Tell Edith to come and see us when she's ready to return to work; we might be able to find something for her. I can't make any promises, but you never know, things have a habit of working themselves out, sometimes.'

The lady gave a little smile. 'Edith wanted me to come in and let you know what she had, and to thank you for all your kindness. She told me she was in a right old state, when you calmed her down.'

Victoria nodded. 'Things are never as bad as we think they are, when we're in the moment. I'm absolutely thrilled it all worked out for you both.'

'I know this is a cheeky question, but Edith asked me to find out what your Christian name is.' The woman leant in slightly. 'I think she wants to name the baby after you.'

Victoria's cheeks immediately flushed. 'Oh no, please don't do that.'

The woman raised her eyebrows, as she waited for an explanation.

'My name is Victoria. My mother always said I was named after our great queen, because she was a symbol for all women, but sometimes I get called Vic or Vicky, and I hate it.'

Edith's mother chuckled. 'Well, that's not so bad; I wondered what you were going to say. I'll pass on the shortened names, as well as the full name, and I'll let Edith decide. I have to say though, I quite like the idea of the little one being named after such a great queen, and a wonderfully kind person, like yourself.'

Guilt flooded Victoria's veins. She wasn't a nice person; look what she had done to Ted and her grandfather. She forced a smile. 'Please give Edith our love and, when she's able to, tell her to bring the baby in to see us.'

* * *

Molly and Victoria walked up and down the aisles, in between the shelving, stacked high with books. Molly looked from side to side. 'Where do we start?'

Victoria shrugged. 'I'm trying to decide whether we should take the books from the basement, or the shop itself.'

Molly reached up to move a book, and dust particles burst into the air. 'These don't look like they've been dusted in a while. Old Leadbetter would go mad, if he saw this.'

'Old Leadbetter would go mad if he saw what?' The familiar deep voice came from behind Molly.

Molly shook her head. 'It's about time I learnt, Mr Leadbetter. You're always close by, when I'm saying or doing something wrong.'

'It's about time you learnt to behave yourself then, but I suppose you wouldn't be the person you are, if that was the case.'

Molly turned around to face him. 'That's true, but I'm not a child anymore either.' She peered back over her shoulder, at the books on the shelves. 'It doesn't look like they have been dusted for some time.'

Mr Leadbetter followed her lead. 'It's not good, but not surprising really. We are so short staffed these

330

days; we can't compete with the wages that the factories pay. Anyway, I came to ask you to take up Mrs Leybourne's position today, or at least until I find someone I can trust, to do it permanently.'

Molly nodded. 'What about my counter in the children's section?'

Mr Leadbetter's lips tweaked at the corners. 'Mrs Leybourne's position is important, because most of the time she can see the door, and down some of the aisles. It's also the busiest counter in the shop, excluding the payment booth. You are only in the children's section because you expressed a desire to bring books into their lives, which is to be rewarded, but you are capable of so much more.'

Colour flooded Molly's cheeks. 'Thank you, Mr Leadbetter. I'm not sure I deserve your kind words, but I love it at Foyles and I will always work hard for you and the Foyle family.'

Mr Leadbetter nodded, before turning to see Victoria pulling books off the shelves, running a rag over them as she went, and dropping them into a box. 'Miss Appleton, are these books for the hospitals?'

Victoria jumped at the sound of her name. She stopped what she was doing and wondered if she was about to get into trouble, for starting before permission had been given. Victoria looked round at his grave face, as he bent to pick up a paperback. 'Yes sir, I know it hasn't been agreed yet but it won't be a five-minute job, so I thought I'd make a start.'

Mr Leadbetter nodded. 'Hmm, James Joyce.' He dropped it back into the box and picked up another one. 'D. H. Lawrence.' He gazed down into the box, and at the books haphazardly placed in it. 'Remember to mix it up a little; not all of the patients will be strong readers, and we don't want to put them off all together. Perhaps look for books that are aimed at older children, and maybe women. Remember, reading is about escaping from our own worries, to another time and place, so try not to put in any war books.'

Relief flooded through Victoria's veins. 'Yes, sir, I hadn't thought of that.'

Molly placed the book she was holding into the box. 'I'll go and stand at Alice's, er Mrs Leybourne's, counter.'

Mr Leadbetter nodded. 'I know you three are as thick as thieves, and your thoughts won't be far away from Mrs Leybourne, but she will be being looked after so please try not to worry.'

Molly giggled. 'You always say that about us, but we are just really good friends that like to be there for each other.'

Mr Leadbetter chuckled. 'Yes, that may well be true, but you have all given me cause for concern, at one time or another. Now, let's get some work done.' He marched towards a waiting customer.

Victoria watched Molly take herself off to Alice's counter, realising how lucky they were to have each other. But what about Stephen and Ted and now there was John and her grandparents as well. Victoria turned and pulled another book off the shelf, and without looking at the title or the author she rubbed her rag over it and dropped it into the box. She glanced across at Molly, who was already smiling, as she served a customer. Victoria realised Molly had come a long way in the last couple of years, but she felt as though she was still in the same place. *That's because you haven't dealt with anything, through to the end. You need to change the way you deal with things and stop running away from everything.* Victoria shook her head. 'It's no good shouting at me; I'm just going to end up in an asylum, if I keep talking to myself.'

'You and me, both.' A young woman's voice came from behind Victoria.

Victoria's conscience immediately went quiet, as she turned to see Lily standing there. She frowned. 'It's Alice, isn't it? Is she all right?'

Lily smiled and grabbed Victoria's hands in hers. 'Yes, and yes.'

'Oh, thank God.'

Lily watched the emotions flicker across Victoria's face, waiting for the penny to drop.

Victoria's eyes widened. 'Wait, has Alice had the baby?'

Lily's face lit up, as she nodded her head.

Victoria gave a nervous laugh; Lily's hands were grasping hers, and she shook them. 'Well, what was it, a boy, or a girl?'

Lily giggled. 'It was a boy; Arthur has a little brother. Isn't that wonderful?'

Victoria jumped up and down, taking Lily's arms with her. 'Have they decided on his name? I think Alice always thought she was having a girl. Does she mind that it's a boy?'

Lilly laughed, as the questions were fired at her. 'No, they had girls' names, but haven't decided on a boy's yet. They're all thrilled, though. I don't think it mattered to them what it was in the end, as long as it was healthy.'

Victoria took some deep breaths, trying to calm herself down, as she realised they were drawing attention to themselves. 'That's true, that is the most important thing.' Victoria paused, as the news began to sink in. 'I can't believe Alice is a wife, and mother of two children.' Her eyes began to well up.

Lily shook Victoria's hand. 'Don't get upset; your time will come, as indeed will mine, once this damned war is over with.'

Victoria gave Lily a watery smile. 'I'm not upset, I'm proud. I'm proud of Alice, and everyone around me.' She hesitated, before continuing. 'To be honest, I'm not worried about me, and everything else is out of my hands.'

Lily nodded. 'I know what you mean, but we can try and influence outcomes, by the things that we say and do.' It was Lily's turn to hesitate. 'You know, you could ask Ted to marry you, instead of waiting for him to ask, especially if he feels he has nothing to offer you.'

Colour crept up Victoria's neck. 'Oh, I could never do that. He might think I'm desperate.'

Lily shook her head. 'Or he might think you love him so much, you don't care about anything else, including what he thinks about you asking him. If the war should have taught us anything, it's that life is too short, and that what we have can be ripped away from us in a moment. Look at Molly with Tony, and then she nearly lost Andrew as well.' She paused. 'Think about what Molly would have missed out on. Think about what Alice would have missed out on; two beautiful boys and a husband who adores her.'

Victoria slowly nodded her head. 'What about you?'

Lily laughed. 'I have to find someone first. I'm not madly in love like you are. Grab it with both your hands. If he says no, you don't have to see him again, but I suspect he will say yes.' She looked around her.

334

'Sorry, I forgot for a moment you were in work, and I don't want to get you into trouble. I know you all think I'm young and impetuous, but please think about what I said.' She pulled Victoria towards her and gave her a hug. 'I've got to go, but think about what I said. Oh, can you let Molly know, otherwise I'll get shot.'

'I will, and thank you.'

Lily nodded. 'I almost forgot, but Ma says can you wait and visit Alice tomorrow, so she can get some rest?'

'Of course.'

Lily waved, as she almost ran towards the door, just avoiding a little girl who came running around the corner, being chased by her mother.

Victoria shook her head. Fancy Lily thinking she should ask Ted to marry her. Whoever heard of such a thing? She smiled. Molly would think it was a good idea, but was she brave enough?

23

Victoria settled into the armchair opposite Daisy, in their basement, covering her legs with a blue blanket. They were down there earlier than usual, under the instruction of the policeman cycling along the road. Mr Leadbetter had mentioned earlier that London hadn't been bombed for a few weeks, so we were probably due, but she had hoped he was wrong. When she walked home from Charing Cross Road to Percy Street, Victoria had noticed the moon shining through the thin mist that hung in the dark, inky sky. She picked up the knitting needles that were permanently by her chair, for exactly such occasions, wrapping the dark wool around her fingers, in preparation of knitting another pair of socks to send to the frontline. Hopefully, everyone would be safely taking cover in their basements, or the underground stations. 'I hope the hospital doesn't get hit; after they bombed that school in Poplar, earlier this year, it makes you realise they don't care who they kill. Those poor children must have been terrified, and God only knows what the parents must have gone through, when they realised their children had died.'

Daisy nodded. 'It must have been terrifying for them.'

Victoria clicked her knitting needles together for a moment, before pulling her wool free, to allow her to carry on. 'I suppose, with Christmas just a week away, we should be making plans. Are you working on Christmas Day?'

'No.' Daisy sighed. 'I am the day after, but I had to do one or the other. To be honest, I haven't thought about Christmas at all.'

Victoria thinned her lips, for a second. 'I'm the same, but I keep telling myself Stephen wouldn't want us to be miserable.' She rested her knitting on her lap. 'Molly was saying that Grace has sent her a food parcel, so they have lots of fresh vegetables to eat.'

Daisy beamed. 'Blimey, that's worth its weight in gold, that is.'

Victoria laughed. 'It is. Molly sent her a box of books to read. It's lovely that they're staying in touch still, but I suppose that's friends for you, sometimes they are better than family.'

Daisy stared at her sister. 'You're thinking about Brighton, aren't you?'

Victoria nodded. 'I don't understand why our grandfather is so against us, or why we weren't told about them. I think the money in the box was for John, in case he had to be admitted into hospital.' She paused. 'I've tried to stop thinking about them, but I can't let go of it, because I don't understand, and now I can't find the diary, which may have held some answers. On top of that, the key is missing from that chest, so we still have no idea what's inside it. I feel like I'm going round the bend, between John and Ted, and that's without me admitting something could have happened to Stephen.' She scowled. 'And now, Lily thinks I should ask Ted to marry me; whoever heard of such a thing?'

'Lily's a modern woman.' Daisy bit her lip. 'I shook the chest and it didn't sound like there was anything in it, to me.'

Victoria raised her eyebrows. 'I suppose I've just

got to stop worrying so much. You know, I haven't even bought any Christmas presents yet.'

'You work in a bookshop, so that's one problem solved.' Daisy gave Victoria a sideways glance, as she pulled her blanket aside and stood up. 'Look, I have a confession to make, but first you have to promise you won't be angry with me.' She paced back and forth, wringing her hands together. 'It's something I've wanted to tell you for a while now, but I've come to the conclusion I'm a coward.'

Confusion flitted across Victoria's face, as she studied her sister. 'I'm sure, whatever it is, we'll be able to cope, so spit it out.' She placed the knitting needles on the side table, next to her chair.

Daisy perched on the edge of the armchair, clinging tight to the blanket. 'I want you to understand that, at the time, I thought I was doing the right thing.' She stopped and peered up, as a familiar rumbling could be heard from above them. 'It's now or never, I don't want to die, knowing I've been selfish.'

Victoria could feel the tension that sat between them. She reached out and took Daisy's hand in hers. 'I don't understand. There's nothing you could do that would come between us, and there'll be no talk of us dying tonight, thank you.'

Daisy shook her head. 'You don't know what I've done.'

Fear ran down Victoria's spine. She held herself rigid. 'What is it?'

Daisy stood up, glancing over at Victoria with hooded eyes, before lifting the cushion that formed the seat of the chair.

Victoria gasped. 'Why?'

Daisy allowed her tears to silently fall. She shrugged

and shook her head. Her grief held her speechless.

Victoria didn't take her eyes off the chair that her sister had been sat on. She moved the blanket to one side, before pushing herself out of the chair, unsure about what to do next. 'Why? You know I've been looking for it. I thought it had been thrown away by mistake.'

Daisy sniffed.

Victoria glanced over, as Daisy brushed her fingers across her cheeks. 'Come here.' Victoria stepped forward and wrapped her arms around her sister. The crying got louder and she could feel Daisy's body shaking with the pain of what she had done. 'It doesn't matter, it's not important.'

Daisy lifted her tear stained face. 'But it does. If I'd given it to you earlier, you would have found John sooner, and maybe, just maybe, we could have had a proper conversation with him. Instead, we're facing the prospect of him dying, without having got to know us at all.' She gasped for air. 'I've been so selfish, and I've known that for some time, but I just didn't want to lose you to them.'

Victoria squeezed her sister tight. 'That would never, ever happen. I've told you that already.'

Daisy lifted her head. 'I know, and since we had that talk, I've wanted to give you the diary, but I was too scared to admit what I'd done and the longer it went on, the more difficult it became.'

Victoria shook her head, before giving her sister another hug. 'The main thing is that you didn't throw it away. Have you read it?'

Daisy stepped back, rubbing her cheeks, leaving red blotches. 'No, I felt you should be the one to read it first.'

Victoria closed her eyes for a second, wondering when life had got so complicated. *The day your parents died on the train from Brighton, that's when.* She shook away the voice that seemed to be continually with her and glanced over at her sister. 'We shall read it together.'

★ ★ ★

Daisy and Victoria had sat up all night in the basement, paging through their mother's diary together, taking it in turns to read extracts, until their candles had died. Victoria could hear her mother's voice, as they read each entry.

It broke my heart to leave John in Brighton; he's only three years old, but I need to think of his health. Maybe we'll be able to bring him home soon. I miss him so much. David's father doesn't make it any easier. Doesn't he know, we would never willingly leave our child with him, or anyone else. The children are so young to be separated. Hopefully, Victoria will soon stop asking when their brother is coming home. I wish I had the answer, she gets so upset about him, maybe it'll be easier for them if they no longer visit him.

In those few words, Victoria could feel her mother's pain, and the tears that had marked the paper. She had flicked through to another entry, to find a lock of hair, wrapped in paper and pressed into the spine of the diary.

I'm heartbroken, not knowing when, or if, I'll ever see my baby again. My father-in-law and husband have had the same argument that brought David to London in the first place. I wonder if he'll ever accept that David is happy being an architect. I don't understand why he can't see that Edward, along with his father Arthur Gettin, has been so good to us. It's time I started to think about Victoria, Daisy and Stephen, even though I'm desperate to bring John home, before his brother and sisters forget about him.

Victoria read the entry again. She hadn't realised that Alice's grandfather and great-grandfather had given her parents a helping hand in some way. She flicked through towards the end of the book, stopping at an entry that had her name all over it.

I am so angry right now. I've just discovered Herbert locked my Victoria in the basement for not jumping to it when he told her to. My poor little girl must have been terrified and I wasn't there to help her. I've been told that was how his father punished him, but surely doesn't that make it worse? Wouldn't he know how scared she would have been? Instead he told my husband it didn't do him any harm, it made him into the man he is today. I can't think about leaving John there for a second longer, it just breaks my heart.

Victoria sucked in her breath as she realised her grandfather was just doing what his father had done to him. He didn't know how else to behave because everyone was too scared to explain there was another way.

Daisy and Victoria had spent hours searching their minds for memories of John, but hadn't come up with anything. They both remembered things about

Stephen, but not John. In the dead of the night, long after Daisy had given in to the exhaustion they both felt, it dawned on Victoria that Stephen was only a year older than John, so maybe some of her memories were being given to the wrong brother.

Victoria gripped her handbag, not wishing to let the diary out of her grasp, now she had it. While Daisy was asleep, Victoria scribbled a note, donned her thick, woollen winter coat, hat, scarf and gloves, and quietly left the house. The heat in her cheeks was at odds with the cold air that hit and burnt into them. It was early; the air was damp. The streets were still enveloped in darkness, with only the moon to light the pavements that sparkled with the winter frost. The large buildings formed eerie shapes up ahead. It felt like London was still asleep. Victoria fleetingly wondered whether, if it snowed, the bright reflection in a dark sky would help the Germans find their targets. Her heels clipped the pavement, as she paced along. A dog could be heard barking, but she couldn't tell where it was coming from. Something ran across her path, causing her to squeal in fright. Without realising it, she was in Soho Gardens. She was tempted to sit down for a few minutes, maybe read the diary again, but common sense told her that wouldn't be a good idea. She needed to be inside, to read. She looked around, knowing this area wasn't as bomb ravaged as some, although the road and the public house outside the Lyceum Theatre, near Covent Garden, had never really recovered, and neither had the road outside the Bedford Hotel, in Southampton Row. There were now craters and bomb-damaged buildings all over London. From what she'd heard, both north and south of the river had been hit, and probably the whole country, but she had given up reading the newspapers a long time ago; it was all too depressing.

Victoria carried on walking, glad to have a day off from Foyles, and had decided to go to the hospital to see Ted, whether he wanted to see her or not. Lily's words bounded into her head. Could she propose to him? Laughter bubbled to the surface. Alice and Molly would be so shocked, if she told them what Lily had suggested.

'Morning.' An old man, pulling a barrow, walked past.

'Morning.' Victoria smiled at the man, but that quickly disappeared as she realised there was no point asking Ted, because he would probably never forgive her for not telling him who she was when she first saw him in hospital. *How do you know that, if you don't ask him?* a voice screamed in her head. She tightened her lips, when she realised that was the advice she had given Molly. It was time she just got on with it. 'Everything's such a mess.' The swirls of her breath disappeared into the night. 'I just need to be honest, and if it doesn't work, at least I know.'

'You talking to yourself, luvvie?' A woman's voice came from behind Victoria.

Victoria blushed as she turned to face the woman.

'Sorry luvvie, but couldn't 'elp 'earing yer.' The woman was leaning on a walking stick, as she shuffled along. 'Yer need to be careful, ovawise they'll be locking yer away in one of them there 'omes, and not many come out again, I can tell yer.'

Colour flooded Victoria's cheeks, as she opened her mouth, but then she shut it again.

The old woman cackled. 'What I will say is yer should always be 'onest, cos 'e won't know yer love 'im

343

if yer not, and life's too short to be messing around.'

Victoria cleared her throat. 'What makes you think it's got anything to do with a man?'

The woman placed her free hand to her chest, as laughter burst out from her. 'Listen, luvvie, when a woman is walking the street in the dead of night, talking to herself, that always means it's man trouble.' A high-pitched cackle escaped again. 'That, or else she's a streetwalker with serious problems, and yer look too well turned out to be a woman of the night, selling yer wares.'

Victoria's eyes widened. 'I'm certainly not a streetwalker.' She felt a mischievous moment come over her. 'So are you a streetwalker then?' She grinned at the unexpected conversation she was having.

The woman's cackle grew in volume; she gasped for breath. 'Yeah, that's why I'm starving.'

Victoria threw back her head and roared with laughter.

The woman's laughter gradually died down. 'So what are yer doing, out on the streets so early?'

'I'm just going through my thoughts, before going to the hospital; and you?'

The old lady nodded. 'I 'ave trouble sleeping, so it helps me to come out for a walk. Anyway, I won't 'old you up. Just remember, stop talking to yerself, and 'onesty is always best.'

Victoria frowned. 'Thank you. Will you be all right, if I walk on?'

The old lady smiled. 'Thank yer for caring luvvie, but I'll be fine, now yer go off wiv yer, and don't forget to tell yer man yer love 'im.'

Victoria nodded, turning away from the old lady, to carry on walking to the hospital. She looked over her shoulder, squinting to see in the darkness, but the old lady was nowhere to be seen. Her hand flew to her chest as panic took hold. She took a couple of deep breaths and ran back to roughly where they had chatted, staring all around her, but there was nothing. What a night, thinking of asking Ted to marry her and talking to an old woman that seemed to have disappeared. Maybe she should be locked away somewhere. With one last look around her, and a shrug of her shoulders, she carried on walking towards the hospital.

The large gates of Endell Street Military Hospital beckoned.

Was Mabel back working? Victoria hadn't seen her since she'd argued with her grandfather. Did that mean they were grieving over John? Wouldn't they have written to her? Maybe it was time she either visited again, or wrote to them, but she didn't want to intrude if they were grieving. She shook her head; as always, her thoughts were in turmoil. Was she doing the right thing? Did it matter? She told herself it was about not living with any regret.

Victoria entered Endell Street Hospital and sat in the reception area. Just one light shone over the receptionist's desk in the far corner, away from the windows. She didn't know how long she had been there, but the clock in the corner made her jump, as the musical chimes rang through the area. Victoria craned her neck to see the time, as several nurses walked past her. She could tell by their looks, they wondered what she was doing there. Women didn't often sit there, waiting. Pushing herself off her chair, Victoria stretched her stiff arms and legs. She flopped back down on the wooden chair, as her sleepless night caught up with her. 'Come on, you can do this.'

A nurse looked round. 'Is everything all right?'

'Yes, sorry.' Victoria forced a smile. 'I'm just trying to get myself moving.'

The nurse nodded and carried on walking by.

Victoria stood up again, craning to see the time; eight-fifteen. She took a deep breath and a step forward. No one would stop her going onto Joan of Arc ward; everyone would assume she was there to work. She stopped at the top of the stairs and steadied her breathing, before pushing open the ward doors.

'Good morning, Victoria.' A nurse smiled. 'I didn't realise you were coming in today.'

Victoria stuffed her scarf and gloves into a pocket, before hanging up her coat on a nearby peg. 'I'm not really, but I wanted to speak to the patient in bed twenty-five, if that's all right?'

The nurse picked up a piece of paper and glanced down the list of names. 'Ah, Corporal Marsden, yes, by all means. He seems to have taken a step backwards and won't eat his breakfast, so any help you can give there will be gratefully received.'

Guilt rushed through Victoria's body. She should have faced the music sooner. Having admitted she had misled him, she should have come back for his verdict on her crime. 'I'll do my best.' She pushed her shoulders back and lifted her chin, wishing she had Alice and Molly by her side, but knew this was something she had to face alone. They would be there, to pick through the pieces of the wreckage that would be the end result. Victoria marched down the ward, keeping her eyes forward; she needed all her focus on what was ahead of her. She stopped just short of bed twenty-five and watched Ted, lying very still. His eyes

346

were shut and, for a moment, she wondered if he'd died. Her heart lurched into her throat, as she quickly stepped nearer. Ted moved his head slightly and Victoria breathed a sigh of relief. She had the urge to run her fingers through his already ruffled hair.

'I'd know that perfume anywhere.'

Ted's slow quiet words reached Victoria. Fear held her hostage, as all of what she was going to say left her.

'You can stay quiet, but I know you're here.' He paused. 'I didn't think you would come back.'

Victoria cleared her throat, but her voice was but a whisper. 'I had to.'

'Had to, or wanted to?'

Victoria wrapped her arms around her waist, holding her sides tight. Pain gripped her chest. She took a couple of shallow breaths. 'For me, it's the same thing.' She stepped forward. 'I've been told you're not eating. The nurses are worried about you.'

A throaty noise came from Ted.

'What?' Victoria edged closer still, her damp hands clutched tight in front of her. 'I'm here to face the music for what I've done, or not done, but you still have to eat.'

'Eat?' Ted's face tightened. 'What were you doing, hedging your bets, by not telling me who you were? Were you frightened you couldn't stay around to look after me?'

Victoria gasped. Her eyes held a steel-like quality, anger quickly replacing the fear that had held her rooted to the spot. 'You have a nerve. You left me seven years ago, without a word of explanation.'

Ted fidgeted in bed, before pulling himself upright. He stared in her direction, trying hard to focus on her. 'Yes, I admit that was a mistake.'

Victoria automatically stepped nearer, to plump up his pillows. 'You have to realise that I thought you were dead, or at best missing, so when I was told to sit with Corporal Marsden, it caught me by surprise.' She paused. 'But when you said there was no one to inform that you were here, well, that cut right through me.' She paced back and forth, wringing her hands, her bravado fading under the spotlight he was putting on her actions.

Ted sat in silence for a moment.

Victoria glared at him. 'I know I was in the wrong for not telling you who I was, but that was only because it felt like it had gone on for too long, and I couldn't see a way out of it.'

Ted stared down at his blue blanket, his hands clenched into a fist, resting on top of the cover.

Victoria pulled up a wooden chair and sat down. Just when she was beginning to think he was never going to say anything, he began to mumble.

'I can believe that, because that's how I felt, when I ran away seven years ago.'

Victoria leant in nearer to him. She breathed in deeply, taking in the smell of carbolic soap, mixing with his body's natural smell. Could she touch him? Did she dare touch him?

Ted interrupted her musings. 'I immediately regretted my actions, but I couldn't see my way back. That's when I joined the army, to try to forget you, but I thought about you every day. I was a coward for not being there for you, when you needed me more than ever.'

Tears began to prick at her eyes, as his words took her back to those painful days. 'It's understandable; I suppose I didn't deal with it very well.'

Ted's face contorted with anger. 'No, I'm not having that. You were sixteen and both your parents had died. You were suddenly responsible for a younger sister and brother; how were you meant to deal with it?'

Victoria shrugged. 'I've been lucky to have Alice and Molly, to keep picking me up when I fall.' She paused. 'They have been really good friends to me.'

Ted nodded. 'Well, let's face it, you find out who your true friends are, when you need someone. I'm sorry, more than you'll ever know. I'm sorry I was a coward and let you down, but I'm pleased you had them both. They are good friends, who no doubt, won't be happy to see me.'

Victoria couldn't take her eyes off him. 'They just want me to be happy, with someone who treats me right.' Without realising it, she shrugged off the weight she had been carrying on her shoulders. 'I'm sorry I didn't tell you who I was, right from the beginning. What I don't understand is why you didn't want the hospital to contact me.'

Ted fidgeted in the bed, moving his legs up and down a few times.

Victoria raised her voice a little. 'Are you going to tell me?'

He frowned and took a deep breath. 'In my mind, I always thought, when I came home, I'd try and make up for everything I'd done, all the hurt I'd caused, before I asked you to marry me. But then I was in here, with nothing to offer you. I had no sight and no job prospects. I didn't want to drag you down with me, and besides, I had no right to ask after everything I'd done.'

Victoria's jaw dropped open. 'You were . . .' Her

349

voice dropped to a whisper. 'You were going to ask me to marry you.'

Ted shook his head. 'I know it's ridiculous, because nothing has changed, I still have nothing to offer you, so I have no right to ask.'

Victoria's gaze darted from side to side. 'It's not about work and what you have to offer, it's about whether you can be trusted not to run away, when things get tough. No one wants to be friends with, let alone married to, someone who lets them down and runs away, when something unbearable happens.'

Ted moved his hands over the bed-cover, searching for Victoria's, and placed his over them.

Victoria gasped, as butterflies flew around her stomach. The urge to hold him close was unbearable.

Ted squeezed her hand. 'I've learnt too, and I want to prove it to you.' He groaned. 'Well I did, before I lost my sight.'

Victoria shook her head, fighting her natural urges that the electricity between them was creating. She suddenly had an insight into how Molly had struggled with Andrew, and how useless some of her advice had been. 'So what's your answer, push me out of your life again, because things are tough?'

Ted snatched his hand away from hers. 'Look, how can I do anything else, if I can't be the breadwinner, if I can't look after my wife and family.'

Victoria gasped. Marriage and family; was she going to lose it all again? 'So it's all up to you, is it? Well, sight or no sight, maybe I would have said no.' Impatience and anger took hold of Victoria. 'It's not about whether you can see or not, it's about how you cope with it. I don't want to be married to someone who thinks of himself as a victim. We're all victims,

350

one way or another, but to always think of yourself as one, destroys you and everyone around you.' Victoria pushed a piece of cold toast towards him. 'Eat your breakfast, and don't think I'm going to be here for every mealtime, to make sure you eat. I'm not your mother and have no desire to be so.'

Ted sat in silence for a few minutes. 'That told me.' He picked up the limp slice of bread and bit into it.

Victoria wanted to laugh. 'I'm afraid I'm not the innocent little sixteen-year-old anymore.' She paused. 'You know, one thing I have learnt, thanks to Alice, Molly and this war, is that we're all stronger than we think. I've also come to realise it takes time to grieve, and to allow you to be built back up again. You have to keep the faith that everything will work out in the end.'

'And that's what you've done.' Ted shook his head. 'I can only admire you, Victoria. You've grown into a strong woman.'

Victoria laughed. 'Alice and Molly might tell you otherwise, but what I can tell you is, it wasn't a choice. It was about survival, and keeping my family together.' She paused. 'You must have had to fight, to survive all this time, so where's your fight now?'

Ted sighed. 'Your letters gave me hope for the future, and I just feel as though the future has been ripped away from me.'

The pair of them sat in silence for a few minutes.

Victoria reached over and took his hand in hers; her skin tingled. The overwhelming feeling of being safe, and at home, wrapped itself around her. She ran her thumb over the top of his soft hand. 'I have something to ask you.' She stared down at his hand, mesmerised by the movement of her thumb. She took a deep breath. 'Will you marry me?'

351

24

Molly paced down one of the aisles in Foyles Bookshop, wishing her legs were as long as her manager's. 'Mr Leadbetter, I've done a sign for the window, telling everyone Father Christmas will be in the Children's Section today, from ten o'clock until four. Is it all right for me to put it in the window?'

Mr Leadbetter turned round, taking in the tinsel that she had clipped into her blonde hair. He laughed at her excitement. 'I can see you're getting into the spirit of things, Mrs Greenwood.'

'Of course, Mr Leadbetter, it's Christmas Eve and I'm determined that we are going to enjoy Christmas, despite the awful war. It will be good for the children not to worry about their fathers for a couple of hours, and just be children.'

Mr Leadbetter studied her for a moment. 'You have a good heart, Mrs Greenwood. Is your husband here?'

'He's in the basement, getting into the red suit and white beard.' She giggled. 'We brought a couple of pillows from home, because he's not round enough.'

Mr Leadbetter threw his head back and roared with laughter. 'It's good to see you're taking it seriously. Make sure you place the sign where everyone can see it.'

'Thank you, Mr Leadbetter.' Molly began to race towards the shop window, slowing down when she nearly collided with an excitable little girl.

Mr Leadbetter grinned as he walked away. He chuckled, as he watched a very rotund Father Christmas come out from the staff area, quickly followed by Victoria. He peered left and right, trying to decide which way to go. Mr Leadbetter shook his head, as Molly was suddenly beside her husband.

Molly hung the side ribbon of the long white beard over Andrew's ears, tweaking a couple of the soft curls that had escaped. She breathed in his familiar musky scent, which filled her with joy, as it aroused memories of their turbulent courtship. She leant back a little, studying Father Christmas. His fur-trimmed red hat sat at a jaunty angle, covering his brown hair. The pillows didn't look out of place, covered by the red coat, and held by the wide black belt. Andrew had taken some of Molly's rouge and smeared it on his cheeks, in circular movements. Molly nodded; he looked jolly, just as all Father Christmas's should. 'Give me a ho, ho, ho.'

Andrew's colour began to rise, mingling with the neatly applied rouge. 'Ho, ho, ho,' he said, at the top of his voice.

Molly giggled. As she studied him, her laughter gradually faded. 'I love you, Andrew.' She went on her tiptoes and kissed him. 'I've had an idea, which could help the men that come home from the front, but we'll have to talk about it later.' She pulled at his arm. 'Come on; let's get you upstairs. I think there's already a queue of very excited children.'

They both went up the stairs and gasped when they saw the line of children, snaking round the section. Their chatter and excitement gradually subsided as, one by one, they realised Father Christmas had arrived.

A little girl ran over to Father Christmas and put her hand in his. 'I'm at the end of the line, with my ma. Will you still have time to listen to what I want for

353

Christmas?'

Andrew stooped down in front of the little girl. 'Of course, Father Christmas has time for all children.'

The little girl beamed and clapped her hands, before running back to her mother.

Andrew stood up and glanced around him. 'It hadn't occurred to me it was going to be this busy.'

Molly smiled. 'There are lots of children that need the excitement of Christmas, especially as their fathers have been gone for so long.'

Andrew nodded, before shouting at the top of his voice. 'Ho, ho, ho, Merry Christmas everybody.'

Everyone yelled back, 'Merry Christmas.'

Molly giggled; the atmosphere was full of excitement and anticipation.

Andrew walked over to a brown, wing-back chair and sat down. He carefully adjusted his padded stomach, to ensure it didn't move position.

Molly walked over to her counter, picked up one of the boxes of children's books and carried it over to Father Christmas, placing it on the floor, next to the chair. She looked at her husband and whispered, 'Are you ready?'

He nodded. 'As ready as I'll ever be. This is scary stuff, you know.'

Molly laughed. 'You'll be all right. Don't forget you're my hero, and I'll be here.'

Andrew raised his eyebrows and took a deep breath, calling the first child over, in his best Father Christmas voice. He guessed her to be about six years old.

A choir burst into song and the words of 'Away in a Manger' filtered up to them from the street below. A couple of customers joined in and gradually, the whole queue was singing. Molly found herself unable to resist singing along with the words of the Christmas carol.

A woman held her little girl's hand, as they took the couple of steps towards Father Christmas.

'Hello little one, and what's your name?'

The little girl looked shyly up at her mother, who nodded her encouragement. 'Susan.'

Andrew beamed at the little girl. 'Well, Susan, that's a lovely name. Would you like to sit on my knee, so we can have a little chat?'

Susan nodded.

Andrew reached out and picked her up. 'Now, do you have a Christmas wish?'

Susan nodded.

Andrew smiled. 'Would you like to share it with me.'

Susan glanced at her mother, before leaning in to whisper in Andrew's ear. 'My pa isn't coming home from the war, so I want a new one, then my ma can stop crying at night.'

Andrew gasped and his eyes widened, as he looked towards Molly for a second. He took his attention back to Susan and spoke to her in low tones. 'Your ma is a good woman and I'm sure you will get a new pa. It just won't be in time for Christmas this year, but I'll see what I can do for the ones to come.'

Susan glanced over at her mother, before beaming up at Andrew. 'Thank you.' She stretched, to kiss Andrew on the cheek. 'It's working already. Look, she's smiling.'

Molly reached into the box of books and pulled out Appley Dappley's Nursery Rhymes by Beatrix Potter, handing it to Susan.

The mother stepped forward and took her daughter's hand, helping her to get down off Father

Christmas' lap.

Susan looked down at the cover. 'Thank you; can I keep this?'

Andrew smiled. 'Of course you can, little one. Enjoy it.'

Susan giggled. 'Look, the mouse is carrying a plate of food.' She held it up, to show her mother.

The mother smiled at Andrew and Molly. 'Thank you. You don't know what this means to us.'

Molly could feel the tears welling up. 'Thank you, it means a lot to us here at Foyles, too.' She watched them walk away, as the next child approached Father Christmas.

* * *

Victoria rushed up the stairs, as quickly as her tired legs would carry her. It was Christmas Eve. Everyone had a busy evening ahead of them, preparing for Christmas Day, but the policeman cycling along Charing Cross Road had put an end to closing Foyles Bookshop, and any thoughts of going home in ten minutes' time. She gasped for breath, as she reached the top, peering into the children's section, thankful that Molly was bringing Father Christmas' job to an end, for another year. She rushed over to Molly. 'We have to get into the basement and bring any customers that are still in the shop. They are expecting the Germans to ruin Christmas.'

Molly looked around. Andrew had finished with the last child, ten minutes earlier. Thankfully the dark, cold evenings had meant customers hadn't wanted to wait around. 'Right, I'll have a quick look around.' She bent down to pick up the fifth box they had emptied of children's books.

Victoria shook her head. 'No, leave all that. We'll tidy up when we know it's safe. I hope Daisy is inside, so she can take cover.'

'Daisy's a sensible girl, so I'm sure she won't be hanging around outside.' Molly dropped the box where she stood. 'I'll have a quick look around.'

Andrew stood up. 'I'll help.'

Victoria nodded. 'Me too; there are so many nooks and crannies in this shop, it would be easy to lose someone.'

The three of them split up and checked every corner, aisle and staircase, ushering staff to the basement.

Molly shouted out, 'I think everyone has either gone home or downstairs.'

Victoria nodded. 'We're lucky it's so close to closing time. Imagine what we would have done with all those children. They would have been so scared.'

'We would have had to entertain them.' Molly forced a smile. 'It's been a tiring day, but what Foyles and Andrew did here was wonderful. Every child went away with a book.'

Andrew yawned and stretched his arms. 'It's certainly been a special day, but mostly it's been heart-breaking. You know, none of the children asked for anything for themselves.'

Victoria shook her head. 'Thank you for doing it, Andrew. It's been a tough few years, especially for the children.' She sighed. 'What did the government say when all this started, "it should be over in four months"? Huh, it's fast approaching four years.'

Molly put her arm around Victoria. 'Don't think about it, it doesn't change any of it. Come on, let's get down to the basement.'

Victoria bent down to pick up the gloves and scarves customers had dropped in their haste to take cover. She noticed the large wheels of a wheelchair sticking out by the payment booth. 'I hope whoever was in that got down the stairs all right, I'm not sure Mr Leadbetter could have carried someone into the basement, and Albert certainly couldn't.'

Molly glanced over to where Victoria was looking. 'That's true.' She gave a cursory glance around the shop. 'There's no one left up here, except us, so you'd assume they worked it out between them.'

The three of them trundled down the stairs, shocked to see how many people had been left in the store and were now filling every corner of the room.

The door thudded shut, behind Victoria. She peered around. Albert was chatting away to a couple of members of staff. Her thoughts immediately went to Ted and Endell Street Hospital. She prayed the hospital wouldn't be bombed.

'Victoria.'

Victoria turned at the familiar voice. Alice was stood in front of her, carrying her newborn baby, almost invisible under all the blankets wrapped around him. Freddie and Arthur were looking at a couple of books that had been on the shelf. 'Alice, how wonderful, I was hoping you'd be indoors and safe.'

Alice laughed. 'Well, to be honest, I missed seeing you girls, so I thought I'd bring the new addition to the family to meet you both.'

Victoria moved the edge of the blanket. 'Can I hold him?'

'Of course you can.' Alice carefully manoeuvred the little one into Victoria's arms.

'He's so handsome.' Victoria lifted him higher, to

358

kiss his forehead. His powdery smell made her smile. Maybe, one day, she would have her own children, but she was happy to be holding this little bundle of joy. 'So what are you calling him?'

'We're not sure yet; we have a number of names in mind, it's just about making the final decision.'

Victoria stroked the soft skin of the baby's hand; his fingers uncurled and wrapped themselves around her finger. She beamed down at him. 'What are the favourites?'

Alice grinned as she watched Victoria. 'We're probably going to name him David Robert Leybourne.'

Victoria looked up at Alice. 'That's got a good ring to it, I take it Robert is after your brother?'

Alice nodded.

Molly sidled through the people sitting soberly, waiting to start their family Christmas celebrations. 'I thought I recognised that voice.'

Alice turned and wrapped her arms around Molly. 'I'm so pleased to see you both, and I want to hear what you have both been up to. It seems ages since we last chatted.'

Molly and Victoria both laughed.

Molly glanced at the small bundle in Victoria's arms. 'Now you can understand how I felt, working at the munitions factory. I felt lost, without you both by my side.' She looked across at Alice. 'Can I have a hold?'

Alice smiled at the girls. 'If you can prise him away from Victoria.'

Victoria kissed his soft forehead and his thin layer of dark hair, before handing him over to Molly. 'I'm sorry we haven't been round; we were coming, but the time seems to have run away from us.'

Alice nodded. 'Have you been to the hospital, to see Ted?'

Victoria kept her eyes fixed on the baby, as she wondered what she should tell Alice and Molly. Her mother's voice was suddenly in her head. 'The truth; honesty is always best, and that's what you told Molly, when she was fighting her feelings for Andrew.' She shook her head and caught sight of Daisy, walking towards her. 'Daisy, what are you doing here?'

Daisy frowned. 'We have a letter.' She handed the brown envelope over to Victoria. 'I haven't opened it. I nearly did, but I thought we should be together when we read it.'

Victoria turned the envelope over and gasped. It was official.

Daisy put her arm around her sister. Alice came and stood the other side of Victoria. Molly stared at the envelope, wishing and praying for good news.

'It's not a telegram.' Victoria turned the envelope over a couple of times, before ripping it open. She pulled out the single sheet of paper. Tears ran down her cheeks.

Daisy looked over the edge of the paper. 'What is it?'

The others stared on in silence.

Molly whispered to Alice. 'It's not a telegram, so it can't be bad news, can it?'

Daisy felt her sister become a weight, next to her. She slowly lowered her into a nearby chair. 'Is there any water down here?'

In minutes, Albert appeared next to her, carrying a small cup of water.

Daisy took it from him and put the cold liquid next to Victoria's lips. Her eyelids fluttered, as she slowly came round.

Molly couldn't hold her silence any longer. 'Is it about Stephen? Is he all right?'

Daisy snatched the letter from her sister's fingers. Her eyes scanned the page before a smile slowly lit up her face. 'Stephen is on his way home, hopefully he'll be here in time for Christmas.'

Everyone cheered and hugged each other.

Molly yelled above the noise of everyone talking at once. 'That's the best news ever, although he'll have to be quick.'

Laughter filled the room.

Victoria murmured, 'Thank goodness; I was beginning to think the worst.'

Daisy held the cup of water to her sister's lips. 'Here, sip this and sit still for a moment. It was a good job I didn't leave you to read it on your own, or goodness knows what I would have come home to.'

'Sorry, it must have got too much for me.'

Alice stroked Victoria's arm. 'Don't worry; you've been through so much lately. It's hardly surprising, really.'

Daisy gave her sister a nervous glance. 'Well, while you're sitting down, I have another surprise for you, or shock, depending on your point of view.'

Victoria's eyes widened, as she looked around her. Everyone was here, except Ted. Had something happened to him? Fear trampled across her soft features.

Daisy beckoned someone forward, from behind Freddie and Arthur.

Victoria felt the little colour she had drain away. 'Mabel, I've been looking for you in work. I thought John must have . . .'

'No.' Mabel stood aside.

Victoria gasped. 'John, how . . .' She wiped away the tears that were now falling down her cheeks. 'I thought . . . I thought I'd never get to have a conversation with you.' She stood up. 'I can't believe it.' She ran forward and thrust her arms around him, squeezing him tight to her. Victoria felt his arms go around her, and they cried together for a few minutes. She pulled back to look at her brother, taking in his sallow complexion. 'Here, sit down; I'll get you a drink. Is that your wheelchair upstairs?'

John laughed. 'Yes, but don't worry, I'm feeling well. I might not tomorrow, but today is the best day of my life.' He turned to Mabel, who was now standing next to his grandparents. 'Thank you, thank you for bringing me here.'

Victoria lifted her hand, to cover her mouth for a few seconds. 'Oh my goodness, I thought . . . it doesn't matter what I thought. Thank you for bringing him here.' Her eyes glistened with unshed tears. 'We can all have Christmas together. I wish Stephen was here to meet you, but at least we know he's coming home.'

A group in the far corner of the basement started to sing 'O Come All Ye Faithful',and people around them started to join in.

Herbert stepped forward. 'I owe you an apology, not just for the other day but for everything. I should have given you a chance to speak, the first time we met.' He looked down at the floor. 'There's a lot of things I should have done differently, but it's too late for all that now.'

Victoria put her arms around her grandfather. 'No, it isn't.'

'Does that mean you can find it in your heart to forgive me?'

'Without a doubt.' Victoria looked over his shoulder at her newfound family and gave a wry smile. 'But it's not my forgiveness you need, it's your wife's along with John and Mabel.'

Colour crept into Herbert's cheeks. 'After you left I'm afraid the flood gates opened, and I've been given some tough home truths.' He paused as his brows knitted together. 'I'm ashamed to say I had unwittingly turned into my father, but I'm working on that.' His eyes welled up, he blinked quickly before reaching out for her hands, squeezing them tight. 'It's too late for my son's forgiveness but hopefully not for the rest of my family.'

Tears rolled down Alice's face as she watched Victoria and her newfound family. 'You must all come to us for dinner tomorrow. Mrs Headley always cooks far too much so there'll be more than enough to go round.'

Victoria nodded her thanks before turning back to her grandfather. 'If we do that then you must behave because Alice's grandfather was the man who gave your son, my father, his job as an architect.'

Herbert stared at Victoria for a moment before nodding and looking over at Alice. 'It seems I owe your grandfather a great thanks, my son was very happy working for him.'

Mr Leadbetter called over to Albert. 'Clear the table of books. It's Christmas and who knows how long we'll be stuck down here, so let's start celebrating early.'

A voice came from down the other end of the basement. 'I have a bag of shopping we can use; it's not much, but there's some bread and cold meats in there.'

Another voice called out. 'I only came to sit on

363

Father Christmas' lap and now I'm down 'ere, but I've got a bag of goodies too.'

Albert looked up in the direction it came from. 'I'd know that voice anywhere, what yer doing 'ere?' He looked back at Victoria. 'It's me trouble and strife.'

Victoria smiled. 'It's nice to meet you . . . '

'Rose,' Albert and his wife answered in unison.

Albert crooked his finger at her. 'Come 'ere and sit on this chair, rest yer bones a while. What yer doing 'ere?'

Rose giggled. 'I came to meet yer from work but then when I got 'ere I fought I could sit on Father Christmas's knee, yer know like the old days.'

Andrew chuckled and leant forward. 'Come on then, Rose.'

Albert laughed. 'Get out of 'ere. I'll borrow the costume and she can sit on my knee.'

The room filled with laughter.

He leant forward and kissed Rose's pink cheek.

Another member of staff shouted across the room. 'I can't think about this conversation Albert, but I do have a bag of groceries, near the door; we can use that too. Merry Christmas everyone.'

A young man edged his way towards the tables. He was dusty from the train journey home. He slowly moved nearer to Victoria and Daisy before whispering, 'Merry Christmas.'

Startled Victoria spun on her heels. Her face lit up. 'Stephen.' All eyes turned to Victoria as she wrapped her arms around him and squeezed him tight.

Stephen beamed as he wrapped his arms around both his sisters. He turned to Alice. 'Is there room for one more tomorrow?'

Alice nodded. She sniffed. 'Without a doubt.'

Mr Leadbetter popped some corks from some wine bottles. 'I knew there was a reason why I bought a bottle each week and stored them down here all year.' He chuckled. 'I was hoping for a momentous occasion, and they don't get any bigger than a family reunited.'

Victoria smiled at her manager, before glancing across at her two friends. She held on to Stephen with one hand and grabbed Daisy's hand with the other and squeezed it tight. 'There might be something else to celebrate as well.' She gave a nervous giggle. 'Last night, I asked Ted to marry me.'

'You did what?' the girls yelled as one.

Victoria laughed. 'It was Lily's idea.' She clapped her hands together and squealed. 'Isn't this the best Christmas ever?'

Acknowledgements

As always I owe a huge thank you to some very special people who have helped me finish this novel with their support, understanding and encouragement.

It was just after I started writing this novel that my husband was diagnosed with Non-Hodgkins Lymphoma, which is a form of cancer. We weren't concerned, and neither were the doctors because it had been caught early — it was actually discovered when he went to give blood. I took my laptop to the hospital when he was having chemotherapy and we tried to concentrate on my novel; it was a good distraction for us both. Suddenly, the chemotherapy stopped working, and on 9th April we were told he had a bleed on the brain and didn't have long to live.

Dave and I had walked together, hand in hand, for twenty-seven years and thought we had many more years ahead of us. We were devastated, but he was concerned about us all looking after each other and that I wouldn't stop writing. It was very hard for us as a family as it hadn't occurred to us he wouldn't survive. I never left his bedside and my husband quietly passed away on 19th April 2019 with dignity and surrounded by love. My undying gratitude must go to the doctors and nurses on Rosewood Ward at Darent Valley Hospital for all their love and support. You were beyond brilliant, thank you.

I owe a huge thank you to the team at Aria, for their understanding and support of how my life has been turned upside down. You have been fantastic and I couldn't have asked for more from you. Thank you.

The biggest thanks must go to my family for dragging me through this nightmare we're living in. James, my eldest son, took a week off work, attempting to step into my husband's shoes, and guiding me through the editing process when all I wanted was to sit in the corner by myself. All five of our children have stood tall and supported each other and me in every way possible.

Dave and I were truly blessed and I can't thank them enough. It is now common to hear 'what would Dave do?' or 'what would Dave say?' in our conversations. He lives on in our hearts and will be forever missed. Thank you Dave, for encouraging and supporting me to write. We started this journey together and I know you were so very proud of me. I will always love you.

We do hope that you have enjoyed
reading this large print book.

Did you know that all of our titles
are available for purchase?

We publish a wide range of high
quality large print books including:
Romances, Mysteries, Classics
General Fiction
Non Fiction and Westerns

Special interest titles available in
large print are:
The Little Oxford Dictionary
Music Book, Song Book
Hymn Book, Service Book

Also available from us courtesy of
Oxford University Press:
Young Readers' Dictionary
(large print edition)
Young Readers' Thesaurus
(large print edition)

For further information or a free
brochure, please contact us at:
Ulverscroft Large Print Books Ltd.,
The Green, Bradgate Road, Anstey,
Leicester, LE7 7FU, England.
Tel: (00 44) 0116 236 4325
Fax: (00 44) 0116 234 0205

Other titles published by Ulverscroft:

THE FOYLES BOOKSHOP GIRLS AT WAR

Elaine Roberts

Working at the Foyles bookshop was Molly Cooper's dream job. But with the country at war, she's determined to do her bit. So she gathers her courage and sets off for the East End — and her first day working at Silvertown munitions factory. It's hard manual labour, and Molly must face the trials and tribulations of being the new girl in addition to the relentless physical work. The happy-ever-afters she read about in the pages of her beloved books have been lost to the war. And yet the munitions girls unite through their sense of duty, and the friendships that blossom in the most unlikely of settings . . .